Kings and Emperors

Kings and Emperors

An Alan Lewrie Naval Adventure

Dewey Lambdin

THOMAS DUNNE BOOKS

ST. MARTIN'S PRESS

NEW YORK

THOMAS DUNNE BOOKS.
An imprint of St. Martin's Press.

KINGS AND EMPERORS. Copyright © 2015 by Dewey Lambdin. All rights reserved. Printed in the United States of America. For information, address St. Martin's Press, 175 Fifth Avenue, New York, N.Y. 10010.

www.thomasdunnebooks.com
www.stmartins.com

Maps copyright © 2015 by Cameron MacLeod Jones

The Library of Congress Cataloging-in-Publication Data is available upon request.

ISBN 978-1-250-03006-1 (hardcover)
ISBN 978-1-250-03007-8 (e-book)

St. Martin's Press books may be purchased for educational, business, or promotional use. For information on bulk purchases, please contact the Macmillan Corporate and Premium Sales Department at 1-800-221-7945, extension 5442, or write to specialmarkets@macmillan.com.

First Edition: February 2015

10 9 8 7 6 5 4 3 2 1

To George and Olga Weiser, my long-ago agents who took a chance on an un-published writer back in 1988, liked what they read, and offered representation . . . which caused me to get "over-served" in celebration. Six weeks later, I had my first two-book contract, and the rest, as they say, is history.

At least I think it was 'cause that was one more reason for donning "beer goggles," and my memories get rather foggy.

Full-Rigged Ship: Starboard (right) side view

1. Mizen Topgallant
2. Mizen Topsail
3. Spanker
4. Main Royal
5. Main Topgallant
6. Mizen T'gallant Staysail
7. Main Topsail
8. Main Course
9. Main T'gallant Staysail
10. Middle Staysail
11. Main Topmast Staysail
12. Fore Royal
13. Fore Topgallant
14. Fore Topsail
15. Fore Course
16. Fore Topmast Staysail
17. Inner Jib
18. Outer Flying Jib
19. Spritsail

A. Taffrail & Lanterns
B. Stern & Quarter-galleries
C. Poop Deck/Great Cabins Under
D. Rudder & Transom Post
E. Quarterdeck
F. Mizen Chains & Stays
G. Main Chains & Stays
H. Boarding Battens/Entry Port
I. Cargo Loading Skids
J. Shrouds & Ratlines
K. Fore Chains & Stays
L. Waist
M. Gripe & Cutwater
N. Figurehead & Beakhead Rails
O. Bow Sprit
P. Jib Boom
Q. Foc's'le & Anchor Cat-heads
R. Cro'jack Yard (no sail fitted)
S. Top Platforms
T. Cross-Trees
U. Spanker Gaff

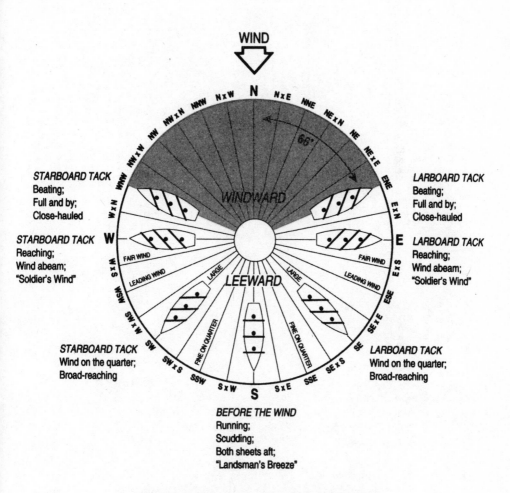

POINTS OF SAIL AND 32-POINT WIND-ROSE

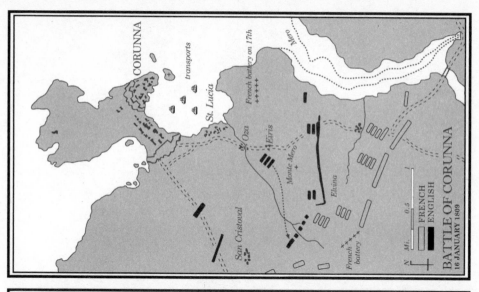

CORUNNA

transports

St. Lucia

French battery on 17th
+ + + + +

Mero

Oza

Eiris

Monte Mero

Elvina

San Cristoval

French
battery

N
Mi.
0.5   1

FRENCH
ENGLISH

BATTLE OF CORUNNA
16 JANUARY 1809

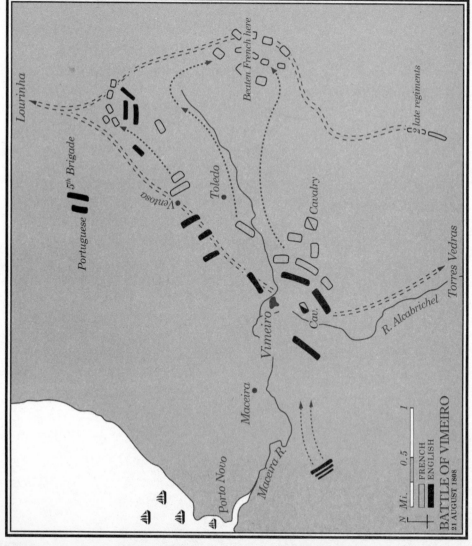

Lourinha

5th Brigade

Portuguese

Venosa

Toledo

Beaten French here

Cavalry

2 late regiments

Vimeiro

Cav.

R. Alcabrichel

Torres Vedras

Maceira

Maceira R.

Porto Novo

N   Mi.
0.5   1

FRENCH
ENGLISH

BATTLE OF VIMEIRO
21 AUGUST 1808

Savoir dissimuler est le savoir des rois.
Dissimulation is the art of kings.
-ARMAND JEAN DU PLESSIS,
DUC DE RICHELIEU (1585-1642)

PROLOGUE

In Fame's temple there is always a niche to be
found for rich dunces, importunate scoundrels, or
successful butchers of the human race.

      -JOHANN GEORG RITTER VON ZIMMERMAN
      (1728-1795)

CHAPTER ONE

Who do I have t'kill t'get out o' this assignment? Captain Alan Lewrie had to ask himself as he beheld his little flotilla of miniature warships close alongside his ship, the 50-gunned two-decker Fourth Rate HMS *Sapphire*, which was firmly anchored by bow and stern off Gibraltar's Old Mole, and, if fresh orders didn't come immediately, that was where *Sapphire* would remain 'til she put herself aground on a reef of discarded beef and pig bones! *Christ on a crutch!* he added after a much-put-upon sigh of frustration.

"They look very smart, sir," Lieutenant Geoffrey Westcott, the First Officer, commented.

"They look like turd barges in Purgatory," Lewrie snarled back.

"Well . . . well-*armed* turd barges, sir," Westcott amended. His wry smile of amusement was well-hidden from his superior, for he knew how much Lewrie detested the duty. In point of fact, Westcott detested the duty, too, and, like his Captain, would rather be back out at sea, ravaging the coasts of Spanish Andalusia, as they had done the previous year.

There were eight of the "turd barges," six of the original rowing boats that *Sapphire* had used to land troops and explosives to make their raids, and an additional two fresh from the Gibraltar dockyards made to the same pattern. They were thirty-six feet long and almost ten feet in beam, and too heavy to be hoisted aboard the hired transport which had borne the soldiers; they'd been towed astern to and from raids.

Now they were converted to gunboats and given official numbers, each armed with a 12-pounder cannon in the bow and a 12-pounder carronade on a pivot mount in the stern, copied by the dockyard superintendent, Captain Middleton, from a design he'd seen done by a home-based dockyard Commissioner Hamilton.

The bastard's promised even more *o' the bloody things!* Lewrie further fumed to himself; *A dozen, two dozen, and more! The bastard!*

When they'd been just landing craft, each one required a crew of nine; eight oarsmen and a Cox'n to steer, and usually with a Midshipman aboard to boot. Now, though, Captain Middleton had out-done himself, adding two more oars for more speed (since the guns made the damned things even slower), and each boat needed at least six hands to operate the long gun and at least five to man each carronade, which took so many men from *Sapphire*'s complement that if attacked whilst at anchor by enemy gunboats, she would have only half her upper-deck gun crews aboard for her own defence!

And, it was not as if those spanking-new eight gunboats would amount to much, since the Spanish already possessed un-told dozens of gunboats just cross the bay at Algeciras, and in the mouths of the Palmones and Guadarranque Rivers, some of them big beasts mounting many, and heavier, guns, and based on the war galleys which had dominated the Mediterranean for centuries. If they ever felt like it, the Dons could sally out and swat Lewrie's boats away like flies, then swarm his ship and board her, and it would be up to the cannon on Gibraltar's sprawling fortresses to save him. If the Army felt like it, that is!

"Well, let's get on with it," Lewrie grumbled. "Hoist signals for Harcourt and Elmes to begin, if ye please, Mister Westcott."

"Aye, sir," Westcott said, turning to the men of the After-Guard on the poop deck to strike the single flag hoist, the sign to Execute.

"Look at 'em," Lewrie groused, "all those eager, bright-shinin' faces, just *strainin'* at the leash t'get going . . . hah!"

The ship's Second Officer, Lieutenant Harcourt, and her Third Officer, Lieutenant Elmes, shouted orders, and the gunboats got under way, separating into two groups of four, with sailors heaving hard on their oars to get the heavy boats going, and Cox'ns at the tillers calling out the stroke. Lewrie *could* hear an enthusiastic cry arise, but that would most-likely be from one of the youngest of *Sapphire*'s Midshipmen, who didn't know any better.

Yay, we're goin' *somewhere!* Lewrie scoffed to himself; *Ain't it just devilish-grand?*

It must here be pointed out that Captain Alan Lewrie, before he had become Sir Alan Lewrie, Bart., had been press-ganged into the Navy by his own father when he was seventeen, in the middle of the American Revolution (to collect an inheritance on Lewrie's mother's side that would save the old rogue from debtors' prison whilst Alan was away and all unknowing), and that Midshipman Alan Lewrie had *never* been a gladsome sailor! Or quite that young, either, to be perfectly honest!

Lewrie fetched his day-glass and mounted to the poop deck to observe the first morning's evolutions. The awnings were rigged over the deck against the Mediterranean sun and the rare rain, even if it was getting on for late November of 1807. Near the head of the larboard ladderway, his collapsible wood-and-canvas deck chair sat most invitingly, but, after a moment's longing look, Lewrie steeled himself to stand and look *somewhat* the Proper Sea Captain. The ship's mascot, Bisquit the dog, had been loafing aft on the flag lockers, but came trotting up for pets. After a proper greeting, and ruffling of his fur, Bisquit hopped into the chair himself, tongue lolling as if he knew he was getting away with something.

"Bloody idle . . . usurper," Lewrie muttered to the dog, smiling even so, then raised his telescope to watch the gunboats manoeuvre.

With wig-wagged hand-held flags, Harcourt and Elmes directed their sections of gunboats into line-ahead, headed out as if to row towards Algeciras and challenge the Spanish, then wheeled them into two separate groups in line-abreast . . . very raggedly, Lewrie thought, even if it was the sailors' first try, but he willed himself to be patient.

The next evolution that he and his officers had discussed would be a bit harder. The 12-pounder guns in the boats' bows were fixed on wheeled carriages, and the whole boat must be slewed about to aim them. Harcourt and Elmes would order their boats to wheel about in their own lengths as if they had fired and would retire to re-load. One bank of oars must stroke ahead whilst the opposite bank of oarsmen must either back-water, or jab their oar blades into the sea for brakes.

The little flags wagged again.

Though the gunboats were over two hundred yards off by then, Lewrie could distinctly hear Lt. Harcourt swearing a blue streak as some of those braking oars snapped like twigs. To make matters even worse, two boats in Lt. Elmes's group had their tillers put hard over in the wrong direction, causing all four of his boats to collide. The helmsmen in that group out-shouted Lt. Harcourt, each blaming the other for the accidents. Lewrie could make out "Tom-noddy!" and "Hen-headed lubber!" and "Cack-handed idjit, ye geed when ye shoulda hawed!" Even more oars were damaged as they'd scraped down each other's sides.

"Lord, sir!" Lt. Westcott said, astonished.

"Show 'em the Recall hoist, Mister Westcott," Lewrie ordered in sad amusement, shaking his head and slowly collapsing the tubes of his telescope, "before the Spanish spot 'em and laugh themselves t'death. This looks like it's goin' t'be a *damned* long day."

Fully armed and manned, the boats were just too heavy for the normal oars used in ships' boats to get them going from a dead stop, to back-water and shift their aim quickly, or bring them to a quick stop; they'd snap every time, leap out of the thole pins that held them, and slam oarsmen hard in their chests.

"Send ashore to the dockyards, Mister Westcott, and my compliments to Captain Middleton," Lewrie decided, "but, what we need on the boats are cut-down sweeps. Bigger oar blades, with thicker, stronger shafts, and perhaps even thicker and stronger sets of thole pins. If he can pad the loom ends so they don't cripple my sailors every time they brake or back-water, we'd all very much appreciate that, too."

The sailors in question, now back aboard for a more detailed explanation of their duties, had a good, appreciative laugh, but the First Officer had to scowl, and a scowl on Lt. Westcott's harsh face was formidable. "Sweeps, sir? I can't recall the last time I've seen even the smallest warship fitted with sweeps, and row-ports. He might not have a one on hand."

"Exactly, Mister Westcott," Lewrie replied with a sly, cherubic grin. "And until he does whip some up, our gunboats are useless."

"Oh, I *see*, sir!" Westcott grinned back, tumbling to it. "I shall go over to the yards myself, sir, with your permission."

"I couldn't deprive you of the experience, sir," Lewrie told him with a wink and a nod. "Now, lads," he said louder, turning to his sailors, "let's gather round the base of the main mast and we'll go over what *should* have happened this morning, hey?"

He put a bold and confident face on for their benefit, even as he thought that the whole endeavour was thankless, pointless, useless, hopeless. . . . *Christ, you can coin a whole* slew *o' new words to describe this shitten mess! Somebody,* anybody, *get me back out to sea!*

CHAPTER TWO

*L*ieutenant Westcott had come back aboard an hour or two later that day with the cheering news that Captain Middleton didn't have any sweeps in store to be cut down. Equally cheering was Westcott's description of Middleton's reaction, how he had all but slapped his forehead, stomped round the wood yard in anger at himself for over-estimating the strength of the usual ash oars and under-estimating how the added weight made his fancy new gunboats so slow and unwieldy. It had been a joy to watch, Lewrie was assured!

Less cheering was the information that, once Captain Middleton had gotten over his "How could I have been so stupid?" and his groans and gargles of *Mea Culpa,* he had assured Westcott that the Gibraltar dockyard had a goodly lot of ash planks in stock, and that he could have enough sweeps fashioned to try out on at least half of the gunboats by the end of the week, and that his artificers would have the rowlocks strengthened on all the existing boats, and strengthen them on the four more under construction, as well!

"Don't s'pose we could sneak over and set a huge fire in the yards," Lewrie had glumly suggested at that news.

"That might not go down well, sir," Westcott had cautioned him. "Sabotage, treason . . . all sorts of court-martial charges."

"Unless we could blame it on the Spanish," Lewrie pointed out. "The authorities ashore have foreign agents on their brains, and Spanish or French spies under every bed. General Dalrymple's sure that a mutiny plot has been in the works for most of this year. Ah well . . . we probably would be caught in the act."

Long ago, Lewrie and two schoolboy chums *had* been caught in the act after setting fire to the governor's coachhouse at Harrow, and sent down, expelled, and denied the grounds forever.

"You'll be dining ashore tonight, sir?" Lewrie's cabin steward, Pettus, asked as Lewrie primped himself at his wash-hand stand. He asked with a straight face and a non-committal tone, since everyone knew by now where Lewrie might be, and with whom when ashore.

"Thought I might, Pettus," Lewrie said, striving for "casual" himself as he dried and put away his razor after a touch-up on his morning shave. "Pass word to Yeovill that he's to prepare something for you, Jessop, and my clerk, Mister Faulkes, but not for me, but I will be back aboard for breakfast."

"Aye, sir," Pettus replied, casting a quick grin at the teen-aged cabin servant, Jessop, who, out of Lewrie's sight, also grinned impishly and made a hole of his left hand, poking a right finger into it.

Lewrie wetted his toothbrush in a cup of fresh water, ran it over a tin of flavoured pumice toothpowder, and began to scrub at his teeth. Once done, he put a hand to his mouth to catch his breath to sample its freshness. He would be dining with his "kept woman," the lovely and intriguing Portuguese, Maddalena Covilhā, and wanted very much to please. In a side pocket of his uniform coat he had a tin of London-made cinnamon *pastilles* for both of them, before and after supper.

In the other side pocket there were three freshly-cleaned sheep-gut cundums, also London-made. Though he did not plan to make the evening an "All Night In" at the lodgings he'd taken for her, it was always best to be prepared for surprises.

Surprises, well; here came one of the furry kind, for his cat, Chalky, sprang to the top of the wash-hand stand and found a precarious perch on one corner, then ambled along the narrow front lip with the skill of a circus rope walker, brushing his mostly white fur on Lewrie's recently sponged waist-coat, butting and stroking his head and his cheeks in affection, or in mischief; with Chalky it was hard to tell.

"Aye, and I love you, too, puss," Lewrie said, giving Chalky a few long strokes from nose to tail as the cat turned about and pressed himself to Lewrie the other way, marking his master as *his* property. He also stuck his nose in the cup of water and had a swipe at the toothbrush.

"Just keep my coat out of his reach 'til I'm ready to put it on, my lad," Lewrie told Pettus.

"Never a fear of that, sir," Pettus promised, "we always hang it from an overhead beam hook . . . though, there is so much stray hair in the air, you're sure to catch a few."

"As I well know, by now, aye!" Lewrie happily replied, taking a last brush of his hair. "Well, shove me in it, and I'll be off."

Oh, Christ . . . him! Lewrie thought with a groan as he espied Mr. Thomas Mountjoy at the top of the landing stage of the Old Mole as his boat ghosted up to it; *What the Devil's he doin' here, and what sort of shit is he lookin' for me t'do for him, now? We weren't to see each other 'til the end of the week!*

Thomas Mountjoy was really a nice younger gentleman, a clever and diligent fellow who ostensibly ran a minor firm's office at Gibraltar, the Falmouth Import & Export Company, Ltd. He was the epitome of a second or third son of some Squirearchy family, sent abroad and into Trade, with a hope that he might make something of himself. Mountjoy was brown-haired and brown-eyed, and nothing remarkable at first impression, sobrely dressed, no flash at all.

What Thomas Mountjoy was, was the senior agent of the Foreign Office's Secret Branch station at Gibraltar, who ran spies into Cádiz to keep an eye on the French and Spanish ships that had been blockaded there since the epic Battle of Cape Trafalgar two years earlier, kept in touch with an host of paid, or patriotic, Spanish informers along the Andalusian coast; into Seville, the regional capital; and even in Madrid.

It had been Mountjoy who arranged for the hire of the transport ship that had carried Lewrie's borrowed soldiers to carry out his raids in the Summer, and he who amassed the information about, and sketches of, the targets they'd raided. It was Mountjoy who had been sent to Gibraltar by his mentors, the coldly calculating old cut-throat, Zachariah Twigg, who'd been Lewrie's bane since the early 1780s 'tween the wars, roping him into one neck-or-nothing affair after the other, and the cool James Peel . . . "'tis Peel, James Peel" . . . who was just as scary.

Lewrie hadn't seen Mountjoy's dangerous side, *yet*, but he was mortal-certain that, with teachers like those, the man had one, and before this active commission in command of *Sapphire* was done, there always was a good chance that he'd ask, or order, Lewrie to perform some "damn-fool" mission. Secret Branch had their hooks in him and they'd never let him off; it was only a matter of time!

What was really disturbing about such a mild-looking man as Mountjoy was that, once, he had told Lewrie that a part of his mission here at Gibraltar was to find a way to turn Spain, which had been at war with Great Britain since late 1804, to abandon its alliance with Napoleonic France and switch sides!

That had appeared to be a chore worthy of Hercules, like mucking out the Augean Stables, but, of late, events had arisen that might make it happen. The slavishly Franco-phile administration of Spain's Prime Minister, Godoy, had signed a treaty with France to let one of their armies march cross Spain to invade and conquer Portugal to force that country to cut off all trade with Great Britain, and at that moment, that army, under a Marshal Junot, was doing that very thing. Would the Spanish people be too proud to abide that?

Damn my eyes, but he's grinning! Lewrie thought, groaning to himself again; *I may be in the "quag" up t'my neck!*

Of course, Lewrie could also consider that Mountjoy had merely got some very good news of late, and had come to impart it, in the usual "ask me first, I know something that *you* don't know" way that most people in Secret Branch evinced . . . the smug bastards! He might even owe Mountjoy a drink at the end!

"Hallo, Captain Lewrie!" Mountjoy called out as Lewrie stepped onto the landing stage and ascended the ramp to the quay. He had his hat on the back of his head, hands on his hips, and his coat thrown back, beaming fit to bust and looking like a fellow who'd bet on the right horse at Ascot or the Derby.

"What's this welcome in aid of, Mountjoy?" Lewrie asked, feigning a faint scowl. "Need my services of a sudden, hey?"

"Why, I've come to congratulate you on your splendid show this morning," Mountjoy teased. "Most impressive, I must say!"

"Impressive, mine arse," Lewrie scoffed as he doffed his hat in salute. "Could you see the Dons laughing?"

Mountjoy had lodgings high up in the town, the upper storey of the house to boot, with a rooftop gallery where he kept an astronomical telescope so strong that he could count nose hairs on the Spanish sentries on their fortified lines, and get a good look at Ceuta, their fortress on the other side of the Strait of Gibraltar, on a good day.

"They were so amused that I fear several of their naval officers herniated themselves," Mountjoy twinkled back. "And, I have come to share the latest news with you."

"If it's something that gets me out of the gunboat trade before the dockyard sets things to rights, and back to sea, it'd be welcome," Lewrie replied, all but crossing the fingers of his right hand for luck.

"Well, it *might*," Mountjoy allowed, "one never knows. Junot is across the border into Portugal, and is dashing on Lisbon as fast as his soldiers' little legs can carry them, and thank God that the roads, or what pass for roads in Portugal, are so shitten-bad, if they exist at all. Come, let us stroll to a tavern, and I'll tell you all."

Lewrie noted, from a corner of his eye, that Mountjoy's second-in-command, Deacon, was at hand and on a careful watch over his superior, whilst seeming to be merely strolling and window-shopping. The grim, craggy-faced ex-Sergeant in the Foot Guards was another of Zachariah Twigg's or James Peel's recruits to an informal secret force of house-breakers, lock-pickers, copyists and forgers, house-maids, and street-waif informers and followers, assassins and disposers of foreign spies. Twigg called them his Baker Street Irregulars, after the location of his London townhouse.

"If the roads are so bad, can the Portuguese army slow them down, block them in all those mountain passes?" Lewrie asked.

"I'm sure they're trying," Mountjoy said with a shrug, "but it's a small army, compared to Junot's, and even if a fair share of their officer corps are British, there's only so much they can do.

"The royal court is packing up and taking ship as we speak," Mountjoy went on. "The national treasury, libraries, and art museums, the gilded royal carriages *and* the horses, and nigh ten thousand retainers, ladies, and courtiers will all sail for the Vice-Royalty of Brazil. Our embassy's packing up, too, and will go along with them, and be back in business. But, Portugal will be lost, in the end."

"Damn!" Lewrie spat. "That won't make Maddalena happy."

"I daresay," Mountjoy sadly agreed, then perked up. "Hopefully, it won't make the Spanish all that happy. This alliance with France has simply *ruined* their country, destroyed the pride of their navy, and put all Spain on short-commons, with half the goods and foodstuffs going to feed France's armies. A horrid bargain, altogether. Marsh sent me a note from Madrid—"

"Marsh?" Lewrie barked. "That insane fool?"

"I know, Romney Marsh is as mad as a hatter, but damn his eyes, he gets the goods, and his reports have been spot-on accurate. Whatever guise, or guises, he wears in Madrid, he's effective," Mountjoy had to admit. "Spying is the greatest *game* to him, a continual costume ball, and they'll get him in the end, but for now . . . ?"

"So . . . what'd he say?" Lewrie had to ask after a minute.

"The treaty that Godoy convinced King Carlos the Fourth to sign to let the French cross Spain to get at Portugal also allows any *number* of French troops into Spain itself," Mountjoy imparted in a low mutter. "They're marching South in several columns of corps, and they're under the command of a Marshal Joachim Murat, one of Napoleon Bonaparte's best generals. One column's bound, so Marsh says, to Madrid, and that one's gotten the Spanish worried that Godoy and all his French-loving, arse-licking allies will sell the whole country out.

"King Carlos is old, witless, and long past it," Mountjoy expanded as they ducked under a gaily-striped awning and took a two-place table outside of a public house. "The Crown Prince, Ferdinand, is a stubborn dunce, too, too much under the influence of one of his aunts, who's just *evil-mad* . . . but he has ambitions. Ferdinand is plotting to usurp the throne, and have Godoy garrotted . . . slowly . . . as soon as he pulls it off, and the Spanish seem just eager for that to happen, by now. Maybe Murat is bound to Madrid to save Godoy's, and the French-lovers', bacon before that happens, get rid of King Carlos, and put Ferdinand the Fool on the throne. We'll see which of them comes out on top."

"But . . . if the French are marching South, what if they come here?" Lewrie asked, frowning in deep thought. "What *else* is in that treaty?"

"Well, we don't know, and that's worrisome," Mountjoy gruffly confessed. "I was up to the Convent earlier today, to see the Dowager, at his request. He told me that his Spanish counterpart in charge of the military district, General Castaños, had sent him a letter saying that Madrid has ordered him to cease all communication with us, and restrict all further trade cross the Lines."

"Mine arse on a band-box," Lewrie started. "That sounds like a joint Franco-Spanish attack on Gibraltar! What did Sir Hew make of it?"

Lieutenant-General Sir Hew Dalrymple, best known as the Dowager for his lack of field experience, governed Gibraltar, and was responsible for its defence and continued existence. During his short term in that post, Sir Hew had fostered a warm and peaceable line of communication with

Castaños, a "live and let live" and a "let sleeping dogs lie" relationship. Lewrie imagined that Dalrymple's headquarters, once a real convent when Gibraltar had been captured from Spain in 1704, would be as topsy-turvy as the city of Lisbon tonight!

"No sign of panic when I was there today, but bags of active scurrying," Mountjoy told him with a grin. "Urgent despatches are being sent to our Army on Sicily, asking for re-enforcements, more are on the way to London, and Sir Hew's dusted off his scheme to attack the Spanish fortress of Ceuta, again. It seems that Lord Castlereagh, our War Secretary, had an inkling that the French would be moving on Portugal way back in August, and sent Sir Hew a letter wondering if Ceuta could be used by the French as a base for an expedition to take Gibraltar from the South. In league with the Spanish, of course." Mountjoy told him with a smirk of how *that* alliance would work. The Spanish had yearned to recover Gibraltar the last hundred years, and there had been siege upon siege, all failures. Would they want the Rock back so badly that they'd tolerate their own country full of Frenchmen?

From where he sat, Lewrie could look down the main town street which led to Europa Point, about four miles South, and picture in his mind the twelve miles of sea that separated Gibraltar from Ceuta. At Europa Point, there were no defensive works, such as there were on the West and North of the peninsula. The last fortifications ended a bit below the New Mole, and the Tuerto Tower, for the very good reason that there were no beaches on which to make a landing, and the bluffs were nigh-vertical, right down to the sea.

No, anyone landin' there'd have t'be a Barbary ape just t'get a toe-hold, Lewrie told himself; *And, can the French get a fleet and a huge convoy of transports to sea, with our Navy keepin' close watch on their main bases at Toulon and Marseilles?*

"I don't see it happening," Lewrie told Mountjoy, and explained why he doubted the French could pull it off. That seemed to mollify the man's worries on that score.

"Well, you're the sea-dog, so I'll take your word for it being nigh-impossible," Mountjoy breezily said, as if a large load had been taken from his shoulders. "But, the Dowager's always wanted to take Ceuta, and now's perhaps his chance. If Lord Castlereagh fears that the place is a risk for Gibraltar, they'd both want it eliminated."

Back in the Summer, before he and Mountjoy put together their raiding force, Lewrie had scouted past Ceuta looking for supply ships which he might snap up as prizes, and he had his doubts about taking Ceuta, too.

"Don't see that happening either," he told Mountjoy, describing how mountainous and rocky, how North African—desert dry was the land on which the great fortress complex was built, the massive height and thickness of the walls, and how many heavy guns he'd counted when he sailed *Sapphire* temptingly close to extreme gun-range. "There's no approaching any gate, or landing at its foot. You can blockade it, but I doubt it can be taken, even if ye *had* God's own amount of heavy siege guns, and even then, it'd take a *year* t'batter down a breach in the walls. Best isolate it and leave it be to starve."

"Well, I'm sure Sir Hew's aware of all that, but he's still so dead-keen on the attempt, I expect he relished Castlereagh's letters," Mountjoy scoffed. "Ceuta's his bug-a-bear."

"Hmm . . . he'd need someone t'go scout the place, wouldn't he?" Lewrie suggested, feeling sly and clever.

"Well, yayss," Mountjoy drawled back, "but only if that person kept his fool mouth shut and kept his doubts to himself. Have anyone in mind?"

"Me, Mountjoy," Lewrie snickered. "Dalrymple's sent off all of his available ships in port t'carry his letters, and who's left here? You're up to the Convent tomorrow? Good, you can suggest that Ceuta needs a close eye-ballin', and remind Sir Hew that I'm familiar with the place from before."

"Anything to get free of those gunboats, right?" Mountjoy said with a laugh.

"You're Goddamned right!" Lewrie assured him.

"I'm to attend a staff meeting just after breakfast, I'll put the flea in his ear then," Mountjoy promised.

After a couple of glasses of a sprightly white Portuguese wine, Mountjoy sloped off for his lodgings for the night, covertly shadowed by ex-Sergeant Deacon, who tipped Lewrie a grim nod of recognition.

Lewrie strode South, further down the quayside street to meet Maddalena for his own supper. There was a lovely and colourful sunset behind Algeciras and the Spanish mainland the other side of the bay, one that was mirrored in the harbour waters, and there was a slight cooling breeze wafting down the Strait from the Atlantic, a breeze that had a touch of

Winter to it, at long last. Looking up at the massive heights of the Rock, Lewrie could see that the sundown colours painted the stark mountain red and gold, and tinted the white-washed stone buildings of the upper town in the same warm hues.

He reached Maddalena's lodgings and trotted up the stairs to her floor, down the hall to the front of the building, and knocked at her stout wooden door.

"Ah, you are here!" Maddalena said as she swept the door open, and quickly embraced him with a fiercer hug than usual. As he stroked her back, Lewrie felt a tenseness in her.

"What is it, *minha doce?*" he asked, using what little Portuguese that he'd picked up from her over the months: *my sweet.*

"It is true, the rumours in the markets?" she fearfully asked. "The French are taking my country? Lisbon?"

"I'm afraid it's true," Lewrie had to admit to her. "They aren't there yet, but they're marching on Lisbon," and he added what Mountjoy had told him of the evacuation of the Portuguese court and all of the national treasures.

"We've a dozen ships of the line to see them to Brazil, along with all the Portuguese navy. The French won't get anything." Lewrie added, "Your Dom João bamboozled Bonaparte and the French, stringin' them along 'til the last moment, promising t'close his ports to British trade, but planning t'flee all along."

"But your country cannot stop them?" Maddalena fretted. "Your army and navy can't . . . ?"

"Not right away," Lewrie had to tell her. "We have t'save Gibraltar first, *then* London will come up with something."

"I never saw Lisbon," Maddalena mournfully said, drifting off towards the wine-cabinet to pour them drinks. "When we sailed from Oporto on our way here, we came close . . . but not so close that I could see the city. I was always told how beautiful it is, and now . . . you must save *Gibraltar* first?" she asked with a deep frown.

"The French are sending several armies into Spain, too, bound here and Cádiz, most-like, t'lay siege here, and get their ships from Trafalgar back. Gibraltar's always held, and I doubt if the French and Spanish together can change that. We're safe. You're safe," he assured her as he took an offered glass, marvelling again at how fortunate he was to have discovered her. She'd been "under the protection" of an army officer, a Brevet-Major

Hughes, when he met them, and a dull and joyless relationship that had been for her, for Hughes was a fool. General Dalrymple had put Hughes in command of the land forces for the raids, and, fortunately for Lewrie, the idiot dashed off in the pre-dawn dark and confusion and was captured by the Spanish, and still languished in their custody, on his parole 'til a Spaniard of equal rank could be exchanged for him. Hughes never knew what he'd had.

Maddalena Covilhã had come down from a mountain town of the same name, Covilhã, to Oporto to make her fortune, struck up with a wine merchant who'd brought her to Gibraltar in 1804 and then died of Gibraltar Fever the same year, leaving her penniless and alone.

Beyond her slim and supple body, beyond her bold good looks, Maddalena Covilhã was also a very intelligent young lady of great sense, who had taught herself English, then Spanish, and was literate and fluent in all three languages.

Such was the fate of all un-attached young women, and young widows, on Gibraltar, unless they'd inherited a family business or a bequest, and could support themselves; they had to be dependent upon a man who would take them "under his protection" and pay for their up-keep. Maddalena might have expected her new keeper to be the same sort of un-feeling brute as Hughes, but both she and Lewrie found their arrangement to be a mutually pleasing, amusing, and affectionate relationship, even knowing that it might not be permanent. He'd been a widower since 1802, and a sailor who could be ordered away any time.

She was wearing a new gown in a russet colour, trimmed with just a bit of white lace, which he thought complemented her dark brown hair and eyes and slightly olive complexion quite nicely. He noted that a white lace shawl and a perky little straw bonnet trimmed with russet ribbons awaited their going-out atop a tall chest, out of reach of her cat, Precious. Maddalena had gone to the set of double doors that led to the harbour-front balcony of her set of rooms, to stare out at the sunset and sip her wine. He went to join her.

"Ye know, *minha doce,* that we'll kick the French out of Portugal, and you'll see Lisbon," he cooed, and she leaned back into him. "Hell, I vow you'll end up a fine lady in Lisbon, in a free country."

"*Sim* . . . yes, I would like that, someday," she whispered back, still looking outwards. She then turned to look at him and put her arms round his waist, with a dreamy look on her face. "You will do that for

me, I know. You're a good man, Alan. Now, will you feed me? And where
do we dine?"

"Pescadore's!" they said in chorus, and laughed aloud, for that seafood
establishment, run by a retired British Sergeant-Major and his Spanish wife
and children, was one of the few really good places on the Rock to dine.

As merry as Lewrie tried to be with her, though, and as merry as she
pretended to be, Maddalena's mood, her sadness and worry, could not
rise to the occasion, and she merely picked at her succulent seafood
supper.

Worst of all, for Lewrie at least, was later when they returned to her
lodgings. When they sat on the settee and began to kiss and fondle, she
laid a reticent hand on his chest.

"Alan, I am . . . how you say, 'under the moon'?" she whispered.

"Under . . . ah!" he realised, then deflated. "Damn. Well . . . ?"

It was Maddalena's time of the month, and those cundums in his coat
pocket would go un-used. He'd never much cared for tupping any maiden
when she was having her bloody flux, and had slept in a separate bed-
chamber when his late wife had hers. It was just too messy!

"I am sorry, dear man," she said, whispering into his neck.

"Don't you be sorry for Mother Nature," he insisted, trying to laugh it
off. "There'll be plenty of other nights. Eh, I don't think I'll sleep ashore,
if that's alright with you. I *adore* sleeping with you, mind, but I'd only get
tempted, and . . ."

"Frustrated," Maddalena finished for him. "*Sim,* I would be frustrated,
também," she added with a nervous little laugh.

It was awkward for both of them, but, after a final glass of wine and a
few hugs and kisses in parting, Lewrie ended up strolling back to the quays
and the landing stage in the dark and mostly empty streets, hand on the
hilt of his everyday hanger, and glad to see the Provost patrols who served
as the Town Major's police force.

"A boat, sir?" a sleepy waterman at the landing stage asked, rousing
himself from a nap.

"Aye," Lewrie told him. "Out to the *Sapphire.*"

My idle ship, he thought.

The large taffrail lanthorns at the stern were lit, as well as smaller lanthorns on the quarterdeck and forecastle. The wee street-lights along the
quay and the main street barely reached her sides, making the 50-gunned

two-decker merely the hint of a wooden ghost out on the calm waters of the bay, and her furled and harbour-gasketted sails seemed more like old parchment.

It's only a day's jaunt, out and back to Ceuta, but I'll take it, he told himself; *I'll take* any *opportunity t'get under way again.*

CHAPTER THREE

*L*ewrie was only half-way through his breakfast, a particularly fine omelet with mushrooms, onions, tomato, and cheese, with toasted slabs of fresh shore bread, when one of *Sapphire*'s Midshipmen standing Harbour Watch hailed an approaching boat. Lewrie perked up, chewing a bite of toast thickly slathered with red currant preserves, cocking an ear to what was occurring just beyond his cabin doors. He faintly made out a call from the boat; "Letter for your Captain!" and sat up even straighter, about ready to cross the fingers of his right hand for good luck. Yes! There was the thump of a boat coming alongside, and the scramble of a messenger up the boarding battens!

He picked up a bit of spicy Spanish sausage with his fingers and popped it into his mouth as footsteps could be heard clumping on the quarterdeck, leading to . . .

"Message for the Captain, SAH!" the Marine Private who stood sentry at the cabin doors cried, stamping boots and musket butt.

"Enter," Lewrie called out, trying to sound *blasé*.

And don't let it be from the bloody dockyards! he thought.

Midshipman Ward, one of the youngest, came round to the dining-coach with his hat under his arm, and a sealed letter in his hand.

"Yes, Mister Ward?" Lewrie said, between sips of coffee.

"A message from Lieutenant-General Sir Hew Dalrymple, sir," Ward stiffly said, laying the missive on the dining table.

"Thank you, Mister Ward, you may go," Lewrie told him, paying it no attention for the moment. As soon as Ward was round the corner into the day-cabin, though, Lewrie snatched it up and tore it open. "Aha! Pettus? Pass word to muster my boat crew, if ye please, I'm called ashore." He reached for the napkin tucked under his chin and almost shot to his feet, but paused. It really was such a toothsome breakfast, too good to be abandoned entirely. He took a few quick bites more of everything, a last slurp of sugared and creamed coffee, then shrugged into his coat, snatched up his sword belt and hat, and left the cabins, still chewing.

Chalky, who had been feeding from his own bowl atop the table at the far end, took the opportunity to raid what was left, paying close attention to the sausages.

The Convent, headquarters and lodgings for Dalrymple and his staff, did not resemble the dither that Thomas Mountjoy had depicted to Lewrie the night before; it seemed almost somnolent and hushed at its normal routine. Lewrie was shown into Dalrymple's offices by an aide-de-camp. There was no breathless council-of-war going on; there was only Sir Hew, standing before a large map pinned to a board on a stand, musing over Ceuta and its environs.

"Ah, Lewrie," Sir Hew said, almost absent-mindedly. "Thank you for coming on such short notice. I need you to do me a small service, if you can."

"Happy to, sir," Lewrie replied, feeling a bit let-down that his imaginings did not match the reality. "What do ye have in mind?"

"*That* bloody place, sir!" Sir Hew spat, jabbing his arm out to tap his map. "London has finally relented to my many suggestions for dealing with Ceuta." Sir Hew turned to face Lewrie. "Major-General Sir Brent Spencer and an army of seven thousand men are being sent to me to do just that. Lord Castlereagh has sent me formal approval to make the attempt."

"And you need someone t'give it a fresh look-over, I see, sir," Lewrie said, his excitement rising.

"That Mountjoy fellow reminded me that you had sailed close to Ceuta several times during your, ah . . . exertions during the Summer, and thought you might be familiar with the number, and calibre, of its artillery," Sir Hew said, twitching his mouth; he had not been enthusiastic about the raids, even if they might have led to Spanish troops being syphoned off from the vicinity of Gibraltar to protect the coast.

"It's a fine day for it, sir," Lewrie chearly said, itching to be back aboard his ship and out of harbour. "I can be off Ceuta by noon and back in port the day after with a report."

"I've heard some rumours, which that *spying* fellow of yours . . . ," Sir Hew said with a sniff.

He's mine is he? Lewrie thought, twitching his mouth.

". . . that Ceuta has been re-enforced," Dalrymple went on, "with more troops and more guns, perhaps two more regiments and two more gun batteries, though there's nothing definite. How that's possible, God only knows. I've observers atop the Rock with strong telescopes."

Lewrie went to look at the map, searching for the landing place that served the fortress. "Your observers can't see round the other side of the peninsula, sir, the Sou'west side at the narrow neck below the fortress. Ships from Málaga and Cartagena could sail wide, almost level with Tetuán, then coast up to the landing. Do it in the dark . . . on stormy nights? Those two big frigates I fought were loaded with supplies, food, and arms. They could have been on their way to concentrate with what's left of the Spanish navy at Cádiz, but now I suspect that they were on their way to Ceuta when I ran across 'em. That's most-like how they did it."

"And our naval supremacy in the Mediterranean could do nought to stop them?" Dalrymple snapped, as if assigning blame.

"Our fleet in the Med, sir, is more concerned with the French, at Marseilles and Toulon," Lewrie pointed out. "When *Sapphire* raided the coast, it was rare t'run into a naval presence 'til we got up to Barcelona, and, once the raids were suspended . . ."

That earned him a deep glower from Dalrymple; he'd been the one who'd ordered that the raids cease, to maintain his amicable relations with his counterpart, Spanish General Castaños.

"In any event, I *do* need someone to make a reconnaissance over yonder, Captain Lewrie," Sir Hew said, stiff-backed and gruffly. "The powers-that-be in London *still* refuse to see the need for a permanent naval squadron at Gibraltar which I may call upon. I thank you for acceding to my request."

"I'll get right at it, sir," Lewrie said, turning to go.

"By the by, how is your progress with the gunboat squadron?" Sir Hew called out.

"Bloody awful, sir, truthfully," Lewrie was happy to tell him. "But Captain Middleton at the dockyard is making adjustments."

"Be sure that once you return with your report that you bend all your efforts to bringing them to fruition," Sir Hew sternly told him.

"But of course, sir," Lewrie had to agree, while wondering if he could send a written report ashore by boat, then sail off to see what was happening off Cádiz, or Lisbon; *anything* but gunboats!

"Welcome back aboard, sir," First Officer Geoffrey Westcott said to him, in his shirtsleeves and sweaty from sword practise. In Lewrie's absence, the crew had been put to an hour of cutlass drill, and the two-decker had rung with metallic clashes before his boat was hailed, and Lewrie's Cox'n, the "Black Irishman" Liam Desmond, had shouted back "Aye aye!" and held up four fingers to tell the men of the watch that the Captain was returning.

"Had enough tinkling, Mister Westcott?" Lewrie asked.

"Well, aye, sir," Westcott said with a puzzled frown.

"Good. Stop the drill and stow the cutlasses away, then pipe Stations for getting under way," Lewrie told him. "Once we're fully under sail and beyond Europa Point, we'll beat to Quarters, to boot."

"At *once*, sir!" Westcott shouted with glee. "Ehm . . . where are we going? Is there a fight ahead?"

"We're ordered to scout Ceuta, and yes, there may be a fight," Lewrie promised. "It'll be un-equal, of course, but we should survive it."

Westcott was still puzzled, scowling fiercely, but inside he was pleased.

"Let's get those bloody awnings down!" Lewrie shouted.

CHAPTER FOUR

*O*ut at sea, there was a decent amount of wind to carry *Sapphire* over to-wards Ceuta under fully-spread tops'ls, t'gallants, all of her stays'ls and jibs, with her main course brailed up against the risk of that great sail catching fire from the discharge of her own guns. It had been several months since the 50-gunned two-decker fired her broadsides in action, and Lewrie hoped that that hard-won efficiency and accuracy that his crew had developed, that his gunners had been able to concentrate against a shore fort under construction to the point that its foundations had been undermined, and concentrated so brutally in *Sapphire*'s fight against two big Spanish frigates that had utterly disabled one and sunk the other, still existed, even if they were now a bit rusty.

"The ship is at Quarters, sir," Lt. Westcott reported, sternly and formally, even doffing his hat in salute.

"Very good, Mister Westcott," Lewrie replied with equal formality, and a doff of his own hat. "Do we have good, deep water with no obstructions, right up to within a mile of the fortress, Mister Yelland?" he asked, turning to the ship's Sailing Master.

"Within a mile, sir?" Yelland replied, sucking at his teeth. "Aye, sir, if you've a mind. Ten fathom right to the shore, except at the narrows, where it shoals to five."

Lewrie nodded agreement, glad that they did not have to enter the chart room on the larboard side of the quarterdeck, for Yelland did not sponge himself as often as he should, nor did he change his small-clothes often, either. Yelland was an excellent Sailing Master, but by God did he reek!

"Mister Hillhouse, and Mister Fywell," Lewrie called out to two of his Mids, one in his twenties, and the other still a lad. "I will admire did ye both place yourselves in the main mast fighting top and take a slate, or paper and pencil, with you. We're going to trail our colours before the Spanish bull, and see how he snorts. I want a count of guns in the fortress, t'see if they have more than the last time we got close to the place. A rough guess as to the respective calibres'd be welcome, too."

"Aye aye, sir," Hillhouse, the oldest, firmly replied. Fywell merely nodded with a wide-eyed gulp, for the fortress of Ceuta mounted artillery equal to 32-pounders and 42-pounders in British measure, and could range out to *three* miles. There already were some thin skeins of smoke rising within the fortress, where roundshot was being heated to red-hot in the furnaces. They *might* be cooking mid-day dinners, but . . . !

"Mister Westcott, you and I will be on the poop deck, where we can use our telescopes to spy out the other details," Lewrie said.

"A grand place to catch a cool breeze, sir," Westcott agreed, despite his understandable worry. This was damn-fool daft!

"I think we'll begin at three-miles' range, then slowly close to two miles, Mister Yelland," Lewrie said, "and I'll trust you and trigonometry t'see to that. We'll not make it easy for them."

"Aye, sir," Yelland said with a throat-clearing *grumph*.

"Just . . . tempting," Lewrie added before mounting the larboard ladderway to the poop deck.

HMS *Sapphire* stood on, with the rocky heights and the fortress of Ceuta almost bows-on for some time, 'til the Sailing Master spoke up. "Three miles off, sir!"

"Very well. Hands to sheets and braces, and make her head Due East," Lewrie ordered, and the Bosuns' calls piped the order, along with loud bawls from Bosun Terrell and his Mates, Nobbs and Plunkett. The helm was put over, and Ceuta swam from being obscured by the fore course and jibs to appear ahead of the bows off the starboard side.

A long five minutes passed as *Sapphire* surged along at seven knots, three miles off from the fortress, with nothing happening.

"What, are they asleep?" Lt. Westcott japed, eager for something to happen, even if it would be dire.

"Wish I'd thought t'fetch Mountjoy's astronomical telescope," Lewrie said, lowering his day-glass in frustration. "I can make out troops on the parapets, sure enough, but evidently they're not tempted yet. Mister Yelland? Alter course and close to two miles' range, if you please, then bring her back to Due East."

"Aye aye, sir!"

Once more, *Sapphire* swung shoreward, gathering a little speed as she took the winds more on her larboard quarters, then swung back East. "Two miles, sir!" Yelland reported from the quarterdeck below Lewrie's position.

"Very well, carry on," Lewrie called back, sensing his ship's loss of speed as she took the winds more abeam. He was still getting used to plodding, after years in sloops of war and swift frigates, and *Sapphire*, like all her sister Fourth Rates, definitely plodded!

"Gunfire, sir!" Midshipman Hillhouse shouted down from the main mast fighting top. "The Spanish have opened upon us!"

"Now, that's more like it," Lewrie said with a satisfied grin.

"The things we do for King and Country," Lt. Westcott said.

The fortress of Ceuta slowly erupted in flashes of flame from the muzzles of her guns, and large yellowish-grey clouds of gunpowder. It was seconds later that anyone aboard *Sapphire* could hear the explosions, and long seconds later before massive solid iron roundshot came moaning and droning towards the ship. The Spanish were in no hurry, for Ceuta's guns tolled down the length of its northern face as slow and steady as a metronome, or a salute fired to honour an incoming ship. Far ahead of *Sapphire*'s bows, far astern, and between Ceuta and *Sapphire*, the shot smacked into the sea, still travelling nigh to eight hundred feet per second, raising great, crystalline pillars and feathers of spray and foam that took forever to collapse upon themselves, and Lewrie thought that they looked quite pretty . . . so long as they were well wide, or well short!

One ball skipped from First Graze, dapping to Second Graze, and finally sank about a cable's distance to starboard. The fortress's guns were mounted so much higher than the ship that grazing, skipping shot was a rarity, much more common between ships in combat whose guns were much on the same level. The bulk of the Spanish fire came in a descending arc, which created those immense pillars of spray.

Whee-ooh! First one, then another heavy roundshot moaned overhead to strike the sea beyond *Sapphire*, higher-pitched as they approached, then going *basso* as they soared high over the mast trucks and sailed out to sea.

"Those'll be the big bastards, their version of forty-two-pounders," Lewrie commented. "Still like the cool breeze, Geoffrey?"

"It's getting hotter," Westcott replied. "Well, warm-ish."

"Just so they don't glow red," Lewrie said, lifting his telescope once more. "Is that everything, East to West, from all their embrasures and the upper parapet, d'ye think?"

"Hmm, it seems to be," Westcott agreed with his own telescope up to his right eye. "Those last shots came from the Eastern end of the fort."

"Mister Yelland, alter course to loo'rd, put us on the wind and get back to three miles' range," Lewrie ordered. "We'll try the East face, next, once we're beyond the point."

"Aye *aye*, sir!" Yelland shot back, quickly issuing the orders to the helmsmen and hands on the sail-tending gangways. He sounded relieved.

Ceuta's gunners had adjusted their aim, and their elevations, and the North face of the fortress tolled again, lashing the sea with shot, but *Sapphire*'s turn to seaward frustrated them. Their 24-pounders and 32-pounders struck well short, and it was only a few of the massive 42-pounders 'round-shot that came anywhere close, but they all missed.

"It doesn't look as if they've had much practice, recently," Lewrie said with a hopeful note in his voice.

"Good Lord, who'd dare *give* them any, sir?" Westcott muttered. "We just *might* be doing them a favour, damn their eyes."

A last 42-pounder shot plunged into the sea roughly amidships of *Sapphire*'s length and only a long musket-shot off, throwing up so much spray that the starboard side was drenched, and everyone could hear a quick hiss and see a gust of steam as it sank. Heated shot!

"A bit more than three miles off now, sir," Yelland reported. "Shall we come back to Due East?"

"Aye, Mister Yelland," Lewrie agreed, noting that the man was fetching his hat from the deck and plopping it back on his wet hair.

The man's had a bath, whether he wanted it or not, Lewrie told himself with a hidden smile.

They turned South once the ship was three miles beyond the end of the peninsula on which Ceuta was sited, and played their dangerous game down the fortress's East face, ducking in and out of range on a "drunkard's walk" of course alterations, counting the guns fired at them. Lewrie imagined that the Spanish would refuse to co-operate and not be drawn, after a while, seeing the game for what it really was, and loath to waste powder and shot, but, evidently the officer commanding Ceuta thought that he was in need of a live target and practice, or his touchy Spanish pride was pricked too sore, for when *Sapphire* turned Sou'west to run in towards the North African coast within two miles of shore, the South face opened upon her, too. After a quick count of the guns in the lower embrasures and the open-air parapets above, Lewrie finally, and secretly much relieved that his ship had not taken any damage, ordered *Sapphire* to turn South and sail away out of range, halfway to the Moroccan port of Tetuán before wheeling seaward to round the Ceuta peninsula by a wide berth.

"Secure from Quarters, Mister Westcott, and I hope the hands weren't too bored," Lewrie said, "standin' round the better part of the day with not a shot fired."

"Oh, I think they'll not mind too much, since there was nothing our guns could've done, even had we gone within a mile or less," Lieutenant Westcott replied. "Ceuta's a right formidable bastard."

"Aye, it is," Lewrie agreed as they descended to the quarterdeck, "and I don't envy anyone who trades fire with it, or tries to take it. The West face, the main gate, and where any besiegers would have t'set up, that's a *killin'* ground. Dalrymple's daft to try."

"If our Navy can keep the French from getting in there, and it can be blockaded proper, maybe Ceuta could be left to wither on the vine," Westcott decided, "as you told me what you and Mountjoy spoke of. If the French *do* get a fleet of transports in there and join up with the Spanish garrison, the only shelter from bad weather is on the Southern side, near the landing places, and even that's wide open to a bad blow."

"Might not have good holding ground, the same as Gibraltar," Lewrie agreed.

"And, if the mountain, and the fortress, disturb the winds as badly as Gibraltar does, sir, anyone anchored there for any time may suffer a clear-weather gust and end on their beam-ends, the same as happens at the Rock!" Westcott exclaimed.

Gibraltar Bay, from the Old Mole to the New Mole, was littered with the wrecks of ships caught un-awares, and driven ashore onto the rocks as their anchors dragged due to the strong, fluky winds.

"Ah, Mister Hillhouse," Lewrie said, acknowledging the Mids as they came to the quarterdeck. "What's the count?"

"Formidable, sir," Hillhouse reported; there was the word, again. "We counted over one hundred fifty guns, altogether, those that fired upon us, and lighter twenty-four-pounders on the upper parapets that could not range us. Fywell's made a sketch—"

"I draw quite well, sir," Fywell piped up, "or so my tutors told me," he added with a blush.

"Indeed you do, young sir," Lewrie congratulated him as he was handed a set of sketches of all three sides of the fortress which had engaged them, and a fourth—sideways view—of the West face and entry gates and the ground at the neck of the peninsula where an army would have to camp, along with the structures along the landing place.

"Sir Hew Dalrymple will be happy to have these, Mister Fywell, and if you hope to advance, would you please put your name on them in a prominent manner? Good," Lewrie bade him. "He might mention you in despatches. I don't know how many guns Ceuta had before, but we have rumours that it's been re-enforced, and someone will know the original number. Thank you both, you've done good service."

"Ehm, thank you, sir!"

"We won't be going back to harbour, will we, sir?" Fywell had to ask. "Not right away?"

"Been anchored so long, sir, we've nigh lost our 'sea legs,'" Hillhouse added.

"No," Lewrie decided of a sudden. "We'll stand off-and-on for the night, and see what the morrow brings. Carry on, sirs."

"Enjoy," Lt. Westcott added.

"Mister Yelland?" Lewrie called out.

"Still here, sir," that worthy grunted in reply.

"Let's take a look at your charts, sir," Lewrie said. "Let's see if we can discover where our soldiers could land and encamp."

"Aye, sir," Yelland said, heading for the larboard chart room.

Lewrie steeled himself for the stink.

It was late in the day, in the middle of the First Dog Watch, and Yelland lit a candle to see by. They pored over the chart for some time, but neither of them could admit to the slightest clue as to where Dalrymple thought to land his army.

"It looks to me, sir, that the coast is too much bluffs and too little beach," Yelland said, scratching his chin. "The North shore is too open to weather, and the South's not much better. Maybe they could go ashore far South of Ceuta, and march there."

"What's this little place?" Lewrie asked, pointing to a mote on the chart. "The Isla de . . . Perejil. What's a *perejil*? It's Spanish, but I wonder if it means something in Arabic."

"I think it means 'Parsley,' sir," Yelland supplied. "Parsley Island. Spanish, for certain."

"D'ye think parsley really grows there?" Lewrie asked.

"Haven't a clue, sir. If it does, some fresh, green parsley would be welcome," Yelland said with a deep chuckle.

"We'll stand off-and-on through the night, but in the morning, I want to take a look at Parsley Island before we head back to Gibraltar."

"Very good, sir," Yelland said, blowing out the candle.

Being out in the fresh, cool air again was very welcome, as was Lewrie's joyful greeting from Bisquit, who'd been down on the orlop and shivering in fear. Whenever *Sapphire* went to Quarters, the poor dog no longer needed someone to lead him below to dubious safety; he dashed down the steep ladderways on his own. Now he was prancing on his hind legs, front paws and head on Lewrie's chest, and his bushy tail a'wag, making happy little whines.

"Good boy! Want a sausage?" Lewrie cooed. Bisquit did!

CHAPTER FIVE

*H*MS *Sapphire* ghosted her way to Parsley Island just after dawn the next morning under tops'ls and jibs, with leadsmen in the foremast chain platforms sounding for the shallows. The only charts available were copies of very old Spanish charts—make that *ancient* Spanish charts—borrowed from the dockyard superintendent. Certainly, no Arabic seamen had made surveys or soundings in the time when the Moors held Spain, Portugal, or North Africa, and made their corsair voyages on "fishermen's lore." To make sure that the ship did not strike some submerged rock or shoal, one of the twenty-five-foot cutters led *Sapphire* by several hundred yards, under a lugsail, with two leadsmen in her bows, as well, and armed with a swivel gun to be fired should they run into any measure less than five fathoms. So far all was well.

"We're really looking for parsley, sir?" Lt. Westcott asked between yawns. "It looks a damned dry place, to me."

"I did a little fiddling over the charts last night," Lewrie told him, "and it appears that this little island *might* not be visible from Ceuta . . . straight-line ruler, bulge of the mountains 'twixt here and there? But, still close enough to Ceuta to be able to take any approaching Spanish or French ship under fire, if there's any way t'mount guns ashore."

"If there's any way to *get* guns ashore, sir," Westcott countered. "It looks damned steep."

The island was not all that big, really, and it put Lewrie in mind of a half-sunk scone, with bald rock cliffs all across the side that they were approaching. Atop of its ragged, erose surface there were hints of desert-like scrub and sere grass, but there didn't seem a way up to the top. *Africa, North Africa,* he thought; *who'd want it?*

"Eight fathom! Eight fathom t'this line!" a leadsman wailed.

Sapphire drew nigh twenty feet right aft, slightly less at the bows, so he considered the going safe for a time more, but the best bower anchor was ready to be let go should the men in the chains call out five fathoms, crewmen stood by to seize upon the sheets and braces, and a pair of experienced helmsmen were prepared to put the ship about into the wind in a twinkling.

"The cutter is showing numeral flag Six, sir!" Midshipman Griffin shouted aft from the forecastle.

"We're about half a mile off the island now, sir," the Sailing Master, Mister Yelland, reported, after a quick peek with his sextant and some figuring on a chalk slate.

"Seven fathom! Seven fathom t'this line!" a leadsman called.

"Put the ship about, Mister Westcott, and prepare to let go the best bower," Lewrie decided.

"Aye, sir. Hard down your helm, there! Topmen, trice up and lay out to take in sail!" Lt. Westcott ordered in his best quarterdeck shout. "Ready brace-tenders to back the fore tops'l!"

Sapphire slowly wheeled about to turn up into the wind, barely making four knots in the beginning, and starting to sag slower as the rudder was put over at such a great angle. The jibs began to flutter as the wind came right down the boom and bowsprit, the fore tops'l pressed back against the foremast, and the ship almost came to rest.

"Let go the bower!" Lewrie ordered, and the large larboard anchor dropped free from the cat-heads to splash into the sea, and the thigh-thick cable rumbled and roared out the hawsehole. *Sapphire* drifted shoreward for a time, 'til the anchor hit bottom and a five-to-one scope had paid out. Then she snubbed, groaned, and was still.

"We'll take the second cutter and the launch," Lewrie told his assembled officers. "Mister Roe, ten Marines into the launch, and I'll take the cutter." Lieutenants Westcott, Harcourt, and Elmes all peered at him, evidently disappointed. "What? D'ye think you're to have *all* the fun? Pass word to my steward that I'll need my brace of pistols, my Ferguson rifled musket, and all accoutrements. Crawley and his old boat crew to man the launch, and my boat crew to man the cutter. And Mister Fywell . . ."

"Sir?" the lad piped up.

"Go fetch your drawing materials and join me in the cutter," Lewrie ordered. "We may have need of some more sketches."

"Aye aye, sir!" Fywell said with a face-splitting grin before doffing his hat and dashing off below to the orlop cockpit.

"Permission to go ashore, sir?" Lewrie's cook, Yeovill, asked from the foot of the ladder in the ship's waist. He held up a woven basket. "If there is parsley growing there, I could pick some, or a batch of wild bird eggs."

"Permission granted," Lewrie said with a nod.

"It *looks* deserted, sir," Marine Lieutenant Roe commented. "Do you think the Spanish might have troops there, anyway?"

"We saw no campfires, no lanthorns or glims during the night, so I rather doubt it," Lewrie told him, shrugging. "We *might* run into a Robinson Crusoe, or some Arab fishermen, but—"

"The boats are coming alongside, sir," Lt. Westcott announced. "Bring me back a mermaid."

"Right up to an Arabic country, I'd have thought you'd ask for a *hareem,* or a *genie* in a bottle," Lewrie teased, for Westcott was a fellow madder for quim than any he'd ever seen.

"Oh, one or two jewels from some sultan's *hareem* would suit me just as well," Westcott allowed, pulling a face.

"Reminds me of Malta, sir," Marine Lieutenant Roe commented as the cutter was slowly stroked towards the shore of Perejil Island, "a vertical rock wall everywhere you look but for Valletta Harbour."

"You've been there, sir?" Lewrie asked, wondering how a young Roe could have served in the Med before, aboard another warship.

"Oh no, sir," Roe said with a chuckle, "but my uncle has been, and he had an illustrated book about the Turk siege of 1565. That's how I formed my view of it. A rather fanciful book."

"Can't see that fort no more, sor," Patrick Furfy, stroke oar and long a member of Lewrie's small entourage, pointed out with a jut of his chin to the East. "They's tall bluffs in th' way."

"No, you can't," Lewrie realised, taking a look for himself. "Thankee, Furfy."

"No place t'land, sor," Cox'n Liam Desmond said.

"Let's go round the East end of it, then," Lewrie decided.

Close in, within a long musket-shot of the shore, the island's bluffs looked to be as tall as the masthead of a ship of the line and just as hard to scale. There might be hand-holds for anyone determined to climb, but sea birds of a myriad of sorts had built nests where one could put a hand or foot, and the narrow ledges would be slick with guano, making that approach almost impossible, if not suicidal.

The two boats rowed round the Eastern end of Perejil, looking for a landing place, but it was much the same there, too, but—

"Damn my eyes, will ye just look at that!" Lewrie exclaimed as he beheld a wide, sheltered bay on the South side of the island, and a jutting headland that daggered at the African mainland, a headland with a pronounced slope. A few more minutes of rowing on calmer waters took them towards the tip of the headland, and Lewrie was even more pleased to see that the headland separated one bay from another to the West, just as spacious and sheltered from strong winds.

"We'll have to take soundings, but each one looks as if more than ten transport ships and smaller warships could anchor in each bay!" Lewrie crowed, clapping his hands together.

The cutter and launch steered into the second wide bay, and Lieutenant Roe raised an arm to point. "There, sir. There's a notch in the West side of the headland, like someone took an axe to it . . . and I think there's a way up."

"Take us over to it, Desmond, and let's see," Lewrie said.

"There is a landing!" Midshipman Fywell exulted.

Sure enough, the split notch began at the foot of the bluffs, by a small patch of gravelly, shingly "beach" littered with rocks the size of cobblestones, and a path led up from that spot to the top of the bluff. Low wind-shaped scrub bush and stunted trees grew in that shelter, here and there.

"Mister Roe, land your Marines from the launch, first, and go scout your way to the top," Lewrie ordered, turning on his thwart to wave the launch ahead of his own boat.

"Fix bayonets and prime your pieces!" Roe shouted over to the Marines in the launch. "We'll be going up first, Sar'nt Clapper."

"Roight, sir!" Sergeant Clapper acknowledged.

"Think there's enough room for two boats, sir?" Roe asked, anxious that he not be separated from his men.

"Take us in, Desmond, soon as Crawley's hands have boated their oars," Lewrie ordered. "We don't want t'snap any more of the things."

At least Midshipman Fywell found it funny.

First the launch, then half a minute later the cutter, ground their bows on the beach, and bow men leapt out with painters to find some place to lash their lines to keep the boats ashore. Marines filed forward to the launch's bows and jumped overside into shallow water, not up to their shins. Lieutenant Roe leapt out of the cutter, drew one of his double-barrelled pistols, and joined them, leading them up the notch.

"Leave four hands from each boat, Crawley. . . . Desmond, the rest follow the Marines," Lewrie said, stumbling forward over thwarts and stowed oars to the cutter's bow to step ashore himself.

Stealth, should any Spanish soldiers be on the island, was out of the question. Issue boots slipped and slid on rocks and hard, dry soil, and their presence stirred up several hundred sea birds to caw and mew in protest and take wing with the sound of flapping canvas.

Have to exercise more, Lewrie told himself as he scrambled up, grasping on to the thin, stunted trees and shrub branches that were so thinly rooted that they could not be trusted, head up and ears cocked for danger. The notch was wider than it had first appeared, but deeper, and steeper a climb, deep enough to cast them all into shade from the rising sun.

"Hold it up, hold it up," Sgt. Clapper was warning in a growl of caution, waving sailors and Marines to hunker down as Lieutenant Roe knelt at the very top of the notch with a Private Marine to each side of him, and was slowly raising his head for a wary look-see.

"Come on up, lads, there's no one here," Roe called down the notch to the shore party. He and his brace of Marines scrambled up to the top of the island and stood, looking round.

"Un-inhabited?" Lewrie asked Roe once he was up.

"Well, sir, there's a rock circle where someone camped out not a stone's throw from the top of the notch, some broken crockery, and a cast-off blanket," Roe told him. "If anyone lit a cookfire, it's been ages since."

"Wild bird eggs, hmm," Yeovill mused, looking about. "A dozen might make a regular-sized omelet. Tiny. But, there's nests everywhere you look."

"An' bird shite," Furfy said with a snort.

"Let's spread out and look around," Lewrie ordered. "If you run into anything interesting, give a shout. If we must run back to the boats, Mister Roe will blow on his whistle."

"That notch, sir," Lt. Roe said, pointing downward. "If that's the only way to get up here, fifty Marines could defend it against hundreds. Fifty men, with a pair of swivel guns, or boat guns?"

"Desmond, you and Furfy scout the top of the bluffs Westward, to the tip of the island, to see if there's another way up," Lewrie told them. "And, if you find a source of water, that'd be welcome."

"Aye, sor," Desmond said, knuckling his brow in salute. "Come on, Pat. We'll work some of our fat off."

Lewrie walked off North, making a bee-line for his ship, which was anchored off and in plain sight from anywhere on the island. He discovered that the roughly flat surface of Perejil was not so flat as it had first appeared. There were rocky outcroppings here and there, and some depressions in which rainwater might gather, where the plant life was a shade greener and healthier than the dried grasses and shrubbery, which were so wind-shaped that they put him in mind of the miniature trees or stylised representations of trees that he'd seen at Canton, China, long ago. There were some wildflowers here and there, wilted by a Summer of Mediterranean heat and a lack of rain, poking up among what he could only call weeds. His late wife had been the one with a green thumb, lovingly tending the back garden of their old house, and the large circular plot before it where carriages could turn around.

"Whoo!" Yeovill shouted, some hundred yards away. "Parsley!"

At least someone's pleased, Lewrie sourly thought.

He turned about to see Midshipman Fywell sketching madly away, unsure what he'd depict first, but eager to limn it all.

Close to the North bluffs, Lewrie stopped and looked right and left, speculating on how much loose rock, some of it large slabs or boulders, there was, and how hard and dense was the soil. A sly grin arose on his face as he imagined several gun emplacements dug into the edge of the bluffs, screened with piles of rock before each for make-shift parapets. He drew his hanger and probed the ground, bringing up little mounds of gravel, sand, and dirt, and smiled some more.

"It's a stone ship of the line," he whispered. "Half a mile long, unassailable, and the Dons can't see it from Ceuta. Hah!"

He walked back towards the top of the notch, found Lt. Roe, and had him blow the recall signal. "Back to the ship, lads! Rally here!"

Desmond and Furfy were the last stragglers to return, blowing with their exertions. "They's no other way up, sor," Desmond said. "It's nigh vertical bluffs right down t'th' tip of th' island."

"Anybody wish t'live here, they'd best bring a water hoy, for they's no water anywheres, sor," Furfy added, licking his lips.

"We've five-gallon barricoes in both boats?" Lewrie asked, and looked at Desmond and Crawley for confirmation. "Good. As soon as we're at the boats, we'll all have a 'wet.' Careful where ye place your feet on the way down, lads, and don't trust the hand-holds. I'd not like any broken bones or heads."

"Ah, but a sprain, sor!" Furfy enthused. "Light duties for a week, that!"

"Take a tumble on purpose, and it'll be bread and water with no rum for those 'light duties,'" Lewrie warned. "Let's be on our way. Clear the pans of your weapons before we do."

He blew the priming powder from his own pistols, eased them off cock, and stowed them in his coat pockets.

Some of the landing party did slide and stumble on the way down, but there were no injuries beyond some scrapes and bruises. They boarded the boats and shoved off, after a break for water, and rowed back to the ship.

"No dancing girls, sir?" Lt. Westcott asked, looking disappointed when Lewrie got to the quarterdeck.

"Only dancing *gulls*, sorry," Lewrie quipped. "Morrocan fisherman, or Barbary Corsairs, might put in here, but it's un-inhabited."

"Ah, well," Westcott said with a large sigh.

"Mister Fywell?" Lewrie called down to the ship's waist, where the Midshipman was sorting through his sketches.

"Aye, sir?"

"Once we have got the ship back under way, I'd admire that you bring all your drawings of the island to my cabins," Lewrie said.

"Very good, sir!"

"Back to Gibraltar, and our damned gunboats, I suppose, sir?" Westcott asked. "So much for freedom, however short."

"Aye," Lewrie told him, with a grunt of displeasure at the prospect. "Hmm . . . you can't see Ceuta from the quarterdeck, can you?"

"No, sir, there's a young mountain in the way," Westcott said.

"Masthead!" Lewrie bawled up to a lookout in the main mast cross-trees. "Can you see the fort from up there?"

"Nossir! It's b'hind a lotta bluffs!" the lookout reported.

"Excellent!" Lewrie exclaimed. "Hands to the capstan, Mister Westcott, and let's get under way!"

CHAPTER SIX

*T*hese are quite good," General Sir Hew Dalrymple said as he looked over Midshipman Fywell's sketches in his offices at the Convent the next morning. "That many guns, though, Captain Lewrie? Damn."

"Those mounted atop the walls, the lighter twelve-pounders and eighteen-pounders, didn't have the range to engage us, sir, and the lightest cannon that protect the West face, where any land attack would come, couldn't fire on us, but we think the count's right," Lewrie said.

"That confirms that the rumours of re-enforcement are true," Sir Hew said with a sigh. "We must assume that the troop re-enforcements are equally true, and that Ceuta now has two more full regiments to defend it. It's much too formidable to be attempted. It would have been a tough nut before. Now . . . ah well."

"It has to be supplied, sir," Lewrie pointed out, "and, did my ship stand off-and-on so no supplies could reach it, and the Isle of Perejil would be occupied, with some artillery emplaced, the Spanish would be cut off and starved."

"Perejil?" Sir Hew said with a scowl, glancing over to his large map.

"This little dot here, sir," Lewrie said, crossing to the map and tapping at it. "There's nobody there. The Spanish named it, so they may claim it, though it's close to the border with Morocco, so they may claim it, too, but the Dons've never done a thing with the place. Look at the chart we made, sir. There's two roomy bays either side of this headland, only one steep path up this notch to the top, and plenty of rock and sand for emplacements. Fifty men could guard the landing place against hundreds. No timber or water, though."

"Fywell?" Sir Hew said. "Peter Fywell? From Hampshire, is he?"

"Ehm, I don't know, sir," Lewrie replied, perplexed.

"Knew a fellow at Eton named Fywell, and this one could be his kin," Sir Hew said, maundering. "Oh, well. Didn't stay long, it was the Army for me, don't you know, and I was with my regiment when I was thirteen. My dear old regiment, ah!"

"One battery, six twenty-four-pounders, could keep the Dons from fetching supplies to Ceuta from Cádiz, sir," Lewrie strongly hinted, before the Dowager could launch into humming his favourite regimental march. "The Dons can't see Perejil from Ceuta, so they wouldn't know what we're up to 'til it's too late."

"Hmm, what if it's really Moroccan territory, and only named and claimed by the Spanish, unlawfully?" Sir Hew quibbled. "I have established good relations with the Sultan at Tangier, and I'd not wish to endanger them. They're touchy enough about Spanish Ceuta."

Why, you just have so many friends, everywhere! Lewrie thought, wondering when the Dowager would see his point, if ever.

"Captain Middleton's yard has scads of timber, and we could establish a regular supply of rations, ammunition, and water for the garrison you put on Perejil, or Parsley, Island, sir," Lewrie pressed on.

"*Is* there any parsley?" Sir Hew asked, as if it was vital.

"Very little, so late in the year, sir, and bitterer than the usual," Lewrie replied. "I didn't care for it as garnish."

Hands t'yourself, and don't *pound his desk!* he chid himself.

"I'd like to go back and sound the two bays, sir, determine the depth—," Lewrie tried again.

"And so you should, Captain Lewrie, at once!" Sir Hew woke up and urged him. "I will send along an officer of the Royal Engineers to determine the suitability of the island for artillery, and siting any guns. There's a Naval Captain available, too, a Captain Ussher, at hand with nothing to do so far. He'll go along with you, too."

Someone who could take charge of the damned gunboats, maybe? Lewrie thought in sudden hope; *Can I cozen the man into the job?*

If Perejil was garrisoned, it would be under the command of an Army officer, surely, with Royal Artillery supported by as much as a half-battalion of infantry, and no place for a sailor.

"Once I drop them off with sufficient supplies, and chart the bays, sir, 'til the island's garrisoned, I can blockade Ceuta from re-supply from Cartagena, Algeciras, or Cádiz," he suggested, crossing the fingers of his right hand for luck.

"Yayss," Sir Hew slowly drawled, "that would be best."

"Well, I shall take my leave, sir, if there's nothing else, and await the officers of your choice to come aboard to begin their survey of the island," Lewrie said, "if they will notify me as to how many in their party they think necessary to accompany them. I must make arrangements for their berthing."

"I will speak to them and have them do so, Captain Lewrie," Sir Hew promised. "By the by, sir . . . you deliberately trailed your colours well within Ceuta's gun range to count their guns?"

"Aye, sir," Lewrie told him.

"And the Spanish obliged? Good God!" Sir Hew exclaimed.

"I expect they were bored with garrison duty in such a dull place, sir," Lewrie told him, tongue-in-cheek. "An exciting time was had by all parties, with no damage done. They're bad shots."

"I cannot determine whether you are intrepid, or mad, sir," Sir Hew declared, goggling at him and shaking his head with a *bit* of bemusement.

"Well, the jury may still be out on that head, sir," Lewrie replied with a laugh.

Sapphire thankfully spent much of the remaining year of 1807 at sea, after the survey of Parsley Island was completed, loitering off the fortress of Ceuta as an ever-present threat, and only departing for deeper waters as stormy Winter weather came on, always returning to just beyond maximum gun range. Thankfully, Sir Hew Dalrymple wrote to Admiralty in London, explaining what Lewrie and *Sapphire* were doing, and requesting a draught of officers and sailors to man the burgeoning squadron of gunboats, so someone else was stuck with that onerous chore.

There was some excitement when the renowned General Sir John Moore and an army of eight thousand men entered Gibraltar Bay on the first of December, bound from Sicily, with orders to land somewhere in Portugal and fight the French. That army spent two days in port, then sailed for Lisbon; they were back at Gibraltar by the tenth. Lisbon and Portugal were firmly in French hands, and there was a small squadron of French ships in the Tagus, and a suspect squadron of Russian warships, too. The Russians were nominally allies of France, but so far had not taken any hostile action against Great Britain; more interested observers than active participants, so far, but no one could know on which side they might fall if challenged.

Lewrie had been in port to re-provision when Moore first arrived, and had had a brief chat with the man at a supper party hosted by Sir Hew Dalrymple, and had found Sir John Moore a paragon of active soldiering. Maddalena thought him handsome, too.

Barely was Moore back, though, when orders came from Lord Castlereagh in London to leave two regiments at Gibraltar and bring all the rest home to England. There was nothing to be done for Portugal in the middle of a rough Winter, and plans would have to be re-thought for the Spring.

Bad weather also delayed the arrival of General Sir Brent Spencer and his 7,000 men who had been counted on to take Ceuta; they were still in England. Parsley Island remained un-occupied.

A little after the New Year of 1808, *Sapphire* was back at Gibaltar to re-place some sprung top-masts and other storm damage, when Thomas Mountjoy sent him a note, inviting him to come ashore and dine. Lewrie sprang at the chance, and had a note sent ashore at once, and was at the landing stage an hour later, in a rare, driving rain.

"You look miserable, like a drowned rat," Lewrie said as he shook hands. "What's that, a *parasol?*"

"They're calling them 'umbrellas,' and every gentleman at home with any sense of style, and wishes to stay somewhat dry, has one," Mountjoy told him, not rising to teasing in his usual manner. He looked drawn, and tired. "*Be* a sailor, *be* a stoic, and we'll see who is the drowned rat. Let's go to the Ten Tuns Tavern, they've a good menu of late."

Lewrie had to shake water from his hat, and briefly, from his uniform coat by the time they arrived and went inside, where it was much warmer, and the wind-whipped rain did not spray into the outdoor covered patio.

"Too bad that Spencer and Moore could not combine their armies, and do something in Portugal," Mountjoy began, after ordering them a bottle of claret.

"We'll see in the Spring," Lewrie said with a shrug. "Better weather, better plans?"

"I've heard from Romney Marsh in Madrid," Mountjoy imparted in a mutter, hinting that there were some new developments, but this time he did so without his usual twinkle of knowing something that Lewrie did not. He sounded tired. "Crown Prince Ferdinand is plotting to usurp King Carlos and arrest Godoy, for real. It ain't a rumour anymore. That painter, Goya? He's doing portraits of the royal court, heard whispers, and passed it on to Marsh. The Spanish people would be all for it . . . *anyone's* better on the throne than Carlos, and they think that Ferdinand will tear up any treaties with France if he does win out, and get them out of this miserable war."

"Napoleon'd never abide that," Lewrie said with a sneer. "He'd be over the Spanish border in force, like he did with Portugal, to put a puppet in charge."

"Perhaps he's planned to do that all along," Mountjoy said with a hint of his former slyness. "He's gobbled up enough of Europe for an empire, already, and if he holds the Spanish throne, perhaps he thinks that gives him all of Spain's overseas possessions, too?"

"Hah!" Lewrie scoffed. "No one in any Spanish colony pays the slightest bit of attention to Madrid, anymore. If France gobbles up Spain, most of 'em would declare independence and say to Hell with European doings. Bonaparte would take an empty purse with not one penny in it, even if the Spanish roll over and beg, which they would not. *Sure* t'be riots and revolution. Then you get your fondest wish . . . Spain comes over to our side. Are you sure you're getting true accounts from Marsh, not just idle rumours? Don't see how he does it."

Romney Marsh could be considered insane, but a perfect spy; he could assume a myriad of identities and carry them off with *panache*. The only question was how he could juggle all his multiple personas and keep straight which one he played at any given time.

"I gather he plays an artistic priest, he draws extremely well, and can play the guitar so he can pose as an itinerant musician in taverns," Mountjoy related. "What else he is in his spare time, I'd not hazard a guess. Napoleon *is* plotting to take all of Spain and her possessions. London's sent me a letter condensing what they've heard from Paris."

"*That* bitch!" Lewrie snarled, meaning Charité Angelette de Guilleri, the worst-named murderess ever, once a Louisiana Creole who had gone pirate to raise money for a French rebellion to take the colony and her beloved New Orleans back from Spain, then a *salon* celebrity in Paris, and part of the force that had hunted Lewrie and his wife to the Channel coast during the Peace of Amiens, where his Caroline was shot in the back and killed. The woman had turned British spy when Napoleon Bonaparte sold New Orleans, and Louisiana, to the United States.

"One of 'Boney's' Marshals, Joachim Murat, is gathering another army cross the Pyrenees, over one hundred thousand men, with orders to pretend sweetness and light, and lie like the Devil so the Spanish don't suspect anything 'til it's too late. He'll march on Cádiz, to free up the French ships blockaded there since Trafalgar, and he'll come to Gibraltar. The treaty that Godoy signed with France proposes an alliance to take Gibraltar."

"Any mention of Ceuta?" Lewrie asked, suddenly concerned.

"Not to do with Murat, no," Mountjoy told him. "When Sir Hew Dalrymple wrote to the Sultan at Tangier about your proposal to take Perejil, or Parsley, or whatever it's named, the French legation at Tangier learned of it at once, and wrote to Paris. Bonaparte was furious, I'm told. He doesn't have the navy or the transports to use Ceuta as a base, not with our Mediterranean Fleet in the way, and fears that we'd use Perejil for a landing to take Ceuta, first. Now we occupy the little speck—"

"We haven't yet," Lewrie had to tell him. "We surveyed it but Sir Hew's still making 'nicey-nice' with Tangier, so nothing's been done."

"Good Christ!" Mountjoy gasped, shaking his head in disgust. "Fine intelligence gatherer I am. Right cross the Strait, and I hadn't a clue!"

"You wish, sirs?" a waiter asked, interrupting their covert mutterings.

"Ah . . . yes," Mountjoy replied, as if coming up for air, "Oh, look! They have macaroni and cheese. *And* roast beef. Must be the weather, or the gloominess lately, but I'm craving something exotic for a change."

Lewrie went for spiced kid medallions *au jus* atop a bed of *couscous,* and a vegetable medley, whatever that amounted to in Winter with all trade cross the Lines shut down by orders from Madrid.

"A basket of rolls to begin with, with herbed oil and butter, and lots of roast beef for me," Mountjoy insisted.

"'When mighty Roast Beef was the Englishman's food . . . It ennobled our hearts and enrich-ed our blood,'" Lewrie attempted to sing.

"You sing, sir, on par with how you tootle on the penny-whistle," Mountjoy said with a wince, and a laugh. Once the waiter was gone to place their orders, though, he leaned closer and lowered his voice to a mutter again. "London also believes that Murat will march on Madrid and oust the Bourbon dynasty, then place one of 'Boney's' brothers on the Spanish throne. Bonaparte's leaning towards Joseph, even though he's already the King of Naples. From our source, whom you despise, we also strongly suspect that Murat dearly wants it for himself. He's seen so many of his old comrades awarded duchies and minor kingdoms, and we gather that he feels he's more than earned one, and it's his due."

"You say the Spanish people want Ferdinand, and no more truck with France," Lewrie replied. "You ought to cheer up, Mountjoy, for if Napoleon does that, Spain *has* to revolt and change sides. That's what they sent you here to accomplish, isn't it?"

"The Spanish are proud enough to rise up," Mountjoy said, looking glum. "But, *will* they, and will it *amount* to anything? There's the rub."

"Then, let's all keep our fingers crossed," Lewrie suggested. "And like my First Officer says they do at the Artillery School at Woolwich, it depends on holding your mouth just right, too. Christ, Mountjoy, cheer up! The prospects are good . . . *and,* the menu shows they've a berry duff for dessert!"

BOOK ONE

Nothing should be left to an invaded people but
their eyes for weeping.

—ATTRIBUTED TO OTTO VON BISMARCK,
PRUSSIAN CHANCELLOR (1815-1898)

CHAPTER SEVEN

"*A*ren't they pretty, sir?" Lt. Westcott said in glee as they stood atop the poop deck to watch the gunboat squadron, now a dozen in number, exercise in the bay.

"So long as it's someone else's bloody gunboat squadron, I'll allow that they look . . . smart," Lewrie said, lowering his telescope. "Speaking of smart, has the dockyard sent us the paint we requested?"

"The Commissioner's clerk says that there's very little paint on hand, at present, unless we prefer green," Westcott told him.

"Well, I don't," Lewrie said with a growl. "Green? Mine arse on a band-box. What's that here for, the walls of the hospital?"

HMS *Sapphire* had spent the better part of the tumultuous Winter at sea off Ceuta, and what she needed was black paint to renew the upper-works of the hull, and whitish-cream buff paint to touch up the gunwale stripes along her gun-ports, which colour scheme was becoming the standard for the Royal Navy, *à la* Nelson.

"It may be some months before an adequate supply arrives, sir," Westcott said. "I suppose the old girl will have to look . . . dowdy for a while more. Any more word from shore, sir?"

"It seems that Spanish spies are as good as ours," Lewrie told him with a bark of mirth. "The Madrid papers printed accurate details of our planned attack on Geuta on the fourteenth of February. By the time General Spencer's main body came in to harbour here, it was given up as hopeless."

The Atlantic had been fierce that Winter, driving most of the expeditionary force back to ports in England, though some ships with three thousand of Spencer's army *did* arrive at Gibraltar in late January much the worse for wear, and Sir Hew Dalrymple did send them on to Sicily, which occupying force had been reduced when London ordered Sir John Moore's eight thousand back to England, not back to Sicily. Now, Spencer had come, with nothing to do, and his remaining four thousand were added to the Gibraltar garrison, in case French Marshal Murat did indeed plan to lay siege to Gibraltar for the umpteenth time since 1704.

"Just waiting for the shoe to drop, we are, Mister Westcott," Lewrie told him, strolling over to the windowed coach-top above his cabins to retrieve his pewter coffee mug and take a sip.

"Pray God it does drop, sir," Westcott said with eagerness to be doing something more than blockading Ceuta, "and flings us into a purposeful action. I'm growing bored."

"You've your mistress ashore to relieve that, surely," Lewrie teased. Finding a wench had been Westcott's first act as soon as he stepped onto the Old Mole, long before Lewrie had found his.

"She proved faithless," Westcott said, heavily scowling. "She found herself an Army Colonel with a fuller purse to keep her. We've been at sea so long, so *uselessly,* that she grew bored, too."

"Ah, well," Lewrie said in sympathy. "I'm sorry for that. By God, you'd think that Spain'd be up in arms, by now!"

French Marshal Murat crossed the border into Spain in the middle of February, they had since learned. On one pretext after another, the French had taken Pamplona, San Sebastian, Figueras, and Barcelona, and were reputedly bound for Madrid, just as Mountjoy had expected. So far, though, there were no agents' reports of any Spanish reaction. Another of Mountjoy's agents, nigh as dashing as Romney Marsh, captained a filthy trading vessel along the coasts of Andalusia, pretending to be a Spaniard. He carried orders and requests for information from informers and brought back fresh news from Spain, and made a fair profit trading Gibraltaran goods to Spaniards starved for grains and luxuries. The harsh Winter seas had penned him in one port or other for weeks on end, but John Cummings, *aka* Vicente Rodríguez, reported that news of the Spanish incursion had not yet reached the South of Spain, and it was *he* who had spread the news to the Andalusians. Now, here it was March of 1808, and the fuse to the powder keg had been lit, but so far, there was no bang!

"Boat ahoy!" one of the Midshipmen standing Harbour Watch shouted to an approaching boat.

"Message for your Captain!" one of the boatmen shouted back.

Lewrie and Westcott crossed the poop deck to the starboard side to see what the fuss was as the boat was rowed to the bottom of the entry-port, and a shoeless boy in his shirtsleeves scampered up the boarding battens to hand a letter over, then just as quickly got back down the battens and into the bows of the boat.

"A letter from shore, sir," Midshipman Spears reported with a doff of his hat after he'd come up to the poop deck.

"Thankee, Mister Spears," Lewrie said, turning the wax-sealed missive over to see that it was from Thomas Mountjoy. Once it was torn open, Lewrie grinned quickly, with a hitch of his breath. "I'm summoned ashore, instanter, Mister Westcott, for a discussion."

"You think . . . ?" Westcott hopefully asked.

"Fingers crossed, mouth held just right, all that. Continue with provisioning whilst I'm away," Lewrie said, almost bounding to the quarterdeck and aft into his cabins for a quick change of clothes.

"Good morning, sir!" Mountjoy's assistant, and bodyguard, said with unwonted good cheer as Lewrie entered Mountjoy's lodgings. Mr. Deacon was usually a cautious, guarded fellow who bore himself in total seriousness, but now his harsh features were split in a smile. "He's waiting for you, sir," Deacon said, pointing a finger to the top of the stairs.

Lewrie trotted up the stairs and went out on the top-floor open-air gallery, where he found Mountjoy in his waistcoat, his shirtsleeves rolled to the elbows, and his neck-stock discarded. He held a smuggled bottle of French champagne.

"We're celebratin' something, I trust?" Lewrie asked, pausing by the glazed double doors.

"They've done it! The bloody Spanish have at last done it!" Mountjoy whooped in glee. "A week ago . . . they're calling it the Tumult of Aranjuez, God knows why . . . it was too much for 'em, all those bloody French, all the cities taken over. . . ."

Is he insane, or drunk? Lewrie had to wonder; *He's babblin'!*

"The Spanish mobs have risen up, they've forced King Carlos to step down, and they've put Ferdinand on the throne, and for all that I know, *he's* finally arrested the Foreign Minister, Godoy, and named a new one! I fully expect to hear in a few days that that treaty with France is torn to shreds, too. Oh, they're teetering on the brink of changing sides, maybe raising armies to drive the French back home. Christ Almighty!" he yelled at the sky, and began to whirl about in an impromptu dance, putting Lewrie in mind of an Ottoman *dervish*. "Have a drink, Captain Lewrie! Have a whole bottle, hah hah!"

"Damned if I won't!" Lewrie hooted, and went to the iron table before the settee to pour himself a glass from a second open bottle.

Neither Mountjoy or Deacon had taken time to cool the champagne in a water-filled bucket or tub, so Lewrie felt as if his mouth was full of foam as he glugged down a goodly measure. He looked to the West, over towards Algeciras, then North to the Lines, and the Spanish fortifications beyond them.

"Mind if I borrow your telescope?" he asked. Mountjoy paid him no mind; he was still dancing and drinking from his bottle, so Lewrie stepped round him and bent down to see if the Spanish troops on the walls had heard the news, too, and if they had, what was their reaction. It was a fine astronomical telescope, able to fill the ocular with an image of the moon when pointed aloft at night.

Right, no reaction, Lewrie told himself; *perhaps their officers haven't told 'em yet, or they haven't heard, themselves.*

Some sentries under arms were slowly pacing their bounds atop the parapets, but most were leaning on the walls, some smoking their pipes or *cigarros*, and one un-kempt corporal was picking his nose and puzzling over what he'd gouged out. He slewed the tube over to look at Algeciras, and the mouths of the rivers that fed into the bay; the many Spanish gunboats were sitting empty at their moorings or along the quays beneath the fortifications there, and that enclave looked as somnolent as the Spanish Lines. A downward tilt showed Lewrie a close-up view of one of the British gunboats wheeling itself about in almost its own length as the exercises continued.

"Maybe you should send some letters cross the Lines," Lewrie told his host. "I don't see any riots in the Spanish garrisons."

"They're military," Mountjoy gleefully stated. "They aren't *allowed* to riot. God, it'd be grand if Madrid sent General Castaños orders to march off and defend their country. Might be hard, though," Mountjoy said, taking another deep swig from his bottle, and calming down. "I've heard that Murat's sent a small advance party to scout our lines, with lots of money and grain, which the Spanish really need. Who *knows* who in their army can be bribed to go along with the occupation of their own nation? Castaños may be too closely watched for him to take action on his own. Yet."

"The Dowager must be over the moon," Lewrie speculated, going to the settee to have a sit-down, and a refill of his wineglass.

"Damned *right* he is!" Mountjoy buoyantly said. "He's still in a quandary whether Gibraltar is threatened, but *very* pleased with the news. If the revolts spread, as we expect, we may have Spain as an ally, and a British army in Spain to assist them. Not from here, ye see . . . not 'til we know one way or another what else the Spanish will do . . . but from England. As soon as the weather at sea is improved, London will be sending an army to re-take Portugal, and you did *not* hear that from me. Maybe Sir John Moore, again. *Or,* we might launch ourselves into Southern Spain from here, depending."

"Well, that's all grand news," Lewrie said, scowling in deep thought, "but it don't signify to me, or *Sapphire*. That's soldier's doings, and I'd still be stuck here at Gibraltar, keepin' an eye on Ceuta."

"Grand events, even so, Lewrie," Mountjoy chortled.

"Aye, fun t'watch unfolding, like watchin' a play, with no part in it but t'clap and laugh," Lewrie sourly commented. "Grand, hah!"

"Lord, but you're a hard man to please!" Mountjoy groused.

"Aye, I s'pose I am," Lewrie admitted. "Last Summer's raids . . . those were just toppin' fine. We were *doing* something, killing Dons and smashing things, burning captured ships and semaphore towers. Now, it's . . . plodding off-and-on the same bloody headland, days on end."

"You could be in charge of the gunboats," Mountjoy pointed out. "Be thankful you're not. You could be ordered to join Admiral Collingwood's blockading squadron off Cádiz, Charles Cotton's off Lisbon, or do your plodding at Marseilles or Toulon as a *minor* part of the Mediterranean Fleet."

Lewrie feigned a shiver of loathing for either of those choices. He no longer had a frigate, and would have no freedom of action to probe and raid inshore, and it would be bloody dull sailing in line-ahead behind larger ships of war, continually under the eyes of senior officers and their Flag-Captains. Except for single actions or small squadron actions in the Caribbean or Asian waters, there had been no grand engagements since Trafalgar, now three years before. France, and her puppet ally, the Batavian Dutch Republic, still built warships, but, once built they sat at their moorings, their crews idling, bored to tears with "river discipline" training, which was not the same as the experience gained through long spells at sea. The best of the Spanish navy had been crushed at Trafalgar, and blockaded into ports ever since, and might *never* dare come out again.

He'd helped in making them fearful a few months back in 1807, when he stumbled across a brace of large Spanish frigates off Cabo de Gata, East of Gibraltar. Fine ships, fine crews, gallant captains . . . with the gunnery skills of so many chipmunks, and he'd taken both on, getting to windward of them and keeping the wind gage through a two-hour battle, forcing one to strike and the other to limp off for the nearest port, sinking an hour later.

The way things are goin', I may never see an enemy at close broadsides again! he fretted to himself; *Twenty-eight years in the Navy, it's been, and it's all been shot and powder stink!*

He frowned heavily again as he pondered the possibility of Bonaparte's eventual downfall, and peace. What sort of life would he have, then? A decade or so on half-pay with no new active commission, slowly going up the list of Post-Captains, a meaningless promotion to Rear-Admiral of the Blue, then a slow ascent of *that* list as elder officers died?

I'll whore and drink myself to an early grave, damned if I won't! he thought; *Just like my useless father!*

"My, sir . . . so morose of a sudden," Mountjoy said.

"So bored," Lewrie amended, "and daunted by the prospects. Is there anything in your line that needs doing?"

"Can't think of anything off-hand," Mountjoy told him. "And for now, Sir Hew needs you off Ceuta. You know . . . the duty you invented for yourself to avoid the gunboat squadron?"

"Ouch!" Lewrie spat, going for the champagne bottle.

"Now, how far afield you carry that task, that may be up to you," Mountjoy suggested with a sly wink. "You never know, Sir Hew may send you to Tetuán to fetch the garrison an hundred head of cattle."

What that filth would do to his ship didn't bear thinking about; there'd be cow piss dripping onto the mess tables and hammocks of the upper gundeck for days, and cow pats piling up as high as the weather deck gunports!

"Tetuán, hmm," Lewrie mused aloud. "Ye know, I've not been to that port, yet. It might be a good idea t'make myself familiar with it."

"Well, if you like slave-markets, and insults 'cause you're an infidel, perhaps," Mountjoy chortled. "If you ain't a Muslim, you'll get the evil eye from one and all, even if they like your money."

"Not much by way of melons, grapes, or vegetables this time of year," Lewrie mused some more, "but surely they'd still have grain in storage . . . wheat, millet, that *couscous*? Sheep, goats, cattle, hmm."

"What are you thinking?" Mountjoy asked, puzzled by the sudden change in Lewrie's mood from despondent to scheming-impish.

"They trade with anyone, right? Even the Spanish if they've solid coin?" Lewrie asked.

"Well, yes, but—," Mountjoy replied.

"Sir Hew's convinced that Ceuta's been re-enforced, with more guns, and at least two new regiments of troops," Lewrie said. "That means more gunners, more mouths to feed. I don't know how much they had in their stores before the re-enforcements, but I doubt that the ships that sneaked them there, from Algeciras, Tarifa, or Malaga, can keep 'em fed. They can't sneak in a second time! It's what, only ten miles by sea from Tetuán to Ceuta? Where *else* can the Dons get their provisions? I think I'll wander a bit more far afield, as you said."

"I stand amazed, Captain Lewrie," Mountjoy announced, standing up and bowing to him with his arms widespread. "Utter boredom inspires and awakens your slyness!"

"Sly? Me?" Lewrie scoffed, goggling at him.

"Or do you prefer . . . low cunning?" Mountjoy teased.

"I'll call it curiosity t'begin with," Lewrie said, laughing, "and if that leads to a little adventure—a successful adventure, mind—I may settle for the low cunning, later."

"We must open another bottle of champagne," Mountjoy decided, turning his upside down to see one lone drop dribble out, frowning in disappointment.

Aye, drunk as a lord in an hour, Lewrie judged him; *as drunk as an emperor by the afternoon.* Lewrie figured that Mountjoy had earned himself a good drunk, after a year or more of scheming, planning, disappointments, and set-backs. The spy trade didn't allow all that many successes, and the few had to be savoured and celebrated, one way or another.

"You'll have t'drink without me, sorry," Lewrie told him as he got to his feet and fetched his hat. He did drain his glass of champagne to "heel-taps," though. "I think I'll ramble down to Maddalena's to see if she'd like to dine out."

"I see," Mountjoy said, sniggering. "I celebrate my way, and you will celebrate your own way."

"Something like that, indeed!" Lewrie told him, grinning.

CHAPTER EIGHT

$\mathcal{B}$oat-work, I see, sir," Lieutenant Harcourt, the ship's Second Officer, said, leaning over an old chart on Lewrie's desk in his day-cabins.

"We draw too much water to go right to the docks," Lewrie told him, tapping the chart with a pencil stub. "Tetuán's a full two miles inland, up this long inlet, which is also too narrow for us. I asked round ashore with various merchants, and they all said it's best to anchor off the mouth of the inlet and send boats in, or a single boat to place orders with the Moroccan traders, and wait for them to barge the goods out. They're used to British ships putting in to purchase foodstuffs, so your presence won't seem remarkable. I wish you to accompany Mister Cadrick, the Purser, who'll buy flour and *couscous,* to give us a good reason to be there, but . . . I want you to keep a sharp eye out for any Spanish buyers, any boats along the quays, to see if the Dons cooped up in the fortress of Ceuta use Tetuán as a source for provisions. With all those new arrivals, they're sure to be on short-commons, and need food from somewhere."

"I'm to 'smoak' them out, sir? Aye, I see," Harcourt agreed.

"All the men in your boat party will be armed, just in case," Lewrie went on, "but the last thing I wish is swaggerin', so keep the men close, and the arms out of sight unless they're *really* needed. I don't have to mention that there's no drink to be had in an Arabic port, so the people in your party must be warned about that. I don't know what Arabs think about whorin', so you'll have to caution them on that head, too. Once Mister Cadrick's business is done, come back out to the ship, making it appear to be business as usual, with your report. Who will you have?"

"Able Seaman Crawley and his old boat crew, sir, and one of the cutters," Harcourt decided quickly, playing old favourites from the ship's former Captain's days.

"Take Midshipman Fywell along," Lewrie told him before Harcourt could request his ally, Midshipman Hillhouse. "He draws well, and art work could be useful."

"Aye, sir," Harcourt agreed, but that was rote obedience.

"The Moroccans have no way to enforce the accepted Three Mile Limit, so once we round Ceuta and come to anchor off Tetuán, we will do so one mile off the mouth of the inlet, where most of our traders and warships do. As I said, business as usual, and no one suspecting what we're really about.

"We'll also take a peek at the dock area on the South end of the neck of land below Ceuta, to see if they've any vessels there," Lewrie continued. "If there are, there may be more boat-work, a cutting-out raid in the dark of night, but that's for later. Right?"

"Right, sir," Harcourt said. "And thank you for the duty, sir."

"Good. Go brief your chosen hands, and we'll be about it," Lewrie told him in conclusion, and dismissal. He lingered after the Second Officer had left the great-cabins, studying the chart for a bit longer, noting that close inshore of the Moroccan coast 'twixt Ceuta and Tetuán there were soundings indicating six or seven fathoms. If *Sapphire* had to chase Spanish coasters into those waters, there would be no refuge for them; his ship could still swim in there!

Satisfied at last, he rolled up the chart, grabbed his hat, and went out to the quarterdeck and the larboard-side chart room to place it back in a slot, then went to the helm, the compass binnacle cabinet to take a peek. At last, he ascended to the poop deck for a long look about.

Sapphire was two miles Sou'east of Gibraltar's Europa Point, on her way to Ceuta once again. She ploughed along at a slow five or six knots under tops'ls, fore course, spanker, and jibs. There was no rush to cross the Strait; it was only twelve miles to the fortress.

Now that Spring had arrived, he found the seas and winds mild and pleasant, the skies bright blue, with no ochre clouds of dust in the air from the Sahara for a change. In high Summer, and even in the Winter when the winds howled out of North Africa, the remnants of dust and sand storms cut visibility to almost nothing, and left *Sapphire* strewn with gritty dust that got into the food and water.

God, who'd live in such country, Lewrie thought; *Unless they have nowhere else to go.*

He'd been to many foreign places during his long naval career, some of them exotic, some dismal, and always got a strong longing for the ordered gentleness of England. He'd even tolerate the rain, if it made the countryside greener!

"Yar, dog, 'at's filthy," a sailor in the After-Guard griped. "*I* won't throw it for ye, fer all th' rum in th' Indies!"

Disconsolate, Bisquit picked up his oldest plaything, a rabbit hide stuffed with wool batt. Half the hair was missing, by now, and Bisquit had mouthed it so long that it was permanently slimy. With a faint hope, he padded to Lewrie's side and made some pleading whines.

"Alright, alright," Lewrie said, ruffling the dog's fur, and taking the damned thing from his mouth, which set Bisquit to prancing. He threw it aft, and off the dog dashed to pounce on it, give it some shakes, then trotted back to drop it at Lewrie's feet. A feint left and right, and Lewrie hurled it again, right to the taffrail flag lockers, resulting in another mad dash. That game went on for five minutes before Bisquit's tongue was lolling.

At least somebody's *gettin' some exercise,* Lewrie thought, glad that the game was over. He wiped his hands on a handkerchief and left the toy on the deck. "Thirsty, Bisquit? I'll bet you are. Let's go down to the scuttle-butt."

Bisquit followed Lewrie down to the quarterdeck, then to the waist, where Lewrie used the long dipper to pour water into his hand so the dog could lap. He knew he was making a comical spectacle of himself, but he didn't care; Bisquit needed a drink.

Sapphire rounded Ceuta and the fortress's guns by four miles, just out of gun-range, to frustrate the Spaniards, then shaped course for Tetuán. She came to anchor a mile off the mouth of the inlet in six fathoms of water. Bosun Terrell took one cutter to row round the ship to see that all the yards were squared, and all the running rigging was set at the right angles, with no lubberly slackness. The other cutter set out for the inlet, first under a single lugs'l, and later oars once they entered the long slash of an inlet, hacked out of the dry hills to either side by centuries of fresh water from some inland river. Just off Tetuán's quays, the waters would be brackish, but that small stream of fresh water had guaranteed Tetuán's existence for all those centuries.

"It seems we have the anchorage to ourselves, sir," Westcott idly commented as they strolled the quarterdeck. "There's no one else in sight. No Spanish merchantmen, certainly."

"They need grain, they get it smuggled out of Gibraltar by any *number* of traders who'd oblige 'em," Lewrie cynically said. "Spies on the side, who knows? Sir Hew Dalrymple has a bee under his bonnet, sure that there's mutiny or civilian revolt just waitin' to explode. For all I know, he may be right. Keeps him up, nights."

"Like a Trojan Horse?" Lt. Westcott scoffed. "Up against the Rock's garrison? Sounds iffy to me."

Lewrie picked up a telescope from the binnacle cabinet rack and went to the quarterdeck's landward side to peer shoreward. "Hmm, there's some shallow-draught boats of decent size up the inlet, just off the quays, it appears. Arabic, I think. Lots of lateen sails furled up round their booms. *Feluccas,* or *dhows?* Here, have a look for yourself, Mister Westcott."

"Hmm," Westcott dared to speculate after a good, long look of his own. "There's one almost big enough to make me suspect that it's a Barbary Corsair's pirate craft. It's hard to tell any more, they've so many captured brigs, schooners, and such, but a big lateener would be fast enough to run down a prize. The rest? We'll know once the cutter's back. If she is a Corsair, we should keep an eye on her, too, sir. Just 'cause we pay tribute for safe passage doesn't mean we can't have a go at one of them if we catch them red-handed."

"At least the Americans had the will to take them on and end *their* paying tribute," Lewrie said, enviously. "Christ, one'd think that with our Navy so big, we could spare a squadron of brig-sloops to put an end to North African piracy, once and for all."

"Now, there's a duty I'd relish," Westcott said with some heat. He bared his teeth briefly in one of his quick, savage grins, looking positively wolfish.

"I think I'll go aft and have a well-needed nap, perhaps play with Chalky," Lewrie decided aloud. "The weather's fair, there's no threat in sight, and the Mids of the Harbour Watch can cope."

"I may emulate you, sir," Westcott said.

"Later, Mister Westcott. Alert me when the cutter's back."

"Aye, sir."

⚓

His cat had been in need of a bout of play, too, a full half-hour of chasing and pouncing and leaping after a champagne cork on a length of twine, 'til he was panting. And when Lewrie stretched out on the settee, Chalky settled down on his chest for pets and praise 'til he slunk down to one side of Lewrie's leg for a well-earned nap of his own. Pettus, his cabin steward, and Jessop, the cabin servant, did their puttering about the cabins quietly, to allow Lewrie perfect rest, at least an hour's worth before there was the rap and shout from the Marine sentry.

"Midshipman Harvey, SAH!" the sentry bawled.

"Uhmph . . . enter!" Lewrie called back, sitting up and getting to his feet.

"The First Officer's duty, sir, and I am to inform you that the cutter is returning," Harvey reported.

"My compliments to Mister Westcott, and I will be on deck, directly," Lewrie replied. A quick trip to his wash-hand stand for some splashes of water on his face, and a quick drink and rinse, and he was awake and headed for the quarterdeck, impatiently waiting for the boat to come alongside, and for Lieutenant Harcourt and Midshipman Fywell to come and report.

"Let's go aft," Lewrie suggested to them.

Fywell had made a rough chart of Tetuán's docks, with pointed ovals to represent the vessels in port. "Here, sir," Lt. Harcourt said, tapping the biggest with a forefinger. "That's an armed ship, a Barbary Corsair, sure as Fate. I counted at least eight gun-ports, and a crew of at least sixty. Dirty looks they gave us, from one and all."

"And a flood of threats and curses in their tongue, too, sir," Midshipman Fywell stuck in.

"Along here and here, the vessels are mostly *feluccas,* lateen-rigged, filthy, and begging for paint, crewed by locals, or traders from Tangier," Harcourt went on. "Further up the inlet beyond the quays, there are some clutches of much smaller boats, all drying their fishing nets. But over *here,* though . . . there are two good-sized lateeners, *but,* they've European crews, not a Arab in sight aboard them."

"And they were *very* shy of the sight of us, sir," Fywell said with a laugh. "They *must* be Spaniards."

"Were they taking on cargo?" Lewrie asked.

"Sacks of grain, sheep and goats, dried fruit, and sugar, is what it looked like, sir," Harcourt said, sounding very sure. "They may even grow coffee round here, so they may have bought that, too."

"Some bigger slabs of meat, wrapped in cloth, don't forget, Mister Harcourt," Fywell said. "If they had no room aboard for live cattle, it looked like they were taking on whole sides of beef."

"I need no prompting, Mister Fywell," Harcourt snapped. "I was about to mention them."

"Aye, sir," Fywell replied, blushing and shrugging into his coat to be chid before Lewrie.

"Two of 'em," Lewrie said. "Makin' a weekly run? Or, do the Dons have four or more, alternating supply runs, not wishing to risk all of 'em bein' snapped up in one go, I wonder? Hmm."

"We could take them, sir, soon as the sun's down," Lt. Harcourt eagerly suggested.

"Not in a sovereign, foreign port, no," Lewrie dis-agreed. "Not if Dalrymple needs friendship with the Sultan at Tangier. Why, he'd have our heads on pikes if we upset the Moroccans! No, we'll wait 'til they're at sea, no matter *how* close they hug the coast. And they won't dare sail 'til we're gone and out of sight. Mister Fywell, did you go to the markets with the Purser?"

"No sir, I kept a close eye on our hands, at the cutter," Fywell replied. "Mister Harcourt told me to keep them out of trouble."

"I'd admire did you pass word for the Purser to come to see me, at once," Lewrie urged the Midshipman. "Off you go!"

"The Purser, sir?" Lt. Harcourt questioned.

"Well, he obviously bought the ship *something* whilst ashore, Mister Harcourt," Lewrie said in a biting drawl. "How much, and when it is to be delivered will depend on how long we must stay at anchor."

"Oh, I see, sir," Harcourt said, crestfallen at the delay.

He's a damned good sailor, a good officer, but my Lord, *he's a dullard!* Lewrie thought.

"The Spanish have long experience with lateen-rigged vessels," Lewrie said to fill the time 'til the Purser arrived. "Picked 'em up from the Moors, and built their war-galleys on the designs of *xebecs*. When we were chasin' privateers off Cuba a couple of years ago, they were a common sight along the coast."

"Indeed, sir," Harcourt said, with a brow up as if he felt that his leg was being pulled. "But only 'til they learned the advantages of square-rigged ships, I'd imagine."

"You've never seen a lateener thrash to windward, closer than any of our ships could sail," Lewrie countered.

Thump-crash of musket butt and boots. "Th' Pusser t'see th' Cap'm, SAH!" from the Marine sentry.

"Enter!" Lewrie called out, glad of the interruption.

"You sent for me, sir?" Mister Cadrick, their paunchy Purser, said, stepping inside with his hat in his hands. He was as well-fed and sleek as a tavernkeeper, and had always made Lewrie think that he ran a prosperous "fiddle," no matter how well his books balanced.

"What did we buy ashore, Mister Cadrick?" Lewrie asked. "And, do we have to await delivery?"

"An hundredweight of flour, sir," Cadrick easily ticked off, "two bullocks, four sheep, a dozen chickens, and small lots of goods for the wardroom, mostly coffee beans, spices, and fruit. Neither your cook nor your steward made any requests, else I would have gotten some items for your needs, sir."

"How long before the goods come aboard, Mister Cadrick?" Lewrie asked him.

"A-rabs have their own sense of time, sir," Cadrick said with a dismissive laugh. "*Inshallah*, they say, 'God willing,' which I took for sometime in the afternoon, perhaps by the start of the First Dog."

"Stringy bullocks, most-like?" Lewrie wondered aloud. "That means those two will only make one meal for a crew this size. Hmm, slaughterin' 'em, carvin' 'em into eight-pound chunks for each mess, and the pumpin' and sluicin' the decks clean, after . . . We'll remain at anchor overnight, then, keepin' a close-eyed watch on those Spanish boats in the harbour, and that damned Corsair."

"Very good, sir," Cadrick said, bobbing his head. "Would you be interested in some of the goods, sir? There are dates, honey, and coffee beans, some of that *couscous*—"

"A bit of each, sir . . . along with a good-sized beef steak," Lewrie said, perking up.

"A pound of dates, a crock of honey, and say, a five-pound bag of coffee beans, for . . . oh . . . two pounds, sir?" Cadrick said, looking crafty.

"Sounds good, Mister Cadrick," Lewrie agreed, sure that he was being over-charged, even so. "You may go, and thankee. Don't forget the steak!"

"We won't act tonight, sir?" Lt. Harcourt asked, disappointed.

"If the winds allow, we'll up-anchor round two in the morning, hopefully as quiet as mice, Mister Harcourt," Lewrie told him. "And hope to be off Ceuta's piers, close to the coast, just before dawn."

"*Then* the boat-work, and cutting-out parties, sir?" Harcourt asked, perking up at the hint of action.

"Hopefully, sir," Lewrie told him. "Once the bullocks've been slaughtered, and the decks are clean, I'll send for all officers, and we'll thrash things out together."

"Very good, sir!" Lt. Harcourt said, taking his leave.

Lewrie bent over the desk, ready to go to the chart room for another peek at the old chart of the North African coast, but halted. Something in Midshipman Fywell's rough sketches caught his eyes, something he'd missed the first time round.

"Just damn my eyes!" he spat as he shuffled through them.

Fywell's quick pencilled impressions of the suspected Corsair showed a three-masted *xebec,* and the two Spanish "boats" that Harcourt had described as *feluccas* were not small single-masted lateeners, but two-masted *dhows,* much bigger than little *feluccas!* The figures that Fywell had shown on their decks made him think that both were about sixty or seventy feet in length, which left bags of room aboard for crews large enough to put up a stiff resistance to any attempt at boarding them, even in the wee hours.

It was like mistaking a brig for a gig!

Scheme yer way outta this, *ye damned fool!* Lewrie chid himself.

He'd promised action by dawn, and should it have to be abandoned, or attempted and result in failure, he'd look like the biggest idiot in all Creation!

CHAPTER NINE

*H*e'd dined alone after the long meeting with Lieutenants Westcott, Harcourt, and Elmes, and Marine Lieutenants Keane and Roe. The steak was fresh and juicy, though a bit tough going. Yeovill found some wrinkled old potatoes, had cut out the bad bits, and made him a spicy hash, with some chick peas and flat local bread, all sloshed down with a very passable Spanish red. Yeovill had done an appetiser with the chick peas, sesame oil, lemon juice, and garlic in which he could dip shreds of the bread, something Arabic he called *hummus*. A few of the preserved pitted dates made a superbly sweet pudding, too.

Chalky was not deprived, either, getting hashed potatoes along with some steak ground after roasting to manageable bites, while Bisquit got strips of meat, and a meaty bone to gnaw after, so he didn't go after Chalky's bowl.

After a turn on deck in the cool darkness, a look at the sky, and an observation of the night's moon, Lewrie determined that their attempt *might* be disguised 'til the last moment. The moon had risen just at dusk, and would be almost below the horizon by three in the morning. There was a slight overcast by the end of the First Dog Watch at 6 P.M., which might thicken during the night. The Sailing Master, Mr. Yelland, had cautiously concurred.

By nine in the evening, *Sapphire* went dark. Her Master-At-Arms, Mr. Baggett, and his Ship's Corporals, Wray and Packer, had gone round ordering the extinguishing of all candles, lanthorns, and glims belowdecks, and the soft amber glows from the gun-ports opened for fresh air disappeared. Below the thick bulwarks, and hopefully out of sight, there remained one tiny glim up by the forecastle belfry so a ship's boy could see his sand-glasses and ring the bells at the proper time, and one glim in the compass binnacle cabinet. Out of the ordinary, and also hopefully unnoticed by anyone ashore, the large taffrail lanthorns were not lit. *Sapphire* was a black mass in a night as black as a boot.

Lewrie napped in his darkened cabins, fully-clothed upon his settee, not *sleeping* exactly, for his mind was going like a galloping Cambridge coach. He might have drifted off for ten minutes at a stretch, at best, before a new worry arose, snapping him back awake. Midnight's Eight Bells were struck, beginning the long, dark Middle Watch. He did drift off and missed the single stroke of half-past midnight, but came round as Two Bells was struck at 1 A.M. A moment later, and there was a knock on his door.

"Midshipman Hillhouse, sir!" the Marine sentry called out, much softer than usual.

"Enter!" Lewrie called back, rising from his impromptu bed.

"Sir, those two Spanish boats are moving!" Hillhouse said in an excited rush as he entered the cabins. "The lookouts spotted them just this instant, coming down the inlet from the quays against the few lights burning in the town."

"No pipes, Mister Hillhouse, *pass* the word for All Hands, and take stations to raise the anchor!" Lewrie told him in a conspiratorial whisper. "Off ye go, instanter!"

"Aye aye, sir!"

Belowdecks, the Bosun and his Mates would be rousing sailors from their hammocks and urging them to the fore capstan, where the long bars had been shipped in place before Lights Out, surely a give-away to one and all that something out of the ordinary would happen; else, hunting them up and shipping them into the pigeon-holes and the drop-bolts fitted, and the light "swifter" line passed through the outer ends of the bars, much less finding the mauls to fleet the messenger cable round the capstan drum, would have been chaos in the dark.

"Fore capstan manned and ready, sir," Lieutenant Westcott reported a few minutes later. "Messenger's fleeted, and the nippers are standing by."

"Very well, Mister Westcott, let's have 'em breast to the bars at once.

Once the bower's free, I'll have spanker, all jibs, and all stays'ls set t'get a way on her." Lewrie ordered, "No music, mind! Let's keep it as quiet as possible."

There was *supposed* to be good holding ground off Tetuán, according to the Sailing Master's books, so *Sapphire* had come to anchor in six fathoms of water, and had paid out a five-to-one scope, meaning the men at the capstan bars only had to haul in 180 feet of cable. It would not be noiseless, though. The capstan pawls clanked as loud as pistol-shots, the thick cable groaned as it came slowly in against the hawsehole's lower rim, and even horny bare sailors' feet drummed on the decks. Despite the need for quiet, the ship's boy "nippers" just *had* to stumble and argue with each other as they dashed back and forth to nip the lighter messenger line to the cable, follow it near to the drum of the capstan, then dash to nip on again to seize onto a freshly-revealed length of cable. And the drumming of the mauls fleeting the messenger up the capstan drum put Lewrie in mind of a dance among the Muskogee Indians in Spanish Florida ages before!

"Short stays!" the word came from the forecastle, followed a very long moment later by "Up and down!" and a harsh voice up forrud calling for the Heavy Haul, for the hands to stamp and go!

"Anchor's free, and haul away!" the Bosun cried.

"Make sail, Mister Westcott," Lewrie ordered. "Hands aloft to the tops'l yards."

The stock of the bower anchor was snagged and "fished," a fluke "catted" and men on the forecastle and weather deck walked away with the "fish," then the "cat" to ring the anchor up to the out-jutting cat-head beam and swung it up for stowage, even as the ship began to get a slight way on her.

"No bite, sir!" Senior Quartermaster Marlowe reported from the doublewheel helm, turning spokes either way. "Her head's fallin' off to starboard. Sou'east."

Aloft, tops'ls were being loosed and let fall, clew lines sang in the blocks to draw them down, and brace lines groaned through theirs. The wooden parrel balls squealed as the yards were braced round to cup wind in the sails, impossible to see, and only imagined in the mind by the sounds of sails pivotting on the masts, and the rustling of canvas.

"Answerin' her helm, now, sir," Marlowe announced, sounding relieved.

"Close-haul her 'til we get some speed," Lewrie ordered. "A cast of the log!" A minute later and some Midshipman aft reported that the ship was making three knots; Lewrie could not differentiate who it was by the screech.

"Aloft, there! Lay out and free the fore course!" Westcott yelled. "Sorry about the shout, sir," he apologised to a shadow on the quarterdeck he took for Lewrie. "Will you wish to tack or wear once we get some drive on her?"

"A wear's safer, Mister Wesctott," Lewrie replied. "Do we miss stays, those Spaniards will get clean away."

Westcott took a long look aft towards Tetuán and must have reckoned that they were now better than a mile out to sea and out of ear-shot, for he yelled aloft for the main course to be freed and let fall. More rustling, groaning, and squealing resulted.

"Five knots, sir!" came the call from the chip-log tender.

"Stations to wear, Mister Westcott," Lewrie snapped. "Thank God our night-time doings last Summer got the people used t'doing their duties in the dark."

"Then I will not disappoint you with a description of what a muddle it was, sir," Westcott teased. "Hands to sheets and braces! Prepare to wear ship!" he shouted.

Lewrie could not see the long commissioning pendant high aloft, but he could judge the direction and strength of the night winds by turning his face left and right; they were light but steady, coming from the East-Nor'east. A peek into the compass bowl confirmed that. Once fully about, the ship could jog towards Ceuta on a close reach, haul her wind to close the coast in pursuit of the Spaniards, and go "full and by" to clear the coast, later.

Unless it changes, Lewrie fretted to himself; *Pray God that it don't. Just a little help here, please Jesus?*

"In all the rush, Mister Westcott, has anyone kept track of our Dons?" he asked. "Have they cleared the inlet?"

"Ehm . . . don't know, sir," Lt. Westcott had to confess.

Lewrie fumbled about for a night-glass at the binnacle cabinet and went up to the poop deck, leaving the wear to Westcott. He could see absolutely nothing! Tetuán lay astern, and there were some weak lights ashore there, but nothing moved across them; the harbour was asleep, with nothing moving. He peered urgently up the coast beyond the entrance to the inlet, knowing that there was solid land there, but it was invisible, and nothing moved in front of it . . . wait!

He was high enough above the sea to barely make out two tiny glows, about one cable apart. The Spanish *had* cleared the inlet and gotten to sea in total darkness just as *Sapphire* had, but they had to see their own com-passes to avoid getting too close to shore and grounding. Their compass bowls were lit, but shrouded by cloth so the helmsmen could take a squint now and then!

"*Got* you, you bastards!" Lewrie growled, just as *Sapphire* began to put about.

Dhows with two large lateen sails could be fast, but *Sapphire,* under courses, tops'ls, spanker, and her stays'ls, had much more sail aloft, and she had a much longer waterline. The *dhows* might be sixty or seventy feet overall, but they were built with a lot of that length in bow and stern overhangs. Once *Sapphire* got a way on her, even in light night winds, she was a lot faster than their foes.

"All officers to the quarterdeck," Lewrie called out, waiting for them to assemble. When they were all present, he amended his plans. "They're over yonder, gentlemen, about a mile alee of us, three points off our lar-board bows, and we're closing on 'em. You can spot 'em by their compass bowl lights, a faint amber glow, with a flash now and then when they take a peek under a burlap covering. They look to be sailin' close together, about a cable apart in line-ahead. I think we can close with both of 'em, about evenly 'twixt both, and open fire on them both at the same time, six-pounders and carronades on one, and the upper-deck twelve-pounders on the second, at a long musket-shot's range. We'll call on them to strike, close one, and board her, while we shoot the second to surrender, but it'll have t'be quick, brutal, and overpowering. No boat-work tonight, sorry, Mis-ter Harcourt, but we'll save that for another day . . . or night, rather."

"Work up ahead of the leader, then haul our wind and fall down with one on the bows, and the other abeam, sir?" Westcott said, getting it in one.

"Exactly, Mister Westcott," Lewrie said. "No pipes, again, and no bel-lowing or drumming, but let's go to Quarters. Here are the keys to the arms lockers, sir."

"Very good, sir," Westcott said, accepting the keys.

"Now, let's be at it," Lewrie said.

While the two-decker rumbled to the tumult of hands turning out to man and load their guns, and the Marines assembled with their weapons on the sail-tending gangway on the larboard side, Lewrie went atop it all to the poop deck, where he could get a better view of the two Spanish vessels, where their shrouded compass binnacle glims showed more clearly. They were still sailing close together, the stern-most *dhow* about three points off the larboard bows, slowly sliding to four points as *Sapphire*'s greater speed out-paced the Spaniards.

God above, he told himself with a grin; *we're* faster *than somebody, at long last? Wonders never cease!*

"Pass word to the gun-decks t'keep the ports closed 'til we're ready to open fire!" Lewrie called down to the quarterdeck in a harsh mutter, not daring to shout aloud. "The Dons may spot us by the glows of our slow-match linstocks and battle lanthorns!"

Slow-match fuse was coiled round the tops of the swab-water tubs, and lit in case the flintlock strikers failed, and thick red-glass, metal-re-enforced lanthorns were usually lit for night actions, so the men serving the guns had some light to work in.

A Midshipman, Lewrie could not say who, dashed below to pass the word, a moving shadow on a black deck, barely made out by white collar patches and white slop-trousers.

He looked North towards the massive fortress of Ceuta, finding its bulk by the lanthorns along its ramparts, and judged it to be six or seven miles off the starboard bows. He had no chance to peek at the chart, but knew that on a course of Due North, *Sapphire* would be closing the coast, which trended Nor'east in a long arc. The North African coast off to larboard was as black as a boot, its nearness impossible to judge, but if the Spanish sailed this short trading route often, he could not go wrong by being to seaward of them; they would know where the soundings shoaled, and were hugging it for safety.

"The leader's almost abeam now, sir," Lt. Westcott announced at the foot of the ladderway.

"Aye, Mister Westcott," Lewrie replied. "Alter course to fall down on them." The helm was put over a few spokes, and Lewrie had to hold his breath and cross the fingers of his right hand that the enemy did not hear the creaks and groans that the yards made as they were eased to cup the night winds at a slightly new angle.

Slowly, slowly, *Sapphire* fell down on the two un-suspecting *dhows*, 'til Lewrie could almost make out their dark bulks and the triangular lateen sails. The lead *dhow* was off the larboard bows, the trailing vessel was just a bit aft of abeam, and he *thought* that the range was less than one hundred yards.

Are they deaf, dumb, and blind? he had to wonder.

"Mister Westcott!" he cried. "Open the ports and run out!"

HMS *Sapphire* trembled as the ports were lowered and hands tailed on the run-out tackles to drive the carriages to thump right against the ship's thick timbers. Eleven squares of red light blossomed down her larboard side as the ports' lowering revealed the ship's presence.

"Take aim at yer targets!" Lewrie shouted, abandoning stealth. "Open fire!"

"Upper gun-deck . . . by broadside, *fire!*" Lt. Westcott howled.

Lewrie shut his eyes to preserve his night vision as the 12-pounders bellowed as one, spearing the night with jets of flame and swirling sparks of burning powder and shreds of flaming cloth cartridge.

"Helm hard down! Ready, six-pounders and carronades!" Lt. Westcott shouted. He was swinging the ship back onto the wind for a moment so the weather deck and quarterdeck guns could bear more easily. "As you bear . . . *fire!*"

Lewrie shut his eyes again, opening them after the last loud roar, though red-amber sparks still whirled amid the dense cloud of powder smoke. He could see *nothing* of their targets, for the smoke was drifting down-wind onto them, masking them completely. Even the aid of a night-glass, which gathered more ambient light, didn't help.

"*There* they are!" the Sailing Master cried, pointing off to the larboard side. "I think the leader's dis-masted!"

"Fall down on 'em, Mister Westcott!" Lewrie called out. "Close with 'em, gunnel-to-gunnel!"

"Hah! Got the both of 'em!" Mr. Yelland whooped. "Damned if the tailing one's not run into the first'un!"

Damned if they haven't! Lewrie told himself.

Their first target, the trailing *dhow,* had held her course, so surprised or stunned that no one had thought to bear away shoreward. The leader had had time to hear the 12-pounders' roars, and *had* hauled her wind to escape into shallow waters and the blackness of the shore, but the 6-pounders and carronades had scythed away both of her masts and long lateener yards and sails, leaving her wallowing in the path of her sister, which had rammed into her amidships, entangling both!

"Boarders, Mister Westcott!" Lewrie shouted exultantly. "Away boarders!"

Sailors manning the carronades and lighter guns abandoned their charges, took up cutlasses and boarding axes from the arms chests, and massed along the larboard bulwarks. Marines were taking individual pot-shots at anyone that moved on the trailing *dhow*'s decks. As *Sapphire* thumped against the stern of the lead *dhow* and the side of the other, Westcott, the Marine officers, and eager Midshipmen waved their swords or dirks in the air and ordered men over the side, and away they went with great, feral cheers. There were opposing shouts from the Spaniards, mostly *"rendicíon!"* and *"clemencia!"*, with their hands in the air, empty of weapons, some kneeling as if at prayer in supplication. A few scrambled from the bows of the trailing *dhow* to the other, and sought refuge right at the other *dhow*'s bows.

There were some screams as a Spaniard was hacked or bayonetted, but it was quickly over, and they made prize of both ships.

"Grapnel to 'em, there!" Lewrie ordered, unwilling to lose his prizes in the dark as *Sapphire* kept a way on her.

Lieutenant Westcott scrambled back up the ship's side, crawling over the closed entry-port, followed by most of the armed hands. He thumped to the deck in a most un-dignified fashion, then made his way to the quarterdeck, where Lewrie met him.

"Have an adventure, Mister Westcott?" Lewrie asked him.

"Not much of one, sir," Westcott griped. "There was no fight in them. Too stunned, I reckon, and I doubt if they had no more than nine or ten hands in each crew, so putting up resistance was out of the question."

"We need to fetch-to," Lewrie told him, "before we all drift shoreward and wreck ourselves. Then, we'll discover what condition the *dhows* are in. You've told off men for prize crews?"

"Aye, sir, ten hands each, with five Marines as guards," Westcott said. "Mister Roe, who's fluent in Spanish, is questioning one of their captains. Mixed bag, really. They were officered by navy men, but half the hands were army conscripts who knew a little about boats, I gathered. Sailing to and from Tetuán may be much preferable to 'square-bashing' and standing guard on the walls at Ceuta. We're grapnelled to them, sir? Best we take in all sail, for now. I will see to it, directly."

"Are they worth saving?" Lewrie asked.

"Taken into Gibraltar, burned where they sit, sir. Either course costs the Dons their cargoes, and makes them tighten their belts," Westcott said with a shrug.

"Sir? Captain, sir?" someone else came back aboard in the dark, stumbling over ring-bolts and thumping up a ladderway to the quarterdeck. "Leftenant Roe, sir! I've been questioning one of the Spanish naval officers. These two vessels aren't the only ones the Dons have at Ceuta.

They've six, in all, and they make the trip to Tetuán at least twice a week, sometimes in threes, for provisions. The other four are alongside the quays at Ceuta, waiting to make their runs later."

"Have they? Damn!" Lewrie spat. "Do ye gather that the Dons in the fortress know when these two will return?"

"Hmm, don't know, sir," Roe replied. "Didn't think to ask."

"Go ask, Mister Roe," Lewrie urged him. "Mister Westcott? I wish the Bosun and his Mates to go over to the prizes and determine if they're able to sail, without sinking. I wish the ship, and the prizes, well out to sea off Tetuán by sunrise, and out of sight of the fortress. I've a nasty idea, if they're seaworthy."

CHAPTER TEN

$\mathcal{H}$MS *Sapphire* entered Gibraltar Bay, firing off a salute to honour the Governor, Sir Hew Dalrymple, and proudly, to draw attention to herself and the four shabby prizes that trailed her to anchorages nearby the Old Mole. As soon as the ship was at rest, Midshipmen Hillhouse and Britton were sent ashore, each bearing reports to Dalrymple at the Convent, and to Thomas Mountjoy's false-front offices further down the town. They had distinguished themselves in carrying the other two prize *dhows* and Lewrie felt that they were deserving of some recognition from senior officers, or even from a spy.

Lewrie had certainly drawn the town's attention to himself and his ship. As his two-decker had ghosted past the Old Mole, he could lift a telescope and pick out the balcony which fronted his rented lodgings, and was delighted to see Maddalena there, smiling fit to bust, and waving a dish cloth in joy of his return.

He could not go ashore right away, though; he was forced to wait for a summons. Midshipman Britton returned aboard with a brief congratulatory note from Mountjoy. It took Midshipman Hillhouse longer to come back aboard. He had a note in his hand, as well.

"Message from General Dalrymple, sir," Hillhouse reported with a doff of his hat, "and a request that you attend him at Army headquarters."

"Very well, Mister Hillhouse, and thankee," Lewrie replied. "I'll take the boat you used. You're senior in the Harbour Watch?"

"Aye, sir," Hillhouse said.

"Carry on, then, and inform Mister Westcott that I will be ashore for some time," Lewrie ordered, then bounded down to the waist and the opened starboard entry-port.

"All hands!" Hillhouse shouted. "Face aft, off hats! Captain is departing!"

"My stars, just what did you do, Captain Lewrie?" Dalrymple asked once Lewrie had entered the Convent and the coolness of Sir Hew's spacious and high-cielinged offices. The old fellow was in good takings; there was a glass of wine offered at once.

"As I said in my report, sir, we put into Tetuán to see if the Dons provisioned there, discovered a brace of *dhows* loading food for the fortress, chased them down in the dark of night and took them, then repaired them far out to sea, and used them as Trojan Horses the next night. We sailed right up to the piers, boarded and carried two more, and set the last pair afire. The Spanish in Ceuta are now deprived of any means of obtaining food from Tetuán, unless they manage to sneak some vessels out of Algeciras to replace them."

"Carried them out under fire from the fortress, did you?" Sir Hew goggled.

"It was a hot corner for a time, sir, but, once far enough out from Ceuta, they lost sight of us in the dark. I cannot speak highly enough of Lieutenants Harcourt and Elmes, or four of my Midshipmen . . . they're named in the report, Sir Hew," Lewrie told him, "as well as some of my more energetic and quick-thinking sailors who accompanied them on the cutting-out raid."

"That's what the Navy calls it, a 'cutting-out'?" Dalrymple mused, with one quizzical (and thickly hairy) brow up. "Well, well, well! Took part, did you, Sir Alan?"

Here, that's nice and chummy of him! Lewrie told himself, glad to hear it.

"Had to stay aboard my ship, Sir Hew," Lewrie replied. "Have t'let the young'uns make a name for themselves. It rubs raw, but at some point, that's the drawback of senior command. How else are they to gain notice, and promotion?"

"Exactly so, Sir Alan," Dalrymple almost cooed. "Might you stay at headquarters for a time, sir? I've sent for our young 'spy-master,' Mister Mountjoy. There are doings ashore among the Spanish that I must discuss with him, and, now that you've reduced the rations of their troops in Ceuta, well . . . let us say that there are changes afoot."

"I'd be delighted, Sir Hew," Lewrie assured him, though he was mystified as to what part he and *Sapphire* might play. "I'll wait in the hall 'til he arrives, then? Won't take up more of your time 'til then."

"If you'd be so kind, Sir Alan," Dalrymple agreed.

There were some very comfortable upholstered chairs out in the hallway, where the thick walls of the Convent, the high cielings and tiled floors made a very cool, and quiet refuge; Lewrie almost nodded off before Mountjoy came breezing in with a jaunty step.

"Captain Lewrie, you rascal!" Mountjoy hooted. "You've been a mean boy to the Spanish again, haven't you?"

"Hallo, Mountjoy," Lewrie said, grinning. "Aye, I've been brutish. Put it down to drink and bad companions." He tugged his forelock and went into a lower-deck accent. "'Twas drink an' bad companions wot made me do it, Yer Honour sir, an' I swear a Bible-oath I'll never do it agin, hah! Sir Hew hinted there's something in the works that we both might have a part in," he added in his normal voice. "Have you anything you'd care to share?"

"Haven't a clue *what* he's in mind . . . really!" Mountjoy said in response to Lewrie's skeptical scowl. "If he's been dabbling in my own 'trade' . . . honestly, it'd be news to me, too."

One of Dalrymple's aides-de-camp, a pink-cheeked young Lieutenant, came from the inner office, spotted them, and summoned them in.

"Captain Lewrie, Mister Mountjoy? The General will see you, now," he said in a thin, high voice.

"Ah, gentlemen, thank you for attending me," Dalrymple effusively said, "and for your patience waiting, Sir Alan. Tea?" he asked as he waved them toward chairs in front of his desk.

A silver tea service and a set of Delft cups and saucers were close at hand on a campaign table. Dalrymple played "Mother," pouring cups for all, and stirring in the desired sugar and lemon or cream. He looked very pleased, almost playful, as he sat down again behind his desk and took a sip before beginning.

"Mister Mountjoy, are you aware of a certain distinguished Gibraltarian gentleman, a Mister Emmanuel Viale?" Dalrymple asked, with the air of knowing something that Mountjoy did not, and more than happy to enlighten his ignorance.

That's the biter bit, Lewrie thought. Usually, it was the game that Mountjoy played on *him*!

"Only that he's large in the grain trade, sir," Mountjoy had to confess, "and an un-official leader of the local business community."

"Spanish, of course," Dalrymple said with a pleased nod, much like an Oxford Don's response to a student's right answer. "But, you have had no dealings with him, even through your, ah . . . trading concern?"

"A false-front, Sir Hew, as well you know," Mountjoy replied, squirming in his chair a tad to have to admit that fact.

"Mister Viale requested a pass to cross the Lines to manage a business matter in San Roque," Dalrymple went on, "and has just come back, bearing a letter from General Castaños to me. The General wishes to re-open our formerly cordial correspondence, and for Viale to be his emissary."

"Indeed, sir?" Mountjoy said, perking up at that, though cautiously avoiding too much excitement.

"The recent abdication of King Carlos, the crowning of Ferdinand, and the French . . . well, call it what it is, a callous *invasion* of an allied nation, has General Castaños and his contemporaries in a stew," Dalrymple explained. "He alludes to military and civil authorities in Catalonia, Aragon, and Valencia who have written him with a call to raise an army of one hundred and fifty thousand men, asking him if his forces will join them, and if they can count on Andalusia, as well. Your ah, agents in Spain, Mister Mountjoy . . . how much have they heard of the sentiments of the Spanish people?"

"Ah, the Tumult of . . . wherever it was," Lewrie popped out. Both men stared at him, almost making him blush. "Well, there must be others, what?"

"The news of the new king, the French armies marching South to Madrid, has only just now begun to filter down to Andalusia, as idle rumours, sir," Mountjoy said, returning his attention to Dalrymple. "In some instances, it has been *my* people who've spread the news, but I cannot yet substantiate any public reaction. The other large concentration of available Spanish troops, other than General Castaños's, are in Cádiz, and I've had little luck getting information from there, or an agent in place. It's known that the governor of the city and its environs, and its garrison, is decidedly pro-French."

"Then would it come as a pleasant surprise to you, sir, that General

Castaños is asking for help from Great Britain?" Sir Hew slowly said with a beamish grin on his face. "And, that if the French take Madrid, that there is a possibility that the new king, Ferdinand, may have to flee into exile, as did the royal court of Portugal, perhaps to here, at Gibraltar, or even to London?"

"My *word*, sir!" Mountjoy responded with a gasp as the implications of those events struck him; struck him dumb-founded, in point of fact. "That'd be . . . world-shaking! Spain would become our ally, at last, and Spain a battlefield."

"Yayss," Dalrymple drawled, "and that is why General Castaños is desirous of bringing the entire garrison of Ceuta over to Algeciras to supplement his own forces, as soon as possible. You told me that Marshal Murat already has officers in Algeciras and San Roque, scouting my defences. If Castaños fields an army against the French, there's no possibility of the French besieging Gibraltar."

"Ehm, a question," Lewrie stuck in, his brow furrowed. "What sort of chance do the Dons stand against Napoleon's Grand Army? Are they any good, or would they fold like the Austrians, over and over?"

"Well . . . ahem," Dalrymple hemmed, clearing his throat, scowling heavily in Lewrie's direction.

From the very first battles along the French frontier in 1793, the much-vaunted Austrian armies, the well-drilled Prussians, and in 1805 even the massive Russian armies, had been beaten like so many rugs. The French marched too quickly, scattered themselves in semi-autonomous divisions across too broad a front, with a knack of concentrating *en masse* at the vital point at the last minute and shattering everyone with their thick attack columns, supported by massed cannon regiments.

"Mean t'say," Lewrie blundered on, "does Spain have a general like Sir John Moore, someone the equal of Napoleon and his marshals? Have the Spanish really fought a big battle, the last fifty years or so, or waged a long campaign against anybody?"

"I would strongly imagine, Captain Lewrie, that the Spanish will require the assistance of a British army, perhaps several forces, to ah . . . stiffen them," Dalrymple archly replied. "That would be simply grand!"

"Starting with Portugal," Mountjoy said.

"Yes, Portugal first," Dalrymple agreed. "Lord Castlereagh has written me that an expeditionary force is being assembled in England to be landed somewhere in Portugal, under a General Wellesley."

"Not Sir John Moore?" Lewrie puzzled. "Who's Wellesley when he's up and dressed?"

"Tell you later," Mountjoy whispered to Lewrie. Louder, he said, "I would much appreciate was I allowed full access to your correspondence with General Castaños, Sir Hew, and a chance to speak with Mister Viale the next time he returns from San Roque. In that way, I can assure you that all my humble facilities will aid you in this endeavour, to the hilt!"

"But of course, Mister Mountjoy," Dalrymple beamed amiably, "and I am certain that both your, and my, informations to the Foreign Office, and Horse Guards, will go off on the very next mail packet."

"Count on that, sir," Mountjoy assured him.

"We are on the verge of a great change in world affairs, perhaps the beginning of the end of Bonaparte's despotic tyranny over Europe. And it will all start *here*, in *my* patch. Thank you for your attendance, gentlemen. I think that will be all for now. Sir Alan, I may call upon you to carry General Castaños's orders over to Ceuta, should the time come, when all the arrangements for their transfer have been agreed to. Do stay in harbour awhile longer."

"Happy to oblige, Sir Hew," Lewrie agreed, looking forward to an idle spell, hot baths, clean clothes, and some "All Nights In" with Maddalena Covilhā.

CHAPTER ELEVEN

*D*amn my eyes, your news just keeps getting better and better!" Lewrie congratulated Mountjoy as they left the Convent. "Everything's goin' your way, and London will be very pleased with you."

"Well, I can't really claim that much credit," Mountjoy said with seeming humility. "It's not as if *I* goaded the French into invading, or the Spanish turning against old King Carlos. Those events were beyond my control, and I'm just riding in their wake. But, they *are* satisfying, even so. I cannot sway General Castaños to join with the others who've written him . . . revolutionary councils, or *juntas,* or whatever they're calling themselves, not unless I had face-to-face access with the man. You know, you almost stuck your foot in it, in there."

"Why? What'd I do?" Lewrie asked. "Because I couldn't remember the Tumult of Oranges right?"

"Tumult of Aranjuez," Mountjoy corrected.

"*Sounds* like oranges," Lewrie japed.

"No, it's when you questioned if the Spanish could face a French army, and if they had any decent generals," Mountjoy told him as they strolled downhill to the main street. "From all I know of Castaños, he's been a peacetime officer . . . never fought a battle in his life. The same as the

Dowager, d'ye see, and that rankled Sir Hew, who has never participated in one, either."

"Oops," Lewrie replied, un-abashed.

"Mind you, Sir Hew dearly desires one," Mountjoy went on. "He has dreams of martial glory, and a chance to fight and defeat French armies in the field may be within his reach."

"What? Sir Hew? Don't joke!" Lewrie heartily scoffed.

"Think of how our British Army chooses officers for their campaigns, sir," Mountjoy cautioned. "Command always goes to the most senior man available, whether they're any good or not. Dalrymple is senior to General Fox on Sicily, Sir Brent Spencer cooling his heels here at Gibraltar after the Ceuta siege went bust, even Sir John Moore who sailed home after the French took Lisbon. Horse Guards *may* promote Dalrymple to Commander-In-Chief for Portugal and Spain."

"Christ, if they do, we're just fucked!" Lewrie spat out loud. "Who in their rights minds'd . . . mean t'say, the Dowager *must* know his limitations, and leave the fieldwork to someone like Sir John Moore . . . wouldn't he?"

"One would hope," Mountjoy gloomily responded. "Care for some wine? Let's pop into the Ten Tuns. Some celebratory champagne, if they have any."

The Ten Tuns did not run to smuggled French champagne, though it did have some fine Italian *pinot grigio* just in from Genoa.

"So, who's this Wellesley, then?" Lewrie asked again once he had half a glass inside.

"He's a 'Sepoy' general, made his name in India against the Tippoo Sultan of Mysore, and then later the Maratha princes," Mountjoy told him. "Of course, his brother, Lord Mornington, was Governor of India at the time, so you can imagine his rapid promotions, and rank nepotism, rankled his fellow officers. He and all his brothers adopted the name Wellesley, because it linked them to aristocracy on one side of the family. When *all* the Wellesleys left India, he got a knighthood, so he's Sir Arthur Wellesley, and *might* have come off with over fourty thousand pounds," Mountjoy chattily gossipped.

"A chicken-*nabob*'," Lewrie said with a smirk. "Must not have been tryin'. A full '*nabob*' comes home with over an hundred."

"Don't I wish!" Mountjoy said with a sigh. "Anyway, Sir Arthur and his family are *Irish* peers, don't ye know, so they have to grub harder than

English peers. He got elected to Parliament for a time, voting with Pitt, then Grenville, was Secretary-General for Ireland 'til Grenville lost office and Portland took over. He was in command at Copenhagen last year when we had to bombard the city to convince the Danes to surrender their fleet before Napoleon could get hold of it, and did the job very well, so . . . he's in favour at the moment, and was fortunate that he and an army were at Cork, waiting to sail to take Venezuela from Spain. Ever heard of a Colonel Miranda?"

"That gad-fly who wants a United States of South America?" Lewrie said with a loud groan. "He was the drivin' force that put a flea in Commodore Popham's ear that sent us from Capetown to Buenos Aires, and *that* series of disasters! The worthless shit-stirrer."

"I'm sure that the Wellesley family had a lot to do with his appointment for that, and for the expedition to Portugal, too. The senior brother, Lord Mornington, is a pretentious seeker of higher grandeur," Mountjoy relished in the telling, "more and greater titles, more land, more esteem. Oh! Here's a tangy tidbit about Sir Arthur . . . when he was younger and poorer in prospects, he fell in love with one of the most beautiful young ladies in Ireland, Kitty Packenham. Her daddy was immensely rich, mind, and Arthur's suit was refused, especially by Kitty's brother, Edward, or 'Ned.'

"He goes off for years, wins his spurs in India, and has one more go at marrying her, sight unseen," Mountjoy said, almost tittering with amusement. "This time, he's rich, knighted, and famous, and Edward Packenham, a soldier himself, agrees. Down the church aisle the bride comes, and Sir Arthur asks Edward, 'Good God, who's that ugly brute?', or something like that, and Edward says 'It's Kitty!' 'She's grown damned ugly, by Jove' says Sir Arthur, but honour demands, and he marries her in spite of her looks. Pig in a poke, what? The years weren't kind to her, and it's rumoured that Kitty had turned *stiffly* religious, to boot, so it's no wonder that Sir Arthur developed a strong lust for pretty young ladies. Not quite as bad as his brother, who should have been castrated at birth, for his own good, but, he *will* dally at the drop of a hat, hah!"

"So, he's senior to other choices, as you said?" Lewrie had to ask as he poured himself another glass, and topped up Mountjoy's.

"*Lord*, no! Interest and influence won out, again!" Mountjoy said with a hoot. "There's dozens of senior Generals on Army List grinding their teeth in rage over it! With any luck, he knows how to soldier. He's won all his battles before, so . . . we'll see."

"Just how d'ye *know* all this, his private life and all?" Lewrie groused. "Get it from *The Tatler*, did ye?"

"Lewrie," Mountjoy said with an arch grin, "you should know by now that Secret Branch knows everyone, and everything, that matters."

"Keep a file on me, do ye?" Lewrie asked with an accusing scowl.

"Pages and pages," Mountjoy said with a laugh.

"Secret Branch keeps lists of useful idiots?" Lewrie gloomed up.

"Old Zachariah Twigg always thought well of you, and said so in his notes," Mountjoy told him. "That arch manner of his, his biting banter, were just his way with everyone from senior ministers to the footmen. He had no patience for anyone who wasn't as clever or intelligent as he was. He treated Peel, me, and you the same. What mattered to him was results, and if you got the job done, that was the main thing. He did not praise, ever!"

"You speak of him like he's dead," Lewrie joshed.

"I didn't tell you?" Mountjoy replied, cocking his head over. "He is. Passed away at his country house just after the New Year . . . pity, 'cause he'd finally been knighted for his long, distinguished service to Crown and Country a bit before Christmas. How remiss of me, not to tell you."

So, the old cut-throat's gone, Lewrie thought, and wondered if he felt mournful, or should.

"I'll wager the announcement was bland and murky," Mountjoy went on, "and made him sound like a long-serving clerk or barrister!"

Lewrie did feel mournful, after all. Twigg had been a part of half his life, and his conniving had driven Lewrie into some of the grandest neck-or-nothing adventures he'd experienced. Twigg's demise was a wrenching reminder of his own mortality, and the fact that those experiences were long gone, never to be re-lived.

"To Sir Zachariah Twigg," Lewrie said of a sudden, raising his glass, "and thanks that we survived his doings."

"Yes, to Sir Zachariah, the greatest of them all," Mountjoy agreed, clinking glasses with Lewrie's.

CHAPTER TWELVE

At least somebody *speaks well of me,* Lewrie thought as he read the latest edition of the *Gibraltar Chronicle,* which featured a brief description of *Sapphire*'s raid and the captured *dhows.* The newspaper was a thin one, and only came out weekly, sometimes twice a month if short of ink or newsprint paper.

"Here, Maddalena, have ye seen this?" he asked her.

"The *Chronicle?* Pooh," she said with a dismissive laugh. "It reprints what it gets from English papers, and never says much of what happens here that is important. I think the Army tells them what not to say. I like the imported papers. What is in it?"

Lewrie had purchased some used wooden furniture for the balcony overlooking the harbour, some slatted chairs and a low table, and Maddalena had made some colourful pads for them. That was where he sat at that moment, whilst Maddalena was puttering round her warbler's cage, which she had brought out to let the bird have some fresh air and sunlight.

"An account of my raid, a bit more dramatic than my report to Admiralty, really," Lewrie told her. "And, they're calling it a deed of remarkable pluck and daring."

"Hmm, let me read it, then," she said, sitting down opposite him. "Well, I must cut this out and save it. Bonito," she said to the bird, "you will have a thinner lining of your cage. No droppings on this. I do not recall any articles of your other raids last Summer, though."

Lewrie was about to blurt out that they had been Secret Branch doings, but said instead, "I imagine that the authorities feared the Spanish would get hold of a copy and find a way to stop my business. The Governor's got spies on the brain, and he's probably right in his suspicions. Too many foreigners on the Rock . . . present company excepted," he added, blowing her a kiss.

He was having a very pleasant morning, at his ease in shirtsleeves, with his neck-stock undone. The town, fortifications, and the harbour lay in a cool shade from the heights of the Rock that towered over all, with a light wind wafting, and it would be late afternoon before the sun's glare made the balcony uncomfortable. Maddalena was dressed down, too, in a white blouse, a colourful woven peasant skirt, and leather sandals, clothing she owned when she'd lived in Oporto and brought with her to Gibraltar years before.

She tapped the side of the coffee pot on the table to see if it was still hot enough, and poured herself a fresh cup, silently offering Lewrie a refill with a tilt of the pot.

"I believe I will, thankee, uhm . . . *obrigado*," he replied.

"I am a woman, Alan. It's *obrigada*," she teased.

"Why, so you are!" he teased back. "That's handy, by God!"

He stirred sugar into his cup, wishing that Gibraltar had any dairy cows, even nanny goats, for a splash of milk. Maddalena leaned back in her chair; she'd taken charge of the *Chronicle* for now, and it was pleasing to watch her reactions to the articles. She'd flash a quick smile, furrow her brow, or move her lips to silently sound out un-familiar words. She suddenly lowered the paper to her lap.

"The riots they speak of, the demonstrations . . . what can the Spanish people do against French armies, Alan?" she asked.

"Well, if their new king has a *dash* of gumption, he'll tear up that treaty that that arse-lickin' French-lover, Godoy, signed and call out his own armies," Lewrie told her. "He may even switch sides and call for British help t'kick 'em back over the Pyrenees."

"Gumption," Maddalena said with a sudden laugh. "The same as courage? *Bom*. Arse-licking? I did not know you could be crude, Alan, *querido*."

"Of course I can be crude, *querida*," Lewrie mock-boasted. "I've been dined out on my crudity for years!"

"Seriously, though," Maddalena pressed him, after a brief laugh, "is

Napoleon Bonaparte attacking us here at Gibraltar, or is he so, oh, what is the word? Arrogant? *Bom.* So arrogant that he thinks he can eat up Spain, too?"

"I'd say it's a little of both," Lewrie replied with a shrug. "He has the treaty to use Spanish armies alongside his own to take Gibraltar, but he may imagine that if he owns Spain, lock, stock, and barrel, he gets control of the whole Spanish Empire by default. He's an ambitious little bastard, out to rule all of Europe, and the rest of the whole world. He may have bitten off more than he can chew this time, though. If Spain resists, and gets British help—?"

"And my country is free, again," she interrupted.

"That's coming, dear," Lewrie told her. "Keep this under your hat, but . . . there's a British army on the way to do just that, under a good general, Sir Arthur Wellesley."

"Not that Sir John Moore we met?" she asked with a frown. He'd made quite an impression on her at that supper, as good an impression as *she* had made among the exalted company for her gown, her beauty, and her excellent English skills.

"I'm assured that he won all his battles," Lewrie said.

"Where?"

"Uhm, in India," Lewrie had to admit.

"But not against the French. Hmm," she said with one brow up in skepticism. "Then we must pray that he is skillful." She turned to stare out at the harbour and the Strait for a long, pensive time.

"Your coffee's getting cold," Lewrie gently prompted, and she turned her head to face him with a very fond smile on her face.

"I like this very much," she told him, "how you do not speak to me of only simple things, but treat me as if I have a mind capable of understanding things like . . . this," she said, tapping a finger on the newspaper. "You are a very dear, rare man, *meu amor.*"

"Well, you're a rare, and dear, young lady, Maddalena," Lewrie purred back. "Most women are all about receipts to cook, gossip, and domesticities, and leave the reading and thinking to the menfolk . . . though back home, most of 'em are into poetry, and long, thrilling novels," he said with a dismissive snort. "Fetching, but empty-headed."

"Domestic . . . hmm," Maddalena said with a pleased look as she lifted her coffee cup, trying out the word and liking the sound of it and its meaning. "At this moment, I feel *very* domestic."

Where the Hell's she goin' with that? Lewrie thought in alarm.

"It is very pleasing," she added, smiling wider, batting her lashes at him before taking a sip of coffee.

"I'm glad you're pleased, *minha doce*," Lewrie replied, hoping that she wasn't planning, or scheming, for more *permanent* domesticity.

I quite like her, I'm fond of her, but, mean t'say! he thought.

Someone rapped on the thick oak and iron-barred door.

"What the Devil?" Lewrie groused. "Who's that?" He sprang to his feet and went through the lodgings to answer it. There was more rapping 'til he flung the door open, and beheld a boy of about twelve.

"Are you Captain Lewrie, sir?" the boy asked.

"I am," Lewrie gravelled.

"Then this letter is for you, sir," the boy said, drawing it from inside his loose shirt. As soon as Lewrie had it in hand, the lad dashed off, clattering down the hall and the stairs in a pair of loose, old shoes.

The sender was *T.M.*, so the ornate looping initials said; from Thomas Mountjoy. "Damn!" Lewrie spat as he tore it open, breaking the wax seal. "Damn!" he said again as he read the brief content.

Ominous developments. Come quick, my lodgings.

Hmm . . . saved me, he just did, Lewrie thought, relieved that Maddalena and domesticity could be avoided a couple of days.

"Who was it?" Maddalena asked, coming inside. She picked up her cat, Precious, and cuddled it in her arms.

"Official business, I fear, Maddalena," he explained. "I must be off, at once."

"Oh, what a shame! We were having such a nice morning together," she pouted, as Lewrie donned his waistcoat and coat, and did up his neck-stock.

"Old Navy sayin', my dear. 'Growl ye may, but go ye must,'" he cited. "I may be tied up the rest of the day, and may have to stay aboard ship tonight." With the cat in her arms, the best he could bestow, and the best he got, was a quick kiss and a brief one-armed hug. A ruffle of Precious's head fur, and he was off.

"What the Hell is so important, Mountjoy, that ye had t'tear me away from a morning with Maddalena? And how did ye know that I'd be there, hey?" he fumed.

"We know everything, remember?" Mountjoy shot back, looking as if he'd been tearing at his hair, and pacing in a fury. "The idiots in Madrid! I got a despatch from Romney Marsh just after sunup, and the news is dire. Marshal Murat and his army has entered Madrid, and *summoned* King Ferdinand, the old king, Carlos, the queens, *and* Godoy, to meet Napoleon at Bayonne, in France, and the damned fools are setting out to do just that! Goddamn such miserable, spineless, idiotic royal clowns!"

"Well, if they didn't go along, Murat would've arrested them and *made* them go," Lewrie speculated, wondering what this meant for him and his ship, and why he'd been summoned.

Maybe Mountjoy just wants to rant at somebody, and I'm handy, he thought.

"Just climbed into their gilded coaches and thrown their crowns away, thrown their *country* away," Mountjoy ranted, and he *did* pace the balcony like a caged tiger. "Mark my words, Napoleon will replace them with one of his brothers, and the deluded fools think that he's going to play arbitrator 'twixt Carlos and Ferdinand?"

"Be a king-maker?" Lewrie asked. "I'll wager old Carlos thinks that 'Boney' will put him back on the throne, and Ferdinand imagines that Bonaparte will put the guinea-stamp on his legitimacy. Godoy . . . I imagine he's going along t'get his job back, and get a chance to worship Napoleon in person, and *really* kiss his arse!"

"As I said . . . deluded!" Mountjoy said, throwing up his hands in disgust. "The people in Madrid can see right through the ruse, even if their royalty can't. Marsh writes that some angry meetings have been held, some *juntas* assembled, though nothing's come of them, yet. He's heard rumours from the North that towns where the French have taken over are ready to riot, but that may be more hopeful than helpful. He puts little stock in them, so far."

"Heard anything more about General Castaños and the *juntas* you mentioned earlier? Have you spoken with that Emmanuel Viale?" Lewrie asked, looking about for something to drink, and wondering if Mountjoy was so vexed that he'd forgotten hospitality.

"*Still* not ready to declare, waiting for more information, the same as me," Mountjoy growled, flinging himself into one of the chairs. "Viale, well. He's a nice-enough old stick, but he only parrots what Castaños's letters tell him to say, shrugging his shoulders and saying that he's only an emissary, not a conspirator. And Dalrymple! God! He's turned as closed-mouth as a statue, lately, playing his own game and keeping his cards close to his chest. Mind you, he wants Spain as an ally, he wants a war, and a big role in it for himself, but he won't trust me, or Secret Branch, to help him get it!"

"No wonder you're frustrated," Lewrie said. "You look like a man who badly needs a drink."

"By God I am!" Mountjoy all but roared, sprang from the chair, and dashed inside his lodgings from the gallery, rooting about for a bottle, and the cork-pull which he was forever mis-placing. Lewrie heard the clink of bottles against bottles, as if Mountjoy was un-decided. "What do you prefer, a Spanish red, or brandy?" Mountjoy called.

"No corn whisky, no 'Miss Taylor'?" Lewrie called back.

"God, that sour rot?" Mountjoy scoffed. "I remember that 'Miss Taylor' from when I was your clerk. *Paint* remover! Ah! I have it."

There was a happy *stoonk* noise as Mountjoy pulled the cork on something, and returned to the outdoor gallery with a bottle of white wine and two glasses.

"A light and flowery Spanish white, as I recall from the first time I drank it," Mountjoy said as he poured them full glasses. "Not much of a finish, but pleasant."

"Do ye less harm, in the long run," Lewrie said, sampling his sip. "No sour mash bourbon whisky?" he teased.

"Not too many American ships put in at Gibraltar, of late. Do you really savour it? Sour mash corn liquour, the description. Ugh!"

"Only after supper, or when I'm completely frustrated," Lewrie told him with a grin, sitting down in one of the padded chairs. "Did Romney Marsh say anything in his report as to how the people of Madrid are acting, now they have a large French army in the city?"

"A little," Mountjoy replied, less agitated now that he had a drink in hand. "Shunning them in the streets and taverns, leaving an establishment if French soldiers show up. What Madrid's whores are doing, he didn't say, but money's money, and I can't imagine them refusing fresh trade. What high-born ladies are doing, I can imagine. Giving the 'cut direct,' the 'cut sublime,' just short of cursing, or staying inside so they won't have to deal with them?"

"The French are barracked inside the city?" Lewrie pressed. "That'll drive the Dons mad. Are they inside, or camped outside?"

"Ehm . . . inside the city," Mountjoy told him, after a quick rummage through a sheaf of papers that he'd abandoned, or hurled away, after his first readings. "Yes, Marsh said inside Madrid."

"Hah!" Lewrie crowed. "There's half your revolution started, already!

Our Army, the French army . . . they reach a town with decent shelter available, and they barge into houses, inns, and taverns, and assign so many soldiers to each. If a family has three bed-chambers, the soldiers'll take over two, and you'll find a notice painted or chalked on the entry door, say 'eight, number one company, umpteenth regiment,' for example. The troops'll use the cooking facilities for their own, too, and whatever the family has in their larders will be fair game. So will the wine and spirits, and if they stay there for long, so will the prettiest daughters.

"Ever read the Yankee Doodle's Declaration of Independence?" he asked. "That revolution wasn't just over tea taxes or the Stamp Act. After the French and Indian War, as they called it, we posted a stronger army in the colonies and expected the Yankee Doodles t'pay for it, but we didn't build encampments or permanent barracks, so we shoved our troops into civilian lodgings, to be fed by the colonists. Pinch-penny government policies like that *forced* the rebellion."

"So, if the French do the same thing, take over the taverns and inns, barge right into the grand houses, eat and drink everything in sight, the Spanish will rise up?" Mountjoy slowly realised, perking up immensely.

"That, and seeing their squabblin' kings coachin' off at the 'Corsican Ogre's' bidding, abandoning them to rape and pillage will take the trick!" Lewrie assured him. "You might wish to find a way to pass that news along to Castaños, who's never seen a conquering army in action. You might even get Cummings t'spread the word all along the coast of Andalusia, too. That'll fire 'em up."

"A believable lie in a good cause is excusable, too. Hmm," Mountjoy pondered, all but chewing on a thumbnail. "If the French haven't committed any atrocities yet, they surely will, sooner or later. And, if I *invented* some horrific tales of rape and robbery, well! They'd *surely* go down well."

"That's the spirit!" Lewrie urged. "No sense tearing your hair out and frettin' yourself half to death, when you can do what Twigg and Peel would do. Lie like blazes!"

"National treasures pillaged, art galleries stripped of their works," Mountjoy mused.

"Oh, what Spanish peasant cares a fig for art galleries?" Lewrie countered. "Pretty girls of good family kidnapped from city parks by French brutes . . . taverners murderered 'cause they wouldn't serve Frog soldiers, houses looted, virgins raped. Hell, *nuns* raped! Churches looted of their plate, shops robbed of their cash. Priests killed protecting their altars, or their parishioners?"

"Rather . . . *lurid*, ain't it?" Mountjoy meekly objected.

"The more lurid, the better," Lewrie encouraged him. "We need some sort of visual proof, though, hmm. I could loan you Westcott, and Midshipman Fywell."

"What for?" Mountjoy asked.

"They're both dab-hand artists. They can draw pictures of any sort of atrocity you wish. Well, I'd leave the rape and all to Westcott. Fywell's the innocent sort, and he'd be better at burnin' homes and taverns, the looting and such. You can sign them with the names of Spanish artists, have the people at the *Gibraltar Chronicle* print 'em up, then get 'em delivered by the bale all along the coast."

"God, do I dare put *Goya's* name on them?" Mountjoy wondered.

"That might make sense, since he is known to live in Madrid, and paints royalty and the rich," Lewrie said with an uncaring shrug. "He ain't here to object, now, is he? Rich Andalusians'd know of him."

"You know, sir," Mountjoy said, getting a sly look on his face, "if I let slip to the local paper that we have it on good authority from a Madrid paper about the kings doing Bonaparte's bidding, they could print it, and some early atrocities, as a news item, Castaños and his officers are sure to obtain smuggled copies. I could *invent* an article about what the French are doing to Lisbon, too."

"D'ye think the Spanish give a damn about Lisbon, or the Portuguese?" Lewrie scoffed.

"But, it's all of a piece, don't you see?" Mountjoy said, in much happier takings, agitated and on his feet once again, but this time he was scheming with evil delight. "Fresh French depredations, the same as they've done from the toe of Italy to the border with Russia! The new Vandals, the new Huns, the new barbarians! We must have pictures of innocent-looking Spaniards, but brutish, hulking, shaggy-haired, ogre-ish-lookin' French, doing their very worst!"

"You could throw in a bridge troll or two," Lewrie cynically stuck in.

Thomas Mountjoy paid that comment no mind, too intent upon his fresh scheme. He dashed inside to his desk for writing materials, and dashed back out, prepared to scribble madly.

"I'll go back aboard and inform Lieutenant Westcott and Midshipman Fywell what's wanting, so they can get a start on the sketches immediately," Lewrie said, realising that he'd not get a sensible word out of Mountjoy that day. "I'll try to keep Westcott's pictures just short of pornography."

"Uhm-hmm," Mountjoy said, distracted.

"No bestiality, hey? No ducks or goats bein' sodomised?" he proposed. "Uhm-hmm."

"Good day, Mister Mountjoy," Lewrie said, then drained his glass and stood up to depart. "See myself out?"

"Uhm-hmm."

CHAPTER THIRTEEN

*O*h. My word, sirs," Midshipman Fywell all but croaked as he caught sight of some of Lieutenant Westcott's pictures. His eyes got as big as a first-saddled colt's. "What are the soldiers doing?"

"That is called 'rape,' Mister Fywell," Lewrie informed him with a straight face, "forced sex with un-willing women. *Not* the sort of thing a British gentleman should *ever* do, but our enemies will."

Damme, they are quite . . . suggestive, he told himself as he felt a slight stirring in his groin; *Westcott knows what he's about.*

There was one with a young nun being carried off over the shoulder of a French soldier much resembling a gorilla, arms out-stretched to her sisters, who were reaching to pluck her back, daunted by other brutish Frenchmen with swords and bayonetted muskets. A church-ish-looking building was burning in the background, and the yard in front of it was littered with cast-off loot.

In another, an innocent young *señorita* had been dragged from her coach, her *duenna* battered with a musket butt, and five French soldiers, also re-sembling massive brutes, were assaulting her, four holding her arms and legs, and the fifth just shoving down his trousers with his bare butt show-ing. Her gown was thrown up, just an inch shy of lewdness.

There were firing squads, there was pillage, bayonetted churchmen, abandoned crying babes sitting next to their slain parents, and any sort of brutality, there were two men in rich-looking clothing being hanged from an iron Liberty Tree, the sort that the French erected in every town they conquered since 1793, as if they were bringing freedom, Liberty, Equality, and Fraternity to people crying out for relief from their former rulers.

Damned if some of the Frog soldiers don't resemble some of Sapphire's crew! Lewrie thought; *Just filthier and more "Jack Nasty-Face."*

"Is that'un supposed to be Bosun Terrell, sir?" Fywell asked.

"I took some from life, Mister Fywell," Westcott said with a simper. "If they all looked like apes, they wouldn't be villainous. They'd be caricatures."

"You do a nice looting, and good burnings, Mister Fywell," Lewrie congratulated the Mid. "I quite like the tavern drunks, too."

"But, none of this is strictly true, is it, sir?" Fywell had to ask. "Mean to say, we don't know if the French are really doing these things."

"It's what we *wish* the Spanish to believe, young sir," Lewrie told him. "They're a proud, suddenly conquered, and sold-out people. Sooner or later, some Frenchman will be insulted, have a chamber pot dumped on his head, they'll kill whoever did it, and these sorts of things *will* happen, then there'll be general riots, to which the French will respond with exactly this sort of barbarity. Trust me that it'll happen. And we *want* it to happen. Then Spain becomes a British ally, and Napoleon gets his nose tweaked.

"Hmm, best sign this'un with a Spanish-sounding name," Lewrie instructed. "Then, I'll take them to Mister Mountjoy."

"Who's he?" Fywell asked Westcott in a whisper.

"A British government official in charge of such things, my lad," Westcott told him, "a fellow in the 'hush-hush' business."

"A *spy*, do you mean, sir?" Fywell asked with a gulp.

Gawd, but is he young! Lewrie thought.

"The man who chose our targets last Summer," Lewrie admitted. "And the least said of him, the better all round. Get it?"

"Aye aye, sir!" Fywell said, half-appalled, half-intrigued.

"Well, thank you both for your efforts, and your good work, sirs," Lewrie said, signalling that the meeting in his cabins was done. Westcott stayed awhile longer than Fywell.

"I didn't show you all of mine, sir," Wescott confessed. "Do you want to see these?" He had a folder in his hands.

"Utterly pornographic, are they, Geoffrey?" Lewrie asked.

"Utterly, sir," Lt. Westcott said, smirking.

Lewrie leafed through several, finding fully de-nuded women, Frogs with their pricks showing (none *too* large, mind) virginal girls being taken in every possible orifice.

"By God, but you *must* get yourself a new mistress ashore, sir!" Lewrie said, a tad wide-eyed. "If I showed these to Mountjoy, he'd be staggered, makin' garglin' noises. He's a prim sod, given his line of work."

"Working on it, sir, working on it," Westcott promised.

"Oh yes, these are excellent, Captain Lewrie," Mountjoy said, leafing through the sketches, nodding and humming over the barbarities, then going wide-eyed over Westcott's "specials," and made some "my words" and "egads."

"Think they'll do?" Lewrie asked.

"Oh, they'll more than do!" Mountjoy said with delight. "For the most part, I'll claim that these events occurred up North, not in Madrid, where the French have already seized cities on false pretexts. The people at the newspaper have aided me most nicely, too. What do you think of those, there on the desk?"

Lewrie looked over a pile of what looked to be snippets from newspapers. He could not make heads or tails of them, for they were all printed in Spanish or Portuguese. "What are these?" he asked.

"Eyewitness accounts of French atrocities, allegedly from Lisbon, or Northern Spanish papers," Mountjoy said with a hint of pride. "See on the backs, there are incomplete articles, as one would expect to see when clipping something out of a paper. I'm passing them on to Mister Viale to give to General Castaños, and read for himself. The *Gibraltar Chronicle* is fitting my work in between their own work, and I've had to dip into my funds to pay them for it . . . dearly, you see . . . but I think it's worth it. They'll be doing some one-sheet tracts, too. I *wish* I could produce *entire* Spanish papers to send along the coast, but that would be asking too much of the *Chronicle*. When the Duke of Kent was here, he wrote a three-hundred-page book of regulations and ordered them to print it. They couldn't put out the paper for two whole months, and swear they'll never miss an issue again."

"Who wrote the articles?" Lewrie asked.

"Deacon and I did, in English first, then got some people here to translate them into Spanish or Portuguese," Mountjoy told him.

"This'un here won't do," Lewrie pointed out, holding one up for Mountjoy to look over. "I don't think the Spanish use the *f* letter to replace an *s* as we do, and ye might have a care with all the tildes, squiggles, and whatnots."

"What?" Mountjoy yelped, astonished, seizing the snippet and poring over it. "Damn! Damn my eyes, just . . . shit!" He went to his desk and read through each article, highly agitated. "Thank God, it's only this one that the paper got wrong, then. The rest will do."

"Well, that's a relief," Lewrie said.

"I'm sending some of the finished product to London, too. They may find them useful," Mountjoy said. "Not the illustrations' original woodcut blocks, I'll still need those for later printings, but maybe my superiors can hire some artists to make their own. Got to stir up people back home, to ready them for a wider war, hey? Distribute them into the rest of Europe to turn people against the French?"

"You really need a printing press of your own, Mountjoy."

"I do, don't I?" Mountjoy said with a wide grin. "The power of the press. Look at that radical, Thomas Paine, and what his pamphlets did for the American Revolution, how his later work prompted the French Revolution."

"How Napoleon uses his *Moniteur* to lie to his own people, and the rest of the world," Lewrie sarcastically added. "Though by now, the French people say that if someone lies to them, they say that 'he lies like a bulletin in the *Moniteur.*'"

"It's the way of the future, war by newsprint," Mountjoy said with glee. "England must lead the way in it . . . even if Bonaparte got to it, first."

"Well, if you're happy with the results, I'll be going, then," Lewrie told him. "I'm going to sail over to keep an eye on Ceuta one more time. Sir Hew Dalrymple asked me to stay in harbour, but hasn't come up with anything to do, and my people are goin' stale."

"But, what if he suddenly has need of you, or I do?" Mountjoy asked.

"I'm only twelve miles cross the Strait," Lewrie laughed off. "He can send a small boat under sail, or light a beacon atop of the Rock . . . if the Barbary apes allow it. I don't know. He can fire off some Congreve rockets, if he has any. I'll send the old fart a note today, and, weather allowin', sail tomorrow after dawn. That's time enough t'prompt him into any request he has in mind."

"Very well, then, Captain Lewrie," Mountjoy agreed. "I have no pressing need of your ship and your services, for now, either."

"Then I'll take my leave. Enjoy your newspaper project, sir, and have joy of it," Lewrie said, bowing himself out.

And so went the rest of April and early May of 1808; calling at Parsley Island, now garrisoned and equipped with batteries of 24-pounder cannon; circling round the fortress of Ceuta and its peninsula at a safe five miles' distance, and fetching-to at night within sight of the frustrated, and hopefully starving Spanish garrison, lit up with extra lanthorns on deck like a garden party. A week of that, and *Sapphire* would return to port for firewood, water, fresh rations, and shore liberty for both watches. Except for Lewrie's visits with Maddalena when in harbour, it was the dullest sort of duty, almost as bad as what he imagined peacetime service was like. He even found himself with the urge to re-black the guns and obtain brick-dust to polish brass like the finicky-est martinet of a Captain!

It came as a great relief one morning, just after *Sapphire* was gotten under way, when a small boat came dashing cross the Strait in her direction. Someone aboard the boat had jury-rigged a short staff ahead of her fores'l upon which she flew a British boat jack.

Lewrie abandoned a fine breakfast to go on deck to await the boat's arrival, leaving his coat and hat in his cabins in curiosity.

"A request for our services from General Dalrymple, might we imagine, sir?" Lt. Westcott said with a hint of eager hope.

"Be careful what ye wish for, Mister Westcott," Lewrie japed. "It could be your tailor sending a demand for immediate payment."

The last time Lieutenant Westcott came back aboard from a jaunt ashore, he'd been sporting a new coat and waist-coat, with a parcel of new shirts and breeches.

The boat crossed *Sapphire*'s stern and surged up alongside of her starboard side, her bow man hooking onto the main-chain platform with a gaff. There was an Army Lieutenant in the boat, one whom Lewrie recognised; the same young pink-cheeked lad he'd seen attending at Dalrymple's offices.

"God, the lubber can't figure out how to scale the side," Lieutenant Harcourt said with a snicker.

The Army officer had one booted foot on the gunn'l of the boat, but kept staggering, reaching out for the man-ropes, but hopelessly short of seizing them.

"Mister Ward?" Lewrie called to the nearest Midshipman. "Do you go down and gather what correspondence he has, so he won't fall in and drown himself."

"Aye, sir!" Ward replied crisply, dashing to the entry-port and down the battens as spryly as a monkey, grinning fit to bust at the chance to further embarass a lubberly Redcoat. He was back in a trice with a wax-sealed letter, which he handed over.

"Thankee, Mister Ward," Lewrie said, tapping his forehead to acknowledge the Mid's doffed-hat salute. He went to the bulwarks of the quarter-deck to look down into the boat. "Hoy, there, sir! Might you wish to return to Gibraltar aboard this ship?"

"Ehm, no thank you, sir!" the young officer called back. "I'm comfortable where I am, thank you!" He was re-seated, in the middle of the centre-most thwart, with both his hands gripping the thwart as if for his very life.

"Very well, then," Lewrie called down to him. "Follow us."

He broke the seal of the letter and unfolded it.

"Aye, we are requested to return to harbour, Mister Westcott," Lewrie told him. "The note does not say why, but I am to attend the General at my earliest opportunity. Shape course for the Rock, sir, and crack on sail."

"Aye aye, sir!" Westcott happily agreed, and as he bawled out his orders to make more sail and alter course, the on-watch hands raised a small cheer that they would soon be back among the taverns and brothels of Gibraltar Town. Getting there would take hours, for the East-set current was dead against the course, making entrance to the Mediterranean easy, but an exit to the Atlantic a long trial. If the winds were light, an all-day's sail could result in a progess measured in a few miles.

"You have the deck, sir," Lewrie told Westcott. "There's my breakfast to finish, and, I s'pose I'll have t'dress up for the occasion."

"Might shave close, too, sir," Westcott said with a grin.

"Pettus! Jessop!" Lewrie shouted as he re-entered his cabins. "Heat an iron for the sash, pin the bloody star on my best coat, and black my bloody boots!"

CHAPTER FOURTEEN

L ewrie found the usually quiet Convent headquarters building a bee-hive of activity, with junior officer clerks moving between various offices with more despatch, boot or shoe heels clacking on the old stone flags or tiles. There were Colonels, Lieutenant-Colonels, and regimental Majors present, gathered in small groups, mostly with their own sort, recognisable by the detailing and colours of their uniform coats' lapel facings and their button-hole lace. Officers turned their heads to peer at him as he approached Dalrymple's office, muttering among themselves.

"The Navy's here," he heard one Colonel bray. "That means we're going somewhere, haw haw!"

Lewrie announced himself to yet another junior Lieutenant of Foot in the anteroom, and the young fellow made a chequemark on his list. "You are to go right in, sir," the fellow told him. "You are expected."

Lewrie entered the offices and left his cocked hat on a side table where there were already several ornately laced and feathered Army officer's bicornes, and one civilian hat.

"Ah, Sir Alan," General Dalrymple said in greeting, waving him to come forward. "Do allow me to name to you General Sir Brent Spencer; Sir Brent, this is Captain Sir Alan Lewrie, Baronet, Captain of HMS *Sapphire*."

"Pleased to make your acquaintance, sir," Lewrie and Spencer said almost as one, and offering their hands briefly.

"Mister Thomas Mountjoy of the Foreign Office, you already know," Sir Hew went on. "It is his news that prompted this meeting. Do inform us of what you have heard, or learned of, Mister Mountjoy."

"Gladly, Sir Hew," Mountjoy said, springing from a chair with alacrity. He was beaming fit to bust. "I have gotten a report from a source in Madrid that, on *Dos de Mayo*, the second of this month, the people of the city rose up *en masse* against the French, hunting down and killing every off-duty Frenchman they could find, arming themselves as best they were able, and slaughtering them. Marshal Murat turned out his troops and resorted to using artillery against the mobs. The riots were put down after three hours' fighting, then the French had a riot of their own, entering every building in sight and dragging suspected rioters out to be shot or bayonetted. It was a great slaughter, 'mongst the guilty and the innocent, and atrocious crimes were committed . . . looting, theft, rape, and pillage on a grand scale, much like what happens when an army breaks into a walled town that resisted a long siege, in mediaeval times. A day later, one other of my sources relates that the garrison troops and the Spanish Navy at Cartagena arose, as well, and that there is great unrest in Seville. I have so far un-substantiated reports that many cities in the North, in Galicia and Catalonia, are also restive."

"For *real*, Mountjoy?" Lewrie had to ask, wondering if the riots were invented to spur Dalrymple into some rash action, on a par with the false reports of atrocities that Mountjoy had spun out of thin air.

"For *real*, Captain Lewrie," Mountjoy stressed. "The Spanish heard that their old kings had been arrested after they met Napoleon over the border at Bayonne, and that King Ferdinand was being forced to abdicate in favour of a king of Napoleon's choice, one of his kin, or one of his favourite Marshals."

"Upon that head, I have heard from General Castaños," Sir Hew Dalrymple imparted to them all. "There is a rebellious committee forming at Seville, what the Devil do they call it, Mister Mountjoy?"

"A *junta*, sir," Mountjoy supplied.

"Yes, a *junta*," Dalrymple continued, "which had been pressing General Castaños to declare for them, and raise a general rebellion in Western Andalusia. Castaños has already written me for British aid should he decide to act. He has raised the idea of evacuating the fortress of Ceuta, and adding those troops, and some of the fortress's lighter cannon to his artillery train, as well."

"By Jove, that'd be grand!" General Spencer exclaimed. "What's stopping him, then?"

"That would be the *other* largest force of Spanish troops in Cádiz, Sir Brent," Mountjoy told him, dashing cold water on Spencer's enthusiasm. "The governor of Cádiz is decidely pro-French, and, with the French warships that escaped into port after Trafalgar to count on to defend him, he could put down any rebellion."

"They can't get to sea, with Admiral Purvis watchin' them," Lewrie supplied, "but they could add their gunfire to defeat any attempt to take Cádiz . . . or bombard the city if the citizens arose against the governor. Their crews could hold the port's forts if the troops at Cádiz march on Castaños if he does join the *junta*."

"You have no news from that quarter, Mister Mountjoy?" Sir Hew asked.

"A tough nut to crack, sir, sorry to say," Mountjoy said with a frown, and a shake of his head. "I've had no luck at getting an . . . a source in. Not for long."

"A *spy*, you're saying?" General Spencer barked as if someone had just cursed him. "That your line of work, is it, sir?"

"Someone must gather intelligence for military operations," Lewrie said, defending him. "Else, you swan off into *terra incognita*, deaf, dumb, blind, and get your . . . fundaments kicked."

"Much of a piece with cavalry videttes making scouts, and gallopers to bring news of enemy movements," Sir Hew grudgingly allowed. "Regrettably necessary, at times. General Castaños informs me that he is also short of arms to give to volunteers whom he expects to come forward once the *junta* in Seville declares. I have on hand in the armouries at least one thousand muskets, with bayonets, cartridge pouches, and accoutrements, and I think I may spare about sixty thousand pre-made cartridges for that purpose, and shall write London to ask for more, at once. If the Spanish wish to send ships to Ceuta, we will allow them to do so."

"And I finally get the fortress, without a long siege, ah hah!" General Spencer cried, clapping his hands in delight. He'd spent long months, cooling his heels, once it was realised that Ceuta had been re-enforced, and could not be taken without a larger army.

"Oh, I fear not, Sir Brent," Dalrymple said with the faintest of smiles on his face. "In light of these new developments, I think that your brigade-sized force would be of more use nearer to Cádiz. That part of your original force, which was sent on to Sicily earlier, I shall recall to join you after you've made a lodgement. To encourage the *junta*, and General Castaños."

"Ehm . . . make a lodgement exactly *where*, Sir Hew?" Spencer asked in sudden shock at a new, even more dangerous, assignment.

"Well, so long as the forts are in the hands of the pro-French governor, it would have to be somewhere *near* Cádiz proper," Mountjoy declared, then turned to Lewrie and raised a brow to prompt him.

"Anyone have a sea chart?" Lewrie asked.

General Dalrymple did not, but an aide-de-camp managed to turn up a map of the city and its environs, after a frantic search.

"Hmm, there's this little port of Rota, though that's a bit far from the city," Lewrie opined after a long perusal. "Closer into the area, there's Puerto de Santa María, on the North side of the bay."

"Captain Lewrie became very efficient at landing and recovering troops along the coast last Summer," Sir Hew said. "If you choose to land near Cádiz, he's your man."

"Well, we only put three companies ashore at one time, sir, for quick raids," Lewrie had to qualify, "without packs or camp gear, rations and ammunition, and no artillery, no horses. If you have to depend on your transports' crews to row your men in, it'll take forever, they're so thinly manned, and the number of boats will be limited. How many troops do you have, sir?"

"At present, just a bit over three thousand," Spencer said, "a little over one brigade. Daunting. Have the French sent one of their armies to Cádiz?"

"General Castaños tells me that there is a French brigade in the city, under a Brigadier Avril," Dalrymple said. "So far, at least, the French have left San Roque and Algeciras alone."

"You could not enter Cádiz itself, sir," Mountjoy warned them, "even if the Spanish *juntas* were suddenly in charge. They would not allow a 'second' Gibraltar under British rule. Their touchy Spanish pride is too great for that."

"I will send for transports, and obtain an escort from Admiral Purvis, now blockading Cádiz," Dalrymple declared. "Boats from those warships, manned by British sailors, will speed the landings, at whichever place you decide, Sir Brent."

"Or, where the Spanish let you," Mountjoy cautioned again.

"We have some idle transports in port, already, troopers, and supply ships," Dalrymple said. "Captain Lewrie, you and your ship will go along as part of the escort. Depending upon whom Purvis sends me, you may be senior in command of the escort, and the co-ordination."

"I *was* wondering why I was summoned, sir. Aye," Lewrie said, grinning. "Happy to oblige."

"Then let us have a drink, to seal the bargain, as it were," Dalrymple happily proposed.

Well, that's one *way t'end my bordeom,* Lewrie thought as wine and glasses were fetched; *but if I get pressed into Admiral Purvis's fleet, will I ever see Gibraltar again, or Maddalena?*

At least it would beat the sight of Ceuta, or hauling cattle from Tetuán, all hollow.

BOOK TWO

Therefore let every man now task his thought
That this fair action may on foot be brought.
-WILLIAM SHAKESPEARE,
THE LIFE OF HENRY THE FIFTH,
(ACT I, SCENE II, 809-810)

CHAPTER FIFTEEN

Should we hoist a broad pendant and name you a Commodore, sir?" Lt. Westcott proposed, craning his neck to look aloft. "Even if it'd be the lesser sort—"

"An Army general gave the orders, and he don't count," Lewrie countered, looking upwards himself. "No, I may command the escorting force . . . such as it is . . . but Admiralty'd never stand for it. I'll stand on as I am."

He lowered his gaze to the clutch of troop ships and supply vessels that wallowed along in passably decent order astern of his two-decker. All that could be scraped up at short notice to protect the convoy was a 32-gun frigate, a Sixth Rate sloop of war mounting but twenty light guns, and two brig-sloops. Lewrie knew that the French warships left over from the Battle of Trafalgar, now closely blockaded in Cádiz, would never come out to harm his charges, but there were still rumours that a large squadron of French ships at Rochefort, and some frigates in the mouth of the Gironde River near Bordeaux, could sortie at any time. Those rumours kept him up at night, and he secretly hoped that he could get General Spencer's troops ashore, and the merchant ships away, without opposition, so they would no longer be his responsibility.

"*Damn* these perverse winds, *and* the currents!" he spat.

Since leaving Gibraltar on the fourteenth of May, and rounding Pigeon Island into the Strait, they had proceeded at a slug's pace, hobbled by the in-rushing current into the Mediterranean. Sailing "full and by" hard on the wind for several days might *seem* swift and bracing, but that was an illusion, for their overall speed over the ground resulted in only a few miles per hour. The convoy's first leg, a long board Sou'west, only got them a few miles West of Parsley Island before they had to tack and cross the Strait to halfway 'twixt Pigeon Island and Tarifa. The second tack Sou'west had fetched them close to the Moroccan city of Alcazar, and the third had gotten them five miles East of Tarifa.

And so it had gone from there, day after day. Lewrie led the convoy out West-Sou'west to get clear of the current, taking advantage of a wind shift, far enough out off the coast of Morocco that a simple turn North would bring the convoy into contact with Admiral John Childs Purvis's blockading ships off Cádiz. Another shift of winds had put a stop to that simple run, that combined with a bout of foul weather, and they all had short-tacked under reduced sail through several half-gales to make their Northing. And, when the gales blew out and calmer winds and seas returned, they ran into a fringe of the Nor'east Trades, into which they butted the wrong way. The Trades were simply grand for *departing* Europe for the Americas or the Caribbean, but nigh a "dead muzzler" for returning.

"Land Ho!" the main mast lookout in the cross-trees shouted down. "Two points orf th' starb'd beam!"

"Any guess as to *what* land?" Lewrie scoffed to his assembled watch-standers. "Mister Yelland?"

"Some part of Spain, sir," the Sailing Master said, sounding as if he'd made a jest. "If we could send a Mid aloft with my book of the coast, I could tell you more."

"Fetch it," Lewrie demanded. "Mister Harvey?" he said to the nearest Midshipman. "Aloft with you and Mister Yelland's book, and tell us what you see."

"Aye, sir," Harvey replied, looking eager for a scaling of the shrouds.

"Don't drop it overside, mind, Mister Harvey," Yelland said as he brought the book of coastal sketches from the chart toom. "Or your bottom will pay for it."

Midshipman Harvey took the larboard shrouds, the windward side, to the cat harpings, switched over to the futtock shrouds to make his way to the main top, hanging like a spider upside down for a bit, and then up the narrower upper shrouds and rat-lines to the cross-trees, a set of narrow slats that braced the top-masts' stays, to share that precarious perch with the lookout on duty. Harvey raised a telescope to peer landward, flipped pages in the coastal navigation sketchbook, peered some more, then shouted down. "It's Cape Trafalgar, sir! Cape Trafalgar, fifteen miles off!"

"Very good, Mister Harvey!" Lewrie called aloft, cupping hands by his mouth. "Return to the deck, *with* the book."

"Aye aye, sir!"

"We'll stand on on this tack 'til Noon Sights, then," Lewrie announced, "when Cape Trafalgar is truly recognised, then go about Nor'west, which'd put us somewhere off Cádiz, and in sight of our blockading squadrons sometime round dusk. Sound right, Mister Yelland?"

"If the winds hold, aye, sir," Yelland agreed. "That'd place us, oh . . . round twenty-odd miles off Cádiz, and *sure* to run across one of our ships."

"I s'pose I'll have t'shave, and dress for the occasion," Lewrie glumly said, rubbing a stubbly cheek. "Called to the flagship, all that? Mister Westcott, best you warn my boat crew t'scrub up and wash behind their ears. Best turn-out, hey?"

"Aye, sir," Westcott responded with a faint snigger.

"I'll be aft. Carry on, the watch," Lewrie said, turning to go to his cabins.

"Why does the Captain dislike dressing in his finest, sir?" Lt. Elmes asked once Lewrie had departed the quarterdeck.

"It's the sash and star of his knighthood he dislikes, Mister Elmes," Westcott informed him in a low voice. "Officially, it was awarded for his part in a fight against a French squadron off the coast of Louisiana in 1803, but he strongly suspects that it was a cynical way for the Government to drum up support for going back to war, by publicising the fact that the French tried to murder him, and killed his wife instead, when they were in Paris during the Peace of Amiens."

"Murdered?" Lt. Elmes gawped.

"The Captain was invited to a meeting with Napoleon at the Tuileries Palace," Westcott explained. "He had five or six swords of dead French officers, and thought to return them to the families, in exchange for an old hanger that Napoleon took off him at Toulon in Ninety-Four, when the

Captain would not give his parole and leave his men after their mortar ship was blown up and sunk. It turned to shit, he angered Napoleon somehow, and the next thing he knew, they were being chased cross Northern France to Calais."

"He's *met* the Ogre?" Elmes marvelled. "Twice? I never knew. What a tale!"

"To make matters worse, when the Captain was presented at Saint James's Palace to be knighted, the King was having a bad day, and got confused and added Baronet," Westcott went on, making a face. "You can imagine how it all left a sour taste in the Captain's mouth. He *earned* a knighthood, *and* a Baronetcy, a dozen times over during his career, mind, long before I met him, and he's done a parcel of hard fighting, since, but . . . that don't signify to him. He doesn't like to speak of it, so . . . don't raise the matter with him."

"I stand warned, Mister Westcott, though . . . I'd give a month's pay to hear the whole story," Elmes said with a wistful note to his voice.

"I'll tell you of the fight off Louisiana," Westcott offered. "The French were taking over Louisiana, and were rumoured to be sending a large squadron to New Orleans for the hand-over, and we were ordered to pursue and stop them if we could, just four ships, three frigates, and a sixty-four . . ."

Late in the afternoon, the winds dropped and the seas calmed, just after lookouts aloft spotted strange sails on the Northern horizon, quickly identified as British ships. *Sapphire* made her number to them once within five miles of them, and the towering First Rate flagship hoisted Captain Repair On Board. The salute to Admiral Purvis was fired off, the cutter was drawn up to the entry-port battens, and Lewrie was over the side and into his boat at once, dressed in his best, with the sash and star over his waistcoat and pinned to his coat, with his longer, slimmer presentation sword at his waist instead of his favourite, everyday, hanger.

"With luck, they'll sport me supper, Mister Westcott. Keep things in order 'til I get back," Lewrie shouted up in parting, and the cutter began its long row to the flagship. Another boat set out from one of the transports; General Sir Brent Spencer would attend the meeting, whether he'd been summoned or not.

It was a long climb from his boat to the quarterdeck of the flagship, past three decks of guns and a closed entry-port on its middle gun deck, one surrounded by overly ornate gilt scrollwork. He was panting, and his wounded left arm and right leg were making sore threats by the time he heaved himself in-board to the trilling Bosuns' calls, the stamp of Marines' boots, and the slap of hands on wooden stocks as arms were presented. He took a deep breath, made sure he was two steps inward from the lip of the entry-port, and doffed his hat in a replying salute.

"Captain Sir Alan Lewrie, Baronet, of the *Sapphire,* coming aboard to report to the Admiral," Lewrie told the immaculately turned-out Lieutenant.

"If you will come this way, sir," the officer bade, motioning towards the stern, and the Admiral's cabins. "Ehm . . . who is that coming alongside, sir?"

"That'll be General Sir Brent Spencer, who's been sent to land near Cádiz."

"Oh. I *see,* sir!"

He was announced to Admiral John Childs Purvis, though taking a moment to gawk over Purvis's great-cabins' spaciousness and elegant *decor.* He had come to think his own cabins were a tad grand, but the Admiral's were magnificent.

"Captain Sir Alan Lewrie, Baronet, sir, of the *Sapphire,*" the Lieutenant said, doing the honours.

"Sir Alan," Purvis replied, slowly rising from the desk in his day-cabin, looking worn and tired, and just a bit leery whether this un-looked-for newcomer might be yet another onerous burden to be borne. "I take it that your convoy bears General Sir Brent Spencer and his troops? I received a letter from General Dalrymple two days ago, but I had not expected the force to be assembled, yet, much less sent on. How many troops does Spencer have?"

"Nigh five thousand, sir," Lewrie crisply replied. "Sir Hew Dalrymple added the Sixth Foot, and some artillery from Gibraltar's garrison. There are more being ordered from Sicily, to come later. Sir Hew sent these latest appreciations for you, sir, and all the intelligence he could gather up."

"Ah, thank you, sir," Purvis said, sitting back down to open the thick packet and scan through them. "Do sit, Sir Alan. Wine?"

"Please, sir," Lewrie replied.

"Hah!" the Admiral scoffed after reading through the gist of Dalrymple's packet. "Dalrymple is rather precipitate to send along the troops so soon. Land in, or near, Cádiz? At present, the place is firmly in the hands of the French, and a pro-French lackey government. I see that he is aware of the French brigade under General Avril, though *not* of the division at Córdoba under a General L'Étang, who could march to re-enforce Avril rather quickly, should Spencer land."

"Perhaps it was General Dalrymple's intent to *precipitate,* to goad the Spanish into action, sir," Lewrie suggested as his wine came. "As you can see, sir, the Spanish have already rebelled in several cities besides Madrid. Their General Castaños is almost ready to act, if he can get the garrison from Ceuta into Algeciras or Tarifa to re-enforce—"

"I am aware of those developments," Purvis peevishly cut him off, "but Cádiz has *not* rebelled, and until it does—"

He was cut off, himself, by a rap on the doors to the cabins. The same Lieutenant stepped in. "Admiral, sir, General Sir Brent Spencer is come aboard, and wishes to speak with you."

"He has, has he?" Purvis snapped, scowling heavily, then let out a much-put-upon sigh. "Very well, very well, have him come in."

Purvis and Lewrie shot to their feet as General Spencer blew in, beaming. "Admiral Purvis!" Spencer bellowed.

"Sir Brent," Purvis replied, rather laconically. "Wine, sir?"

"*Relish* a glass, thankee!" Spencer answered, coming to the desk with a glad hand out. Purvis waved both of his guests to sit, then plopped himself down behind his desk, again.

"B'lieve Sir Hew Dalrymple wrote you of our coming, and what my little army's to do, hah?" Spencer began.

"He has, sir, but, as I was just explaining to Captain Lewrie, here, that until the situation in Cádiz changes, there is no chance of that," Admiral Purvis declared.

"But, my men are cooped up, elbow-to-elbow, and as crop-sick as so many dogs, sir!" Spencer protested. "I must get them off those damned ships soon! If we land somewhere near Cádiz, surely the Dons would rise up and welcome us, and kick the French out!"

"Well, I will allow that I've gotten word from sources ashore that the city's taken on a distinctly anti-French mood, of late," the Admiral cautiously said, "so much so that the French consul has abandoned his residence and offices, and taken refuge aboard one of the French warships anchored in the sheltered bay behind the peninsula on which the city, and the fortifications, sit."

"You have agents in Cádiz, sir?" Lewrie asked, amazed. "That would be welcome news to Mister Thomas Mountjoy, at Gibraltar. He's tried to place agents inside, so far with poor results."

"Mister Mountjoy would be one of Foreign Office's . . . *shadier* sorts, hey?" Purvis asked with faint amusement.

"He is, sir," Lewrie admitted.

"As I say, 'til the Spanish rise up, I fear your troops must stay aboard their transports, Sir Brent," Admiral Purvis repeated. "And, even if they do, and declare themselves allies of Great Britain, you would not be allowed in the city, or the forts."

"Captain Lewrie, here, mentioned some alternatives, sir," Spencer blustered on, fidgeting where to place his ornately egret-featherd bicorne hat as a cabin steward fetched him a glass of wine. "Somewhere near Cádiz? What were they, Lewrie? Porto-something, or . . . started with an *R*?"

"Puerto de Santa María, or Rota, sir," Lewrie supplied. "But, with the French warships, there'd be no safe way to enter the Bay of Cádiz. Same for Puerto Real, on the same bay. There's San Fernando, South of the city, but quite close. Rota is North of the city by some eight to ten miles."

"Oh, totally unsuitable, then," Spencer quibbled. "But, there must be *some* place. God knows *I'm* fed up with ships, already. Even getting aboard this one, brr! Being slung up and over like a cask of salt-meat? Mean to say!"

General Spencer meant that he'd not tried to scale the battens and man-ropes, but had been hoisted aboard the flagship in a lubberly Bosun's chair, like a cripple, or drunk. Admiral Purvis and Lewrie shared a brief smirk of amusement.

"San Fernando is near the base of the peninsula, and landing there *might* cut off the land route to the city," Admiral Purvis said, "but, that would be up to the Spanish, once they *do* rebel, and manage to oust the French on their own. At any rate, the situation may not be my responsibility much longer. My active commission is coming to an end, and Admiralty has informed me that Admiral Cuthbert Collingwood is to relieve me on this station."

"Admiral Collingwood, sir? I'd dearly love to meet *him*!" Lewrie gushed out with boyish enthusiasm.

"What, Captain Lewrie, am I not famous enough for you?" the Admiral rejoined with a peevish look.

"Oh, I didn't mean *that*, sir!" Lewrie gasped. "Perish the idea! I merely meant, ehm . . . !"

"It is of no matter," Purvis said, waving a hand to dismiss any thought of being insulted. "Perhaps General Dalrymple, being an Army man, has not enlightened you, Sir Brent, on Sir Alan's adventurous accomplishments at sea. He's reckoned as one of our most daring frigate captains, and even saddled with command of a poor older 'fifty,' he's still raising devilment. The *Naval Chronicle* featured action reports of his doings along the Andalusian coast last Summer, which were bold."

"You do me too much credit, sir," Lewrie replied, putting on his modest face. "Just raising some mischief."

Ye going t'fill Spencer in on some, or will I have t'dine him aboard and do my own braggin'? Lewrie thought.

"I dearly wish that I could have remained on-station just long enough to see Cádiz fall to us," Purvis said with a weary sigh. "And sail in and make prize of those damned French ships that escaped us at Trafalgar."

"That'd be grand, sir," Lewrie told him. "Though, after anchored idle so long, they might not be in good material condition, and there's little the Spanish yards could do to keep them up."

"Even so, it's more the satisfaction than the price a Prize-Court places upon them," Purvis countered. "Claim them, and rub the Corsican Ogre's nose in it one more time, remind Bonaparte of his worst defeat at sea, in a long string of them. Know what he is rumoured to have said when he heard about Trafalgar? 'I cannot be everywhere,' hah! As if that lubber would be a better Admiral than any of his!"

"Well, if he had been, sir," Lewrie slyly replied, "we'd have bagged the lot of 'em, French *and* Spanish, captured 'Boney,' and hung him in chains at Execution Dock!"

"Hear, hear!" General Spencer crowed.

"I had planned to dine my officers in this evening," Purvis said, as if quibbling. "If you gentlemen would care to join them?"

He sounded as if he'd rather not, but could be gracious.

"Topping!" Spencer cried. "Sure to be better than the swill I get aboard my transport, what? I accept with pleasure, sir."

"I'd thought to return to *Sapphire*, sir," Lewrie begged off, sure that that was the right thing to do. Any time with General Sir Brent Spencer was too much time, he was learning.

"Oh, if you insist, Sir Alan," Purvis replied, much too quickly, and with a relieved grin.

"I am certain that you may regale Sir Brent," Lewrie said.

"Oh . . . indeed," Purvis said, almost pulling a face.

CHAPTER SIXTEEN

*T*he last days of May, and the first days of June of 1808 were spent sailing off-and-on under reduced sail, a bit out to sea of Rear-Admiral Purvis's ten sail of the line, waiting for word from shore, or further orders from Gibraltar. Aboard HMS *Sapphire*, live gun drill was held, cutlass drill, pike drill, and the striking and hoisting of top-masts, just to keep the ship's people's skills from going rusty. The weather was fairly decent, the convoy was well-protected by the ships that Purvis led, and it could almost be termed "cruising and claret."

Lewrie was bored, of course.

He *tried* to bear boredom stoically, with much play with Bisquit and Chalky, and with sword-play with his officers and senior Midshipmen. He'd fetch a chair from the dining-coach and sit out on his stern gallery, with the improvised screen door secured so that Chalky could not dash out, leap onto a cap-rail, and go overboard, and practice on his penny-whistle, quite ignoring the whines and howls from the poop deck above from Bisquit, who was either greatly distressed, or trying to sing along; it was hard to tell which.

In private, stripped to the waist so he wouldn't sweat up one of his linen shirts, he would exercise with wooden pails with various weights of swivel gun roundshot, lifting, swinging, and grunting with effort, to the amusement (well-concealed, of course) of his steward, Pettus, and cabin-servant, Jessop.

He'd been skewered in the left thigh by a Spanish bayonet up the Appalachicola River during the tail-end of the American Revolution, had had his left arm shot at the Battle of Camperdown, and had been shot in the right thigh off Buenos Aires two years before, and his workouts made them all let him know that he was getting older, and that he was not the hale and hearty fellow he'd been before, but he persisted. Fourty-five was not *that* old, after all; was it?

"Cool tea, sir?" Pettus asked after his last efforts.

"Christ yes, thankee," Lewrie eagerly said, sponging himself off then towelling, and flinging himself into a comfortable padded chair. "With lots of sugar. Whew . . . woof!"

"Keeps you a fine figure of a man, sir," Pettus commented.

"Lotta work, if yer askin' me," Jessop muttered.

"I don't do half what you do, Jessop," Lewrie reminded him. "Ye wished t'be more of a sailor, servin' a carronade, climbin' the masts, tailin' on sheets, halliards, and gun-tackle. That's *your* exercise."

"'At's just work, sir, wot I'm s'posed t'do," Jessop rejoined.

"Ages ago, aboard my first ship, the *Ariadne,* there was a Marine officer," Lewrie told him, "who suggested that the ladies *prefer* a fit man over a gotch-gut, one who's light on his feet and can dance well, not thunder round like 'John Bull.' All that exercisin' I did at my father's farm t'heal up from gettin' shot two years ago, t'make myself fit for command, again . . . ye took part in that, and you're a fit and spry young fellow, yourself. Ain't he, Pettus?"

"He is, yes, sir," Pettus agreed as he fetched a tall, cool glass of lemoned and sugared tea, "the delight of all the girls at Gibraltar, the young rogue."

"All 'at heavin' an' liftin' beat muckin' out th' stables an' barns, sir," Jessop said with an impish grin. "I wasn't havin' any o' that. I ain't a farmer, nor wish t'be. Gimme Portsmouth or London, anytime."

The Marine sentry outside Lewrie's cabin doors rapped the deck with his musket butt, and stamped his boots. "Midshipman Griffin t'see the Cap'm, SAH!"

"Shirt, Pettus," Lewrie bade. "Enter!" he called out once he was partially presentable.

"The flag has made our number, sir, and signalled Captain Repair On Board," Midshipman Griffin reported.

"Well, just damn my eyes," Lewrie spat. "The Admiral will have t'settle for slovenly, if he wants me straightaway. Thankee, Mister Griffin. Muster my boat crew, if you please, and I'll be on deck, directly."

"Aye, sir."

Lewrie had not shaved that morning, and was dressed in loose and comfortable slop-trousers, white wool stockings, and a pair of buckled shoes, not his Hessian boots. With Pettus's help, he got a fresh shirt done up and his neck-stock bound, shirt-tails crammed into the trousers' waist-band, into a waist-coat and a plainer, older coat.

"Dress sword, sir?" Pettus asked from the arms rack.

"No, give me the hanger," Lewrie decided, "and me older hat."

"What will Admiral Purvis say, sir?" Pettus fretted as he provided the requested articles.

"That I was prompt?" Lewrie japed. "Keep the cat amused."

It was a long and nigh-boisterous journey under lugs'l to the flagship, several miles off, but at last he made it and went up the battens and man-ropes to be greeted with the due ceremony. Once on deck, he noted that a Bosun's chair was being rigged.

"For General Spencer, I presume?" Lewrie asked the Lieutenant who had been assigned to see him aft.

"Aye, sir," the officer said with a snigger.

When Lewrie arrived in the Admiral's cabins, he found that he was one among many; the Captains of all ten ships of the line were present, including Purvis's Flag-Captain.

"Ah, Captain Lewrie . . . Sir Alan, excuse my casual address," Purvis said.

"It's a Captain Lewrie day, sir, and no matter," Lewrie offered.

"So I *see*," Purvis said with a brow up. This day, he did not appear quite so worn or tired as he had upon their first encounter.

Somthing's lit his fire, Lewrie thought; *feagued him like an old horse with ginger up its rump.*

Beyond the cabins, there were more Bosun's calls, the squeals of pulley-blocks. General Spencer was arriving. Right after he was admitted to the great-cabins, he looked for a place to stow his hat, and peered about as if looking for a drink.

"Sir Brent, welcome," Purvis said. "We have heard from shore, at last.

Wine for all, if you please," he directed his servants, and ordered all to find a seat.

"We're landing my damned troops, at long last, are we, sir?" Spencer boomed out, clapping his hands in delight.

"Here is what we know," Purvis went on, standing behind his desk. "The city, and the Spanish garrison of Cádiz, has risen, and the pro-French governor, and some of his aides and hangers-on, have been dragged into the streets and murdered."

"Huzzah!" one Captain shouted.

"We are *not* to enter the city, or the bay, however," Purvis went on, lifting a quieting hand. "Word has come that the Spanish are to deal with the French ships in harbour. They're moving bomb vessels and gunboats, and positioning fortress guns to take them under fire if they do not strike. The French Admiral, Rosily, seems determined to resist, though there's little hope for him. If the Spanish don't set them afire with heated shot, then they'd face us if they sortie, so . . . in the interests of supporting our new . . . ally," he spat the word, "I must leave the honour of capturing those ships to the Spanish."

"Oh, sir!" one of the officers commiserated. "After all of our hopes, and yours!"

"I know, I know," Purvis replied, looking stony for a moment, then perked up, possibly for their benefit. "The silver lining to it . . . the Supreme *Junta* in Seville has declared war upon France, and upon Napoleon *personally,* if one can imagine that. General Castaños at San Roque has been named Captain-General of the Army of Andalusia, and I have been requested to allow merchantmen currently anchored in the Bay of Cádiz to sail for Ceuta, to take off a major portion of the fortress garrison and transport them to Algeciras, to augment General Castaños's forces.

"I have also gotten a request to provide a ship to bear a delegation from the Supreme *Junta* to London, to begin formal negotiations to end the war 'twixt Great Britain and Spain, and I am eager to do so. Any suggestions?"

"Part of my convoy escort, sir," Lewrie quickly offered, "the *Barbados* frigate, a thirty-two. She's fast and weatherly."

And, she ain't the Sapphire, Lewrie thought; *Better anybody than me. I want t'stay and see what happens!*

"Thank you for the suggestion, Captain Lewrie," Purvis replied. "Aye, once the French ships have been captured, it will be safe for *Barbados* to enter port and take the emissaries aboard."

"Then I can land my troops at Port María?" Spencer pressed.

"Ah . . . no, Sir Brent," Purvis had to inform him. "The *Junta* will not tolerate the presence of British troops in, or near, Cádiz, though if threatened by the arrival of a French army, that may be allowed at a later date. They have suggested Ayamonte, instead."

"Where the bloody Hell's Ayamonte?" Spencer groused, turning red in the face.

"It's a small seaport at the mouth of the Guadiana River, Sir Brent," Purvis said, almost with a sly look. "Your troops won't have to be ferried onto a beach, but can land directly on the quays, and the transports may moor alongside, making the un-loading of your artillery and supplies much easier."

"Wasn't on *my* maps," Spencer gravelled.

But it was on Lewrie's sea charts, and he recalled where it was; he had to hide his amusement.

"Ayamonte is on the South bank of the Guadiana, Sir Brent," he took some delight in telling him. "Portugal is on the North. As far as the Spanish want you to Cádiz, and still be in Spain."

"The stiff-necked, prideful bastards!" Spencer screeched.

"Look on the bright side," Lewrie quipped. "You can be rowed over the river and liberate Portugal, if you've a mind."

"Rear-Admiral Sir Charles Cotton, blockading Lisbon, reports that his informations place only four thousand French soldiers at Lisbon," Purvis said with a shrug. "He thinks a British force of six thousand could take the city, though personally, I doubt his figures. They seem too low, to me."

"We know that Marshal Junot led *fifty* thousand troops into Portugal, and there *is* a lot of territory to cover," General Spencer said with a hopeful note. "Hmm, Lisbon, Oporto, the ah . . . other cities to occupy. Your man Cotton might be right."

"Temporarily, Sir Brent," Purvis cautioned, "but if you march on Lisbon from Ayamonte, Junot could summon re-enforcements quickly, and I believe that we have all seen the Napoleonic way of war, by now, and how quickly French armies can move. Portugal must be left to the expeditionary force under General Sir Arthur Wellesley. On my part, I shall add one of my Third Rates to the escort and retain the *Barbados* frigate to transport the Spanish delegation to London, when it arrives in Cádiz from Seville. So, you may begin your landing at Ayamonte at once, Sir Brent."

"Then let's be about it, shall we, sir?" Lewrie prompted the General, who was still looking peeved. "With weather permitting, we can have you and your troops on dry land by the eleventh or twelfth."

"A toast all round, gentlemen," Admiral Purvis proposed, waving his empty glass in the air to summon his cabin servants for re-fills. And once all the glasses had been re-filled or topped up, Purvis paused in thought for a moment, then said, "We could call for victory, or we could call for peace with Spain, but I think a general sentiment may cover the situation presented us. Gentlemen, I give you Death and Confusion to the French!"

"Death and Confusion to the French!" they all chorused lustily, and those seated pounded their fists on their chair arms, stamped their feet on the hard oak deck, and punctuated the air with more huzzahs.

After that, most officers gathered up their hats and made their way to the weather decks to depart. Lewrie was certain that he was the junior-most Captain present, and would be first down the side to his boat, but Purvis crooked a finger at him.

"Bide, Captain Lewrie," Purvis said. "I shall write orders for the *Barbados* frigate's Captain, and would admire did you forward them to that worthy."

"Of course, sir," Lewrie agreed.

"Sorry you will not have an opportunity to meet Collingwood," Purvis said, "but, he's off to Gibraltar to confer with Dalrymple."

"It is of no matter, sir," Lewrie shrugged off.

"Good, then," Purvis decided. "I will assign the *Norwich* to be *Barbados*'s replacement in your squadron. Her Captain caught a fever and passed over, recently, and her First Lieutenant, Abercrombie, is Acting-Captain. I note that you do not fly a broad pendant?"

"No, sir," Lewrie told him. "My appointment as senior officer was by luck, and a request from General Dalrymple, so Admiralty had nothing to do with it. If a man senior to me had shown up among the assembled ships, I would not be drinking your excellent wine."

"Had you not made a name for yourself as a fighting Captain, sir, I'd take you for a scape-grace!" Purvis said with a faint laugh.

"Well, it's still early days, sir," Lewrie japed back.

"Hah! Whilst I write my orders, you should have another, then," Purvis decided. "Re-fills here!" he called to his servants.

"Have you any news to share, sir?" Lt. Westcott asked once Lewrie had gained his own quarterdeck, and sent his boat over to the frigate with new orders.

"Grand news, and a fair parcel of it, Mister Westcott, which I *will* share,"

Lewrie told him, grinning, "just as soon as you can call all officers aft to my cabins. Mister Hillhouse?" he asked the senior Midshipman standing watch. "I have need of Mister Harcourt for a while, and would admire did you take charge of the quarterdeck."

"Aye, sir," Hillhouse replied, straightening up.

"We're off to Ayamonte, Mister Westcott, as soon as one of the Third Rates joins us," Lewrie said.

"Where's Ayamonte?" Westcott wondered aloud.

"The arse-end of Spain, right by the Portuguese border," Lewrie said. "If the Dons don't want us in Cádiz, we'll have t'go in the back entrance. Mister Yelland? Fetch your charts for the coasts North of Cádiz, will you? We're landing a British Army in Spain!"

CHAPTER SEVENTEEN

"*G*rubby-lookin' place, ain't it?" Lewrie mused aloud after a long look through his telescope, now that *Sapphire* was safely anchored in the Guadiana River, in the middle of the stream and just a few hundred yards from the town of Ayamonte. The troop transports and supply ships, which drew less water, had preceded the two-decker to the town and its piers. Lewrie had thought to leave the sloop of war and brig-sloops at the mouth of the river, several miles below, to guard against the slight risk of the rumoured French squadron at Rochefort appearing to crush his little *ad hoc* force. They would cruise off-and-on the coast. The 74-gun *Norwich* he had ordered to anchor in the mouth of the river as a floating battery to deny an enemy an entrance to the river. He would have liked to stay down there with her, but, he had to be close to General Spencer, and had to carefully feel his way up to Ayamonte.

"Anchored fore and aft, sir, with springs on the cables as you wished," Lt. Geoffrey Westcott reported. "Hmm . . . the land about the river and the town is fairly level. Should there be French troops in the vicinity, we should be able to support General Spencer 'til he's got his artillery ashore."

"Not a lot to the place, is there, Geoffrey?" Lewrie asked the First Officer. "It *could* be almost picturesque, if somebody thought to re-paint and sweep up the trash."

"Count on the Spanish for that, sir?" Westcott said, snorting in derision. "Not in our lifetime. It looks to be fairly prosperous, though. Lots of large fishing boats and coastal trading vessels . . . warehouses, there, behind the quays? They appear not to be locked up and idle, like the ones we saw along the South coast last Summer. It may be there's a decent trade here."

Lewrie crossed to the other side of the poop deck and took a long look at the Portuguese side of the river. There was a wee town over there, named Castro Marim on Mr. Yelland's charts, and they had passed a larger town on the way up-river, Vila Real de Santo António, which also looked fairly prosperous. Evidently, the French invasions of both countries had not reached such un-important places, yet, and the war had left this corner of Spain alone.

There were small boats working the Portuguese side of the river, some heaped with huge mounds of what looked like seaweed or riverbank reeds, and Lewrie wondered what in the world they did with it; eat it? Several curious folk were gathered on the Portuguese shore where a road ended, and a ferry rested, and they were pointing and talking animatedly, but looked like they'd flee like rabbits if anyone glared at them the wrong way.

Ayamonte's citizens were more in a dither, with some saddling up horses or hitching up teams, and loading immediately necessary belongings into waggons or carts. Others more bold were gathered in taut, angry bunches, some armed with cudgels, swords, kitchen knives or cleavers, and a few firearms. Lewrie could even see a few lances for hunting wild boar being waved aloft, and one ancient pike. Most of the Spanish seemed wary but curious.

Most of the ten companies from one of General Spencer's battalions were already ashore and formed up in the streets and large plaza that faced the quays, a band was playing, and a colour party was parading the Regimental Colours and the King's Colours.

Lewrie could spot Spencer and some of his staff in conversation with some well-dressed civilian men and several priests, and he hoped that Spencer had thought to include some Spanish-speaking officers in his force, for there was a lot of head-shaking, hand-talking, shrugging, and confused looks between all. One of the civilians wore a sash cross his chest, perhaps the town mayor, and he began to smile. One of the priests dashed inside the nearby church and bells began to ring as the group of soldiers and civilians shook hands. It was almost comical to watch as the town mayor mounted the church steps and tried to address the crowd while the bells pealed on and on. Finally, the eldest churchman sent another priest inside to silence the clanging.

After a time, the mayor's address evoked loud cheers, clapping, and huzzahs. Spanish flags appeared from windows and balconies.

"I think it's safe for heretical English to go ashore, now," Lewrie declared. "Muster my boat crew, and fetch the cutter up from astern, Mister Westcott."

"Aye, sir. If you discover some decent wine, the wardroom will appreciate news of it," Westcott hinted. "Or, if you spot a fetching young *señorita* or two . . . ?"

"If we're here for a while, I'll allow you shore liberty, and you can hunt up your own," Lewrie assured him. He looked aloft and then peered at the steeple of the church ashore. "Might be a good idea to keep a lookout in the main mast cross-trees. If there are any French forces in the neighbourhood, we'd have a better view of them."

"I shall, sir," Westcott agreed.

Once overside and in the cutter, Lewrie looked over his boat crew. "Listen, lads. It's a small town, a Spanish town, and I warn you t'mind your manners. The girls might be willin', but I'd wager their menfolk'd not look kindly on any dallying. Stay close to the quays, and do *not* get drunk. Right, Furfy?"

"Arra, sor," Furfy moaned. "Iff'n th' Dons're grateful for us t'be here, it'd be un-friendly t'turn down a swig or two if they offer."

"We stay ashore th' rest o' th' mornin', sor, we'll miss th' rum issue," Furfy's long-time mate, Cox'n Liam Desmond, pointed out. "Mayhap a cup or two of wine'd make up for it?"

Even the usually-sobre bow man, Michael Deavers, was looking eager to set foot ashore and get a drink. "Aye, it would," he said.

"Pass word for Midshipman Britton!" Lewrie shouted up to the quarterdeck watch. "He's to come ashore with me!"

That put his oarsmen in lower spirits. Midshipman Britton was a Tartar when it came to finding sailors "drunk on duty" and have them at Captain's Mast.

"Aw, sor," Furfy said with a sad shake of his head.

"If offered by grateful Spaniards . . . assumin' they're all *that* grateful . . . you *can* take a drink, but Mister Britton will see that you don't get drunk," Lewrie promised them.

Britton came scrambling down the battens and agilely stepped onto the gunn'l then aft to sit near the stern thwart near Lewrie and Desmond.

"If I need messages passed 'twixt the shore and the ship, I'll need you to bear them, Mister Britton," Lewrie told him. "I'll also want you to mind the men's consumption of any offered wine."

"Aye aye, sir!" Britton crisply answered, with a warning glare at the hands.

"Shove off, then," Lewrie ordered.

"Ah, Captain Lewrie, come to see the sights, have you?" General Spencer boomed as Lewrie strolled onto the plaza.

"I came to see how things are going, sir," Lewrie replied. "I assume the Spanish are giving you a good welcome?"

"Ah, the bloody Dons," Spencer griped, snatching off his ornate bicorne hat and running impatient fingers through his hair. "They claim that I must encamp my troops beyond the town, instead of lodging them in houses. There's some low hills a mile or so to the Northeast and East, and we'll have to march out there and set piquets on the hills, and set up tents and all behind them. They *will* allow a small party in town, atop the church tower, but that's about all the co-operation we're going to get."

"I'm keeping lookouts posted aloft, sir," Lewrie said. "They can see farther than anyone in the tower. They're higher up. Maybe you could erect a semaphore tower at your camp to speak your sentries in the church tower, and run a message to me, should the French show up. If you have to fall back and be evacuated, my guns could dissuade the Frogs from pressing you too closely."

"Fall back and evacuate?" Spencer bristled up. "No, Captain Lewrie. Unless an entire French division marches here to confront me, I fully intend to stand my ground and chance a battle. That's what I was sent to do . . . even if it's the arse-end of this shitten country."

"So, there are no French anywhere close?" Lewrie asked.

"Well, there's L'Etang's division at Seville, and there's General Dupont at Córdoba, but those are rather far off, and couldn't be here for days," Spencer allowed, "even if your Admiral Purvis is of the opinion that the French can fly like so many sparrows from one place to the next. The nearest we're aware of is the brigade under General Avril, and they're nearer Cádiz than I am, dammit all! Where I *should* be is Cádiz, but will the Dons allow me? Gawd!"

"How are the locals receiving you, sir?" Lewrie pressed, turning to look at Ayamonte's residents, who were back to their usual routines, now that most of the excitement was over. "I should think they would be thrilled to hear of the uprisings, the *Junta*'s declaration of war, and all."

"Cagily!" Spencer said with a contemptuous snort. "Be careful where you camp, don't pick fruit, don't cut any olive trees for firewood, don't look at our women, don't go inside their churches. The rich ones are haughty, and the rest are scheming for money . . . as if your average British soldier *has* any. I've had to *hire* waggons and carts, teams and drivers, to carry all my supplies and ammunition out to the campsite, and pay *dearly*! The rest of them goggle at us like we're lepers, and give us what the Sicilians call the 'Evil Eye.' Lord, what a country! Poor as church mice, as illiterate as so many goats, as lazy as butchers' dogs, yet as testy of their honour and pride as mad bulls. Must be some miasma specific to Mediterranean countries, Sicily, Malta, Italy, Spain, and Portugal, they are all alike. They are just *not* like the English, the Scots, or even the bloody *Irish*. A bad race to love, or fight for."

"I was not aware that the transports didn't bring along any horse or mule teams, or waggons," Lewrie said with a frown. That was damned poor planning, to his lights.

"The original plan was to land at Cádiz, and garrison in town," General Spencer continued to grouse. "At any rate, unless we ordered some from Sicily, there were none available at Gibraltar. I'll write Dalrymple to be sure that the remainder of my troops coming from Sicily fetch some along. If I am *finally* allowed into Cádiz, I'll have to *march* there, by Christ!"

"You'll go by sea, sir, it's fastest," Lewrie assured him.

"If the French do not come to assail me, I may end up crossing the river and marching on Lisbon," Spencer said, turning to look over the river into Portugal. "Might be good to place a battalion yonder, anyway. Guard the back door, and my arse, hey?"

"I'm sure the toll for the ferry will be steep, sir," Lewrie said with a wee laugh.

"You do nothing to reassure me, sir," Spencer bristled again. "And, I do not need reminding about money."

"Sorry, sir," Lewrie apologised. "If you need anything, the Navy's ready to assist you."

"If I do, you'll hear of it," Spencer assured him. "I must be off. Too much to see to before sundown."

"I'll take my leave, sir," Lewrie replied, doffing his hat in parting salute.

He strolled back towards the quays, taking in the town of Ayamonte, and its citizens. They did indeed seem a wary lot, who would not make eye contact. There were some pointing and laughing, though, as a second of Spencer's battalions marched out of town. They were making fun of the battalion's camp followers, the soldiers' wives.

Every British regiment on Army List usually maintained two battalions at permanent home establishments. When a regiment was ordered overseas, one battalion would pack up to go, while the second would remain in barracks to recruit, drill, and train, and flesh out for the day when, after several years, the first battalion would be ordered home, and the second battalion would sail overseas to take their place. If the deployed battalion suffered casualties in action, or decimating diseases, if enough men were crippled for life, the home battalion would send out a trained draught of replacements.

The cruelty of that system was that when a battalion was sent out, only sixty or so of the soldiers' wives or camp girfriends were allowed to go with them, chosen by drawing straws or marked slips of paper from a shako. The ones left behind might never see their men again, their children would never see their fathers, and the pay of a soldier was never enough, even at home in peacetime, to support those families, and what little a deployed soldier could allot from his pay couldn't, either.

"*Putas, putas!*" some Spanish women were accusing, sure that the women were whores, for who else would follow soldiers overseas.

And, the battalion's wives *were* a rough lot, poorly dressed, hard-handed, clumsily shod, and could curse like the women mongers at the Billingsgate fish market, or the coarsest sailor. They did present a rather unappetising picture, with rarely a fetching one in their ranks, carrying packs like any soldier, cooking utensils, haversacks, and jute bags of possessions. On the march, they would help dress wounds, cook their husbands' rations, do the sewing and mending, tend their children, and even give birth in camp when the time came upon them.

Lewrie had seen them in action after the battle that had broken the Dutch at Cape Town, two years before. They had swarmed over the dead and wounded Dutch to strip them of anything of value like harpies. They would pick fruit trees and berry bushes bare, forage to steal chickens, goats, or piglets, were as eager as their men for spirits, wine, or beer, and would get just as hoggish, screeching drunk as the men. Many of them marched by chewing quids of tobacco, or had fuming pipes in their mouths.

Lewrie doffed his hat to them, saying "Good morning, ladies."

"Ahn't he a grand'un!" one crone commented.

"Ladies me arse!" another hooted.

"Ye drop y'or sister one more time, an' I'll tan y'or hide!" one stout hag chid a boy carrying a swaddled baby along with a satchel.

"Arr, make 'em bloody damn' Papists shut th' fuck up! They's poorer 'an *we* are!"

Lord God, who'd be a soldier in our Army? Lewrie thought; *Or marry one! Nothing t'look forward to but lice, fleas and sleepin' rough.*

He went back to the boat, where his sailors were talking with some Spaniards, or attempting to. Bottles of local wine were being passed, despite Midshipman Britton's loudest efforts to prevent it.

"Sir, I think the whole lot should be put on charges," the Mid cried as Lewrie approached. "The Spanish gave them drink, and I could not stop them. I wasn't sure whether I should, not entirely, and it got out of hand . . ."

"Because the Spanish are being friendly, for a change, and you didn't wish t'turn them against us, Mister Britton?" Lewrie asked.

"That was my thinking, aye, sir, but . . . ," Britton sputtered.

"Lads!" Lewrie said in a quarterdeck voice. "Leave off, before ye fall down dead drunk. I said a *cup* or two, not a barrico."

An unshaven Spaniard came up to Lewrie and offered him a bottle, gabbling happily away in rapid Spanish, and wheezing a foul, garlicky breath on him.

"Oh, Christ," Lewrie muttered, but plastered a smile on his phyz and took a swig of what tasted as raw and foul as Navy-issued "Black Strap." He swallowed it manfully, and patted the man on his back, handing the bottle back. *"Gracias, mucho gracias,"* he said in his little knowledge of Spanish, but that set the fellow off into a fresh bout of incomprehensible lingo.

"Does anyone know what he's saying, sir?" Britton asked.

"Hell if I know," Lewrie told him. "Look here. The army is going to march inland to those hills, yonder, and set up a semaphore tower. They'll have another in the church tower, and I wish to establish a small shore party here at the quays, should they send any messages to us. We'll keep one of the cutters here day and night, with one Midshipman and a boat crew to fetch off any news. Someone get this oaf off me, hey? Yes, yes! *Sí, sí, buenos mañana, buenos dia?* Ehm, *Adios?* Back in the boat, lads, we're off. Bye *bye!*"

The Spaniards seemed sorry to see them go, eager to give them a "stirrup cup" as the hands sat down on the thwarts and un-shipped their oars.

After the cutter was around one hundred yards off the quays, out in the river and stroking for the ship, Lewrie turned a stern and "captainly" glare at his miscreants.

"How the Devil did ye get so much t'drink so quickly?" he asked in a growl.

"Remember, those blank papal dispensations that were taken out o' the prize afore we got to Buenos Aires, sor?" Liam Desmond asked. "Them that nobody knew what t'do with? The ones we took ashore and doled out like money to the whores and inn-keepers?"

"Good God, you still *have* some of 'em?" Lewrie gawped.

"Nossir, but doffin' our hats, smilin', an' makin' th' sign o' th' cross does just as good," Furfy told him. "An' ain't th' most of us good Catholic Irishmen?"

Lewrie clapped his lips shut and shook his head, thinking that sure as Fate, every sailor sent ashore would hear of that ploy, and try it on. Of course, they'd have to practice "breast-beating" before they set off!

"Back to the ship, you rogues, and don't give me cause t'put the lot of you on bread and water," Lewrie told them.

CHAPTER EIGHTEEN

*G*ood God, what are you doing up here, Captain Lewrie?" General Spencer asked as Lewrie rode up on a hired mount.

"I was bored, sir, and wanted to see how you were doing with your defences," Lewrie told him, with a smile. "Admire my horse, do you?"

General Spencer guffawed in answer, for Lewrie's rented horse was a shaggy, un-curried shambler, more like a plough-horse than one bred to the saddle.

"I'd ship him home and enter him in the Derby, if the voyage didn't kill him," Lewrie japed. "His hire is closer to the price of an outright purchase . . . damned Spanish 'sharps.' This is your camp, sir? And your defences lie beyond?"

"We've settled in quite nicely," Spencer grumpily allowed after a quick look round to see that all was in order. "My troop lines are there, the Spanish volunteers, there," he said, pointing beyond the orderly lines of canvas tents to a shambolic encampment off to the North. "There were several hundred of their soldiers that the French had dis-armed and imprisoned, down South of here. When Cádiz arose, their gaolers were called back to Avril's brigade, and they were left to fend for themselves. I've distributed all the arms I had to spare, with accoutrements and ammunition, but that leaves half of them armed with scythes, swords, or boar spears. As for boots, clothing, tents, and camp gear, they'll have to get by as best they can. The officials in Ayamonte think that I should feed them, but the rations I brought won't stretch that far, and the Spanish *won't* see to their own, damn them."

"Are they worth anything?" Lewrie asked.

"They *claim* that they were trained troops, once, but now they are a shabby joke," Spencer gravelled. "Shoeless armed bands of Gypsies would be more dangerous. So . . . bored, are you, sir?"

"To *tears,* sir," Lewrie eagerly confessed. "I almost wish the French would come down from Lisbon to the border, so I could shoot them t'Hell."

"I'd admire did the French try me on, too," Spencer admitted, with a wistful note to his voice. "The horse I was forced to buy off the Dons is much of a match to yours, Captain Lewrie, but, if you wish a tour of my lines, I'll have it fetched."

"Thankee, sir," Lewrie told him.

He was indeed bored to distraction. Remaining anchored far up a river with little room to manoeuvre if trouble came, idle and feeling useless and cut off from imagined grand doings elsewhere gnawed at his patience. He had moved *Sapphire* closer to the town quays so his guns could cover the ferry landings and the road on the Portuguese side of the Guadiana, and closer to communications with the signalling party in the church tower. He had worked himself to a daily sweat at sword-play, with his pails filled with shot; he'd paced the length of the ship for a full hour each morning, and had gone ashore for long, vigourous strolls. He had hoped that a brisk canter out to the army encampment would be distracting, but his poor hired mount would not go beyond a bone-setting, jouncing trot.

The line of hills that Spencer had thought to entrench turned out to be a series of pimples, with long slopes from the encampment to the tops, and long, gradual slopes down to the plain beyond. Spencer showed him where he had emplaced his few pieces of artillery, set up in redans made of wicker baskets filled with earth, and disguised with shrubs taken from the hedges that bordered individual farm plots or pastures. Lewrie thought that the disguising might have made sense a few days before, when the shrubs had been green, but they were now going sere and brown.

"Do the French come, I intend to mask the bulk of my infantry at the back of the slopes, and have had the men dig a line of chest-high entrench-ments," Spencer explained as they rode along the crests of the hills, look-ing down to the open plains. "Were I a Frenchman, and wished to attack this position, I'd set up my gun batteries out there, round that farmhouse, barns, and such, and pound away, hoping to kill as many men as possible before sending in my columns. That's what they've done since Ninety-Three. Napoleon was an artilleryman, and he loves to mass his guns in big batteries."

"That will tear up a lot of hillside, but your men'll be safe," Lewrie grasped, "unless they have howitzers. But, they don't possess bursting shot, Colonel Shrapnel's shells."

"Exactly so, Captain Lewrie," Spencer beamed, sounding somewhat surprised that a sailor would understand. "And, in the earliest days after their revolution, when they launched the *levée en masse*, they've stuck with the column for the attack, not the advancing line. Think of it . . . a whole battalion formed up two hundred men deep and thirty across. It's a *wondrous* target for direct roundshot *and* bursting shell, and when it gets into musketry range, my men, in ranks two-deep, can direct their fire right in their teeth. Rolling platoon fire in continual volleys, hah! The Frogs haven't run into *that*, yet, and when they do, they are going to be in for the bloodiest surprise of their lives! I fully expect a great slaughter."

"Ehm, they'll have cavalry, and you don't, sir," Lewrie had to point out. "What keeps them from riding round both your flanks? And, these slopes are so gentle, what's to stop them from galloping right up to where we sit?"

"I've also had my men dig patterns of rabbit holes beyond the farthest extents of the hills, and along the back slope," Spencer boasted. "About eight inches across and a foot deep. There are more round the bounds of the encampment to prevent them sweeping through it. Won't stop them, but it will slow them up long enough to shift my men to face the threat, and besides, Avril's the closest threat, and he's in brigade strength, with probably no more than eight or ten guns and few cavalry. What, one squadron? I think I can hold, and bloody his nose."

"If things go badly for you, my guns can cover your retreat to the quays, sir," Lewrie offered. "At full elevation, my six-pounders and upper-deck twelve-pounders can throw shot about a mile."

"Good God, don't!" Spencer exclaimed, aghast. "You would do me more damage than the French! Firing blind? Pah!"

"Did it once before, when our army was in Haiti," Lewrie said. "Of course, the range demanded was much shorter, not over five hundred yards, but with proper flag signals established to tell me where the shot falls, up-down, left-right, it can be done."

"Well, if I am falling back, there won't *be* flag-signalling, and my own guns will be setting up in the streets of Ayamonte," General Spencer strongly objected. "You can maul the French in the town with direct fire, but I never *heard* the like, and don't wish for you to experiment, not with *my* troops. Bang away all you like does Junot send troops down from Lisbon to take me from the rear."

"Very good, sir," Lewrie replied, crest-fallen. He *had* thought it a good idea!

Lewrie got to clamber down into the entrenchments, crawl over the artillery sites, and get a good look at Spencer's defences, but it was a bust of a day's outing, and he wasn't even offered a glass of something before dismissing himself and going back to town. And the horse, no matter how kicked in the ribs, would *not* go at a pace beyond its shambling trot!

After another week of idle uselessness, the crew began to go restless. Ayamonte did not want them ashore, so there was no shore liberty. The demands of Spencer's brigade, and the power of his pay chests full of silver to buy up most of the cattle, sheep, goats, and pigs, kept *Sapphire*'s people on salt-meat rations, and even the wardroom's, and the captain's, tables were reduced to what beasts could be spared from the forecastle manger for their meals.

Weapons drills, make-work, scrubbing and painting, and many Make and Mend half-days, could distract them only so long. Watch-against-watch competitions at how fast they could ascend and descend all three masts, who could sing the best, who could dance the best, and boxing, palled after a time.

Lieutenant Westcott got his chance to go ashore, but came back aboard looking glum. He had fresh-laundered clothing, but little else, and certainly without tales of conquest of any fetching *señorita,* and that with his coin purse much reduced by the prices the Spanish were charging. For the other officers and Mids, it was much the same.

"Christ, you can't even *ogle* them," Westcott carped, "else the men of the town threaten to tear you limb from limb! Breaking into a Sultan's *hareem* would be easier!"

Lewrie dipped into his own funds and sent the Purser, Mister Cadrick, ashore with orders to fetch back sufficient hogs, fruit, and baked bread for a feast, or don't come back at all, and Cadrick managed to haggle, plead, and succeed at his task. There was not a single pence that came back in change.

Fast cutters or packet brigs came in every now and then with orders or news, and everyone got their hopes up that London or Gibraltar would send word for a change in their condition. Sometimes there was mail for *Sapphire* included, and Lewrie could take his mind off his ennui to read newspapers, even if they were weeks out of date by then, or catch up on family and friends. His youngest son, Hugh, was now in a frigate after his first ship paid off, and having the time of his life in the Mediterranean. His eldest, Sewallis, was aboard a new ship, another Third Rate 74, still on the Brest blockade, and did not sound so enthusiastic as his brother, seeming to have had second thoughts of his rash decision years before to run away to sea and *forge* his way into uniform. His daughter, Charlotte, did not write him, but Lewrie's brother-in-law, Governour Chiswick, and his wife, Millicent, wrote for her. If Lewrie would pony up the money, Governour strongly hinted, it might be good to prepare Charlotte for a London Season, and her debut in Society, to catch her a good match.

There were letters from old friends, too; Benjamin Rodgers, Anthony Langlie, and his wife, Sophie, formerly Lewrie's orphaned ward after the evacuation of Toulon, Ralph Knolles also in the Med in his Sixth Rate frigate. There was one breezy, chatty letter full of gossip from his father, Sir Hugo St. George Willoughby, and a packet of letters from Maddalena back at Gibraltar; fond ones that made him wish most fervently for a quick return there. Anywhere!

If we're anchored in this bloody river, anchored to Spencer and his damned army, much longer, I'll go mad! he told himself; Swear *I will!*

At the very least, he could occupy himself answering all those letters, scribbling away for hours on end, so engrossed in the doing that he could forget his miserable circumstances.

"The cutter's coming offshore, sir, and there's an Army officer aboard her," Lieutenant Harcourt announced from the quarterdeck where he'd been idly taking the air.

"Umph!" Lewrie replied, rising from his collapsible chair on the poop deck, and laying aside his book. "So there is. Thankee, Mister Harcourt. D'ye think they've run out of mustard for the officers' mess, and wish t'borrow a pot or two?" he added as he sauntered down to the quarterdeck.

"They'll not get mine, sir!" Harcourt said with a short bark of a laugh.

"Boat ahoy!" Midshipman Spears called to the boat.

"Letter for your Captain!" came the shouted reply.

The boat came alongside the main mast chains, the Army officer managed to scramble up to the entry-port and take the hastily gathered salute from the side-party, then came aft and doffed his hat to Lewrie, and handed over a sealed letter.

"What's this in aid of, sir?" Lewrie testily asked.

"General Spencer has just received orders from London, sir, and informations from Cádiz," the young Lieutenant replied with an eager smile. "General Sir Arthur Wellesley's army is to land in the Tagus, but we will not be marching to join him at Lisbon."

"That was the plan?" Lewrie said.

"It was contemplated, yes, sir," the army man said, "but it seems that London is of a mind that our brigade would be of more use closer to Cádiz, to aid and encourage the Spanish Army of Andalusia, and the Spanish have finally agreed to allow us to do so."

Lewrie ripped the letter open and turned away briefly to read it. "Thank bloody Christ!" he whooped after a moment. "Puerto de Santa María! Not Cádiz *exactly*, but it'll do. General Spencer is packing up and ready to go aboard the transports?"

"As we speak, sir," the Lieutenant happily told him. "He wishes to be away in three days, weather permitting."

"I can't wait t'shake the dust of Ayamonte from my boots, either," Lewrie told him, feeling like breaking out in a hornpipe dance of glee, "not that I *gathered* much dust in the bloody place. Assure the General that the transports await, and we'll be ready to sail as soon as he's got all his force off. And, inform him how delighted that every hand is t'hear of it, me included."

"I shall relate that to him, sir," the Army officer promised, equally pleased that they would go.

"Pettus," Lewrie called, spotting his cabin-steward idling on the larboard gangway and fiddling with a fishing line, "do you fetch this officer a glass of wine before he returns ashore. We'll liquour his boots for his ride."

"Thank you, sir!" the Lieutenant exclaimed.

Word quickly spread, as it usually did aboard ship, fetching off-watch officers from below, with Westcott in the lead, even before Pettus could pour that glass of wine.

"Do I hear right, sir?" Westcott asked, looking hopeful.

"Hear what, Mister Westcott?" Lewrie could not help teasing.

"Why, that we're out of this flea-ridden hovel!" Westcott replied.

"We are," Lewrie assured him. "Off for Puerto de Santa María on the Bay of Cádiz, as soon as the Army can be got off."

"I hope you pack quickly, sir," Westcott said to the stranger.

"Closer to a larger city, your odds'll be better," Lewrie japed. "For your . . . hunting?"

"Perhaps the ladies of Cádiz bathe more often than the women of Ayamonte, aye," Westcott said, sniggering.

"Oh, Lord," Lt. Harcourt said, shaking his head, for Harcourt was a man who could be described as a Decent Sort, one more prone to seek a wife, should he ever get a command of his own and more pay.

As the army officer drank his wine, Lewrie could hear a stir among the crew. Off-watch men were coming on deck, people were whispering behind their hands, breaking out in grins, and looking aft for confirmation of the "scuttle-butt." A fiddler even struck up "One Misty, Moisty Morning"!

Aye, they're ready t'sail away, Lewrie thought; more *than ready t'go somewhere else!*

CHAPTER NINETEEN

*C*ádiz had fallen, the French were ousted, and the important naval port was back in the hands of the Spanish, and the Supreme *Junta* in Seville. The Bay of Cádiz, sheltered and protected by the peninsula on which sat the old city and the fortresses, was crowded with ships. There were Spanish Navy ships of war, too-long blockaded in port and neglected for lack of supplies and money, looking positively dowdy by then. In only slightly better condition were the French navy warships which had survived the Battle of Trafalgar, their Tricolour national flags drooping low on their sterns, with Spanish royal colours flying atop them to show just who had forced them to strike.

Spanish merchantmen, also trapped in harbour and unable to make a profit, were hastily being fitted out for voyages to Spain's colonies in the Americas to re-assert Spain's complete dominance of trade 'twixt them and the home country. When ready for sea, they would most likely bear officials and royal orders to colonial goverors to bar any intra-colonial trade except for Spanish ships, and stop mercantile activities with anyone else.

The revolution against French conquest had arisen so quickly that British, or other neutral European, merchants might take months to make their appearance at Cádiz with valuable, greatly desired, cargoes, but they would come later. For now, it was only the hired transports and troopers of General Spencer's little army which were present.

With the need for blockade over, several Britsh warships from Rear-Admiral Purvis's squadron had been allowed into harbour, mostly for firewood and water. There would be no shore liberty here either, though, for the Spanish were still touchy upon the presence of too many *ingleses* in town, sure that there was still a plot by the perfidious British to take the place by force and turn it into a second Gibraltar, then keep it forever!

Lewrie got his wish to meet Vice-Admiral Cuthbert, Baron Collingwood, but that resulted in a very brief encounter, a nod of a head and a gruff "Ahd ye do, sir?", and Lewrie would not gush like a schoolboy a second time.

"Happy now, sir?" Purvis asked with a wry expression.

"Sorry 'bout that," Lewrie replied, ducking his head and turning red to be reminded of his embarrassment. Up close, Collingwood was a tall and lean old stick, morose and tired-looking, and going bald.

"Well, he was one of Nelson's 'band of brothers,' but I'd have rather known Nelson," Purvis idly said.

"Might I ask, sir, what's to become of *Sapphire,* now that the army is landed?" Lewrie had to ask. "I've been on Independent Orders at Gibraltar for the last year and a half, but with the Spanish up in arms 'gainst the French, my presence there may not be necessary."

"Hmm," Purvis mused aloud, pondering. "I could order you to join my squadron, Collingwood's now, really, but with Cádiz ours, the need for another blockader is gone."

"I might be better employed up North with Sir Charles Cotton's squadron blockading Lisbon, d'ye imagine, sir?" Lewrie wondered. "If General Wellesley's army is to land in Portugal soon . . . ?"

"Aye, you might be more useful with him, but, Dalrymple, and those furtive Foreign Office gentlemen might not be through with you yet. Best sail for Gibraltar and see. Upon that head, you can carry despatches from Collingwood and me on the way," Purvis told him.

"Capital!" Lewrie exclaimed. "I can give my people shore liberty somewhere they're welcome, where most people speak English!"

"Aye, join the Navy, see the world, and be gobbled at by foreigners," Purvis said with a rare laugh. "We'll have our despatches in your hands soon, Captain Lewrie, then you can be off."

"Thank you, sir," Lewrie replied, doffed his hat, and took his leave.

⚓

Free of plodding transports at last, *Sapphire* made a fast passage back to Gibraltar, almost racing through the Strait with currents and wind combining to speed her along, daring to skate past the guns at Tarifa and Cape Carnero, reducing sail and speed as she rounded Pigeon Island into the bay. The Spanish gunners, who normally would have taken any British ship in range under fire, were silent. And at Algeciras, and in the mouths of the Palmones and Guadarranque Rivers, the hordes of Spanish gunboats lay idle. There were more Spanish merchant ships at Algeciras, but no more warships.

Sapphire rounded up into the wind and dropped anchor off the Old Mole, took in sail, and came to rest. Even as that evolution was going on, one of the cutters was brought up from being towed astern, manned, and Lewrie was down the ship's side and into it in a trice, with a canvas satchel full of mail and despatches slung from one shoulder. As he was rowed to the landing stage along the quay, he could cast an eager look lower down the town, and was delighted to see Maddalena on her balcony, waving a towel at him.

Soon, girl, he thought; *soon as I'm done with the Dowager!*

He was shown into General Sir Hew Dalrymple's offices immediately, where the Dowager shot to his feet and almost *dashed* to take hold of the despatches, idly ordering wine for Lewrie.

"Ayamonte first? Quite a long way from Cádiz," Dalrymple commented after he'd read the first one. "God above, the Spanish!"

"They only allowed us into port for firewood and water, sir," Lewrie told him, thanking God for the Convent's deep cellars, where wine could almost chill, as he took a long sip. "General Spencer has built defences round Puerto de Santa María, but he's also despatched four battalions and some artillery to Xeres, further inland, to buck up the Spanish army."

"He's aware that under no circumstances is he to march along with Castaños when he moves? I'll not trust the fighting prowess of the Spanish against the French, and risk losing a sizable body of ours in the process," Dalrymple grumped.

"He is, sir," Lewrie assured him. "I was told that there's yet a French brigade under Avril, lurkin' somewhere between Seville and Cádiz, if it hasn't gone off to join L'Étang there, or Dupont at Córdoba. I gather that

General Spencer will remain near Cádiz 'til he knows whether General Avril will march upon him."

Lewrie took note that Sir Hew's map stand no longer featured Ceuta and the fortress, but now displayed a large map of the entire Iberian Peninsula, with bits of ribbon pinned to various Portuguese or Spanish cities. He assumed that the blue'uns represented French-held cities, and the gold'uns stood for places where the Spanish had risen up. Sir Hew set aside the next letter for a moment, rose from his desk more slowly than before, crossed to his map, and stuck a gold ribbon on Cádiz, then stepped back to admire his map with a satisfied sigh.

"What's the red ribbon for, sir?" Lewrie asked. It was stuck in the ocean, not the land, up near Corunna in Northwest Spain.

"It represents General Sir Arthur Wellesley, Sir Alan," Sir Hew told him as he returned to his desk, and his despatches. "London sent me a letter that he might land there, first. I eagerly await news of that."

"Rather a long march to Lisbon, ain't it?" Lewrie asked. "Even the roads close to the coast are sure t'be bad. But, if the French confront him in force, he could always be taken off by sea, from Vigo or Oporto, if need be. Wellesley's idea, that?"

"Lord Castlereagh's, most likely," Dalrymple said, frowning and stroking his chin. "I know of the Wellesleys, but little of Sir Arthur, but for his reputation gained in India. I do not know his fighting qualities, or whether he is a cautious man or an audacious one. Flighty Hindoos are one thing; the French are quite another. I'm not aware of any 'Sepoy' generals of note who have fought well against the French." He almost sneered.

"Well, so far, Sir Hew," Lewrie drawled, "our Army's not done all that well against them, no matter their generals' *bona fides*."

"Think so, do you?" Dalrymple snapped, coming to the defence of his service, but he could not deny the truth. "I see that the French fleet in Cádiz is neutralised, with the honours going to the Spanish? No prize money in it for the Navy? How sad."

That was a definite sneer. Lewrie shrugged it off, sure that the interview would soon be over.

"Any ideas of how you might employ my ship, given the change in circumstances, Sir Hew?" he asked anyway. "She's too slow for a despatch vessel. Ye need frigates and such for that."

"An orphan, are you?" Dalrymple posed, sounding as if he was still nettled by Lewrie's comments about the Army and its generals. "If

Admirals Collingwood and Purvis found no use for your services, perhaps you might call upon your Mister Mountjoy. You were sent here
partially under his auspices, were you not? You still operate under Independent Orders."

"I shall do that, Sir Hew," Lewrie replied, shifting in his chair, prepared
to rise and depart. "Anything else you need from me regarding the situation at Cádiz?"

"No, I believe the despatches speak for them," Sir Hew said. "You may
go, and good luck to you finding employment." He shooed Lewrie off as
he would a fly.

"Very good, Sir Hew. I'll take my leave," Lewrie said, and rose to deliver a brief bow. When he looked back for a second, he caught Sir Hew
Dalrymple gazing at his maps with a contemplative grin on his face, and
his eyes alight with *some* scheme.

There was nothing for it. As much as he wished *rencontre* with Maddalena,
he would have to go speak with Mountjoy first.

"Is he in, Mister Deacon?" Lewrie asked at the ground-floor entrance
to Mountjoy's lodgings.

"He is, sir, and was just about to send me to find you," that craggy-faced,
grim, and ever-vigilant worthy replied with a taut grin. "Go right on up.
There's wondrous news to be shared."

The interior rooms were empty, but there were some plunking noises
coming from the rooftop gallery that overlooked the bay, and the Lines,
and that was where Mountjoy could be found. Lewrie walked out under
the canvas awnings to find the local chief of Secret Branch seated on the
settee, with a book of musical notes on the table in front of him.

"Good God, what's that?" Lewrie asked.

"This," Mountjoy happily told him, "is what the Spanish call a guitar.
I got it down at the markets, once free trade was opened cross the Lines."
He moved the fingers of his left hand and strummed some chords with his
right, tapping a foot to keep time, and screwing up his face in concentration. "Haven't gotten good at it, yet."

"Aye, so I *hear*," Lewrie gybed, sweeping off his hat and going for a
comfortable chair. "You've been out-done, ye know. Purvis, off Cádiz, and
Cotton off Lisbon, have gotten agents of some kind ashore, where you
couldn't."

"Ah, but in the meantime, I've discovered hundreds of patriotic Spaniards, just eager to send letters down, telling me of French movements, and towns that have risen up," Mountjoy countered, laying his guitar aside. "Almost *weekly* reports from Marsh in Madrid, and from others at Seville, Córdoba, Málaga, and Granada. It's definite. Napoleon's deposed the old king, the new king, and put them under a rather comfortable house arrest in France. I'm told that the Foreign Minister, Talleyrand, is saddled with them at his estate, and is not happy with the arrangement. Joseph Bonaparte is on his way to Madrid to be crowned the newest King of Spain, and all's right with the world, as the old saying goes. There are rebel *juntas* springing up all over Spain, and there's been fighting 'twixt the Spanish Army and the Frogs. I've gotten reports of victories, though I'll take those with a grain of salt 'til truthful results are in.

"What's more intriguing are the reports I've gotten concerning the Spanish people, themselves," Mountjoy gleefully related. "Oh, my manners. Deacon? Fetch us all some wine, will you? That tangy and sparkly white? Thank you."

"What *about* the Spanish people?" Lewrie had to ask.

"There are bands of men in the back country who have taken up what arms they own," Mountjoy said, practically bubbling over with delight. "They're ambushing despatch riders and small foraging parties where they can, slitting French throats, and taking *their* arms and ammunition to use against them. They gallop in, kill or capture the French soldiers, loot them, then gallop away, quick as you can say 'knife,' and disappear into the hills and woods, and I've word that the French are tearing their hair out, unable to chase them very far, or in units small enough to pursue quickly . . . too many of those have been ambushed and murdered, themselves. Heard of Zaragosa?"

"Went down with the Spanish Armada, didn't he?" Lewrie japed. "Ye know I haven't."

"It's a city, capital of Aragon," Mountjoy said, casting his head over to one side and making a face at Lewrie's idea of wit. "It is under siege, after the citizens rose up and slaughtered the occupying French garrison. Spanish troops marched in to aid them, and the city's holding out, just laying Frenchmen dead in windrows when they try to break in. I've sent a letter about it to London, with a drawing . . . invented here by an artist with the *Chronicle* . . . about a heroine, a girl named Augustina, whom the Spanish report defended her own burned-out house with a sabre, dressed in pantaloons. *She's* real enough, even if the drawing's not. It's sure to make all the London papers. War by the press, hah hah!"

"Well, that's all fine . . . ," Lewrie began to say, but Deacon showed up with a bottle of wine and three glasses.

"Best news of all, Lewrie," Mountjoy said with a twinkle in his eyes, "the latest mail packet in from England bore word that the peace treaty with Spain has been *signed*, she's a British ally, now! We're united against the French!"

"Well, no wonder they didn't shoot at me when I sailed in," Lewrie replied, with less enthusiasm than Mountjoy might have wished. "Aye, that's toppin' fine. You pulled it off. Congratulations."

"A deed that can't be celebrated often enough, Captain Lewrie," Deacon said, baring a rare smile as he poured the wine for them.

After drinking half his glass, clinking with the others to celebrate, Lewrie leaned back in his chair and asked, "Now that the Dons are allies, what did you have in mind for me to do?"

"Hmm," Mountjoy paused, frowning in puzzlement. "Haven't given it a thought, since you sailed off with Spencer's convoy. I didn't know if I'd get you back."

"There's the arms, sir," Deacon suggested. "A lot more than John Cummings's coastal trader can carry at one go."

"He's still alive?" Lewrie blurted. "*There's* a wonder."

"Alive, and thriving," Mountjoy said with a laugh, "though he *still* avoids Estepona. Yes, do you recall early on last Summer, that some of our sources on the Andalusian coast requested arms to counter the French invaders? Good. We've managed to assemble five thousand muskets, with bayonets and accoutrements, and half a million pre-made cartridges. The requests have come, again, but I have no way to get them where they're needed."

Of course, John Cummings, who posed as Vicente Rodríguez, had to avoid Estepona; it was the home port of that dowdy coaster that Lewrie had taken for espionage use the last Summer, and he would've been lynched or garrotted had he sailed her in there.

"Does Dalrymple know of the arms?" Lewrie asked, wondering if Mountjoy was playing a double game. "After we landed Spencer at Ayamonte, he gave all his spare weapons to the Spanish, but he could only arm about half of 'em, and that was about all that Dalrymple could spare, either, for Spencer, *or* Castaños. And just where did ye think t'land 'em?"

"Let's just say that my superiors sent the arms along in case I *could* get them to the Spanish," Mountjoy said, going cat-sly as he did so, "and foment an uprising before the real thing happened."

"Málaga's forts are still occupied by a French garrison," Mr. Deacon informed him, "but the *junta* at Granada could use them. The closest place along the coast would be Salobreña."

Christ! Lewrie thought; *Where we got our noses bloodied last year. What sort o' welcome would we have after killin' Spanish troops?*

"The road from Salobreña to Granada is decent, and direct. The Spanish could cart them on from there." Mountjoy added, "I know, it cuts rough to go back there, but I'm assured that there are eager volunteers in need of arms."

"*El Diablo Negro,* returnin' to the scene of the crime?" Lewrie scoffed. That was the sobriquet *Sapphire* had earned during her raiding forays along the Andalusian coast in 1807.

"They *are* our allies," Mountjoy pointed out.

"Anyone told *them*, yet?" Lewrie countered.

"They'll chair you through the streets, most-like," Mountjoy cajoled. "Deacon, here, will go along as my representative. He has excellent Spanish."

"And I don't," Lewrie said with a grunt.

"Bless me, we're all glad that you can speak *English*!" Mountjoy hooted.

"How soon must they have their guns, then?" Lewrie said, surrendering.

"As soon as you can take them aboard and sail," Mountjoy told him. "General Castaños is of a mind to try his hand against General Dupont, now at Córdoba, and he'll need all the armed troops that he can muster."

"A day to take on firewood and water, a day of shore liberty for my crew, a day of lading your arms, and I could be off on the fourth day—," Lewrie decided.

"Wind and weather permitting!" Mountjoy interrupted, using one of Lewrie's usual qualifiers.

"Aye, wind and weather permitting," Lewrie agreed.

"Hmm, I fear your crew may have to forgo their liberty for a time," Mountjoy said upon second reflection. "Getting the arms to the Spanish is paramount. If you could begin taking them aboard as soon as you complete loading your ship's immediate needs, that would be simply topping."

Damme, he's givin' me outright orders, *again!* Lewrie thought in a moment of resentment. He knew that he *was* seconded to the young man, but it did rankle, now and then, to be bossed about by civilians.

"Well, if it's that urgent, I s'pose I could," Lewrie drawled. "What? You want the arms off Gibraltar before Dalrymple knows you have 'em?"

Hah, hit a sore spot there! Lewrie thought, congratulating himself as he saw Mountjoy's cheek wince; *Well, at least I get* one *day with Maddalena.*

CHAPTER TWENTY

*T*he sleepy fishing port of Salobreña had not been a victim of HMS *Sapphire*'s shore bombardments, none of its fishing boats or coastal trading boats had been burned right in the harbour, but some of the prizes which *Sapphire* had run down, taken, and burned close to shore had surely come from there. Only the semaphore tower high up behind the town had been burned, after a brisk pre-dawn skirmish with Spanish troops who were not supposed to be there, according to Mountjoy's informers, but some Spanish commander had sent them down from Órgiva on a route march to keep them fit, or to punish them, and they *had* been there, sleeping in Salobreña's taverns, when the alarm was raised. For sleepy, half-drunk soldiers, they had put up a decent but brief resistance before breaking and running off into the bracken behind the town.

"That's the semaphore tower, Captain Lewrie?" Mr. Deacon asked as he peered shoreward with his own smaller telescope. "Doesn't look like much to die for."

"I'm sure those who did, or were crippled for life, thought the same, Mister Deacon," Lewrie replied.

"They never re-built it, it appears," Deacon said after a longer perusal. "Mister Mountjoy said that his reports tell much the same tale of the others you burned, and the batteries you blew up or shot to bits."

"The French drained so much from the Spanish treasury that the whole country's 'skint,'" Lewrie replied with a shrug. "Now they own Spain as a conquest, it'll be their job t're-build. *Their* soldiers mannin' and guardin' the bloody things. Hmm . . . if I could round up troops, boats, and a transport or two, we could start maraudin' all over again, against the French this time."

"If General Dalrymple could spare troops, again, sir, which I doubt," Deacon told him. "I also doubt the French could man and guard a new line of towers. If the Spanish people are becoming *guerrilleros*, it might take two companies to each tower to protect them."

"*Gueri* . . . ?" Lewrie gawped. "What the Devil's that?"

"Roughly, *guerrilla* comes close to 'little war,' sir," Deacon said with a grin, "with irregular fighters, ambushers, throat-slitters, those sort of attacks that Mister Mountjoy was so excited about. The French haven't seen anything like them in any of their other conquered countries, and it'll drive them mad. More like Red Indian warfare on the American frontiers."

"And the French are a very European army," Lewrie replied with sudden good humour, the opposite of his qualms over how the Spanish would receive their sudden appearance, even if they were bearing them gifts. "God help 'em, then. Saw my share of Indian fighting in Spanish Florida during the Revolution. Brr! Vicious!"

"Seven fathom! Seven fathom t'this line!" one of the leadsmen called back from his post on a foremast chain platform.

"We'll stand on 'til we strike six fathoms, Mister Yelland," Lewrie called down to the Sailing Master on the quarterdeck.

"Aye, sir, six fathoms, and we round up," Yelland agreed.

"I think I see Spanish troops on the quays, sir," Lt. Westcott pointed out. "The *French* wear blue uniforms, mostly, and this lot's white. Do the Frogs wear that colour?"

Lewrie looked to Deacon for an answer; he'd been a soldier in the Guards, and should know, but all he got from that worthy was a shrug and a puzzled face.

"Wish we had a Spanish officer with us, then," Lewrie said. "I would've thought that Mountjoy could whistle one up from General Castaños' staff."

"A rush job, Captain Lewrie," Deacon said, winking. "No time to look for one."

"Six fathom! Six fathom t'this line!" a leadsman shouted.

"Fetch-to, Mister Westcott," Lewrie snapped. "Round up into the wind, and ready the best bower."

"Aye aye, sir!" Westcott called back, then began to bellow orders to steer up into the wind, take in sail, and drop the larboard anchor.

"We'll take the thirty-two-foot pinnace," Lewrie told Deacon as they descended from the poop deck to the quarterdeck. "It's more impressive than a cutter, and has more room for all."

They ain't shootin' at us, yet, Lewrie thought in trepidation as the pinnace came alongside the quays, as the bow man gaffed the piers and sprang to tie off a line to a bollard, as another sailor did the same at the stern.

Deacon plastered a smile on his craggy face and made cordial noises in fluid, fluent Spanish. A Spanish officer came forward to palaver with him. The Spaniard was an odd bird, Lewrie thought, wearing a cocked hat twice as big as any he'd ever seen, with tall dragoon boots with knee-flaps on his legs, and a long smallsword tucked up under his armpit instead of slung on the hip. His mustachio was long, pointed, and looked waxed. The Spanish officer frowned a lot, then broke out in a smile, turned to face the townfolk who had gathered in curiosity, clapped his gloved hands, and began to babble in rapid Spanish. Whatever he'd told them set off tremendous cheers.

"Commandante Azcárte, it means he's a Major, sir, says that we and our arms are more than welcome," Deacon translated as the fellow turned back to face them. "Someone in contact with Gibraltar alerted them that we would be coming, and Major Azcárte was sent from the Granada *junta* to escort them inland, with waggons, carts, and a strong escort. I'm naming you to him now, sir, though I don't know how to render 'Baronet' in Spanish."

"Makes no matter," Lewrie shrugged off, beaming fit to bust, himself, and nodding pleasantly. He made out *"Capitano"* and *"Caballero," "la Marina Real Británica,"* but the rest was higgledy-piggledy. When Deacon drew breath, Lewrie doffed his hat and bowed from the waist; there was no way to make a formal "leg" while still standing in the pinnace.

"Honoured to make your acquaintance, Commandante Azcárte," Lewrie replied. "Uhm, Deacon, ask him if the locals can help get the arms ashore with their boats. It'd take hours, else."

"I will, sir," Deacon said, and launched into more gibberish. Major Azcárte nodded vigourously, replied with more smiles, and turned to the citizens of Salobreña to ask them to help, which launched a rush of fishermen to their boats along the quay, to break out oars, and begin to stroke out towards *Sapphire.*

Lewrie and Deacon scrambled up atop the quay, and Deacon began to ask many questions anent the local situation, the nearness of the French, and the latest news from Granada. Before he could get any answers, Major Azcárte stepped up to Lewrie, threw his arms round him in a bear hug, and bussed him on both cheeks, babbling away.

He got *"muchas gracias,"* but the rest was nonsense sounds.

"He expresses his thanks, sir," Deacon translated.

"Got that part," Lewrie said, wishing the oaf would let go.

"How grateful all Spain will be . . . how grand it is to be allies . . . how despicable the French . . . their cruelties and depredations," Deacon said, hitting only the high points. At least Major Azcárte *had* let him go, and was now stamping a booted foot, gesticulating wildly with his hands, and even going so far as to spit dramatically, fortunately far away. "If you make some agreeing noises, I'll lay it on as thick as he likes, sir," Deacon said, sounding as if he found this most amusing.

I'm a Punch and Judy puppet, by God! Lewrie told himself, but he expressed how much he had always hated and distrusted the filthy French, that English people called them Frogs, that the invasion of Spain was outright thievery, and he was more than glad to help the "brave people" of Spain fight them and throw them back across the Pyrenees, killing as many as they could in the process. All of that was just "the nuts" to Azcárte, who was practically cooing by then.

"He invites us to a tavern, sir, for wine and something to eat," Deacon said at last.

"Hell, yes, let's go," Lewrie was more than happy to say.

That, however, involved meeting more of Major Azcárte's junior officers, all of whom looked to be idling and cooling their heels at the tavern, and may have been for some time, given the sleepy, drunk looks on their faces. Slurred Castilian Spanish with its lisping was hard enough to decypher, and drunk Castilian gave Deacon a trial.

"Boasting of what they'll do to the French, now they have weapons," Deacon idly translated as some rough, raw local red wine showed up, and toasts were given. "Major Azcárte suggests that the next time your ship comes, you could bring blankets, boots or shoes, and food. I gather they're short of everything."

"Tell him that Great Britain will do what we can, but that all depends on how quickly our Government can gather up the goods and get 'em here," Lewrie responded. "Don't promise him the moon."

"Yes, sir. He apologises for the wine, which even he deems as swill, and suggests we switch to brandy," Deacon said.

"Tell him I think I'll go see how the un-loading is going," Lewrie replied, "and if he has his waggons and such handy. Bad as the wine is, I can't imagine the local brandy bein' a whit better."

He rose, clapped on his hat, and went outside. Between the local boatmen and his sailors, quite a lot of the weapons had gotten ashore already, crate after crate of muskets, of bayonets, of cartridges, and leather accoutrements in bundles were already piled high on the quays. Yellow-jacketed Spanish cavalry were coming down the road from Órgiva, alongside slow, creaking, and squealing ox-drawn waggons.

Another party of cavalry in different-coloured uniforms were clattering into Salobreña from the West on tired-looking horses wet with ammoniac white-foam sweat, shouting something in alert, or joy to find a tavern, it was hard for Lewrie to tell which.

"What're they sayin', Mister Deacon?" he asked.

"Ehm, they say the French are coming, sir!" Deacon said with gravel in his throat. "Fifteen miles back, near Almuñécar, at least a demi-brigade. That'd be about two thousand men. Infantry, thank the Lord, so they won't be here anytime soon. Uhm . . . they saw no cavalry, and that's a blessing."

That news stirred Major Azcárte into a frenzy of shouting and windmilling his arms, sending his junior officers scurrying to leave the tavern, retrieve their shakoes or cocked hats, arm themselves, and disperse to their waiting, drowzing soldiers. Locals began to dart about, some helping to load the waggons, and some to begin hitching up their own waggons so they could flee.

"Major Azcárte says the French garrison at Málaga has been re-enforced, and is sending troops out along the coast roads," Deacon managed to pick up from Azcárte's ravings. "He apologises for haste, but he must get the waggons loaded and up into the mountains before they arrive, and God help the people of Salobreña for what the French will do to them when they get here. Tell him *Vaya con Dios,* sir, and bid him goodbye," Deacon added in a harsh whisper.

Lewrie did as Deacon bade, doffing his hat and bowing again, then turned to see to his men in the pinnace. The 29-foot launch and both 25-foot cutters were alongside the quays, un-loading the last of the boxed cartridges, under Midshipman Hillhouse.

"That the last of it, Mister Hillhouse?" Lewrie demanded.

"Aye, sir, the very last scrap. What's the trouble?" the senior Mid asked, looking round at the seeming panic.

"French troops coming from Málaga, in strength," Lewrie told him, on his way to the waiting pinnace. "Let's get our people back to the ship."

"Aye aye, sir!"

"You, there!" someone was bellowing in English. "British officer! Don't leave without me, for Christ's sake!"

Lewrie turned about to see a party of armed civilian men, some of the *guerrilleros,* come clopping into Salobreña. With them on a weary-looking poor prad of a horse was a British Army officer, red in the face, and his elegantly tailored uniform much the worse for wear.

"Mine arse on a band-box!" Lewrie spat in shock.

"Escaped before the French slung me in prison," the man babbled as he almost fell off the horse in his haste. "Was on my parole at Málaga, got helped out of the city . . . Captain *Lewrie?*"

"Aye, Major Hughes," Lewrie replied. "Get your arse in the boat."

It would have been a toss-up, in point of fact, which of the men was more shocked by the other's appearance, Brevet-Major Hughes, or Alan Lewrie.

Thought we'd seen the last o' that bastard fool when the Dons captured him last Summer! Lewrie thought in disgust; *Right here up by the semaphore tower!*

Hughes had been appointed to command the landing force for the raids along the coast, and a fine muddle he'd made of it once ashore.

Oh God, what'll Maddalena make of his resurrection? Lewrie had to wonder.

CHAPTER TWENTY-ONE

*N*eed a Bosun's chair?" Lewrie asked Hughes as the pinnace came alongside the starboard boarding battens.

"Not a bit of it, Lewrie," Major Hughes said with a *harumph* of displeasure. "I've been up the side of your ship before. After you, sir."

"Senior officers are first in, last out, sir," Lewrie corrected. "Up ye get, then."

Hughes looked as if he would argue the point, going squinty-eyed, but stood, teetered on the gunn'l, made his leap and grab, and began to scale the battens. Lewrie looked up and smiled a bit at the sight of Hughes's breeches; elegant white had turned a pale shit-brown round the rump, most-like from a saddle's badly cured leather. Hughes was not aware of it, but Lewrie thought it a good excuse for a ribbing, for later.

"Major Hughes!" Lewrie heard Westcott say above as he climbed aboard. "Look what the cat dragged in, I must say! Wherever have you been?"

Marines stamped their boots and slapped muskets as Lewrie got to the main deck amid the piping of Bosun's calls, and hats were doffed by all hands as Lewrie raised his in salute.

"All boats secured for towing, all hands back aboard, sir, and ready for orders," Lt. Westcott said to Lewrie.

"Very good, Mister Westcott," Lewrie replied. "Stations to up-anchor and make sail."

"Aye aye, sir! Bosun Terrell, pipe Stations to Hoist Anchor!" Westcott bellowed, turning away.

"Might I prevail upon your hospitality, Captain Lewrie? I find myself in great thirst," Hughes said.

"But of course, sir," Lewrie offered, whether he cared to or not. "Let's go aft, but only briefly. We'll be under way in a bit."

Once in the great-cabins, Lewrie requested Pettus to fetch out some Rhenish, then satisfied his curiosity. "Whatever *did* happen to you, sir? How the Devil did ye get captured? Once the Dons ran off, we couldn't find hide nor hair of you."

"Utter confusion was the cause of it, sir!" Hughes said with a dismissive snort. "Three detachments separated too far, not in one organised line. I had to dash over to the left to see to one of them, rein them in before they got too far away, and tripped over a rock in the dark. Next thing I knew, five or six foul-looking Spanish soldiers were all over me, seized my sword and pistols, gave me a bash on the head with a musket butt, and dragged me away. They took me to their cantonment at Órgiva, first, slung me in their gaol for a few days, then got word to fetch me to the fort at Málaga, where there *finally* was someone who could speak passable English, and put me on my parole. Ah, a decent Rhenish, at last! 'Til I got my pay sent on from Gibraltar, I was 'skint,' hardly had tuppence upon me, and had to drink the *vilest* peasant reds." Hughes polished off his glass of wine in four swift gulps and held out his glass for a re-fill. "You sail without the transport, sir? What of our amphibious unit?"

"Dis-banded last Fall, when the French invaded Portugal and Spain, and the Spanish began t'make nice with us," Lewrie told him, taking a few sips from his own glass. "Dalrymple thought it better that we did not make war on the Dons after that."

"Pity, we were just getting good at it," Hughes said.

Did better after we lost you*!* Lewrie thought.

"You still have that damned cat, I see," Hughes said with a scowl as he espied Chalky, who was hunkered into a defensive lump on the day-cabin desk. The cat had never taken to Hughes, perhaps sensing Lewrie's feelings. "Once I got settled in passable lodgings in the town," Hughes went on, "it wasn't so bad, but for the fact that Spain doesn't feature much roast beef on their tables, not where I ate. It was pork, pork, pork, in one form or another, breakfast to supper, and it got tiresome. Then, when Marshal

Murat marched into Madrid, and the Dons got so angry, they let me go, just shooed me off to make my own way to Gibraltar."

"Went the wrong way for that," Lewrie commented.

"The French were in Córdoba and Seville, by then, and marching down to Gibraltar, so heading East and hoping to throw in with armed irregulars or the Spanish army was my best bet," Hughes said, shrugging it off. "You're bound for Gibraltar?"

"Aye, after droppin' off arms and ammunition for the *junta* in Granada, a quick out-and-back," Lewrie replied, setting his half-empty wine down on the brass Hindoo tray table.

"Your turning up was a miracle, sir!" Hughes exclaimed, taking his ease in one of the chairs with his legs stretched out. "I'm damned glad you did, and can't wait to get back to Gibraltar, let me tell you! Back in my regiment's mess, clean clothing, decent food, and a romp or two."

"I must return to the deck," Lewrie said as he heard calls for "short stays," and Westcott shouting for topmen to "trice up and lay out" to make sail. "Take your ease here, whilst we get under way, then come join us when you feel like it. There's a spare cabin in the officers' wardroom that you can use, and 'twixt the three officers' servants, I'm sure they can see to your needs."

"Maddalena, recall her, do you?" Hughes speculated with a grin. "Ever run into her when you were ashore? Poor chit's probably taken up with another who would keep her. Well, soon as I'm back, I'll *see* about *that*! And, by God, he better *not* be anyone I know, hah hah!"

"Seen her around," Lewrie lied, then picked up his hat and left the cabins. That was a conversation for later.

Once *Sapphire* was free of the ground and fully under sail, Mr. Deacon sidled over near Lewrie on the windward side of the quarterdeck, something that anyone in the Navy would not dare do unless delivering information.

"Bit of a wrench, his turning up again, sir?" Deacon asked in a low voice. "An *efficient* fellow, a grand organiser right down to the number of cork musket tompions, but the very worst sort of parade ground officer, as Mister Mountjoy and I agreed."

"I'll get it settled," Lewrie replied, sure that Deacon was talking about Maddalena Covilhā, since both he and Mountjoy had been aware of Lewrie's taking up with her, and being smitten by her long before Hughes had disappeared.

"Settled, sir?" Deacon said, befuddled. "I was talking of his military qualities, and pitying the rankers of his company after he rejoins his regiment. Oh . . . *that* settled!" he went on with a knowing smile.

Lewrie was looking upon Deacon with new eyes. When they were first introduced the Summer before, he had taken Mr. Deacon as just one more of Secret Branch's hired muscle, a very dangerous and menacing sort who'd do the skulking, house-breaking, *head*-breaking, and elimination of the King's enemies. He certainly looked the part; wide-shouldered and slim-hipped, with big, strong hands just made for strangling, and a harsh, craggy face. After this jaunt to deliver arms, though, Lewrie found that Deacon was more than bodyguard or errand-runner. For an ex-Sergeant in the Household Guards, he possessed a brain, and a fine, clever wit, with linguistic skills far better than Lewrie's own.

"Mountjoy once warned me off her," Lewrie admitted, "so long as we needed Hughes. Now he's lazing round my settee, sure that he'll only have to whistle t'get her back, with an idea to thrash whoever's taken up with her."

"Remember the old adage, though, sir, 'Great talkers do the least, we see,'" Deacon said with a grin that could turn most men's blood cold. "I doubt *his* sort will even sulk for more than a day or two, then drop the matter. And, if he *doesn't*," Deacon imparted with a bit of threat in his voice, "he can always be quietly done away with, hmm?"

"Good Lord, Mister Deacon!" Lewrie exclaimed.

"Just saying, sir," Deacon replied, sporting another evil grin. "I might just do it to spare his troops, if his regiment ever takes the field against the French. I can't *abide* his sort of officer."

"No, Mister Deacon, does it come to a duel, I'd rather do him in, myself," Lewrie told him. "It won't get that far, though. You're right. His sort doesn't cherish women proper, and most-like doesn't give a fig for 'em beyond havin' one handy. He'll sulk, then search out another."

"Either way, the offer stands, sir," Deacon said with a shrug, and turned to go to the lee bulwarks.

"A moment more, Mister Deacon, if ye please," Lewrie bade with sudden inspiration. "Major Azcárte said that a French demi-brigade was on the road from Málaga. How big is a demi-brigade? I've never heard of one."

"I believe it would be about two thousand men, sir," Deacon said with his head cocked over in study. "Three regiments of six hundred men each, with some artillery and gun crews. That's right, he said they had no cavalry, which is odd, sir. I'd think they'd have at least one squadron of horse for scouting, at the least. Azcárte may be in big trouble if the report was wrong. The French could be all over him before he gets his slow waggons into the hills."

Lewrie looked round the quarterdeck for the Sailing Master, but could not spot him. A few steps aft and he was in the captain's clerk's office, which had been converted into a chart room, and waving Deacon to join him. The coastal chart from Málaga to Cabo de Gata was laid out on the angled desk-top, much marked from previous raids, up-dated for their own use with information that Mountjoy's informers had given them the year before.

"The road from Almuñécar to Salobreña is right along the coast," Lewrie said, tapping the chart with a pencil, "and there's a section where the road goes round this steep hill, just a mile or so beyond Almuñécar. Hmm. I wonder."

"Are you thinking of slowing them down, and giving Major Azcárte some breathing room, sir?" Deacon asked, looking evil and expectant again.

"The shoals, though, hmm," Lewrie speculated. "If I can get within less than a mile without runnin' aground, maybe. The chart says six fathoms, some five-fathom stretches."

"Thirty feet, and you draw about twenty, sir?" Deacon asked.

"You've been swotting up on salty stuff," Lewrie japed. "Best not let Mountjoy know, he'd fear we'd steal you away."

"I prefer skulking round city taverns, sir, thankee," Deacon said with a rare laugh.

"The five-fathom line is . . . ," Lewrie said, picking up brass dividers, then aligning them on the distance scale, ". . . half a mile offshore. *Well* within gun-range! Ah hah! Let's try it."

He went back out into the fresher air of the quarterdeck, had a squint aloft at the set of the sails and the wind direction which streamed the commissioning pendant.

"We will alter course, Mister Elmes," he said to the Third Lieutenant, who stood the watch. "We will close the coast, reducing sail as we do so, to within half a mile." To Lt. Elmes's puzzlement he added, "There's a French brigade on the coast road, and I intend t'give 'em a big, noisy greetin'."

"Aye aye, sir!" Elmes perked up with glee. "Bosun Terrell, pipe hands to stations to alter course, and reduce sail!"

"Pass word for the Sailing Master," Lewrie ordered.

This'll give Mister Yelland the "squirts," Lewrie thought.

The door to the Sailing Master's sea cabin on the larboard side of the quarterdeck squeaked open and Mr. Yelland stepped out, rumpled and sleepy-eyed from a nap. "Something up, sir?"

"I'll send for strong coffee for you, Mister Yelland," Lewrie offered. "We're goin' *very* close ashore, and we've need of all your expertise."

"Ehm . . . aye, sir!" Yelland said with a grunt of surprise, then winced with dread, scrubbing sleep from his eyes.

High Summer had drummed upon Southern Spain, browning it and drying it out. The forests looked dusted, and only the growing crops were still green. If there had been a paved Roman road along the coast, it had long ago been ripped up for houses, so the road was dry, packed earth. As HMS *Sapphire* slowly ghosted shoreward under tops'ls, jibs, and spanker, with her courses brailed up, the dust plume created by the demi-brigade on the march was visible even from the bulwarks. From the poop deck, Lewrie could begin to make out details with his telescope. There were a few mounted riders, which he took for officers and aides. At the rear, making higher and longer-lasting clouds of dust, he could espy several pieces of artillery, and behind them were many supply waggons, some canvas-covered, and some odd two-wheeled carts with wheels taller than a man. He assumed those had been taken from the Spanish and put to use to supplement French equipment. They were painted in gay, bold colours compared to the French waggons.

"Six fathom! Six fathom t'this line!" a leadsman shouted.

"We should be coming onto the five-fathom line soon, sir," Mr. Yelland said, taking off his hat and mopping his face with a calico handkerchief. "Warm today."

"And soon t'get warmer," Lewrie promised. "Assumin' we don't touch the bottom."

"Starboard guns are at Quarters, sir," Lt. Westcott reported. "Think there's a need to rig anti-boarding nets?" he joshed.

"Only when pigs, and Frenchmen, can fly, sir," Lewrie hooted back. He raised his telescope again. He could make out the infantry, not marching but shambling along and scuffing the road, raising more dust. Blue uniforms on the bulk of them, with white, gold, green, or red sleeve markings and epaulets. Their muskets were slung any-old-how, by the hip, over the shoulder, or laid upon the back of their necks with their arms up-raised to hold them like a farmer's rake.

He'd seen that before, recalling an ambush he made on the Côte Sauvage when blockading the Gironde River, and how the poor French soldiers about to die had shambled along, joshing and sharing tobacco, before his watering party opened fire. It had been a complete surprise for them then, and he hoped that *Sapphire*'s guns would be an even greater one today.

"Five fathom! Five fathom t'this line!" the leadsman called.

"Alter course to parallel the coast," Lewrie ordered. "Stay in five fathoms." The head of the long French column lay about one point off the starboard bows. "Mister Deacon? Enlighten me. How fast can infantry march?"

Deacon had been on the quarterdeck under the overhang of the poop deck, near the doors to Lewrie's cabins. He poked out in sight and ascended the starboard ladderway to join him.

"March, sir?" Deacon said. "If those people yonder were really marching, they *might* do two or three miles an hour. Allowed to route-step as they are, maybe only two miles an hour, or a bit less. Hmm, that makes me wonder if they even *know* about the arms delivery. Did they know, they'd be going a lot faster. Major Azcárte may be safe as houses, after all. Is that smoke yonder, from Almuñécar? What *have* the French been up to?"

"Same as Bayazit the Thunderer," Lewrie speculated. "A Turk general. The Turks marched all round Greece and the Balkans on a regular basis, massacring and burning, just t'keep the Greeks and Serbs fearful. Maybe yon Frogs've been up to some bad mischief, and deserve what they're about to get."

He raised his telescope again, taking in how steep and close to the coast road the foothills were along this stretch. Once he'd opened fire, there would be nowhere to run but back to Almuñécar, or on East for Salobreña. He looked aloft, pleased with the wind's direction, and estimated that the head of the column was now two points off the starboard bows. "Cast of the log!" he called aft, and a minute later, Midshipman Carey reported that the ship was making a slow, sedate five knots.

"Five fathom! Five fathom t'this line!"

"Mister Westcott, the gun crews may load," Lewrie snapped in rising excitement. "Double-shot with grape. The lower deck will open, first, followed by the upper deck, then the weather deck six-pounders. Keep the ports shut 'til we're ready t'run out."

"Aye, sir," Westcott replied. "By God, this will be fun!"

Lewrie looked down at the quarterdeck to see Major Hughes come out of his cabins, yawning and stretching his arms.

"Sorry 'bout that, Captain Lewrie," he said, looking up. "Had another glass of wine, and nodded off for a bit. What's acting?"

"We're about to kiss a bunch of Frogs, Major Hughes," Lewrie told him, jerking an arm to point shoreward. He liked what he saw; the head of the French column and the mounted officers were just at the bend of the road where the foothills shouldered it out closer to the sea, and they now lay five points off the starboard bows, coming slowly abeam, where the ship's guns in their narrow ports could aim in broadside. Another minute or two more and the column would be only half a mile away.

"Someone see Bisquit below," Lewrie asked. "Mister Carey?"

"Aye, sir," the lad replied, sounding disappointed to miss the opening broadside.

"Hurry back," Lewrie bade him as the Midshipman took hold of the dog's collar and led him down to the orlop.

"Half a mile's range, I make it, sir," Mr. Yelland said after taking a sight with his sextant and some scribbling on a slate with a stub of chalk.

"And just about beam-on," Lewrie agreed. "Mister Westcott, open the gun-ports and run out! Pass word for them to aim well."

"Aye, sir!" Lt. Westcott said, then bellowed orders and sent Midshipmen scampering down to pass the word. Word came back, shouts of "Ready!"

In Lewrie's ocular, he could see French soldiers looking back at *Sapphire,* mostly curious and unaware, so far; sweaty, dusty faces, mustachios and beards, heads turning to look seaward, then back, to speculate with their mates, as *Sapphire* rumbled and screeched as the guns were run out.

"Mon Dieu, merde alors, mort de ma vie—" Lewrie tittered with mockery of imagined French expressions of sudden alarm.

"Lower deck, by broadside . . . *fire!"* Westcott roared.

The discharge of all eleven 24-pounders shoved *Sapphire* a foot or two to larboard, and made her feel as if she squatted in the sea. A massive cloud of spent powder smoke jutted shoreward, spiked with reddish-amber jets of flame and swirling wee embers of serge cartridge bag remnants.

"Let the smoke clear a little!" Lewrie called out.

"Now, sir? I can see the shore again," Westcott urged.

"Now, sir. Serve 'em another," Lewrie agreed.

"Upper deck, by broadside . . . *fire!"*

Mr. Deacon had a short pocket telescope of his own to one eye and was gloating. "I can see horses and riders down, the head of the first battalion's colour party down . . . Damn the smoke!"

"A glass, somebody!" Hughes demanded. "The bloody Dons stole mine!"

"Smoke's clearing, sir!" Westcott pointed out.

"Fire away, Mister Westcott!" Lewrie told him.

"Weather deck guns, by broadside . . . *fire!*" and the 6-pounders crashed out, their discharges lighter and shriller than the others. Fewer in number, and their smoke dispersed quicker, giving everyone on deck a good view of what they had wrought, and it was devastation.

"*Goddamned* good shooting!" Lewrie cried. "Have we the best gunners in the Fleet, or not? Pour it on, Mister Westcott, *skin* the bastards!"

The leading regiment in the long, snaking column had sported a few flags, the Tricolour national emblem topped by a large silver bird of some kind, and company flags used as rally points. There was no sign of them, now, except for a few of the lesser ensigns being rushed back West. French soldiers were simply mown down in windrows and heaps of dead and broken wounded, and the rest were fleeing.

"Hah!" Lewrie laughed, turning to Deacon. "How many miles per hour can French regiments *run*, Mister Deacon?"

"Lower gun-deck, by broadside . . . *fire!*"

The massive 24-pounders belched smoke and fire, flinging solid shot and clouds of plum-sized grapeshot right into the heart of the fleeing mass of soldiers, scything down dozens more. The second regiment in line was engulfed by the frantic stampede, bringing it to a panicky halt.

"Upper-deck guns, by broadside . . . fire!"

That avalanche of iron struck all along the length of that seething mass of soldiery, and, when the smoke cleared, all three of the French regiments were in flight back to Almuñécar, over-running the artillery pieces and ammunition caissons, the panic making the horse teams rear and scream.

"Six-pounders, by broadside . . . fire!" Lt. Westcott screeched, and dozens of Frenchmen were tossed aside like lead toys. There were some cleverer soldiers who abandoned their packs, hangers, cartridge pouches, and muskets and were scrambling frantically up the hills that forced the coast road so close to the sea, sure that shipboard guns could not elevate that high. The rest were running, stumbling, shoving slower compatriots out of their way, trampling over the fallen in their haste to find some safety, and leaving wounded friends to their own devices.

"Do my eyes deceive me?" Major Hughes shouted, pointing with one arm as he held a borrowed telescope to his eye. "They're un-limbering their artillery, the damned fools!"

"Brave fellows," Lt. Westcott commented, his voice raspy from shouting orders.

"Damned idiots!" Mr. Deacon spat.

"What might they have, Mister Deacon?" Lewrie asked. "You're my expert on military matters."

"I'd think that they have six or eight twelve-pounders, Napoleon's favourites," Deacon surmised, "and at least a pair of howitzers."

"No bursting shot? No shrapnel 'specials'?" Lewrie pressed.

"The latest intelligence in our possession says not," Deacon assured him.

"Lower-deck guns, by broadside . . . fire!" Westcott yelled, and the horrid scene was blotted out by a thick fog of powder smoke. As it cleared, Lewrie could see fresh *heaps* of bodies, round which the lucky survivors fled on.

"Pass word below to target the French artillery, Mister Westcott," Lewrie ordered. "We can't allow them a single point of pride."

"Aye, sir. Mister Fywell, pass word to the gunners to target the French guns," Westcott said, sending the Midshipman dashing off.

"God, it's wondrous, sir!" Midshipman Carey, who had taken the dog to the orlop, marvelled. "Horrible, but wondrous all at the same time."

"Soldiers just can't fathom a ship's firepower," Lewrie took time to tell him. "Our twenty-four-pounders are the equivalent of an army's entire siege train, only used to knock down fortress walls. They can't imagine them turned on *them*! Why, one of Napoleon's *armies* fields only *half* our number of barrels."

"Ooh, look at the pretty ship," Deacon quipped, "so harmless, and— *ack!*"

"How's Bisquit?" Lewrie asked.

"Curled up and shivering in Pettus's lap, sir," Carey replied. "And Mister Tanner's much the same, between three kegs of salt-meat."

Tanner, the Ship's Cook, a veteran Greenwich Pensioner with a leg missing, had no role at Quarters, and was allowed to hide below.

"Shivering?" Lewrie scoffed.

"It's hard to say which whines louder, sir," Carey said with an impish grin.

"Upper gun-deck, by broadside . . . fire!"

The French guns had been detached from their limbers and caissons, the horse teams had been led behind, and men were hastily ramming bagged powder and shot down the muzzles. Officers and gun-captains were bending over their crude sights, adjusting the elevation screws, and gunners were lifting the trails of the carriages to adjust their traverses. They were just about to step back and apply their burning linstocks to the touch holes when *Sapphire*'s eleven 12-pounders lit off at the top of the up-roll, when the ship poised steadiest. When the smoke thinned and wafted alee, half the battery was wrecked, the barrels knocked off their carriages, wheels smashed and carriages lying at odd angles. Several team horses were down, and many of the others were screaming, kicking, and dashing off among the panicked French soldiers who had been streaming West behind the guns.

"Six-pounders, by broadside . . . fire!"

That finished the horrid work, slaying dazed gunners, dis-mounting or disabling the rest. A lucky hit on a powder caisson caused a great explosion and a massive yellow-white blossom of powder smoke. Burning embers of the waggon landed on the others, setting them on fire, and the gun battery's powder supply and all its limbers and caissons were destroyed. Even if the gun barrels could be salvaged and carted away later, the French would have to force some Spanish arsenal and its unwilling artificers to build new ones before those guns could be used again.

"Take on the supply train, Mister Westcott," Lewrie ordered. "Let's make it a clean sweep. Let 'em starve."

"Aye, sir," Lt. Westcott happily agreed. He and Lewrie shared a look, and both men's faces were wolfish with success and feverish delight; "gun-drunk."

"Five fathom! Five fathom t'this line!" a leadsman intoned.

"Alter course a mite to starboard," Lewrie said. "I recall that this five-fathom line takes a turn seaward, and a four-fathom line lies ahead. Do you concur, Mister Yelland?"

"That should be about two cables afore the bows, sir," Yelland told him. "Aye, it's a good time to edge seaward."

"See to it, if ye please," Lewrie bade. "I will tend to the smashing. Shift aim to the waggons, Mister Westcott."

"Pass word below to take on the waggons, Mister Fywell," the First Officer ordered, and Midshipman Fywell, who had barely returned from his last task, knuckled the brim of his hat and dashed off, with nary a chance to witness or savour their destruction. Carey, who was still on the quarterdeck, shot him a smug look.

"Lower gun-deck, by broadside . . . fire!"

The carters and waggoners had long fled their charges as the three shat-tered regiments swarmed round them in their haste, some of the fleeing soldiers cut reins and harnesses to try to ride to safety, but most of the draught horses were also panicked, and not broken to the saddle, or the weight of a rider, and would have none of it. The colourful, high-wheeled Spanish carts sat cocked down on their tongues, and the French army wag-gons sat at all angles as their waggoners had tried to turn round or force a way through the fleeing throngs before joining the rout.

"Hah! Ah hah!" Major Hughes was shouting at the sight of the wag-gons or carts being smashed to kindling, of tents, blankets, spare boots, and cook pots being hurled into the air. Subsequent broadsides caused am-munition waggons to explode and burn, scattering burning bits among the whole close-packed train. "That's the way! Oh, capital, look at that! Whoo! Burn, you devils!"

"Damn my eyes," Lewrie groaned. "I've made him happy!"

"Well, that won't last, will it, sir?" Deacon cagily said.

At last, *Sapphire* sailed closer to the seaport town of Almuñécar and ran out of targets. The French were surely taking refuge in the houses fur-thest from the shore, huddling in the town square, but the risk of killing Spaniards precluded.

"Cease fire, Mister Westcott," Lewrie called down to the quarterdeck. "Alter course three points to larboard, and secure from Quarters. Fun's over."

"Look there, sir!" Midshipman Carey yelped, leaping and pointing shoreward.

The citizens of little Almuñécar had gathered along the quays and docks, and even with angry French soldiers a street or two behind them, were daring to wave caps, hats, bonnets, dish towels, and one Spanish flag in celebration! The daring demonstration didn't last long, and most of them dashed or slunk away feigning innocence as a few French soldiers appeared in the side streets.

"Unfortunately, they'll pay for that, in lives and torture," Mr. Deacon sadly concluded. "The French will lash out, and there will be Hell to pay."

"Aye," Lewrie agreed with a grim nod.

"Well, sir!" Lt. Westcott said, beaming his harsh smile. "We might em-ulate that Dutch Admiral, De Ruyter, and sail into Gibraltar with a broom lashed to the main mast truck. A clean sweep, indeed."

"That's a damned good idea, Mister Westcott, and I thank you for it,"

Lewrie said with a laugh. "Inform the Purser, Mister Cadrick, that the second rum issue of the day will be 'Splice the Mainbrace.'"

"Aye, sir!"

There had been no need to clear the ship for action, so the great-cabins were as Lewrie had left them. Pettus and Jessop were back from sheltering on the orlop, and so were Chalky and Bisquit. The dog was still shivering and whining his terror of loud noises, eager for stroking and petting from anyone who'd pay him attention. Chalky ran to Lewrie as soon as he sat down on the settee, leapt into his lap and clung to his coat, making fussing noises and butting his head on Lewrie's chin. Bisquit quit his rapid circling of the cabins and came to the settee, too, hopping up on it and laying his paws and head in Lewrie's lap, whining for assurance.

"Sometimes I wonder if it would have been kinder t'leave him on my father's farm," Lewrie said, stroking both creatures 'til their distresses had ceased. Chalky began to purr, rattling away, and the dog closed his eyes and slunk the front half of his body onto Lewrie's lap and thighs. His bushy tail began to flit, lazily.

"Cap'm's Cook, SAH!" a Marine sentry announced in the usual loud fashion.

"Enter," Lewrie responded, remaining seated.

Yeovill came in, and Bisquit hopped down and went to him for pets, and a lot of snuffling; Yeovill smelled like good food and was liberal with treats.

"Scrounger," Lewrie accused the dog.

"I was wondering, sir, if you had plans to dine your officers in tonight, in celebration," Yeovill posed.

"Aye, I thought I might," Lewrie told him. "Major Hughes will also be dining here. He's a roast beef and potatoes sort, but . . . I wonder. What can you serve that *ain't*, Yeovill? Something exotic or foreign."

"Oh, well, sir," Yeovill pondered. "Let me think on it for a bit. I found a receipt at Gibraltar for a French dish, Chicken Marengo . . ."

"Had that in Paris," Lewrie commented. "Good!"

"Onions, tomatoes, eggs . . . though I don't know *what* to replace the crayfish with," Yeovill maundered on. "Salt-fish? Hmm. A berry trifle for sweets, and we've lashings of fresh green beans. Potatoes with cheese and bacon . . ."

"*Couscous*, with cheese sauce," Lewrie suggested, instead.

"With some chicken gravy to moisten it, yes, sir," Yeovill said with a nod. "Chick peas, turned to *hummus*, with stale bread for dipping. And, we've more rabbits than God."

Long ago, Lewrie had served under a Commodore who'd insisted that rabbits and quail made a topping-fine alternative to salt-meat, and he had emulated him. They bred quick, too.

"Sounds good, Yeovill," Lewrie praised. "I'm certain you will produce a triumph, you always do."

"Thank you for saying so, sir," Yeovill replied, smiling with delight. "Exotic and foreign, hey? Then that's what it will be."

"Good man," Lewrie said.

"Cool tea, sir?" Pettus offered, and Lewrie was more than amenable to that, too.

I can't wait t'see Hughes's ruddy face when he gets served that! Lewrie thought. He'd seen how much Hughes disliked any foreign "kick-shaws," and he fully intended to make him as uncomfortable as he could.

CHAPTER TWENTY-TWO

*T*he days on passage back to Gibraltar were a trial for Lewrie, since Major Daniel Hughes was aboard, and most of the time as chatty as a linnet or parrot, underfoot of the crew's work on deck, and an outright pest in the wardroom, where he was lodged in the spare cabin to starboard, right aft. Certainly, he was out of touch with world affairs and eager to hear of Ceuta being evacuated, of Cádiz's fall, of how widespread the Spanish rising had become, but he was full of so *many* questions that the officers when off watch got to entering their flimsily-built cabins to sham sleep just to avoid him. Hughes lurked the quarterdeck and the poop, taking the air, pestering the Midshipmen with his tales of recent battles—in which they'd been active participants and saw them differently—his capture, which became a fierce fight before being overcome the more it was related, and his treatment at Órgiva and Málaga, his release by Spanish patriots who'd taken pity on him—now a story of derring-do and brave escape—and his long ride to Salobreña just chock-full of close pursuit and narrow escapes.

Worst of all, Hughes had the idea that if he'd been allowed Lewrie's great-cabins once, and was dined in several times out of teeth-grinding hospitality, then he could breeze in and plunk down on the settee and order up a glass of something every time he felt a thirst. "The Rhenish, Pettus, there's a good fellow. I'm dry as dust, what?"

The last straw was when Hughes seated himself in Lewrie's wood-and-canvas collapsible deck chair, propped his feet up, and began reading one of Lewrie's racier novels! That had resulted in an altercation with Mr. Deacon that went roughly thus.

"I wouldn't do that, sir," Deacon cautioned. "Like the windward side of the quarterdeck is only for the Captain, so's his chair."

"What?" Hughes had grumped back. "He ain't usin' it at the moment."

"He'll be dis-pleased does he discover you in it, sir," Deacon remonstrated.

"Who are you to tell me, Deacon?" the Major barked. "I'll not be ordered about by a jumped-up *ex-Sergeant*, or a spy's 'catch-fart' minion! Bugger off!" He returned to his novel, fussily.

"I don't know whether to challenge you to a duel . . . *sir* . . . or simply kill you where you sit . . . *sir*!" Deacon replied, bristling up and exuding a palpable air of menace.

"Captain's chair, Major Hughes," Lt. Harcourt, the officer of the watch, snapped, coming to the top of the larboard ladderway to the poop deck. "If you would be so good."

"You hear what this . . . common enlisted man just told me?" Hughes gravelled.

"Didn't hear a thing that passed between you, Major Hughes," Harcourt told him. "This gentleman was doing you a service before Captain Lewrie caught you in his chair, right, Mister Deacon?" Harcourt asked, stressing "Mister" as Deacon's due honourific.

Hughes scowled his dis-pleasure, went red in the face, but got to his feet and slunk off to the wardroom, leaving Deacon seething and Lieutenant Harcourt shaking his head.

"Do *not* kill him while he's still aboard, Mister Deacon, hey?" Harcourt bade him. "If you need a second, I'm offering, however. I'm of a mind to be first in line, myself. God, what a pain he is!"

At last, HMS *Sapphire* dropped anchor and came to rest off the Old Mole of Gibraltar, and with that broom lashed to the main mast truck as Lieutenant Westcott had suggested.

"Might I offer you a lift ashore, Major Hughes?" Lewrie asked, once all the topmen had descended from the yards, after all sail had been brailed up in harbour gaskets.

"Thank you, Captain Lewrie," Hughes replied, stiffly formal. "I would much appreciate it."

"I'd also suppose we're both bound to the Convent to report to General Dalrymple," Lewrie went on, searching for something pleasant to say with the man while Desmond and his boat crew went down the man-ropes and battens to man one of the cutters. "He'll be astounded t'see you, I'd imagine. Back from the dead, all that?"

"I would imagine so as well, sir," Hughes said, "though he's likely filled my old position as his aide, by now."

"Yet, you sounded delighted to return to your regiment and its mess, your fellow officers," Lewrie said.

"Oh, yes, that'll be topping," Hughes agreed.

"Though, you may give up your brevet promotion," Lewrie simply had to say, to get a sly dig in.

"Yes, unfortunately," Hughes said, scowling.

"Met a fellow once, a Lieutenant promoted to Commander and sent home with a prize," Lewrie related, "but, Admiralty didn't confirm his status, and he was stuck ashore, without a ship, and in a year's worth of arrears t'pay Admiralty back the difference in pay."

Hope the Army does the same, ye beef-to-the-heel lummox, he happily thought.

"Your boat is manned and ready, sir," Lt. Elmes announced.

"Very well, Mister Elmes," Lewrie said, going to the lip of the entry-port to take the ritual of departure, doffing his hat to his crew, and the flag. Hughes carefully made his way down the side of the ship and thumped himself down on a thwart in the sternsheets nearby to Lewrie. A leather satchel was lowered down on a line, and a moment later, Mr. Deacon descended, right spryly, to take a seat between Pat Furfy, the larboard stroke-oar, and the starboard oarsman, facing the pair of them.

"Enjoy the voyage, did ye, Mister Deacon?" Lewrie asked him.

"Delightful, Captain Lewrie, thank you," Deacon said, beaming his pleasure, and pointedly ignoring Major Hughes.

"Shove off, bow man," Cox'n Desmond ordered. "Back-water, starboard." He put his tiller hard over. "Poise . . . out oars, larboard. Now, stroke, all together now."

"All in all, the results were most pleasing," Lewrie said to Deacon. "Success for your business, and for mine."

"Mister Mountjoy will be over the moon, sir," Deacon agreed. "He'll pass the news of the destruction of a French demi-brigade to London, and all the newspapers will pick it up. One *might* say that British arms won their first victory over France in Spain. A sign of things to come."

"Hope they spell my name right," Lewrie joshed.

"I'm of a mind to write Horse Guards of my adventures as well," Major Hughes piped up, intrigued by the possibility of his account being published, of being "mentioned in despatches" and "Gazetted."

"Your observations on the state of the Spanish army, sir?" Lewrie asked.

"A churlish lot," Hughes barked in sour amusement. "The senior officers are clueless peacocks in grand uniforms, the junior officers are so loutish and lower class that the fine ladies of Málaga despise them, and their soldiers, rank and file, even in barracks, are slovenly sheep. Badly shod, if shod at all, most in sandals, I ask you! I believe if they have arms, they're short of powder, if well-armed, they're short of rations. Their army is a sad joke. They'll stand no chance against the French, none at all. It'll take a British army in Spain to beat the French."

"Headed for the Convent, first, sir?" Deacon asked Lewrie.

"Aye, for a while, if Dalrymple has time for me. If not, I'll go have dinner and leave my written reports," Lewrie replied.

"Dalrymple, then my quarters," Hughes stated, though no one had really asked him. "Un-pack my stored chests, settle back in, and dine *decent*, for once."

"Ye don't think your fellow officers might've auctioned your goods off, do ye?" Lewrie teased. "I've heard it done."

"They would not dare," Hughes growled. "It's not as if I'm *dead*!"

"In your long absence, sir," Deacon said, addressing Hughes for the first time since their *contretemps* aboard ship, "might your Colonel have requested your replacement from England?" Deacon said it with a sobre face, but Lewrie had to bite his lip to keep from guffawing. "Can't let a company be led by a subaltern, not for long."

"Well, if one's promoted to Brevet Captain . . . ," Lewrie mused, "but, I s'pose he can always revert back to bein' a subaltern."

"If they have promoted an officer to my old place, he'll have to give it back, as soon as dammit," Hughes asserted, growing testy with the trend the conversation was taking.

I'd wager they shoved you at Dalrymple as an aide 'cause they couldn't bloody stand ye, Lewrie thought with evil delight.

"Slow stroke," Cox'n Desmond ordered as the cutter approached the landing stage below the stone quays. "Ready with yer gaff, Deavers. Toss oars, all. Ehm, yair sittin' on th' aft dock loine, sor," he said to Hughes. "Ya moind passin' th' coil t'me, Yer Honour, sor?"

Oh God, now Desmond's *mocking him, layin' the "brogue" on as thick as treacle,* Lewrie thought, feeling like sniggering.

Emulating naval protocol, Mr. Deacon was first out of the boat with his satchel, followed by Hughes, after Lewrie waved him to start. Lewrie exited last, and they all strolled up the wooden ramp to the top of the quays.

Oh, Christ! Lewrie thought; *The cat's outa the bag!*

For not only was an eager Thomas Mountjoy on the quay to greet them, but so was Maddalena Covilhā, dressed in a summery pale blue sheath dress, with a gay bonnet on her head, and a parasol twirling in her hands.

"Why, Maddalena!" Hughes exclaimed, holding out his arms as if she'd come for him. "M'dear! I'm back!"

Maddalena coyly danced right past him with barely a glance in his direction, went straight to Lewrie to plant a kiss on his cheek, and put her arms round him!

"You!" Hughes accused. "You?"

"*Sim,* him," Maddalena said to Hughes with an impish expression.

"But . . . !" Hughes gargled.

"Me," Lewrie told him.

"You are back, at last, *meu querido,*" she cooed to Lewrie.

"It's grand t'see you, *minha doce,*" Lewrie cooed right back.

"Well, just goddammit," Hughes growled, astounded, then stomped his way off.

Poor bastard, Lewrie gleefully thought; *There's no good news for him, or welcome, either! About what he deserves!*

BOOK THREE

"Let there be light!" said God, and there was light!
"Let there be blood!" says man, and there's a sea!
                    –LORD BYRON (1788-1824),
                  DON JUAN

CHAPTER TWENTY-THREE

L ieutenant-General Sir Hew Dalrymple was in a very good humour when Lewrie entered his offices in the Convent. He was standing at his large map of Iberia, hands in the small of his back, rocking on the balls of his booted feet, with a satisfied smile on his face.

"Aha, Sir Alan! Relished your report!" Sir Hew declared. "Positively relished it! A half-brigade slaughtered, what?"

"Well, I can't claim an outright *slaughter*, Sir Hew," Lewrie countered. "It was closer to a decimation, with only ten percent or so killed or wounded. Losing their artillery and baggage train was the worst blow."

"And their pride and confidence," Dalrymple added. "The *esprit de corps* of a unit matters as much as weaponry. A very good show, all in all, along with the delivery of arms to the *junta* in Granada. Do sit, sir. Wine, or tea?"

"Tea, sir," Lewrie replied, easing into a comfortable leather chair in front of Dalrymple's desk as Dalrymple rang a china bell to summon an aide.

"Lord, the Spanish," Dalrymple said, shaking his head as he sat behind his desk. "Rival *juntas* are springing up all across Spain, which is welcome. But, just because Seville was the first does not mean they will all look to Seville as the sole authority. Each one swears they will raise their own army, but co-operation among them, well . . . that will take some doing, I'm afraid. Without a king, and a united court, *and* a definite chain of command over all the armies, the Spanish stand little chance against the French in the field. It will still take a British army to lead the way, and coax our allies into working together. A senior British general with the nicest of diplomatic skills."

You, for one, Lewrie cynically thought; *what the man's always wanted.*

"At least our Andalusians can work together," Dalrymple went on, rubbing his hands and smiling again. "We've just heard that the forces of General Castaños, and the forces assembled round Granada, have met and defeated a French army under a General Dupont near a town called Bailén. It took them six days of fighting, but, Castaños took the surrender of over seventeen thousand French. Bonaparte has not lost that many prisoners at one go since the army he abandoned in Egypt surrendered to us in 1801! Isn't that grand, sir?"

"This is confirmed, sir, not a wild rumour?" Lewrie charily asked. "You know foreigners exagger—"

"Confirmed," Dalrymple insisted, still beaming. "The arms you delivered played a part in it, and smashing that French column most-like freed up Spanish re-enforcements who would have been pinned down guarding against a thrust from Málaga, so you may take great satisfaction in your recent sally, Sir Alan."

"Oh, I see, sir," Lewrie replied, wondering if Dalrymple made note of his contribution in his report to London; he could use some good credit with Admiralty.

A smartly-uniformed Private, most-likely Dalrymple's personal batman, entered with a tray and tea set, pouring for both and offering sugar, lemon, or cream as stiffly as a Grenadier Guard on "sentry-go" at St. James's Palace. Once done, he jerked to Attention, stamped boots, saluted, turned about, and marched out, closing the double doors softly.

"Sir Brent Spencer's force moved inland to support Castaños," Dalrymple casually related, legs crossed and stirring his tea, "not actually *with* the Spanish, setting up a depot at Xeres."

Lewrie looked at the large map but could not find it.

"Now that Dupont has been defeated, and Seville, Cádiz, Granada, and Córdoba are free of French occupation, I have ordered him to get back to the coast at Puerto de Santa María, and sail North to unite with Sir Arthur Wellesley's army. I wish you to go to Cádiz Bay and provide escort for his transports 'til Admiral Cotton's squadron can take over the duty."

"Of course, Sir Hew," Lewrie dutifully answered, even though the idea of more convoy-work almost made him gag. "Where will they be going?"

"Wellesley intended to land at Corunna in Northwest Spain, but he learned that the French had just defeated a Spanish army in the near vicinity, and the Galician *junta* was fearful of drawing too much attention to themselves," Dalrymple told him. He took a sip of his tea, nodded with pleasure at its taste, but set cup and saucer aside to go to his map. "Vigo is also out, but Admiral Cotton chose Mondego Bay, right here," he said, tapping the map, "just by Figueira da Foz. There is a French garrison in the fortress at Coimbra within an easy march to Mondego Bay, but it is thought to be too weak to hold the fort *and* intervene with the landings, Spencer has nigh five thousand men, Wellesley has nine thousand five hundred, and there are units of the Portuguese army still free and available. That should make a decent force to take on Marshal Junot's army."

"That's about an hundred miles North of Lisbon, is it, sir?" Lewrie asked, abandoning his own tea to go to the map.

"Yes, thereabouts," Dalrymple agreed, all his attention on the map, his head turning back and forth as if following the marches of large armies on a long campaign.

Winnin' a war in his head, Lewrie sourly thought.

"Junot has fifty thousand, though," Lewrie commented.

"Yes, but he can't hold the entire country," Dalrymple objected. "It's been determined that he's concentrated at the frontier fortresses of Almeida and Elvas, that small garrison at Coimbra, and the bulk of his force is at Lisbon, below a line 'twixt Abrantes and Peniche. A Portuguese *junta* is centered at Oporto, and *their* partisan irregulars and their regular army have been savaging a force under a General Loison sent into the interior, who has pulled back closer to the main French army round Lisbon to lick his wounds. It's good odds that Wellesley will prevail, though he *may* find that the French are more dangerous than hordes of Hindoos."

"How soon must I sail, sir?" Lewrie asked.

"As soon as possible, Sir Alan," Dalrymple told him.

"Very well, sir," Lewrie replied with a nod, "but, I *would* like t'finish my tea," he japed.

"What?" Dalrymple gawped, scowling at him for a second before catching on. "Aha, I forget that you are possessed of a merry wit, sir!"

"I get it from my Midshipmen, sir," Lewrie explained tongue-in-cheek. "They're always an impish lot."

⚓

"Pass word for the First Officer," Lewrie told a Midshipman of the Harbour Watch as soon as he'd taken the salute to welcome him back aboard HMS *Sapphire*. "I'll be aft. Best summon Mister Yelland, too."

Men on deck perked their ears up and began to speculate, for a summons like that always meant a quick return to sea. *Sapphire*'s crew had been looking forward to a run ashore by watches, which would mean at least two days in port, with firewood, water, shot, and powder, and fresh provisions taken aboard which might mean a third day of rest and even a Make and Mend half-day of idleness to nap, repair their clothing, read, or write letters home.

No helpin' it, Lewrie thought as he hung his hat on a peg on an overhead deck beam; *I'm bein' deprived the same as them. One supper with Maddalena tonight, and we're off, dammit to Hell.*

"First Orf'cer t'see th' Cap'm, SAH!" his Marine sentry loudly announced.

"Enter!"

"Bad news, I take it, sir?" Lt. Geoffrey Westcott said with a gloomy expression as soon as he entered the great-cabins.

"Aye, Geoffrey. Take a pew," Lewrie told him.

A moment later, and Mr. Yelland was announced and given leave to come in.

"Sailing, are we, sir?" Yelland asked, looking as glum as a hanged spaniel. Whatever that worthy had lined up ashore did not bear imagining, but what pleasure he was now denied hurt him sore.

"Wellesley is to land at Mondego Bay, in Portugal, and we're to see Spencer's little army there t'join him, Mister Yelland. Have you charts of the place?" Lewrie asked.

"Aye, sir, though I'll have to dig them out," Yelland replied. "If you will excuse me for a moment?"

"Of course, Mister Yelland," Lewrie said. Once the Sailing Master had departed, Lewrie pulled an apologetic face for Westcott. "Sorry about this rush, but there's no helping it. How ready is the ship for sea?"

"We've the firewood and water, we've replaced what little we consumed by way of victuals," Westcott told him, "but replacement shot and cartridge bags are wanting, and the Purser has yet to lay hands on livestock, or fruit. The wardroom's short of wine and brandy, and all my small-clothes need washing, and my under-drawers itch me, sir. Other than that, we could get under way by dawn tomorrow."

"Is she *that* fetching?" Lewrie teased, sure that Westcott's grumbling was over his girl ashore; no matter where they went, one could count on Westcott finding himself some female comfort.

"Aye, she is," Westcott said with a chuckle and one of his brief, harsh grins. "A fair-haired girl from Genoa. Can't make out damn-all what she's saying half the time, but what does that matter? Italian's not my strong suit."

"But young women are," Lewrie said, grinning as well.

"Well, one has to be good at *something*!" Westcott laughed.

"Sailin' Master t'see th' Cap'm—," the Marine bellowed.

"Aye, enter!" Lewrie said with impatience, and Yelland bustled in with several rolled-up charts in his hands, and they all gathered round as Yelland spread them out on the dining table.

"Figueira da Foz, here, sir," Yelland said, "and Mondego Bay here. It looks to be a good, long beach, running from the city to the Nor'west to Cape Mondego. Better there than a bit North, sir, along the, ah . . . Dunas de . . . Qui-ai-os, however the Hell you say it. God, foreign tongues! No roads shown there, sir. If the army artillery and waggons land there, they'd bog down."

"And once there, they're to march all this way to Lisbon?" Lt. Westcott posed. "Best of luck to them."

"That's the intention," Lewrie said, summarising the locations of French forces in Portugal, and remembering that Dalrymple had put a pin in his grand map at Setúbal, on the other side of the peninsula below Lisbon and the Tagus River, where French Marshal Junot had placed more of his invasion force. "I'm also told that there's some French warships at Lisbon, and there's speculation that eight or so Russian ships are there, and have been taken over, or are now allied with the French."

"Damme, didn't Russia issue *some* sort of declaration of war against us, already?" Mr. Yelland asked, sounding exasperated.

"If they did, they've not taken any hostile action against us, yet," Lewrie told him. "Just closed their ports to our merchantmen as part of Napoleon's Berlin Decree. If those ships *do* hear about Wellesley's coming, or Spencer moving t'join him, they *might* sortie, so we'd best keep a keen lookout."

"How many other ships are available for the escort, sir?" Lt. Westcott asked.

"Dalrymple's writing to the Captains of the ships in harbour to assemble an escort," Lewrie said. "There's *Newcastle* seventy-four, and a brace of frigates. *Newcastle*'s Captain's most-like senior to me, so we're just along for the voyage . . . and I won't have t'think a lot. 'Yes, sir, no, sir, two bags full.'"

"The coast of Portugal offers quite a few places where the soldiers can be extracted, should the French force them to," Yelland speculated, leaning closer over his chart.

"Once at Mondego Bay, we'll meet up with Admiral Sir Charles Cotton's squadron," Lewrie informed them, "and we'll be as safe as houses. Puerto de Santa María to Mondego Bay? Five-hundred-odd sea miles?"

"About that, sir, about that," Yelland agreed, though pulling a face, "as the crow flies. Might take a week, depending on the direction of the wind, and all. Fifty miles right up to windward can turn out to be two hundred in tacking. Hmm, I believe I must go ashore for a bit, sir. It might be a good idea to look for a *map* of Portugal, not just a sea chart. It might be good to know what's beyond the first line of hills and mountains that a chart shows us."

"Good idea," Lewrie agreed. "Know where the army's going."

"You just want *ashore*," Westcott teased.

"Christ, who doesn't, Mister Westcott?" Yelland exclaimed. "I have your permission, sir?"

"Aye, go and fetch us some maps," Lewrie allowed, "something t'fill in the white voids two miles inland."

Yelland rolled up his charts and departed, looking too cheerful for words, while Westcott scowled at his back.

"Thank God," Westcott said, waving a hand under his nose. "He is *riper* than usual. Does he *ever* bathe or change clothes?"

"A good navigator, though," Lewrie said. "He must be borne."

They heard a Midshipman hailing an approaching boat.

"Lord, what now?" Lewrie asked, fetching his hat off the peg, preparing to go back on deck to see what it was about.

"Orders for your Captain!" a voice shrilled from the boat.

Lewrie heaved a sigh and went out to the quarterdeck, whiling the wait away by petting the ship's dog, Bisquit, who was always up for attention and affection. A Midshipman came to the deck from the boat and handed a sealed letter over to Midshipman Harvey, with an exchange of stiff, doffed-hat salutes, and the stranger was back over the side. Harvey brought the letter to Lewrie, bowing as he uselessly announced, "Letter for you, sir."

"Thankee," Lewrie replied as he tore it open to read it. "Mine arse on a band-box!" he exclaimed a moment later. "Jemmy Shirke?"

He hadn't seen or heard a thing about his former mess-mate in ages, and perhaps that was a good thing, for when they'd been Midshipmen together in the old HMS *Ariadne* in 1780, Jemmy Shirke had been a pain, a surly, teasing, and practical-joking lout who'd tormented Lewrie with one prank after another, playing "scaly-fish" to "the newly." Shirke had been a guest when Lewrie was thrown a "wetting down" party to celebrate his Lieutenancy on Antigua, which Keith Ashburn had turned into an noisy orgy worthy of the old Hell-Fire Club, which had been raided by the other patrons of the Old Lamb in Falmouth Harbour, and broken up early.

Last I saw o' Jemmy, he had his head 'tween some whore's teats, and goin' "brr," Lewrie thought, with only a modicum of fondness; *How the Devil did he ever make "Post"?*

However it had happened, Jemmy Shirke advanced through the Lists, and was now senior to Lewrie, and as Senior Officer Present, he would command the escort to the convoy bearing General Spencer and his troops to Mondego Bay. The letter was addressed to the Captain of the *Sapphire*, not by name, inviting him to dine aboard with the captains of the two frigates; it was not a peremptory Captain Repair On Board.

Hmm, wonder which of us'll be the more surprised, Lewrie wondered.

CHAPTER TWENTY-FOUR

*L*ewrie?" Captain James Shirke exclaimed as he greeted him by the entry-port of HMS *Newcastle,* his Third Rate 74. A second's astonishment was followed by a crafty look. "Come up in the world, ain't you. My *Steel's* is out-of-date, else I'd've known who it is I'm feeding. My Lord, a knight-hood? When did that happen?"

Just to make sure that Shirke didn't pick up where he'd left off in the early days, Lewrie had tricked himself out in full regalia.

"About four years ago," Lewrie told him. "The King threw in a Bar-onetcy, to boot. Must've been he was havin' a bad day. I'll tell ye about it over supper. Good t'see ye again, Jemmy, and congratulations to your-self. When *did* ye make 'Post'?"

"Late Ninety-Six," Shirke said, turning wary. "You?"

"Spring of Ninety-Seven," Lewrie said, and Shirke looked relieved. "How *did* that party end, by the way? I slipped out with my wench, through a side door."

"Hah!" Shirke let out a bark of humour. "They turfed us all out in our small-clothes, the girls half-nude, and it was the Hue and Cry all the way back to the piers!"

Jemmy Shirke had put on a stone or two, and his smug face had thick-ened a bit, yet, for age, he appeared about the same as he had in the old days; a prominent forehead, a slightly pouted mouth, and a pair of clever brown eyes.

"Boat ahoy!" one of *Newcastle*'s Mids called to another approaching gig.

"Aye aye!" came the shout, signifying the arrival of another Post-Captain.

"That'll be the Captains of *Tiger* and *Assurance*," Shirke said. "Our frigates. Hayman, and Fillebrowne."

"*William* Fillebrowne?" Lewrie asked, startled.

"I think he is, aye," Shirke told him. "Know him?"

"We've . . . met," Lewrie said through gritted teeth.

That arrogant bastard! Lewrie thought.

A moment later and there he was at the lip of the entry-port, taking the welcoming honours and doffing his fore-and-aft bicorne to the flag and officers. Fillebrowne came from great wealth, and was always elegantly tailored and expensively uniformed, the second or third son of immensely rich people. When Lewrie had met him at Elba in the '90s, he almost took a liking to him in the first minutes, but Fillebrowne had revealed himself a tad too much, and Lewrie happily loathed him a minute after.

He'd had HMS *Jester*, Fillebrowne had had HMS *Myrmidon*, in Thom Charlton's small squadron sent to the Adriatic to counter the French and disrupt their trade in oak for ship-building. Fillebrowne was more interested in using naval service as a chance to amass treasures, artworks, jewelry, and priceless relics from the impoverished French Royalist exiles than in seamanship. His elders had done *their* Grand Tours of the Continent and come home with Greco-Roman riches and grand art, so why could he not, as well?

Idle, flip, sure of his superiority, was Fillebrowne, a top-lofty sneerer, with a mumbling Oxonian accent; a lecher, too, almost as mad for quim as Westcott, but so arrogantly boastful about it.

The worst was Fillebrowne throwing his "acquisition" of Lewrie's former Corsican mistress, Phoebe Aretino, in his face with a leer, and almost daring him to do something about it! In Venice, when the man had found that Sir Malcolm Shockley's younger wife was known to Lewrie, Fillebrowne had gone out of his way to cuckold Sir Malcolm with Lucy, *née* Beauman, a love of his from long ago on Jamaica, to boot!

After taking the salute from the side-party, Fillebrowne took a glance aft, spotted Lewrie, and spread a slow, superior smile upon his phyz.

"Welcome aboard, Captain Fillebrowne," Shirke said. "Allow me to name to you Captain Sir Alan Lewrie, Baronet, an old shipmate of mine. Captain Lewrie, I name to you Captain William Fillebrowne."

"Lewrie," Fillebrowne replied, un-graciously. "Been a while, has it not?"

"Willy," Lewrie purred back. "Aye, it has."

Fillebrowne was not used to people addressing him with the diminuitive of his Christian name, and that threw him off stride, making him clear his throat in sudden pique, and go red in the face.

Another officer came aboard to join them, a Post-Captain of less than three years' seniority, with only the one epaulet on his right shoulder. John Hayman replied properly to the introductions, addressing Lewrie as "Sir Alan." He looked to be a serious young man, but one with an unfortunately smallpox-scarred face.

"Well, sir, shall we go aft?" Shirke said, waving towards his great-cabins. As expected of a larger Third Rate 74, Shirke's cabins were bigger than Lewrie's, and leaned toward the Spartan plain-ness that the Navy approved, though the paint colour, the choice of furnishings, the style of carpeting over the painted black-and-white deck chequer, and the abundance of shiny pewter, polished brass, and fine crystal was quite tasteful, over-all. Shirke had not mentioned if he was married, but Lewrie suspected a woman's touch in the choices, right down to the upholstery, and the bed coverlet.

They were offered seats, and glasses of wine were produced at once.

"Seen Phoebe lately, have you?" Fillebrowne idly enquired with a taunting brow raised.

"'La Contessa Phoebe Aretino was at a *levee* I attended at the Tuileries Palace in Paris during the Peace of Amiens," Lewrie was glad to inform him, refusing to take the bait; that amour was long gone and done with. "She's become the queen of the city's *parfumiers,* and to the Empress Josephine. Still quite a delectable dish."

"What, Paris?" Shirke exclaimed. "What the Devil were you doin' there?"

"Tryin' to swap dead Frog Captains' swords for a hanger that I lost to Napoleon at Toulon," Lewrie told him, leaning back in his chair, quite at ease, and paying Fillebrowne no further mind. He explained how his commandeered French *razée,* converted to a mortar vessel, had been sunk right out from under him by Napoleon's guns, and a lucky hit in the forward mortar well, how he'd made his way ashore with the survivors, and been confronted by Bonaparte himself. "With so many Royalist French in my crew as volunteers, I couldn't just abandon 'em, so I refused t'give my parole, and he rode off with it, just before some Spanish cavalry rescued us. The one Lieutenant Kenyon gave me, remember, Jemmy?"

"Vaguely," Shirke replied. "I *think* you wore it at your shore party to celebrate your Lieutenancy, but that was ages ago. What *did* happen to Kenyon? I recall him from *Ariadne*. An odd sort, he was."

"He perished in a raid on a coastal town in the Gironde, when we took on two forts," Lewrie said, "and aye, he was an odd sort."

A secret "Molly," murdered by his own crew, and the least said of that, the *better,* Lewrie grimly thought. Kenyon's brig-o'-war had been paid off, the crew scattered throughout the Fleet, and the whole unsavoury matter had been hushed up, for "the good of the Service," and Kenyon's cohorts of his same stripe never employed again.

"So, you have actually met Bonaparte *twice*, Sir Alan?" Captain Hayman tentatively asked, with a tinge of awe in his voice.

"Aye, Captain Hayman," Lewrie told him. "The second time, in Paris, I must've rowed him beyond all temperance, for the next thing my wife and I know, we're bein' chased all the way to Calais by his police agents, lookin' t'murder us."

"Indeed," Fillebrowne said with a lazy, half-believing drawl.

"It was in all the papers, just before the war began again," Hayman said. "My condolences, sir, late as they may be."

"Thankee, Captain Hayman," Lewrie said with a grave nod.

Hayman noted his medals, and Lewrie explained his presence at the Battle of Cape Saint Vincent, and how Nelson's ship had wheeled out of line and practically *forced* Lewrie's *Jester* to go about, or be rammed, else, and join him in countering the Spanish fleet, just two ships in the beginning. Yes, he'd been at Camperdown, too, just after escaping the Nore Mutiny, right after making "Post." He had been at Copenhagen, too, but there was no commendation for that.

"I was at the Glorious First of June, too, sir," Lewrie said, "but that was accidental. I was bein' chased by two French frigates, and stumbled into it."

"I was at the Nile," Shirke announced, "still a Lieutenant in a frigate, and we couldn't see much of it, really. Except for when *Ocean* exploded. Cannon fire so loud, you couldn't hear a thing, then *boom!*, and it went so quiet, you could've heard a cricket chirp for nigh-on a quarter hour."

"My son, Hugh, was at Trafalgar," Lewrie reminisced. "With Thomas Charlton. Just a Mid, then. And my other son, Sewallis, was under Benjamin Rodgers for a time. Remember Rodgers, from our time in Charlton's squadron, do ye, sir?" he asked, addressing Fillebrowne.

"A . . . capable fellow," Fillebrowne idly allowed with scant praise. "Rather fond of champagne, as I recall."

"Aye, wouldn't put a toe out t'sea without several dozen-dozen in his lazarette," Lewrie replied. "A *grand* fellow, is Rodgers. I've known him since the Bahamas in Eighty-Six."

Shirke's steward announced that their supper was laid, and they all repaired to the dining-coach to take seats.

"Worked with your old First Officer, Stroud, in Eighteen-Oh-Three," Lewrie commented. "He had the *Cockerel* frigate, when we were sent t'hunt down a French squadron all the way to Spanish Louisiana, just before the Frogs sold it to the Americans."

"Indeed?" Fillebrowne replied between spoonfuls of ox-tail soup, as if it was no matter to him.

"I was First Lieutenant into her round the time of Toulon," Lewrie went on, " 'til they needed sailors t'man some captured French warships."

"Stroud, well," Fillebrowne said, dabbing his lips with his napkin. "I am surprised he was made 'Post.' A good-enough organiser and 'tarpaulin' sailor, but he always struck me as a dullard, a most un-imaginitive man. Takes all kinds, I would suppose. He stayed aboard when we were anchored at Venice. Had no curiosity, nor any urges to savour the city's pleasures, either."

"That's the First Lieutenant's job, is it not, sir?" Hayman joshed. "To present his Captain a going concern, no matter what his own preferences might be?"

"And allow his *Captain* his runs ashore among the pleasures, hmm?" Lewrie posed, with a glance at Fillebrowne.

" 'Til *he's* made 'Post' and has *his* turn, hah!" Shirke laughed.

"What a city is Venice," Lewrie slyly prompted, "and so full of valuable things goin' for a song at the time, with everyone fearful of the French marchin' in and pillagin' the place. I recall you did well there, Captain Fillebrowne."

"Oh, well, I suppose I did," Fillebrowne agreed, perking up. "I obtained some paintings, furniture, and a marvellous pair of Greco-Roman bronzes that had just turned up on the antiquities market, found in shoal water off the Balkan coast."

"Captain Fillebrowne is a collector, with an eye for values," Lewrie told the others. "Runs in the family, don't it?"

"Yes, it does," Fillebrowne said, breaking a smile, at last. "Father, uncles, aunts, and my elder brothers all did their Grand Tours, and I was exposed to such things early-on. Could not help developing a discerning eye, what?"

"I thought t'give it a flutter," Lewrie went on in a casual way, "but an old school friend of mine, Clotworthy Chute, warned me off. He and Peter Rushton were in Venice, lookin' for a way out when we were there, and he told me that the bulk o' such were shams, moulded over forms, then put in salt water for a month or two, so even *he* couldn't tell whether the things were made in Julius Caesar's time, or last week. He's an eye, too, and runs a reputable antiquities shop in London, now."

In point of fact, Lewrie knew that Fillebrowne's treasured old bronzes *were* shams, 'cause Clotworthy Chute had *had* them made, then sold them to Fillebrowne for hundreds of pounds, laughing all the way to help Lewrie get his own back!

"Indeed," Fillebrowne archly replied, looking worried. "As I recall, this Chute fellow was the one who authenticated them for me, and brokered their sale."

"Well, there you are, then!" Lewrie jovially said. "Nothing t'worry about. As for me, Chute found me some dress-makin' fabrics and some drapery material, toys, and a brass lion-head doorknocker."

Fillebrowne peered closely at Lewrie as if wondering if he was being twitted, but the cabin servants cleared the soup course and set out the grilled fish, and the bustle of activity seized Fillebrowne's attention.

Over port, cheese, and sweet bisquits, Shirke briefly outlined his plans for convoying, assigning Lewrie and *Sapphire* to a flanking position, with Captain Hayman's *Tiger* to be the "bulldog" or the whipper-in at the rear of the convoy to chivvy slow sailing transports to speed up and keep proper order. Lewrie made it plain that his ship was not fast enough for that role, and that Hayman might have to give *Sapphire* a reminder to keep up. "I *plod*, sirs, even on the best days!" he said with a deprecating laugh.

"If you will not stand on the order of your going, sir, I wish a word," Shirke said as they went out to the quarterdeck once supper was done.

"Well, of course," Lewrie agreed, wondering what Shirke had in mind. Tradition demanded that Lewrie debark first, but . . .

He and Shirke doffed their hats to salute Fillebrowne's departure, then

Hayman's. Shirke pulled a slim *cigarro* from a pocket and leaned over the compass binnacle's lit lamp, opened it, and got his *cigarro* afire, and took a few puffs.

"May I offer you one, sir?" Shirke asked.

"Never developed the habit," Lewrie told him. "Thankee, no."

"Hayman seems a nice-enough young fellow, don't you agree?"

"Nice? Aye, I s'pose so," Lewrie said, canting his head over to one side. "Eager t'win his spurs, with his first frigate, and his promotion. He didn't even look disappointed t'be the 'bulldog.'"

"Were I in his shoes, I would have pouted," Shirke confessed with a chuckle. "*Ad hoc* squadrons, thrown together at the last minute . . . perhaps we'll learn to rub together on passage to Cádiz, before we pick up the troop convoy. Fillebrowne, though. You worked with him before. What the Devil is he, a naval officer, or an art collector?"

"A bit of both, really," Lewrie said with a shrug. "He did as good as one could expect in the Adriatic, but with little to write home about. His storerooms and part of the orlop stowage were full of valuable acquisitions, so he may have been touchy about taking too much damage. I can't recall him being engaged on his own, and when we were sailing as a four-ship squadron, we took prizes without more than challenge shots bein' fired."

"Is there bad blood between you two?" Shirke asked.

"The arrogant prick took up with two women close to me, and boasted of it, slyly," Lewrie admitted. "One a former mistress, the other the wife of a patron, a 'cream-pot' love of mine during the American Revolution, and neither such a loss, or a wrench, to make me kick furniture. I don't know what his problem is, but for my part, I just don't like him for bein' an idle grasper. That's not t'say that I can't work with him. I'm senior to him on the Captain's List by at least a year, and seniority's a wondrous thing if one's feelin' spiteful," he concluded with a wry laugh.

"Yes, and I'm senior to you," Shirke pointed out with a sly twinkle.

"Feelin' spiteful?" Lewrie teased.

"Not a bit of it," Shirke told him. "What passed between us in the old days was youthful skylarking, and nothing personal."

"The molasses in my hammock?" Lewrie asked. "Sendin' me aloft t'pick dilberries? The paintbrush full o' shit when I was the figurehead when we played 'buildin' 'a galley? Good God, but I was so naive! 'Gild the figurehead's face!'."

"Aye, you were the most *clueless* sort of 'new-come,'" Shirke said, and they both laughed over long-gone Midshipmen's pranks. "I simply wished to see if you still held a grudge against *me*."

"You were never a Rolston, just a prankster," Lewrie replied. "Like you say, it was all youthful skylarking, and no harm done, to my body or my mind."

"Good!" Shirke said, offering his hand. They shook; then Shirke drew on his *cigarro* for a minute. "Whatever did happen with Rolston, after old Captain Bales broke him to a common seaman?"

"He made Able, grew a beard, and was one of the mutineers in my crew at the Nore, under a false name," Lewrie said. "I saw him drowned in chains, as we transferred prisoners once we made our escape. Very . . . eerie, it was."

"Didn't help him along, did you?" Shirke asked, wide-eyed.

"Let's just say that a *lot* of eerie things happened with the *Proteus* frigate, her odd launch, the drowning of her Chaplain, how her first Captain went mad, and swore the ship was out to kill him?"

"Good Lord, a spook ship?" Shirke exclaimed.

"She was t'be *Merlin*, but she stuck fast on the ways when they called out 'success to the *Proteus*,'" Lewrie told him, feeling a bit of a chill run up his spine, even long years after. "An Irish sawyer and his son laid hands on her forefoot, whispered something, and off she went. Her first Captain and Chaplain were Anglo-Irish cater-cousins, and when they boarded one night, the Captain said the man-ropes stung him like wasps, makin' them both fall into the water. Never found the Chaplain's body, then the Captain went ravin' mad a day or two after. I never had a speck of bother from her, but, maybe that's because some say I'm touched with a lucky *cess*."

"And, maybe *Proteus* killed Rolston," Shirke slowly said, with his brows knitted in awe. "He was a murderer, *and* dis-loyal to *her*! Gives me the shivers to even think about that!"

"There were some, me included, who thought her touched by the old pre-Christian gods," Lewrie told him. "A better name might've been HMS *Druid*, or *Wizard*. Ye ever cross hawses with her, doff yer hat to her and speak respectful," he suggested with a wink.

"Rather stand well aloof to windward," Shirke confessed. "Well, it's good to see an old companion from the old days, and know that he ain't out to gut me. I hope to get under way by tomorrow's dawn, weather permitting. I'll dine you in when we drop anchor at Cádiz."

"Hope ye like Spanish cuisine, Jemmy," Lewrie said, offering his hand one more time. "It ain't all bad."

"On your way, Alan, and good luck," Shirke said in parting.

Once back aboard *Sapphire*, and padding round his great-cabins in stockinged feet as he prepared for bed, Lewrie felt a strong urge to reminisce. Yes, he'd been the worst sort of fool when he first went aboard old *Ariadne* in 1780, sulky, feeling wronged that his father had shoved him into the Navy, just to lay his hands on an inheritance from his late mother's side to clear his many debts, with him all far away and un-knowing how he'd been cheated. He'd been a right pain, and not for his nautical ignorance, but for his arrogant, cynical, and selfish attitude, feeling surrounded by slack-wit fools or un-feeling brutes.

Fond memories of my Midshipman days? he thought; *Not hardly! I can laugh about it, now, but it wasn't all that much fun. Jemmy Shirke, well. Hadn't given him a thought in* ages*! I've no hard feelings. His pranks were cruel fun, but he meant nothing by them.*

He had released Pettus and Jessop from duty and had the cabins to himself; just him and Chalky. He poured himself a wee dollop of brandy at the wine-cabinet, took the lone lit candle into his sleeping space, and found Chalky waiting for him with his front paws tucked under his chest, slit-eyed with drowsiness. That didn't last for long. The cat rose and arched his back, going on tip-toes to stretch.

Lewrie finished his brandy, set the glass atop one of his sea-chests, snuffed the candle, and rolled into bed, with Chalky crawling up one leg to his chest to demand pets.

Fillebrowne, now . . . what t'make of him? Lewrie wondered.

It struck him as odd that Fillebrowne showed no curiosity at the mention of Thom Charlton, Benjamin Rodgers, or his First Officer in *Myrmidon*, Stroud. The man had *tolerated* Shirke, Hayman, and himself, and their tales of past experiences, offering none of his own, almost seeming impatient with their supper conversation.

We aren't good enough for his *sort,* Lewrie decided, yawning; *He thinks himself so far above the bulk o' Mankind, I wonder if he has a* single *friend he thinks worthy.*

"I just don't like the bastard, puss," Lewrie whispered to the cat, stroking its chops and under its neck as Chalky sprawled even closer and began to rumble. "And he doesn't like *anybody*. He's an amateur at this business, and I doubt the Navy was his decision. What's a second or third son t'do, if your family says 'go find your career, or else'? Good God, he might've been *pressed,* the same as *me*! I still don't like him, though. Don't trust him, either."

Chalky belly-crawled up nearer his chin and began to lick and head swipe.

"G'night, Chalky. I love you, too."

CHAPTER TWENTY-FIVE

*M*ondego Bay was aswarm with troop transports and supply ships when the convoy bearing General Spencer's five thousand men arrived, and the few piers in Figueira da Foz had been claimed by the first arrivals, the army under General Sir Arthur Wellesley. Most of his troops and supplies were ashore and encamped, so their convoy vessels could go close to the shore and ferry everything to a broad, deep hard-packed beach. All of *Sapphire*'s boats, and the larger cutters or launches from *Newcastle*, *Assurance*, and *Tiger* were put to the task.

"Hmpfh!" Lieutenant Geoffrey Westcott said with a snort after looking the scene over with his telescope. "Are we landing an army, or a parcel of visitors to Brighton? Look there, sir, at those soldiers skylarking."

Lewrie raised his own glass to one eye and beheld what looked to be utter chaos. Dozens of ship's boats were stroking shoreward to the beaches, soaring as they met the moderate waves of surf, and all crammed with piles of crates, kegs and barrels of rations, and infantrymen sitting upright between the oarsmen with their muskets held vertically 'twixt their tight-squeezed knees. But in the surf, pale and naked men were splashing, swimming, floating, or standing in thigh-deep water to let the incoming waves break over them. Further up the beach, barely dressed and bare-chested men were basking or footballing as if the entire army was having a Make and Mend day of idleness.

"One can only hope that French soldiers are as thin and spindly as ours," Lewrie said with a sigh. "They look as pale as spooks."

"They're in the boats' way!" Westcott groused.

"Uhm, no, I don't think so," Lewrie disagreed after a longer look. "Someone's planted posts and flags along the beaches to clear a long stretch where the boats can land. The swimming areas are outside of that. Damme! Someone in *our* army half knows what he's doing, for a change! The whole affair looks . . . organised."

"Oh, now that you point it out, I see it," Westcott said in a much milder voice, sounding as if he was disappointed that he could not have himself a good rant.

"Ye know, I've never been to Brighton," Lewrie admitted. "I've taken the waters at Bath, but they say that saltwater bathing is good for you. Half-freezin' your arse in the Channel, well. The seas here surely are warmer. I'm tempted t'take a dip, myself."

"As I recall, though, sir, you cannot swim," Westcott reminded him.

"I said 'dip,'" Lewrie replied, "not 'plunge.' Wade, perhaps, and let the surf have its way with me, with my feet firmly planted in the sand. On such a warm day, well, it looks refreshin'."

He swung his telescope back to the boats as they hobby-horsed the last fifty yards or so to ground their bows in the sand, rising on the incoming wave, surging onward as it broke and foamed round them. Sailors leapt out to walk the boats over the last incoming surge and steady them as the soldiers began to debark over the bows. Soldiers from other units came down from the low dunes and barrow overwashes to help the boat crews unload and stack crates, bundles, and kegs ashore.

Beyond them, lines of four-wheeled waggons and carts with two man-tall solid wooden wheels stood waiting. The half-battalion that had just set foot on shore stacked their arms up by the waggons, and began to carry all those goods to the waggons, where civilian Portuguese drivers and carters began the loading, under the supervision of British officers in shakoes or elegant bicorne hats.

It struck Lewrie that this landing was better organised than any he'd seen before, at Toulon, at Blaauberg Bay two years before at the invasion of the Dutch Cape Colony, certainly that shoddy mess at Buenos Aires. He suspected that the initial landing of General Wellesley's army a day or two before had been just as efficient. Someone had given a long thought upon how to get troops, guns, waggons, and horses ashore quickly and smoothly, ready for battle the day after if necessary.

And all those waggons and carts . . . They were definitely *not* British Army issue, for upon a longer look, he could not discern more than four that looked similar, as if local towns in Portugal built their own styles. They were all the colours of the rainbow, as well, much like the lot that *Sapphire* had shot to smouldering kindling on the coast road from Málaga to Salobreña.

That must've cost Wellesley a pretty penny, Lewrie thought.

When they had landed General Spencer's small army at Ayamonte, or Puerto de Santa María, the cost of hiring or leasing Spanish carts and waggons was as dear as *purchasing* them outright, and Spencer was as tight as the worst penny-pinching miser when it came to dipping into his army chest, practically weeping over every spent shilling. This General Wellesley, it seemed, had a much fatter purse, and was not averse to spending freely to keep all his supplies close by the heels of his soldiers, ready for issue or use.

"They'll have their supplies in the waggons and be ready to march off in the next hour," Lewrie predicted, lowering his telescope. "That regiment's other half-battalion will be ashore with 'em by then, tents, cookpots, and all. We may have all of Spencer's force off the ships by the start of the First Dog this afternoon."

"Who knew our army had it in them, sir?" Westcott said in sour wonder. "Is this one of Sir John Moore's famous reforms?"

"Could be," Lewrie whimsically replied. He turned away from the starboard quarterdeck bulwarks, put his hands in the small of his back, and peered upward at the long, streaming commissioning pendant for a hint of the wind direction, had a look seaward for signs of a change in the weather, then turned to look back at the beaches. The sea seemed a bit more boisterous further North of the bay, at Cape Mondego, but the bay itself, rather open to the prevailing Westerlies, looked safe, so far, for boat-work, and the surf that growled on the beaches was not too high.

Sea-bathing; it *was* tempting even if he could not swim a lick. The day was hot, and it wasn't even close to Noon. He had already shed his uniform coat and hat, but still felt sweltering in waist-coat, shirt, neck-stock, breeches, and boots. The King, "Farmer George," had begun the fad and made Brighton what it was today, with thousands of people of all classes who thought it fashionable to dunk themselves in perishing-cold water. He'd liked the springs at Bath; they were heated.

George the Third's as batty as yer old maiden aunt, Lewrie told himself; *Perhaps he was daft back then when he took his first dip!*

"Signal from Admiral Cotton's flagship, sir!" Midshipman Kibworth piped up. "Oh! Sorry, sir. It's *Newcastle*'s number, and Captain Repair On Board, not Captains."

"Dinin' Jemmy Shirke in, is he?" Lewrie quipped. "Well, I've seen Jemmy eat with a knife and fork before, and he does it elegant. Oh, *this'll* be embarrassin'. All our boats are away helpin' with the landings, and *Newcastle* doesn't have a *raft* available."

Lewrie went to the larboard side of the quarterdeck to watch the show. *Newcastle*'s signal halliards sprouted a series of flags that repeated the flagship's hoist. They remained aloft for a moment, then were struck down to be replaced with a single flag; the Unable.

"Oh, poor bastard!" Westcott whispered under his breath.

Cotton's flagship sent a new hoist aloft, jerking swiftly to be two-blocked. It was Explain, spelled out.

"No . . . Boat . . . Available," Midshipman Kibworth slowly spelled out, referring to his code book. "Request . . . Send . . . Boat."

Explain was lowered so quickly that it appeared as if Admiral Sir Charles Cotton had tailed on the halliards himself, and in a fit of dire pique.

"Handy bloody word, 'Request,'" Lewrie smirked. "Oh, do, pretty please?"

"With sugar on it," Lt. Westcott added, chuckling.

"Send . . . ing . . . Boat," Kibworth read off, at last.

"Whatever *was* planned for dinner, Shirke'll be dinin' on cold crow, or his own hot tripes, after Cotton rips 'em out for him. Well, things seem t'be goin' well, and I've a book to read," he added, with a longing look up to the poop deck and his collapsible wood-and-canvas deck chair.

"Then, with you on deck, and the Mids in charge of the Anchor Watch, I think I'll go below and have a nap, sir," Westcott said. He tapped two fingers on the brim of his cocked hat by way of salute and departed for the wardroom.

He read 'til time for his own mid-day dinner, came back to the deck and read some more, and drifted off round three in the afternoon, for the warmth was a soporific, not entirely dispelled by a breeze from offshore. Lewrie was roused by the tinging of Eight Bells being struck at the change of watch at 4 P.M.

There was something heavy and warm on his right thigh, and when he opened one gritty eye, he found Bisquit sitting close by his chair with his head and forelegs draped over him, smelling distinctly doggish, and panting with his tongue lolled out. Lewrie gave Bisquit a pat on the head, and ruffled the fur on his throat and ears. That was a mistake, for Bisquit took it as an invitation to hop up onto his chest and stomach like a hot, hairy blanket, and a heavy one, too.

"Oh no, no, me lad!" Lewrie chid him. "That'll never do. Get off me." He struggled to rise, to shove the dog off, but Bisquit was having none of it, whining to stay.

"Here, Bisquit, here, boy!" Midshipman Fywell coaxed, snapping his fingers and whistling. "Want a bite of bisquit?" he asked, producing a corner of a half-consumed ship's bread from a pocket. That freed Lewrie, though the dog's quick leap and shove with his rear legs made Lewrie let out an "Oomph!"

"Thankee, Mister Fywell," Lewrie said, getting to his feet, at last. Bisquit flopped down by the forward railings and crunched away.

"Mister Midshipman Hillhouse's respects, sir, and he sent me to report that our boats are returning."

"What, the landings are done?" Lewrie asked, scrubbing sleep from his face with both hands.

"Aye, sir, it appears so," Fywell went on. "The last boat-loads of soldiers and their supplies went in an hour ago, and the General's transport . . . the Agent Afloat aboard her, that is . . . hoisted a Discontinue about a quarter-hour ago."

"My respects to Mister Hillhouse, and he's to make sure that all the scuttlebutts are topped off, Mister Fywell," Lewrie ordered. "The hands'll be hellish-thirsty when they return. I'll be in my cabins. Carry on."

"Aye, sir," Fywell replied.

Once in the relative coolness of the great-cabins, Lewrie called for a glass of cool tea, and a pint of wash water. He stripped off to the skin, soaked his washcloth, and swiped his body down from head to his toes to freshen and cool himself. He thought of dressing, but the idea of clothing, especially a wool broadcloth uniform coat, just palled. He padded into his bedspace and donned a light linen dressing robe, then went to fling himself onto the settee with his bare feet up on the brass Hindoo tray table to savour his sweetened and lemoned cool tea, gulping it down and calling for a re-fill.

Chalky joined him for some "wubbies" and head butts, and he felt comfortable, at last. All the sash windows in the stern transom were opened at the top halves, and the jury-rigged screen door to the stern gallery let in a halfway decent breeze, though some of the thin twine looked in need of re-roving over the nails; Chalky was relentless in his urge to get out onto the stern gallery and its railings to hunt sea birds.

"Midshipman o' th' Watch, Mister Hillhouse, SAH!" the Marine announced with a stamp of boots and his musket butt.

Lewrie opened his mouth to shout back "Oh, just bugger off!", but thought better of it, and called back "Enter!" instead.

My officer's dignity be-damned, he thought.

"Ehm . . . uh, sir," Midshipman Hillhouse stammered to find his Captain a'sprawl in a robe. "There has come a signal from *Newcastle*, sir, an invitation to dine aboard her, at seven of the evening, sir."

"And I won't have t'request he send a boat?" Lewrie asked, giving Hillhouse an owlish look.

"Uhm, no, sir," Hillhouse replied with a smile; though he had not been on deck at the time, he'd been told the tale of Captain Shirke's embarrassment.

"Very well, Mister Hillhouse," Lewrie said, "make the reply expressing my thanks and pleasure to attend."

"Aye aye, sir," Hillhouse answered, backing out of the cabins and ducking his head, sure to spread his tale of how he'd found the Captain.

"Damn!" Lewrie spat once Hillhouse was gone. "Just when I get cool, Pettus, and now I'll have t'dress, again!"

CHAPTER TWENTY-SIX

*I*t was marginally cooler that evening when Lewrie scaled the side of HMS *Newcastle* and doffed his hat in reply to the salute from the side-party. The boats from *Assurance* and *Tiger* were alongside with his, and he steeled himself for a few more unpleasant hours with Fillebrowne.

"Welcome aboard, again, Alan," Captain James Shirke said in greeting, and offering his hand. "Well, it's done. The army is now ashore, and our boring duty's done, so I thought we'd celebrate."

"Pleased to accept your kind invitation, Jemmy," Lewrie told him. "Ehm, just how big a celebration did ye have in mind?" he japed.

"Well, we've no musicians, and no half-clothed dancing girls, but we'll cope," Shirke promised. "Let's go aft and join the others."

Captains Hayman and Fillebrowne were already there, seated, and they rose when Lewrie and Shirke entered. A cabin servant offered glasses of champagne. "Aah!" Shirke said with pleasure as he drank deep of his, smacking his thick lips in delight. "A hot damned day, was it not? Sit you down, gentlemen, sit you down."

He plunked into a chair himself, took another sip, and called for a refill. "I wish I could find a way to rig one of those Hindoo fans in here. Even with the sash windows open, it's close and warm."

"A *pankah* fan, d'ye mean?" Lewrie asked after a sip or two of his own champagne. "You've served in the Far East?"

"No, but I met a fellow who had, and he told me of them. A tax collector with 'John Company,'" Shirke replied. "Came home a 'chicken *nabob*' after ten years in someplace called Swettypore."

"That was his joke, I expect," Lewrie said with a laugh. "*Every* town, fort, and cantonment in India's just *perishin'*-hot, and ye sweat like blazes, even after dark. *Sweaty*-pore."

"You served in the Far East, sir?" Captain Hayman asked.

"Not officially," Lewrie told him with a chuckle. "It was 'tween the American Revolution and the start of the war with France, Eighty-Four to Eighty-Six. The French were urgin' the local native pirates to raid the shipping routes to China, and I was aboard *Telesto,* disguised as a merchantman t'keep an eye on 'em, and smack the pirates when we could, under direction from some secretive Foreign Office types. Calcutta to Canton and back, round the Spratly Islands and into the Phillipines. Ye don't need a *pankah* boy in turban and his breechclout, Shirke. The Chinese and the pirate kings had these big feather fans and servants standin' behind 'em, thrashin' away. There's no need to rig up the ropes and pulleys . . . though I'm certain the Navy'd have a 'down' on you carryin' a Turk on ship's books."

"I would love to hear about that, sir," Hayman urged. "It all sounds quite intriguing."

"Old sailors' tales?" Lewrie scoffed. "We're here to celebrate, so I'm told, not hear me spin old yarns."

"Indeed," Fillebrowne pointedly said, with a throat-clearing sound, then turned to Shirke. "Just what *is* it we are celebrating, sir? The end of our convoy duties?"

"That, and our release back to our regular posts in the Med," Shirke announced. "Ah, me. No chance to hoist even the *inferior* broad pendant!" he added, rubbing his short-haired pate.

"We'll not remain with Admiral Cotton's squadron?" Captain Hayman exclaimed in surprise, sounding disappointed.

"Once I managed to get *aboard* the flagship, mind you," Shirke said, laughing off the embarrassment and causing the rest to laugh with him, "the Admiral told me he's more than enough ships available to guard the coast, and extract the army should they run into trouble with the French. He's none too keen on this new 'Sepoy' General that London sent down.

He gives him good marks for efficiency and organisation in getting his troops ashore, but I gather that he finds General Wellesley to be a very cold and haughty fish, a most rigid and aloof man."

"Other than Sir John Moore, he's said to be the best we have, though," Hayman offered. "I just wish we could have stayed, in case the French came out from Lisbon or Rochefort, and we'd have had a hot action."

"After Trafalgar, I doubt the French have any stomach for ventures at sea," Shirke said with a shake of his head. "Thank your lucky stars, sir, that you're *not* called to idle all the way down to Lisbon under reduced sail, and barely under steerage way, playing the army's right flank. It's a nasty lee shore, and if foul weather blows in on the Westerlies, you could be hard aground and pounded to pieces."

"*And* bored to death," Lewrie stuck in.

"Hear, hear," Fillebrowne seconded.

"Besides, sirs," Shirke said with a crafty, sly look, shifting in his chair, "Admiral Cotton as good as told me that he doesn't *want* us. The French and Russian ships at Lisbon are his, and his alone, and he means to have them, come Hell or high water, and we'd dilute the share-out of the prize money when he takes them!" Shirke barked in laughter as he told them that. "There may be as many as eight Russian ships of the line anchored in the Tagus River, and there's a fortune just waiting to be reaped."

"Hmm, would they be Good Prize, though, I wonder?" Lewrie objected. "Russia ain't *exactly* at war with us, unless their boy Tsar, Alexander, has gone as mad as his predecessor. Mean t'say, he shut down all trade with us t'make Bonaparte happy, but—"

"The Russians *did* send London some official note from Saint Petersburg," Fillebrowne interrupted, sounding superior and dismissive. "Though people I know in Government have assumed that the Tsar is merely posturing to please Bonaparte, without presenting an *actual* declaration of war. A top-up, if you please," he said to a servant.

"Just because he and 'Boney' met on that raft at Tilsit, in the middle of the river, doesn't make them bosom companions," Shirke said, scoffing. "If France didn't have Spain and Portugal on their plates at the moment, they might have a go at *him*! And, we all know by now that Napoleon Bonaparte's word is worthless. If I were the Tsar, I'd sleep with one eye open."

"He'll not be satisfied 'til the whole world's his," Hayman agreed. "The man's rapacious!"

"That's the second time today I've heard that word," Shirke said with good humour. "Admiral Cotton used it referring to *you*, Captain Lewrie. S'truth! And don't look so amazed."

Lewrie was caught with his mouth open.

"He had the most recent copy of *Steel's*, so he knew who commanded all our ships, and he cautioned me to keep a close rein on that 'rapscallion "Ram-Cat" Lewrie' from having a go at the ships in the Tagus, either, and he said that you're 'a relentless, rapacious reaper of prize money,' hah hah!"

"Well, I *have* had good fortune over the years, but I haven't gone . . . reaping on *purpose*," Lewrie rejoined. "I've just had good *luck*."

"You aren't known as the 'Ram-Cat' for your choice of pets," Shirke pointed out. "Good God, cats! Can't abide them!"

"*I* thought you were better known as 'Black Alan,'" Fillebrowne fussily added. "For when you stole those dozen Black slaves to crew your ship."

"*Liberated*, not stolen," Lewrie corrected. "Their idea, too."

"Stood trial for it," Fillebrowne went on.

"Honourably acquitted," Lewrie pointed out.

"You saw that French *corvette*, and that big Spanish frigate at anchor at Gibraltar, Captain Fillebrowne?" Shirke asked him. "Alongside those Spanish *xebecs*? Those are *Sapphire*'s prizes, all in the last year. Lord, in the old days, *none* of us thought you would make a sailor. You were the *worst* cackhanded, cunny-thumbed lubber we'd ever seen!"

"I think it was all the time I spent 'kissing the gunner's daughter,'" Lewrie japed, thankful that Shirke had praised him and defended him. "Though, I must confess that the *first* time I was warned with that, I thought the girl must be a *real* dirty puzzle if they meant it as a threat! As little as I knew then, I thought it *marvellous* that they'd allow girls aboard, and wondered where was mine, and what's her 'socket fee'! After a few times, I felt . . . *inspired*!"

"We couldn't recognise him by face, and wondered if he could stand erect, he spent so much time bent over a gun," Shirke wheezed with glee, "and our Bosun and his Mates could swing a starter so hard, they could have lit off the priming powder at a gun's touch hole with one blow, hee hee!"

"Raised sparks on *my* arse," Lewrie said, laughing along. "You know, I can't remember either you or Keith Ashburn *ever* bein' whipped."

"That's because we were never caught out at our duties, Alan," Shirke reminisced with joy, "nor caught at our games and skylarking, either," he added with a tap on the side of his nose.

"Excuse me, sir, but supper is laid and ready," the senior steward announced, and they rose to enter the dining-coach, where Shirke had allowed himself a few more luxuries in good sterling silver and glass-ware and china.

Lewrie noted that Fillebrowne had merely pretended to laugh along with the others, and he caught his agate-eyed glances as they sat down. He looked almost archly surly, which pleased Lewrie.

What is he, jealous, or irked? he wondered; *He keeps that up, and I* will *tell Hayman one or two o' my yarns!*

CHAPTER TWENTY-SEVEN

*A*ll four ships of the escort returned to Gibraltar, and turned their sailors loose on the town's taverns and brothels. After a day or two of provisioning, though, Captains Fillebrowne and Hayman took their frigates back to sea to rejoin their commands in the central Mediterranean, and the following day Captain Shirke and *Newcastle* departed, leaving *Sapphire* by herself, again, and Lewrie was glad to see the back of them, Fillebrowne especially.

He had treated them all to a shore supper at Pescadore's, the seafood chop-house in the upper part of town near the Convent, and it went well. The next night, though, he and Maddalena had supped at the Ten Tuns, and who should pop in in the middle of their meal but Captain Fillebrowne and Captain Hayman! It was impossible not to ask them to join them. Hayman was the soul of discretion, but Fillebrowne had skirted the edge of propriety, attempting to flirt mildly and taking over their conversations, as if laying the groundwork to assume possession of *another* of Lewrie's mistresses.

"He assumes a lot," Maddalena had commented on their walk back to her lodgings. "I thought all English gentlemen behaved like gentlemen." She had even clutched her arms cross her chest and darted glances behind them, as if in fear that she'd see Fillebrowne skulking after them.

"Well, we both know that *that* ain't true, Maddalena," Lewrie had said, trying to cosset her. "There's Captain Hughes, for a shabby example." He'd tried to laugh it off, but inside he was fuming, too.

There's un-finished business 'twixt me and that arrogant shit, Lewrie had thought; *Don't know what it is, but, I just hope we don't cross hawses again. Is he tryin' to row me so angry that we'd have to duel?*

Fortunately, though, a shared bottle of sparkling wine, and a night with Maddalena, in which she assured him who *truly* had her affection, was passionate enough to distract him from his qualms.

"Going anywhere *soon*, are you, Captain Lewrie?" the Foreign Office's chief spy, Thomas Mountjoy, asked with mock urgency as they met in the street in front of Mountjoy's lodgings a morning or two later. "If you are, I'm sorely tempted to go with you."

"French assassins're after you?" Lewrie asked. "Or, is it a woman you spurned?"

"There's a diplomatic disaster just waiting to explode, and I wish to be half a continent away when it does," Mountjoy told him in what Lewrie recognised by now as real urgency.

"Whatever's the matter, then?" he asked him.

"That ship that came in yesterday, the *Thunderer*?" Mountjoy said, stabbing a finger at a two-decker Third Rate in the harbour. "She's just come in from Sicily with a brace of pretenders to the throne of Spain aboard. One's Prince Leopold of the Kingdom of Naples and the Two Sicilies, King Ferdinand the Fourth's heir—"

"Is he as ugly as his father?" Lewrie asked, suddenly amused by Mountjoy's distress. "Does he run a waterfront fish shop, same as his Daddy?"

"I don't know, I haven't clapped eyes on him . . . what? Fish shop? Where did you get that?" Mountjoy demanded, most perplexed and thrown off his rant.

"Met Ferdinand ages ago, when my ship put in to Naples, back when Sir William Hamilton was our ambassador, and his wife, Emma, was still slimm-ish. We ate at Ferdinand's shop, where he cooked for us himself. Quite tasty, really."

"Emma Hamilton? *Nelson's* Emma Hamilton?" Mountjoy gawped.

"Umhmm," Lewrie rejoined with an idle leer. "She was tasty at the time, too. So. What's young Leopold doin' here?"

"Offering himself to the war effort, so long as his military post is suit-

able to his *illustrious* rank," Mountjoy scoffed, "and offering his father, Ferdinand, as either a king or a regent. The other passenger is Prince
Louis-Phillipe, Duc d'Orléans, the eldest of the French royal family, who
would have succeeded to the French throne, if the Revolution hadn't come
along. He's offering himself, a French Bourbon to replace a Spanish Bourbon. It's all impossible, of course, and the Spanish *juntas* will never hear a
word of it, and Dalrymple's in a dither, trying to put out fires and soothe
the Spanish, saying that *neither* of the sods are a British idea.

"Worst of all, there's rumours that Archduke Charles of Austria might
be on his way to get a seat at the table, too," Mountjoy went on. "What
good relations we've built in Spain could be out the window if they think
we approve of a foreign king, regent, or emperor, or . . . *generalissimo*! Dalrymple hasn't allowed either of the princes to set foot ashore, yet, *Thunderer*'s captain wants them off as soon as dammit, and the whole thing could
be an *utter* mess by the end of the week.

"Wait," Mountjoy said, ceasing his nervous tirade and peering at
Lewrie. "*You* and Emma Hamilton? Really?"

"In one of her melting moments, she distinctly said, 'I don't know what
it is, about me and sailors,'" Lewrie boasted, laughing out loud.

"My word!" Mountjoy replied in awe. "You never *cease* to amaze."

"Hmm, well, perhaps I do have my moments," Lewrie brashly confessed,
all but polishing his fingernails on a coat lapel.

"The princes are the last thing to have on Sir Hew's plate, at the moment,
and that old meddler, Emmanuel Viale . . . he was Dalrymple's envoy to
Castaños for a time? . . . he and the Vicar of Gibraltar have *both* written
the Seville *junta, praising* Prince Leopold of Naples, and it's riled them
almost beyond all temperance. British scheming and meddling, they
think. And, Dalrymple doesn't have much time to settle the matter. London's appointed him Commander-In-Chief of all operations in Portugal
and Spain, and he'll be off to join Wellesley's army in a few days, dump-
ing the mess on Major-General Drummond."

"What?" It was Lewrie's turn to gawp in astonishment. "Commander-
In-Chief? *Dalrymple?* Are they stark-ravin' *daft?*" He said that loudly, and
didn't much care who heard him. "The Dowager hasn't seen a real battle
since . . . God!"

"Well, not many of our generals have, either," Mountjoy pointed out.
"With any luck, he'll leave the fighting to Wellesley and do the general
directions, himself. Well, leave the fighting to Lieutenant-General Sir Harry
Burrard."

"Who the Devil is he?" Lewrie had to ask.

"London may be having second thoughts about trusting the endeavour to a 'Sepoy' General," Mountjoy told him in a hushed tone, so passersby could not hear. "If Wellesley is successful, Burrard will take over, until Sir John Moore arrives with a much larger army that is gathering as we speak. Burrard's senior to Wellesley, after all."

"But, is he *worth* a tuppenny shit?" Lewrie sneered.

"God only knows," Mountjoy had to tell him, shrugging. "But, Burrard is spoken of as 'Betty' Burrard."

"Now, what does *that* tell you?" Lewrie scoffed.

"That he dresses up in women's clothes?" Mountjoy japed.

"This whole thing could *really* turn t'shit!" Lewrie breathed in disgust. "I've half a mind t'stay in port and have a good laugh, and half a mind t'bugger out. Here, now! I'm still technically under *your* authority. If ye don't wish t'stay here and get smeared with the disaster, can't you *order* me, us, to sail off somewhere?"

"Lewrie, you are a genius!" Mountjoy suddenly exclaimed. "That I could, and yes, we could. Let's go to the Ten Tuns and have an ale or two and plot this out!"

"I don't s'pose you could *write* 'genius' in your reports to London, could you?" Lewrie asked once they were seated, and two pints of pale ale had been drawn for them. Some crisp-fried fish tidbits with a spicy dipping sauce had come with them as *tapas*.

"Don't know if I'd write them, at all," Mountjoy replied. "The less they know of my movements, the better, even if a reply from my superiors would take a fortnight. Sorry."

"After decades of bein' thought a lucky dunce, I'd hoped," Lewrie said with a sigh. "Ah, well. Where would you like to go?"

"I'd thought of Cádiz, to try and establish an intelligence network there," Mountjoy wistfully said after a deep, meditative draught of his ale. "Tap onto the informers that Admiral Purvis developed, but Dalrymple's aides there, and at Seville, are reporting on a regular basis, so that's out. I've people at Tarifa, cross the bay in Algeciras, Málaga, and Cummings and his boat bring news from every port in Andalusia, now. Portugal's not in my bailiwick, so—"

"Why not Portugal?" Lewrie asked him. "Or, does Secret Branch already have fellows like you in Lisbon, Oporto, and Vigo, or with the army?"

"I really don't know," Mountjoy said, wincing a little to confess his total lack of knowledge. "If there are, they certainly won't tell *me*. I'm allowed to know only what I need to know. Portugal, hmm. Now, that's an
intriguing thought. I know that Dalrymple already sends everything he
learns to Wellesley, mostly of the situation anent the Spanish, their politics, and what their armies are up to. If our army succeeds in getting Lisbon back from the French, we could benefit from a Secret Branch presence
there, in the interim before London sends out a man to oversee it, at least."

"And the fellow who took that initiative would be well-thought-of in
London," Lewrie said with a sly cock of his head, and an encouraging wink.
"Get to know the Generals, Wellesley and 'Betty' Burrard, and what *they*
wish to know?"

"He might also be thought of as a gad-about indulging his curiosity at
Government expense," Mountjoy countered, looking glum of a sudden.

"But, curiosity could be taken for energetic intelligence gathering," Lewrie rejoined. He found that his mug was empty, and waved for a re-fill.
"We could even see a battle, and find out if Wellesley is half the general
that people make him out to be."

"Curiosity also killed the cat," Mountjoy reminded him. "Most likely
trampled to death, if Wellesley fails, and his army is routed. Yet!"

Mountjoy got a dreamy look on his face, mulling over the idea so intently that he didn't notice the arrival of a fresh mug of ale set before him,
and the removal of his empty one.

"Why the Devil not, then!" Mountjoy suddenly exclaimed, thumping
a fist on the tabletop. "I'll see Dalrymple at once, and tell him I'm off to
Portugal. Surely, Sir Hew will have last-minute despatches that we can
carry along with us, and he'll see the need for the trip. How soon can
we sail?"

"Day after tomorrow, wind and weather permittin'," Lewrie told him
with his usual *caveat*, which made them both smile. "D'ye think that Deacon can handle your affairs while you're away, or would he like to come
along?"

"No no, I fear that Mister Deacon must carry on here, he's more than
capable of keeping an eye on things," Mountjoy replied. "Deacon is a sly
man of many parts, I've come to discover. Where he developed his wits,
God only knows. Certainly not the barracks and drill grounds of the Guards
Regiment. He's a future with Foreign Office."

"You must send me formal orders, of course," Lewrie told him, sipping
his ale in celebration to get his ship back to sea, instead of idling uselessly

while grand affairs were happening somewhere else. "Damme, sometimes it's *good* t'have friends in high places, even those in your line o' work!"

"And the rest of the time?" Mountjoy teased.

"The rest of the time, people in your line o' work sling me into impossible tasks and dangers," Lewrie said, laughing. "Hang me out on a tree limb like laundry in a hailstorm."

"Mind, though," Mountjoy said. "If we do get to see a battle, we'd *both* be up to our necks in the 'quag,' for once."

"Then come well-armed," Lewrie cautioned, and he was not trying to tease.

CHAPTER TWENTY-EIGHT

*H*MS *Sapphire* skirted the Portuguese coast after standing into Mondego Bay and turning South, with no sign of the army, or the fleet of transports and supply ships that Lewrie had expected to find; should the army need immediate evacuation, this Wellesley would surely keep them close at hand, he reckoned, but the coast that slipped by, and the major seaports of Nazaré and the fortress town of Peniche, where the French were rumoured to have a garrison and over an hundred guns, drowsed in sleepy Summer heat, as peaceful as anything.

In point of fact, though, it was not "all cruising and claret," for General Sir Hew Dalrymple had indeed felt an urgent need to convey his latest informations to General Sir Arthur Wellesley, and had sent one of his aides-de-camp along with his despatches to liaise with Sir Arthur—none other than the idled Captain Hughes, returned to his old substantive rank but *still* considered surplus to requirements by his own regiment.

"Oh, good Lord," Mountjoy had whispered in dread when Captain Hughes was piped aboard. "Not Hughes!"

"It's worse for you, Mountjoy," Lewrie whispered to him as the fellow had doffed his bicorne in salute at the lip of the entry-port. "You'll have t'share that spare cabin off the wardroom with him, hee hee! I'll dine him in in *my* cabins, of course, but he's all yours most of the time."

"Old Zachariah Twigg was right about you, Captain Lewrie," the spy-master hissed. "You *do* have a vindictive streak!"

"Aye," Lewrie gleefully agreed with that assessment, "and I'll have my cook, Yeovill, serve as many foreign kickshaws as he can think of when I *do* feed the bastard."

Poor Hughes; he seemed full of himself to be entrusted with a mission so vital for the new Commander-In-Chief, strutting about and puffing with pride to be thought useful, again, his abilities fully employed, and ready to tell everyone how he was anticipating that he would be Dalrymple's aide-de-camp in the *field,* taking part in grand battles where his skill and experience would be proven.

"I don't know whether t'feel sorry for the sod, or chuck him over the rails," Lewrie said with a groan. "But, I *am* becoming tired of his presence. Where's our bloody army when ye need it?"

"Pray God that General Wellesley finds him indispensable, then," Mountjoy commiserated in the privacy of Lewrie's stern gallery after a midday meal. "Then we're *both* shot of him. God, how he snores! And, whatever you're serving him, he's the *windiest* fellow ever I've had to share a cabin with. That Yankee rebel, Benjamin Franklin, wrote an essay about farting proudly, but God!"

"At least he don't talk in his sleep . . . or does he?" Lewrie asked in jest.

"No no, nothing human-sounding," Mountjoy replied, grimacing. "It's all grunts, moans, and bear-like rumbles and rattles."

"Sail ho!" a lookout in the main mast cross-trees shouted. "One ship, fine on the bows!"

Lewrie fetched a day-glass and mounted the poop deck to spy the strange sail out, but found that the inner, outer, and flying jibs were in the way. Mouthing a curse, he descended and paced forward, all the way to the fore-castle, leaning far out over the larboard cat-head beam for a clear view. Low on the Southern horizon, he finally spotted a set of t'gallants and tops'ls, identifying whoever it was as a three-masted, fully-rigged ship . . . but whose? He lowered his glass and took a peek to larboard, for the coast of Portugal. *Sapphire* was sailing within view of the mountain ranges' peaks, perhaps no more than twenty miles off. He reckoned that the strange sail could not be a merchantman sailing on her own; that would be too risky for her. Besides, the coastal trade of Portugal had pretty-much ceased after the French invaded. No Spanish ships, merchant or warship, would be this far along the coast, either, and no British-flagged merchantman would be sailing alone.

"No idea who she is, sir?" Midshipman Ward asked at his elbow.

"No, Mister Ward," Lewrie told him, raising his telescope to an eye again. "Run aft. My respects to the officer of the watch, and he is to hoist our colours and make the Interrogative signal. If she's one of ours, she'll make her number in reply. If she's an enemy, then we'll see. Off ye go, scamper!"

"Aye, sir!" the lad said, and turned to make haste astern.

The sight of the Captain on the forecastle, the report of a strange sail on the horizon, and Ward's rapid run aft stopped the men of the watch at their various duties, forcing some to lean far over the bulwarks for a look, others to ascend the shrouds for a view of that strange sail, and caused still others to gather in knots to talk it over and speculate. When Lewrie turned about to look aft to see if their national ensign and signal flag had been hoisted, he was pleased to see how many of the crew were looking eager for action. After the boresome escort-work *Sapphire* had done under her old Captain in the Baltic, her people had come to expect a good fight, and lashings of prize-money to follow another prideful victory. Lewrie's mouth curled into a wee smile as he made his return to the quarterdeck down the larboard sail-tending gangway, nodding confidently to the sailors and Marines he met, acknowledging some by name with a cheery "good morning" but not answering any questions, yet. He felt a spurt of pride as he considered that he'd created a happy, confident ship and a crew that knew its business when called to Quarters.

"Any reply?" Lewrie asked Lt. Elmes.

"Not yet, sir," Elmes replied, casting a quick look aloft to the signal hoist to reassure himself that it was not masked by the sails and upper-works.

"Deck, there!" the lookout shouted. "She makes her number, and shows British colours!"

"Four . . . Two . . . Four," Midshipman Griffin slowly read out as he clung to the mizen's larboard shrouds, half-way to the cat-harpings.

"Ehm . . . ," Midshipman Ward said, fumbling this month's secret signals code book until he'd found a match. "She's the *Sabine*, Sixth Rate frigate. Captain . . . Artemis Fleet."

"Another hoist, then," Lewrie said, feeling a little disappointed that they wouldn't have a fight. "Ask her where we can find the army."

"Aye, sir," Ward said, going to the poop deck and the taffrail flag lockers.

"One of ours, then?" Mountjoy asked. "Perhaps she's standing guard over the army's latest access to the sea."

"Might very well be, Mister Mountjoy," Lewrie agreed. "Useful, the Interrogative flag," he mused aloud. "We once spoke one of our ships near the Greater Antilles. Neither of us had seen the sun for nigh a week, and we'd both been runnin' on Dead Reckoning. She showed the Church flag, the one ordering to hold services, spelled out Where, and the Interrogative. The up-shot? Oh God, Where Are We? Hah hah!"

"That's much like the one I saw done when I was Fifth Officer in a seventy-four, sir," Lt. Elmes reminisced with a grin. "We were alongside Gun Wharf, and another ship was waiting to tie up where we were. Her Captain hoists How Long Will You Be, spelled it all out, and *our* Captain replied with numerals and spelled out Foot. One hundred eighty feet!"

"Good one!" Lewrie chortled.

"Naval humour," Mountjoy bemoaned. "Like sailors' slang, it's indecypherable."

"Reply, sir!" Midshipman Griffin shouted down to them. "*M . . . A . . . C . . . I . . . E . . . R . . . A* . . . Bay! Maciera Bay!"

"Mister Yelland? I'd admire a look at the charts, if you please," Lewrie asked, steeling himself to be in the cramped chart room on the larboard side of the quarterdeck, and hoping that Yelland had sponged off in the last week.

"Ah, here, sir," Yelland said, tapping an ink-stained forefinger on the rolled-out chart of the coast of Portugal. "It's not much of a bay, though. There's a wee river, or large creek, that runs down to the sea 'twixt these steep, rocky hills. There isn't much of a beach to speak of, and ah . . . aye, we'd have to anchor far out, since the chart shows that the bay approaches are shallow and sandy. Maybe not the best holding ground, either. Do you wish a safe five or six fathoms, we'd be at least a mile or better off-shore."

"We'll go in sounding the leads, and I will feel better if we anchor in six or *seven* fathoms," Lewrie decided, not liking the sketchiness of the chart's information. "We're about here, now?" he asked as he tapped the chart near Praia de Ariea Branca.

"Uhm, I'd say near level with Lourinhã, sir, a bit further on than that," Yelland corrected. "Still about twenty miles seaward of the coast."

"Very well, sir," Lewrie said, "we'll alter course to the Southeast 'til we strike this twenty-fathom line, come level with Maciera Bay, then alter course again Due East and find safe anchorage."

"Aye, sir," Yelland said, pinning the ends of the chart down with books so he could duck in and out of the chart space to reference it as often as

needed in the next few hours. They then both left the chart space and returned to the quarterdeck, with Lewrie wishing that he could fan away
Mr. Yelland's sour, stale aromas.

Captain Hughes, who had been lounging in the officers' wardroom, came
up from the upper gun-deck to peer about, and see what all the excitement had been. He had taken time to dress properly, and now was slowly
pacing with his hands in the small of his back, as if it was just not done to
appear too curious, or alarmed.

"I heard some shouting," he said at last. "'Sail ho,' what?"

"We've spotted one of our ships down South of us," Mountjoy told him.
"We've found General Wellesley's army, and we're making our way there."

"Have we? Capital!" Hughes said with a bark of delight. "Then I shall
tell my man to pack my traps. It will be good to dine ashore this evening,
even if Sir Arthur's officers' mess will most-like serve salt-beef and such.
Field rations, ah!"

"They've been marching through country un-disturbed by the enemy,
in high Summer," Mountjoy supposed, "so they've surely managed to buy
or forage the best of the local crops. Portugal is known for its own style
of bullfighting. Perhaps they've found some fresh beef?"

"If they have, I'd relish it," Hughes declared. "*Relish* it, I tell you. I've
been bilious ever since I set foot aboard this ship."

"Oh, my dear fellow!" Mountjoy pretended to sympathise. "You found
naval fare distressing? My condolences."

Lewrie bent over to give Bisquit some "wubbies" to hide his delight.
When he stood back up, his expression was bland again.

"Mister Elmes, we will alter course to the Sou'east and close the shore,"
he directed. "Hands to the braces, ready to ease the set."

"Wasn't Navy victuals," Hughes carped, stifling a left-over breakfast
belch. "Not actually." He threw a frown at Lewrie.

"I found them quite toothsome and delightful," Mountjoy said. "Captain Lewrie sets a fine table."

"If you say so, Mister Mountjoy," Captain Hughes leerily said. "Well,
I shall get out from under-foot of the sailors, and see to my despatches."
And with that, he descended to the weather deck and went down the steep
ladderway below.

Lewrie shared a look with Mountjoy, quite satisfied with the exchange,
and with Mountjoy's sly wit.

⚓

By sundown, HMS *Sapphire* was safely anchored bow and stern in about fourty feet of water. Hughes; his batman, a long-suffering Private from Hughes's old regiment; and Mr. Mountjoy had gone ashore in the launch, and Lewrie was shot of both of them for a time, able to take the evening air on the poop deck in peace. There were several supply ships and troop transports closer to the shore, ships of less than half of *Sapphire*'s burthen which drew less water. Beyond them, past the two high headlands which framed the Maceira River, the night was aglow with campfires, where half-dressed soldiers took their ease by pale tan tents and cooked their rations with their arms stacked close by. It all looked quite peaceful, but once Lewrie employed his telescope, he could make out a chain of torches snaking down to the sea, and the rowing boats drawn up on the banks of the river and beach. There were even some carts trundling along, slowly and carefully. A closer look showed litter-bearers, and men on those litters.

"Permission to come up, sir?" Lt. Westcott said at the base of the larboard ladderway.

"Aye, Mister Westcott," Lewrie allowed. "What the Devil?"

Westcott had stopped at the glim which lit the compass binnacle, to ignite a Spanish *cigarro,* and was puffing away.

"Thought I would indulge, before Lights Out is ordered," Westcott explained.

"When did you develop the habit?" Lewrie asked.

"A week ago, on a run ashore at Gibraltar," Westcott told him. "I find tobacco . . . restful, especially after a good shore supper, and with the trade cross the Lines so open, now, they're damned near five pence for a dozen."

"Those torches," Lewrie pointed out to him, handing Westcott his telescope, "they look like wounded, bein' rowed out to the ships for care. What does it look like to you?"

"I'd say you're right, sir," Westcott said after a long minute. "There's been a battle, it looks like."

"Beyond, the army's camped in what looks t'be good order, so . . . dare we imagine that Wellesley's met the French and beaten them?" Lewrie wondered aloud.

"Hmm, high Summer, bad food or water," Lt. Westcott mused, "it may be sick men coming off the shore, not wounded. Disease will kill quicker than a bullet. Happens to every army that takes the field."

"I think I'll go ashore tomorrow morning," Lewrie decided. "I want to know, either way."

"And I must remain aboard to keep an eye on things, *again*, sir?" West-cott said in mock distress. "Damme, but you have all the fun."

"If you made Commander and had a ship of your own, you could go play silly buggers, too, Geoffrey. I keep throwin' opportunities at you," Lewrie told him with a grin.

"When *Sapphire*'s active commission is up, I *will* pursue such," West-cott vowed, "though it'll be a wrench to part us, at last."

"Aye, we've become good friends since we got *Reliant* in Oh-Three," Lewrie agreed, "and I trust we will always be, no matter where the Navy sends us. If I can, I'll even dance at your wedding."

"*My* wedding!" Westcott suddenly hooted with mirth. "*That'll* be a cold day in Hell. Ain't in my nature, no. I'd put that off 'til I make 'Post,' and find a sweet little 'batter pudding' half my age like Hyde Parker did. Or *less* than half my age. Yum yum."

"You're incorrigible," Lewrie chuckled.

"Said the pot to the kettle," Westcott happily rejoined.

"Well, I'll leave you to your 'Devil's Weed,' and go prepare for sup-per," Lewrie said. "Don't go settin' the bloody ship on fire."

"Good night, then, Alan sir," Westcott bade him, his harsh, brief smile baring his teeth which showed stark white in the glow of the taffrail lan-thorns.

CHAPTER TWENTY-NINE

L ewrie had a change of heart and told Lieutenant Westcott to arm himself and go ashore with him, at the last moment. But when the cutter landed them on the North bank of the Maceira River, they had to wander about for a time to find the means to go further. At last, a young infantry officer on a nondescript horse accosted them with a shout and a laugh.

"Halt, who goes there, sirs!" he hoorawed. "What do we have here? Two French officers in blue, and under arms? Never *do*, sirs!"

"And who might you be, young sir?" Lewrie replied in a like manner, with a grin on his face. "We've come ashore from our ship to see what's happening. Are there any mounts available?"

"Allow me to name myself to you, sirs, Leftenant John Beauchamp, of the First Battalion of the Ninth Foot," the young officer gaily said, and doffing his bicorne with a bow from the saddle.

"Captain Sir Alan Lewrie, and my First Officer, Lieutenant Geoffrey Westcott," Lewrie replied, doffing his cocked hat in kind.

"A pleasure to make your acquaintances, sirs," Beauchamp said. "Horses? Only if you will settle for poor local 'bone-setters' like mine, sirs, but I can round a couple up. We're damned short on cavalry remounts. Follow me, if you will."

Lewrie and Westcott took station to Beauchamp's larboard side and strolled along up the river-bank into the draw between the headlands. "We saw wounded coming off last night, sir." Lewrie asked, "Has there been a fight?"

"Indeed there *was*, sir, and we sent the French packing in short order!" Beauchamp boasted. "We marched down to a fortified town by name of Óbidos, the French general, Delaborde, didn't like the odds, and retreated to a line of steep hills South of the town. You'll see them in a bit, once we're further inland. Here's our remount service, such as it is," he said, making a face and leading them to where some locally commandeered Portuguese saddle horses waited, their forelegs hobbled to keep them from grazing or running off. Several were already saddled, and Beauchamp breezily ordered the grooms to lead out a pair.

"I assume that sailors know *how* to ride, sirs?" he teased.

"It'll come back to me," Lewrie replied as he took the reins of a plain brown horse, hiked a booted leg, and swung up into the saddle.

Beauchamp led them on into the plain and the army encampment.

"Up yonder, sirs," the Army officer said, pointing to the North. "There were steep hills, with deep gullies between, and a rough stone wall laid all along the tops of the hills, an incredibly strong position, yet . . . !" he enthused, "we went at them like lions, steep as it was, and threw them off and sent them swarming down into the plain, here. Three guns were captured, and an host of prisoners taken. But for a lack of cavalry, we could have pursued their broken ranks out onto the plain. The French had *swarms* of cavalry."

"So, the French were beaten," Lewrie stated with delight.

"Decisively, sir," Beauchamp hooted. "Decisively! Now, they're South of us, and to the East of us. There's perhaps nine thousand under a chap named Loisin, coming West from Abrantes, and Delaborde still lurks down that way. The General fully expects that there will be a bigger battle to come, and soon. We're told that we're to be re-enforced with another four thousand men, when General Sir Harry Burrard and his convoy show up in the bay."

"He's senior to Wellesley," Lewrie said. "He'll take over?"

"God, I *hope* not, sir!" Beauchamp said, grimacing. "We're doing just fine with Sir Arthur. General Burrard has not seen action since the Dutch expedition in Ninety-Eight, and made no grand show of his abilities, then. He's over seventy years old!"

"Those are Portuguese carts and waggons yonder?" Westcott asked as they drew near a rather large conglomeration.

"Army Commissariat, Portuguese we've hired," Beauchamp told him, "with solid silver shillings, not chits, too. The rest are Irish, if you can believe it. The General hired them before we sailed here. He told my Colonel that he'd learned in India that arrangements for a big commissary train are absolutely necessary. Not that Horse Guards will believe that, though."

"Those casualties we saw last night," Lewrie pressed. "Was it dearly won?"

"Oh no, sir!" Beauchamp said; he was irrepressibly cheerful. "We lost about four hundred and eighty, and the French lost nigh five hundred, plus the prisoners we took. Not bad at all, really. Aha! We're coming to the Portuguese lines. *Do* keep a hand on your purses, sirs. They're nowhere near so bad as Irish regiments, yet . . . ! They are light infantry, called *Caçadores*. Quite good, really, under one of ours, Colonel Trant."

"Their Portuguese officers ain't up to snuff?" Lewrie asked as he took in the foreign troops, mostly uniformed in brown coats.

"From what I've heard, they're *miles* better at their trade than the Spanish," Beauchamp told him with a deprecating laugh, "but, over our long, good relations with Portugal, many British officers served in their army. Trant, now, sirs. He's most capable and aggressive, but the General *was* heard to say that he's a very good officer, but as drunken a dog as ever lived, hah hah! Uh-oh!" Beauchamp sobred quickly and put on a stern face as they rode deeper into the encampment, making a great display of pointing things out to Lewrie and Westcott.

There was a rider approaching with a pack of hounds scouting at his mount's flanks and rear, a grim-visaged fellow wearing an un-adorned bicorne hat and a long-skirted dark grey coat, with only a gilt-edged belt at his waist, and a sword upon his left hip, to denote him as an officer of some kind.

Lt. Beauchamp doffed his hat to the fellow, and Lewrie thought it a good idea to do the same, and throw in a "Good morning to you, sir" for good measure, which earned him a scowl and a brisk nod of his head, which, admittedly, gave Lewrie a faint chill. The man was thin-lipped, haughty, his eyes cold and contempuous beneath a set of full brows, and that nose! It was a prominent hawk's beak.

"Who was that?" Lewrie asked, turning to look astern from his saddle once they had passed.

"That was Sir Arthur Wellesley, sir," Lt. Beauchamp said with a sigh of relief that he had escaped the Presence without a tongue-lashing for idling about, far from his battalion lines, and playing tour guide to a pair of idle sailors.

"A *stern* damned fellow," Lt. Westcott commented in a low voice.

"Oh, indeed, sirs," Beauchamp agreed with a shiver.

"He didn't look particularly happy to see us," Lewrie said.

"Well, we *are* taking a tour, sir," Westcott said.

"It may be that he expected that General Burrard had come into the bay, and that you were part of the convoy escort, sir," Beauchamp dared speculate. "That's where he was riding, to the river mouth, to see if Burrard had arrived."

"Well, no wonder he gave us the cold-eye," Lewrie said. "In his place, I'd've stuck my tongue out at us, too."

That tongue-in-cheek statement gave the young Army officer such a pause that he burst out laughing, amazed that a senior officer of a high rank could be so droll.

"What about Marshal Junot and the rest of his hundred thousand Frogs, though, Mister Beauchamp?" Lewrie asked, using the naval parlance. "When and if General Burrard arrives, you'll have how many men against all of Junot's?"

"Oh, about sixteen thousand British, two thousand Portuguese, altogether, sir," Beauchamp told him, looking off to the far distance to do his sums in his head, "but, we've information that the bulk of Marshal Junot's forces are still far South, round Lisbon and Torres Vedras . . . just *miles* away! We would have been much nearer to Torres Vedras ourselves, but for the word of General Burrard's arrival here in Maceira Bay. The General marched us over to the coast to cover the landings, pick up the re-enforcements and more guns and cavalry, before resuming our march on Lisbon."

"General Sir Hew Dalrymple's coming, too," Lewrie said with a scowl of dis-approval. "He's to take supreme command over Wellesley *and* Burrard, God help you. He's known as the Dowager."

"That's not good, either, I may take it, sir?" Beauchamp said with a visible wince.

"Not good at all, sir," Lewrie gloomily told him.

They were in the middle of the British lines by then, surrounded by tents, and soldiers in all manner of un-dress, and the aromas of unwashed bodies; horse, mule, and oxen manure; the sour reek of campfires burning green wood; salt-beef or salt-pork cooking; and a tang of illicit rum or locally-procured wine. Soldiers' wives sat and sewed or idled, some with pipes or *cigarros* in their mouths. The few children allowed along with each regiment were whooping, running, and playing round between the tents and along the lanes between the tent lines, as ragged a bunch as their fathers, and just as rough.

Lewrie looked South to scan the prospects, taking in the plain that stretched from Óbidos and Roliça, and the line of hills that lay beyond, to the Sou'east.

"What's beyond those hills?" he asked, pulling his telescope from a side pocket of his coat for a better look.

"Some scattered villages and hamlets, sir," Lt. Beauchamp told him, squinting to recall them all. "There's a Toledo, a Porto Novo on the coast, a wee place called Fentanell, and the village of Vimeiro. Some cavalry videttes have scouted down yonder, and I heard that it's pretty broken country, and that the road's horrid. But then, *every* road we've seen so far has been horrid. It's getting on for tea time. Might you gentlemen care to partake at my regimental mess?"

"Thankee, no, Mister Beauchamp," Lewrie said, shaking his head as he lowered his telescope, "but I think that Mister Westcott and I will return to our ship. We might have to shift *Sapphire* out of the way of the arriving convoy and its escort. I'm grateful for your taking the time to show us round."

"Very well, sirs," Beauchamp said with a grin, doffing his hat to them in parting salute. "Leave the horses at the remount station. Don't know if they'll be available, later, but, if you wish to come ashore and witness the battle to come, the best of luck to you."

Lt. Beauchamp put his mount to a stride and headed off for his mess, and his tea, whilst Lewrie and Westcott turned theirs round and ambled back to the beach at a slow walk.

"At least *he* seems confident, sir," Westcott commented after a long, quiet moment. "But, he *is* a younker. All flags and bands, and glory."

"Aye, we know better by now, don't we," Lewrie cynically agreed. "But, ye know . . . I think I *would* like to see how this army does when the time comes."

"I would, too, sir," Westcott strongly hinted. "If only to relieve the boredom. We've spent too long at escort-work, with nary one sight of an enemy sail, or the prospect of a fight. I fear that you have spoiled me, and our crew, you know."

"We *have* had a good run at it, haven't we, Geoffrey?" Lewrie mused.

"Until the French went missish, and lurk in port, scared to risk themselves at sea any longer."

"Five whole years of excitement," Westcott summed up with a longing sigh. "God, it's so dull, we might as well be at *peace!*"

After half an hour, they reached the remount station and surrendered their tired mounts, then continued on foot to the banks of the shallow Maceira River.

"There he is, again," Westcott pointed out as he espied the mounted man they now knew for Lieutenant-General Sir Arthur Wellesley. He was peering out to sea with his own pocket telescope, looking both intent and angry. His horse had its head up, too, looking seaward, as were the hounds that accompanied him, who sat on their hindquarters with their tongues lolling, panting in perfect patience as if awed by their master's mood, and barely bothering to scratch at their fleas.

"What's he looking at?" Westcott wondered aloud, but in a soft voice, as if he was daunted, too.

Lewrie pulled out his glass and had a long look, then handed it to Westcott. "There are dozens of ships out there, Mister Westcott, tops'ls and t'gallants above the horizon. They might be hull-up by mid-afternoon. If it ain't the French, it's Burrard and his brigades, come at last."

"No wonder he looks so black, then," Westcott said with a wee laugh.

Wellesley heard that, and snapped his head about to glare at them both for a second, his face all "thunder and lightning." Those thin lips half opened for a hurled curse, then clapped shut just as quickly before he returned his steely gaze to the incoming ships.

"Let's get back aboard," Lewrie said, "before he has us flogged at a waggon wheel."

CHAPTER THIRTY

*T*he troop transports, "cavalry ships," and supply vessels came to anchor off Maceira Bay in droves, with the convoy escorts anchoring further out. HMS *Sapphire*'s four boats were manned and sent off to aid the
dis-embarkation that proceeded throughout the afternoon and long into
the night. Lewrie stayed on the poop deck no matter the heat of the day,
swivelling his telescope about to take it all in, finding that General Wellesley's efficiency applied to the new arrivals, too, for the whole bay hummed
with activity, and battalions, batteries, and horse troops went ashore with
an alacrity rarely seen, making those landings at Blaauberg Bay at the Dutch
Cape Colony in 1806 look like a perfect shambles by comparison.

General Burrard's re-enforcement did not extend to many pieces of artillery, though, and Lewrie could count only about 240 cavalry horses to
add to the 180 or so that Wellesley had had at the Battle of Roliça. And
those poor horses, both the cavalry mounts and the gun-team horses! They
had been at sea so long that they seemingly had lost the ability to walk.
Once they'd been swum ashore and led to assembly points, it was almost
comical to see horses saddled up, cavalry troopers swung up astride, and
see the horses just fold their legs up and squat to the ground under the
weight!

"Hmm," Lt. Westcott said, his face contorted by a wince as he witnessed that. "*That* don't look promising. That Beauchamp fellow told us this morning that the French had *scads* more cavalry than we do. What use are *those* poor prads, if they can't even stand up? If you *do* go ashore to see the battle, sir, pray Jesus you don't get offered one of *them*!"

"A good clue t'that, Geoffrey," Lewrie said, shaking his head as he watched, "is that the new-come horses all have docked tails, but the local Portuguese horses we got didn't."

"Don't see the sense of that, sir," Westcott said. "How else do they keep the flies off them, if they don't have long tails. Poor beasts. A Hell of a thing our Army does with their horseflesh. Not as bad as the French, I'm told, though. They ride them to death, with open saddle sores so bad that you can smell them coming."

"S'truth?" Lewrie gawped. "There's another good reason t'hate the French like the Devil hates Holy Water."

"At least they leave their tails long," Westcott agreed. "My word, on the riverbank yonder. Where all the torches are lit? Isn't that Wellesley getting into that boat?"

Lewrie lifted his glass once more and peered intently at the shore. "Aye, I think it is, by God. 'Captain Repair On Board,' and all that, hey? The poor bastard's on his way t'get his marchin' orders from Burrard, most-like, gettin' replaced before he's fought his battle. I wonder if he's thinkin' that he'd've done better to march off South without waitin' for extra troops."

"Sir?" Midshipman Harvey reported from the bottom of the quarter-deck ladderway. "Our boats are returning from their ferry-work."

"Very well, Mister Harvey," Lewrie absently took note. "My compliments to the Purser, Mister Cadrick, and he's to see that the boat crews get their evening rum issue . . . them only, mind . . . and that they are fed their proper rations right after."

They had rotated the hands who manned the boats right through the start of the First Dog and into the Second Dog, and these last few sailors had been deprived, away from the ship when the evening rum issue was doled out, and the evening meal was served up from the cauldrons.

"I'll see to it, sir," Westcott offered.

"Thankee, Mister Westcott," Lewrie said with an incline of his head. He pulled out his pocket watch and studied it in the light from the taffrail lanthorns. "It's almost time for your supper, and mine. Sure ye aren't deprivin' yourself?"

"The wardroom mess can start without me," Westcott said with a shrug.

"Then I will leave it to you, sir, and go below," Lewrie said, closing

the tubes of his telescope and trotting down the ladderway to the quarterdeck, and the door to his great-cabins.

He barely had time to hang his hat on a peg before his cook, Yeovill,
came breezing in with his heavy covered brass barge, and a cheery "Good
evening, sir!" and a description of what he had prepared: beef broth with
peas, carrots, and onions; a small roast quail done in herbs; salt-pork well-
soaked in fresh water to remove the crusted preservative and fried; with
a roasted potato, split and drizzled with a cheese and bacon sauce; and green
beans.

Of course, there were some shreds of everything for Chalky, along with
his usual wee sausages, and Yeovill assured him that the ship's dog,
Bisquit, had already gotten a bowl of broth, rice, and cut-up sausages,
too, which he was devouring in his cubby beneath the starboard poop deck
ladderway on the quarterdeck . . . after a foraging journey along both
gun decks among his friends in the crew.

There was a very nice Portuguese white wine with the quail, and Lewrie took a whole glass before his first bite, asking for a re-fill.

"Ehm, before ye turn in tonight, Pettus," Lewrie said after a few spoonfuls of broth, "I'm still of a mind t'go ashore round dawn, t'see what the
army's up to. I wish my over-under pistols and the brace of single-barrel
Mantons cleaned and oiled, and my Ferguson rifled musket seen to."

"Ehm, if there is to be a battle, sir, you'll be wishing for a silk shirt and
silk stockings?" Pettus replied, pausing in the act of pouring that re-fill.
"Just in case?"

"Aye," Lewrie said, ravenously working his way to the bottom of the
soup bowl. "And I'll need some bisquit and cheese, and some of the sausages, too, t'take with me."

"Fearsome, wot boots'll do t'yer stockin's, though, sir," his cabin
servant, Jessop, grumbled. "Darnin' silk's impossible."

"Rouse me at the end of the Middle Watch," Lewrie instructed, beginning on the quail and the potato and green beans.

"A bowl of porridge before you go, then, sir?" Yeovill asked.

"Aye, that'd do nicely, Yeovill," Lewrie agreed.

"I'll send your hanger to the Armourer for a fresh edge, too, sir," Pettus
suggested.

"Oh! See Mister Keane!" Lewrie added. "I'll have need of one of the
Marines' canteens, for water."

"I'll see to it, sir," Pettus said, though his face wore a wary look, and
Lewrie missed the worried expression that Pettus shared with Jessop and

Yeovill. Their Captain was off in search of adventure and excitement . . . again . . . and was sure to find it, the risk be-damned, and no one with better sense could talk him out of it.

"Ye have a care, now, sor," Cox'n Liam Desmond muttered as the cutter grounded on the banks of the Maceira a little past 5 A.M.

"An' may th' Good Lord keep ye in His hand, sor," Pat Furfy added in a solemn voice, crossing himself. "Though, if ya need some stout lads at yer back—"

"I've the army, at my *front*, Furfy, don't ye worry," Lewrie said as he waded the last few feet to dry land. "Back to the ship, you lot, and I'll see you later."

"Aye, sor," Desmond said, sounding doubtful.

It was still dark, before pre-dawn, and the warmth of a Portuguese August had evaporated overnight, leaving a dank, clammy, coolness. There was a faint breath of wind off the sea.

Lewrie trudged along the path he had followed the day before, stumbling over rocks in the dark, headed for a series of torches and the faint glows of campfires beyond the gap between the headlands and the banks of the river. He could not see the remount station; it had been moved somewhere further along.

"Damn!" he spat to the dawn. "I'll be on 'Shank's Ponies' like the poor, bloody infantry! All the way to . . . where?"

I'm already regrettin' this, he thought; *Maybe I should just find a unit in the rear, and scrounge a mug o' tea.*

He hiked on, tripping and stumbling over tussocks of long grass and nigh-invisible irregularities in the ground, through the gap and out onto the plains, and stopped in shock. Half-seen in the first wee greyness of pre-dawn, the encampment he'd ridden through the morning before was just gone! The long, orderly lines of tents had been struck, the campfires extinguished, and the army had marched off South. What few fires still lit the night were those of the baggage train, and they looked to be ready to trundle off in the army's wake, with mules and oxen harnessed or yoked, and the waggoners and carters standing round the few fires to gulp down their last morsels of breakfasts, and their lasts swallows of water or tea.

"Hoy, there! Who are ye, an' what're ye doin' here?" A challenge was called out. He heard the clank of a musket cocking.

"Captain Alan Lewrie, HMS *Sapphire*!" Lewrie shouted back, half-alarmed out of his skin. "Royal Navy?" he added.

"Corp'ral o' th' Guard?" that voice bellowed. "Post Two, we've got a visitor!"

A lean, fox-faced fellow shambled over from one of the fires with a lanthorn held aloft, had himself a good look, and deliberately spat tobacco juice. "Lor', 'e *is* Navy! Wot're ya doin' wand'rin' about this time o' night, sir?"

"Looking for the remount station, for a horse," Lewrie said in calmer takings, for though the sentry had lowered his musket, it was still fully-cocked, and the bayonet tip flashed in the light from the lanthorn, and they both peered at him as if they'd caught themselves a French spy. "I wish to ride up to the main body of the army."

"A'ready gone, sir," the Corporal informed him, "an' remounts is up with 'em. Fear ya haveta walk all th' way, or, ya might hitch a ride with th' baggage train, if yer that eager."

"A ride'll do me quite well, Corporal," Lewrie quickly agreed.

"Pass, then, sir," the Corporal allowed, waving his lanthorn in invitation to approach the mass of waggons. "Christ! Beggin' yer pardon, sir, but ya come armed for it," he said, noting all the weaponry that Lewrie carried stuffed into his coat side pockets, hung from his waist-band, at his hip, and upon his shoulder.

Once Lewrie was far enough off, the Corporal turned to the Private and spat another dollop of tobacco juice. "Bloody, damned officers. Ain't got a lick o' sense in their heads. You an' me, we'll stick with th' waggons, an' stay safe as houses."

He'd picked up *some* Portuguese from Maddalena, but he doubted his ability to converse with any of the hired waggoners, so he went to the Irishmen hired on by General Wellesley, moments before they began to creak and rumble off.

"Could I get a ride?" he called to a burly, beet-faced fellow with a shock of red hair. "I wish to go up to the army."

"Iff'n ye do, yer outta yer fackin' mind," the waggoner shot back with a dis-believing scowl, "but so was I when I signed on fer dis mess. Aye, climb aboard, an' hang on."

That took some doing, for the box was high off the ground and hand-and foot-holds took some figuring out before he was seated alongside the waggoner, who pulled a pipe from a coat pocket and lit it off the candle lanthorn hung ahead of him. Satisfied that his pipe was drawing well, he lifted his reins and gave them a shake, calling out to his four-horse team. At once, there came an appalling screeching from un-greased axles and several sideways lurches as the waggon got a way on.

"Told ye t'hang on, sor," the waggoner grumbled. "It ain't no coach-an'-four. Iff'n ye wish t'say somethin', ye'll haveta shout, for it's a noisy bashtit, t'boot, har har!"

The whole column of waggons and carts was extremely noisy, loud enough to be heard coming for miles. Oxen bellowed in protest, mules brayed now and then, long whips cracked so often that they sounded like sporadic musket fire, and the carters and waggoners continually cursed their beasts, loud, foul, and inventively.

"Royal Artillery, air ye?" the waggoner asked after the first mile, mis-taking Lewrie's blue coat. "Late t'th' party if ye air."

"Navy," Lewrie told him.

"Den yer daft as bats," the man said with a sniff, leaning over to lar-board to hawk up a load of phlegm, then took time to re-light his pipe. "Ye won't git me on a ship, again. Sailin' here was th' worst time o' me life. Mind yer fingers," he cautioned as the waggon gave some more, alarming lurches which made the whole assembly groan as if it would come apart, turn-ing hand-holds into mousetraps as boards worked against each other.

"Rough road," Lewrie commented.

"What ye say? Rough, de man says! Dey ain't no roads in dis bloody country, at all. Half de time, we been in dry creek beds when we couldn't even *find* th' roads, e'en when de maps say they're there!"

"What are you carrying?" Lewrie asked.

"Half a ton o' bisquit, wot passes fer bread fer the bloody fools who went for soldiers," the man griped, "an' dey're welcome to it. Me an' me mates, we bake *real* bread fer ourselves each night. Breast to, ye fackin' four-legged hoors!" he howled of a sudden and cracked his long whip at his team.

So passed the second mile.

The sun slowly rose, and the landscape round the column became vis-ible, as did the dust stirred up by thousands of hooves and wheels. The broad valley of the Maceira narrowed as the waggons neared hills, the hills that Lt. Beauchamp had pointed out to Lewrie the day before. The shal-low river turned into a creek off to the right where it issued from between the hills, and just ahead sat a lop-angled wood signpost announcing that the village of Vimeiro was ahead on their right.

"Caught up with de bloody army," the waggoner said, spitting.

Atop the nearest hill, and strung along the others that rose to the East and Northeast, there were soldiers in black shakoes, red coats, and grey trousers, some assembled in formal rank and file near their Regimental and King's Colours, but most of them on the back slopes of the hills were sprawled or seated at their ease, doing what any soldiers did since Roman times; waiting.

There were more troops in the village of Vimeiro, and what little cavalry was with the army was posted round the village, and Lewrie could spot several dozen horses watering along the northern bank of the Maceira.

"Think I'll get down here," Lewrie told the waggoner, "and get a horse from them," he said, pointing at the remounts.

"Man, ye iver *see* a battle?" the waggoner gawped, leaning back in astonishment. "Man on a horse, he's the finest target in de world! Ah, on yer head be it," he said, drawing rein.

Lewrie clumsily clambered down from the box and headed for the town. He spotted a face he recognised from the remount station, and cajoled the soldier to give him a mount, another of those non-descript locally commandeered Portuguese horses, a dull brown one with black mane and tail, equipped with what looked to be cast-off reins and saddlery, and stirrup straps that looked as if they'd come apart if too much pressure was put upon them.

Leery and cautious, Lewrie swung himself aboard, reined the horse around, and clucked his tongue to get it moving, but no; it took the heels of his boots to encourage it to move, and that only at a sedate walk into the village proper and past a plain two-storey house that, by the presence of so many officers, he took for Wellesley's headquarters.

Mounted messengers, that the army termed gallopers, were coming and going, young fellows of spirit who could not resist the urge to make a great show of their duties and their temporary importance.

Lewrie drew rein a bit beyond the headquarters house to watch, and turned in the saddle to look astern as bugles and whistles blew, and some troops to the West left their positions and began to march through the village to the East.

"What's happening?" he asked of a passing mounted officer.

"Change of position," the officer replied, giving Lewrie a dis-believing look. "French columns have been spotted more to the Southeast, so we're going up to the next ridge over. What the Devil are *you* doing here, sir? The ocean's back that way, hah hah!"

"Curiosity," Lewrie replied with a grin.

"That killed the cat, don't ye know," the fellow cast over his shoulder as he paced along beside his troops.

Lewrie decided to follow the regiment that was passing through Vimeiro. He let his horse have a drink from the Maceira, then forded it and went up the Eastern hills above Vimeiro. Once atop, he found a good view of the countryside, and began to get a grasp of the ground.

Stretching out towards the East and Northeast, there was a long ridge, nearly two miles long, he estimated. The Maceira, now a creek, ran along the ridge's South foot, below an irregular slope which was rather steep in places, but approachable at most, though he thought anyone climbing up would be out of breath by the time he got to the top. To the South and Southeast there lay a rolling set of hillocks that made a second plain, well-timbered in places, and beyond there, what he took for another drop-off to lower ground, a narrow valley in between yet another row of hills.

There was movement all along the ridge as regiments marched further on to shift the whole army's positions to counter . . . something. Lewrie pulled out his smaller pocket telescope and searched for a reason why, and, after a time, found it. There were clouds of dust in the Southeast, and, now and then, glints of morning sunlight off metal, perhaps brass shako plates or bayonets; he did not know, but strongly suspected.

He had loaded and primed all his pistols the night before, but had left the Ferguson un-loaded. Now, he felt the urge to load it. He cranked the long brass trigger guard–hand grip one turn, lowering the sealing screw to expose the breech of the barrel. From the cartridge box on his right hip he withrew a pre-made paper cartridge and bit off one end, using a dribble of powder to prime the pan, then shoved the rest of the cartridge, bullet-end first, into the breech and screwed the weapon shut. A final fiddling with the screw of the dog's jaw that held the flint tight, and he lay it across the front of the saddle, ready for use.

Lewrie thumped his heels to get his horse moving again, along the ridge for a better view of what the newly-placed regiments were doing. He saw green-jacketed soldiers who carried shorter weapons than the Land Pattern Tower musket, men with silver hunting-horn insignia on their shakoes, who were moving downslope in pairs, spaced far apart from other pairs, and wondered who they were; red was the colour of soldiers, after all! The regiment closest to him was taking position along the backside of the ridge, detaching their Light Companies of skirmishers downslope a few paces, and along the crest. With another prompting thump, he goaded his horse for a closer look-see.

"Good Lord, a sailor, up here?" an Army Captain brayed, and let out a guffaw. "Lost your way, old man?"

"The French don't seem all that eager t'oblige me at sea any longer, so I thought I'd see how they fight on land, sir," Lewrie told him in a genial manner.

"Well, you'll see a fine show in an hour or so," the Captain said with a twinkle of eager anticipation. "Horsley, sir," he said to name himself, and his regiment.

"Captain Lewrie, of the *Sapphire*," Lewrie said in return. "Who are those people in green down yonder?"

"The Rifles, sir, the 'Greenjackets,'" Horsley told him with a roll of his eyes. "Think they hung the moon, they do. They fight like skirmishers, in pairs, march at the quick-step, and consider themselves *chosen*, above the common run of soldiers. They're armed with Baker rifles, which are considered to be quite accurate, but damned slow to load. I've tried one, and it's the very Devil to get a ball rammed down with a greased leather patch round it. Might as well use a hammer, haw! They specialise," he imparted with a scowl, "at picking off officers and senior sergeants, at nearly two hundred yards, and God help us do they give the French the idea to emulate them. I see you came well-armed, sir. Well, you just might need all of that, do the French get up close. A custom musket, is it?"

"A breech-loading Ferguson rifled musket, sir," Lewrie told him. "Got it at Yorktown, when I was a pup."

"Egads, a Ferguson! I've never seen one. Might I?" Horsely pleaded, and Lewrie handed it over, explaining how it loaded.

"With hard practice, I could get off five or six shots each minute," Lewrie told him, "though I've not had call for such speed in ages. Two hundred yards' range is average."

"We've trained our lads to get off four a minute," Horsley said as he handed the Ferguson back, "but, they can manage more if they spit the ball down the muzzle and rap the butt on the ground to settle it all at the breech, with no need for the ram rod. Aha! Look there!"

Lewrie looked in the direction Horsley was pointing, and saw a French Tricolour flag at the head of a long column of fours, and the glint of a shiny symbol on a pole, as it emerged from the far trees, the advance regiment or brigade of an entire army.

"Eagles," Captain Horsley said.

"Eagles?" Lewrie asked.

"Bonaparte issues all his regiments a silver spread eagle as a mark of distinction," Horsley explained, "not just to units which have done something grand and brave. *His* Imperial eagles, d'ye see. Makes them think they're as grand as his pampered Grenadiers, and it's said they'd rather die than lose one, like the eagles of the old Roman legions. Be a grand thing to take one. Maybe today's the day, hey?"

"How come most of your regiment's back below the crest?" Lewrie asked, most of his attention drawn to the sight of more French regiments emerging and forming all along the lower ground, with hordes of brilliantly uniformed cavalry trotting up alongside, and artillery in the rear.

"Oh, that's His Nibs's orders," Horsley said with another roll of his eyes. "A queer way to fight, if you ask me, waiting 'til the last moment to rush up, form line, and give them volleys, but, what's a fellow to do if a General tells you to." Horsley pulled a pocket watch out and flipped the lid open. "A little past nine of the morning. We may have ourselves a battle by ten. Ehm, a slight suggestion, Captain . . . Lewrie did ye say? I've left my mount down behind the ridge line, and it might be good for you to do so. A mounted man is a grand target for the French artillery, and you might draw a bit too much attention to my men who are in the open."

"I'll just ride on, have a look-see," Lewrie decided, bidding Horsley a good morning, and ambling on Eastwards.

He rode on to the next regiment, staying near the crest of the ridge so he could witness as much of the field as possible, now and then drawing rein to use his telescope. It was frustrating, for his pocket telescope was much narrower and shorter than the glasses used aboard ship, the "fetch 'em ups." The view in the ocular was narrower, too.

"Wot th' bastards doin', Corp?" a soldier just behind the crest of the ridge called out to another soldier who stood in plain view.

"Formin' up in bloody blocks!" the Corporal shouted back.

"Silence in the ranks!" some officer snapped.

Lewrie's attention was drawn to what the French were doing, as well, and he couldn't quite understand it. Regiment after regiment were coming together, elbow to elbow, rank after rank, creating dense blocks that looked to be thirty men across the front file, and fifty or more in depth.

Other soldiers with bright green epaulets, as opposed to the men in the masses who wore red epaulets, were loosely drawn up on either flank and out in front of the massed blocks, and there were some cavalry troops between, a bewildering array of brass helmets with leopard skins, long horsehair plumes, some in polished back-and-breast armour, some in shakoed headgear, intricately laced and multi-buttoned dolman jackets, with pelisses thrown back over their shoulders. There were even lancers in silly-looking helmets that put Lewrie in mind of exaggerated hats worn by Oxford dons!

"Ah, good morning to you, sir," yet another infantry officer said in greeting as Lewrie ambled up near his Light Company. "They seem to have brought it all, don't you think? Lancers, Hussars, Dragoons, even Cuirassiers, but no *Grenadiers au Cheval*. Those would be with Napoleon himself, his mounted Grenadier Guards. You'd know 'em by their tall bearskin hats. Don't know why, but the French call 'em *Les Gros Talons*, the 'Big Heels.' Oh well, no matter. Cavalry is just for show, today. We have the slope of them, and they'll find it difficult to get up with us."

Lewrie was relieved that this officer didn't make a jape about a sailor being out of his element, and he *did* sound knowledgeable, so Lewrie at last dis-mounted and walked over to him.

"Why are they making those big blocks?" Lewrie asked.

"Ah, that's their way, isn't it?" the Light Company Captain rejoined with a titter. "They always attack in large columns, several of them abreast of each other, and so far, they've been unstoppable. Ask the Dutch, the Austrians, and the Russians. Look closely at the centre of each column. See the drummers, all the flags, and eagles?"

Lewrie raised his telescope and found the Tricolours, other banners displayed on horizontal cross-pieces which bore wreathed *N*'s for "Napoleon," and those silver eagles.

"Out in front and on the flanks, those fellows with the green epaulets, those are their *voltigeurs*, and *tirailleurs*," the Captain said. "Light infantry, much like our Light Companies. *Voltigeurs* . . . it means 'Leapers,' or maybe 'Grasshoppers.' Who'd be a *Grasshopper*, I ask you?" he said with another titter. "Never live it *down*! *Tirailleurs*, well . . . 'Shooters' is close, but if the French had any sense, they'd issue rifled weapons, not smoothbore muskets."

"Let's hope they don't, sir," Lewrie said, faking a shiver, "else our own officers get knocked off quicker than theirs."

"Oh, then we can't have *that*!" the Army officer said with another of his titters, almost a bray this time. "How else would our troops be controlled? We fight battles, not Irish riots. Ah, I believe that the curtain is about to go up. Look there, over to the right."

French artillery was in position, the gunners had done all their fiddling with train and elevation, the barrels were loaded, and sudden spurts of yellowish-white smoke gushed from the muzzles, silently at first, the ground-shaking explosions coming a second or two later and rattling the ground, preceded by the howl of roundshot that climbed the scale as they neared, then keening away as most of the shot went soaring over the top of the ridge line. Some few lucky shots landed just short to graze along the crests, but most struck well below the positioned regiments on the ridge and ploughed into the ground with great gouts of thrown-up earth.

"Don't know about you, sir, but I'd see to my horse," the Captain of the Light Company cautioned. "Far from a thoroughbred, what, but do recall poor Richard the Third, 'a horse, a horse, my kingdom for a horse!, hey? Besides, he ain't battle-trained, most-like, and he'll take fright and gallop off if he ain't well-tended."

"Good idea, sir," Lewrie said, eying his nervous mount, which already was showing the whites of its eyes and tugging at the reins. Lewrie crossed the ridge to the reverse slope, where hundreds and hundreds of soldiers sat or lay in shelter, found this particular regiment's officers' mounts being tended by grooms, and bade them to look after his, then returned to the crest of the ridge.

The French cannonading continued for some time, but the only people that he could see harmed by it were the few skirmishing companies posted on the forward face of the ridge line, below the crest, and since the roundshot was slamming into the ground and caroming on, only one soldier in a group would suffer for it, while the rest were spared. At the crest of the ridge, there were enough men standing in two-deep ranks to make good targets, but very few were killed or injured; the balls might graze the crest, but then sailed off well over the sheltering men on the back slopes.

They can keep that up all day, but it won't help 'em much, he told himself; *Shootin' uphill's a total waste.*

Artillery got its best results on flatter ground, where shot could strike a bit short, rise up from First Graze, then go skipping along at eight hundred feet per second or better to plough into tight ranks like a game of bowls, scattering broken bodies like nine-pins.

"Your poor horse run away, yet, sir?" the Captain from the Light

Company asked as he strolled up to Lewrie, his sword out and whacking shoots of long grass.

"Not yet, no, sir," Lewrie said with a smile, introducing himself at last.

"Captain Samuel Ford, sir, and happy to make your acquaintance," the other fellow told him, offering his hand. "Wonder if the French gunners are growing as frustrated as we are, what? All that powder and shot, trundled here all the way from Lisbon . . . wasted."

There were now at least ten of those massive blocks of troops below them on the upper plain, all standing at attention, it looked like, waiting stoically for . . . what?

"There, Captain Lewrie, a bit to our right," Captain Ford said, pointing, after a long moment. "I do believe that two of the columns are advancing, at last. Not for us, more's the pity. Damn all French, root and branch, but they *do* know how to stage a fine show."

Those two massive columns were lurching forward, marching to the beat of drums, about three or four hundred yards apart from each other, with their light infantry out front as skirmishers and flank guards. They put Lewrie in mind of magic blue carpets creeping along as they began their slow ascent to the ridge. In his ocular, he could see them sway left and right, elbow to elbow, in perfect step, with their muskets held vertically against their right chests and shoulders, at Carry Arms. They were *spiny* creeping blue carpets, for the blades of their fixed bayonets winked and twinkled in waves as they swayed.

The drums thundered in an almost hypnotic beat, over and over, then came a brief pause as nigh two thousand men gave a great shout together, *"Vive l'Empereur!"* and the drums thundered *Boom-buh-buh-boom*. Then *"Vive l'Empereur!"*

Christ, what if they are *unstoppable?* Lewrie thought with a sudden chill in his innards; *And if they are, can my bloody horse be made t'gallop?*

CHAPTER THIRTY-ONE

*T*he initial French thrust seemed aimed closer to the village of Vimeiro, off to Lewrie's right, perhaps in hopes that those massive, bludgeoning columns would push through and cut the British lines in two, and reach the Maceira River valley to cut off any hope of extraction.

Boom-bub-buh-buh-boom, then the pause and the shout of *"Vive L'Empereur!"*, louder now as those two columns got closer, and Lewrie could begin to make out details, the brightly polished metal shako plates, and the differences between them from one regiment to the next, even the large brass numbers, the stiff plumes that rose from the sides of their shakoes in different colours. He could almost make out individual faces; tanned as brown as sailors from weeks or months in the field, coated with dust stirred up by their own boots, and the abundance of short beards or long mustachios among the soldiers.

"Scruffy lot," Lewrie muttered, half to himself, and thinking that there was a great difference between the Sunday parade ground and the field. The French wore ragged, faded, and patched uniforms, stained and dusted, whilst a quick look down the line of the ridge showed the British troops still in mostly new-issued and clean kits.

"When's our bloody artillery going to—?" Ford grumbled, cut off by the first, welcome, shots from British guns. Thin and sketchy trails of smoke marked the passage of their shot as they descended in quick arcs onto those massed columns.

"Shrapnel shot!" Lewrie crowed with delight when he realised what he was seeing. The fuses of the shrapnel shells, ignited by the explosions of the gunpowder in the artillery's barrels, left those thin trails. A second later, and they burst, some at ground level among the French soldiers, but most exploded above their heads, scattering irregular chunks of the shells, and the musket balls packed inside them, to strew death, dismemberment, wounds, and consternation in a wider burst radius.

The French columns staggered and reeled for a second or so, but the insistent drums forced them onward, and ranks and files came back together, shoulder to shoulder, stepping over their casualties at the same implacable pace. Far behind those columns, the elegantly clad French cavalry units still came forward at a nervous, head-tossing gait, waiting their chance 'til the infantry had punched through, so they could charge into the confusion and exploit the breach in the British lines. A pair of artillery guns showed them some attention, too, emptying saddles and scything down screaming horses with their bursting shot, but it was the columns that were the guns' main targets.

"What do they do when they get close?" Lewrie turned to ask Ford. "Do they just tramp straight on, or what?"

"Well, at some point, they bring the rear ranks out to form line, three or four deep, and open fire with musketry," Ford told him. " 'Til then, no more than the first two or three leading ranks . . . ninety men or so . . . and the men in the outer files down the flanks, can use their weapons."

"Don't make good sense, t'me," Lewrie commented with a shake of his head. " 'Til then, the columns are just big, walking targets."

"They've worked for the French, so far, sir," Ford replied. "Perhaps they think that they've such a large army that they can replace all their great losses. It's brute and crude, but columns have broken everyone in Europe, even the Prussians."

The few British guns with the army continued their cannonading of those two columns, the gunners stoically shrugging off the French guns' attempts to silence them with solid shot. More shells burst over the columns, knocking down more soldiers in circles under them. Much like dropping pebbles into thin mud, the circles quickly disappearing as the French stepped over and round their dead and wounded comrades and marched on, to the harsh orders of the French version of "Close Up, Close Up!" Those two columns got a little shorter, and a bit thinner than thirty men across the front ranks, but still they came on as if nothing in the world could ever stop them.

Lewrie lifted his pocket telescope and scanned behind those columns, and what he saw put a wicked smile on his face. There were dozens upon dozens of bodies strewn in their wakes, fallen in roughly circular blots where the shells had exploded practically on the tops of their shakoes.

Now, he heard the thin crackle of musketry, and turned to scan the face of the ridge, where powder smoke was rising from long-range Baker rifles. A quick look at the head of the nearest French column showed officers and sergeants out in front, waving their swords to encourage their troops onward. Here and there, Lewrie could see those officers struck down. He could barely make out where the riflemen were positioned among the scrub, and surely the French could not see them, either, but they were being shot down by ghosts, out of the blue. Red-coated soldiers of the various Light Companies could be seen, but not the Rifles, firing volleys then retreating up the ridge, shooting beyond the effective range of their muskets but with those columns such broad targets, even their fire was taking grim effect, and the front of that nearest column was now stumbling and stepping over their own casualties.

"Lord, they're almost up within musket shot!" Captain Ford fretted, his own telescope glued to one eye. "*Is* there no stopping those snail-eatin' shits?"

The crest of the ridge before the French columns was suddenly full of British troops, hastening to array themselves two ranks deep from their shelter behind the crest. The men of the skirmishing companies were rushing to join them, out of the line of fire, then, at less than one hundred yards, they opened fire.

"Oh, just lovely!" Ford chortled.

Over three thousand muskets opened up, the first rank kneeling to shoot, followed a second or two later by the discharge of the rear rank soldiers who stood behind, and Lewrie jerked his gaze to the column's front, which looked as if it was simply melting away! French soldiers were tumbling down in windrows, taking those punishing volleys from the front and both flanks, trying to spread out to form a matching line and employ their own muskets in reply, but they were dying too fast for that to prevail.

The first ranks of the British infantry volleyed again, then the rear rank men fired theirs, and the insistent French drums were silenced, at last. Then, with a great, screeching shout, British regiments were dashing down the slope with bayonets fixed, howling like so many imps from Hell!

It was too much for the French. The men at the front of that column turned their backs and tried to run, shoving rear rankers out of their way and spreading panic that twitched down the long length of the column. Somewhere in that mass, a bugle was braying the call to retire, but any hope for an orderly retirement was out of the question; it turned into a terrified rout! Frenchmen in the rear were bowled over by the ones in the middle, the men in the middle were trampled by the ones that had borne the brunt of those volleys, and were scurrying like witless chickens to get away from those wickedly sharp bayonets. Some Frenchmen were trying to melee with their own bayonetted muskets, but they were being swamped over and skewered, and some who could not run fast enough were throwing aside their weapons and kneeling, their arms raised in surrender. British blood was up, though, and not all of those who gave up survived, bashed in the head with heavy musket butts as British soldiers raced past them, or bayonetted.

The fastest of the French soldiers to escape reached the cavalry, which had come to a full stop at the sight of such a debacle, going helter-skelter through the drawn-up horsemen. In the meantime, the British artillery resumed firing with bursting shot into that fleeing horde, creeping their fire up to the cavalry units, too, and forcing the elegant French horse to wheel round and retire from the field at the walk, or at the trot, their usefulness dashed.

"By God, the other column is broken, too!" Captain Ford cheered, turning to the men of his Light Company. "See that, lads? That's the way to deal with a column!" and his soldiers gave out a great, mocking cheer to see the French on their way.

"It's hard to tell with all the smoke, but I do believe that the other column fared no better than this'un," Lewrie said, pointing further West at another amorphous blob of blue-coated soldiery which was retiring in rapid order, leaving a long bloody trail of dead and wounded, great heaps of dead where it had been shot to a stop, and the survivors stampeding over the long trail of bodies that they had left in the wake of their approach, pursued by the irregular *Crump!* of shrapnel shells bursting over the largest concentrations.

The British regiments which had launched that bayonet charge were now drawn up in good order and retiring to the crest of the ridge; unlike British cavalry, they had kept their heads and not gone far in pursuit, once the French had broken and run. They herded some whole prisoners and walking wounded along with them, ignoring the pleas from badly wounded

Frenchmen who lay where they had fallen and would not be tended to 'til either night had fallen, or the battle was won, one way or another.

"Well, I *thought* columns made no bloody sense, and it appears they don't," Lewrie summed up, bringing his borrowed canteen round to uncork and take a welcome sip. "What a horrid waste of soldiers!"

"I'd not speak *too* soon, Captain Lewrie," Ford cautioned, "for it seems it's our turn, next. See there? Two more columns are forming a bit to the left of our direct front. Care to go down the slope with me and my company, sir? Pot a few Frogs with your musket?"

"Tempting," Lewrie mused, "but, that'd be askin' a sailor to walk too much. I think I'll watch it play out from up here."

Orders were being shouted, the regiment's line companies were being brought forward to form up on the crest, with the bulk of the unit still in shelter. A runner came to Ford's side with orders for his Light Company to go downslope to take up skirmishing positions, as he had expected.

"Have it your way, sir, and take joy of the excitement," Ford bade him.

"And the best of good fortune go with you, Captain Ford," Lewrie offered, extending his right hand to shake with him.

There came the thuds of hooves from several horses together, and the snorts and pants from a group of mounts being urged along the ridge's crest, and Lewrie turned to look. It was that Wellesley fellow and some of his staff, coming to the scene of the next French attempt. This morning, General Sir Arthur Wellesley was not wearing the gilt-laden red coat of a British officer, but a plain grey coat that fell to his knees and the tops of his boots, with a gold-laced belt round his middle that held his sword. He drew rein to survey the enemy columns that would come against this part of the ridgeline, using an ivory pocket telescope. There was a stern scowl on his face, one that turned even harsher as he swivelled about and espied Lewrie. One quizzical brow went up as he peered down that long, beaky nose, then turned his gaze away to matters at hand, and urged his horse to pace further East along the ridge to the other regiments.

Lewrie *thought* he heard a *"Hmmph!"* from Wellesley over his presence on a battlefield, but could never swear to it in later days. Struggling, thrashing artillery teams, pieces, caissons and limbers, came tearing by to take up quick emplacements further along the ridge, and Lewrie wandered in their wake over to the nearest line company, unslinging his Ferguson off his shoulder and resting the butt on the ground.

"Come to see the show, sir?" an infantry Lieutenant joshed.

"Something like that, aye," Lewrie replied with an easy grin.

"It won't be long coming," the officer said, perking up to the thin, distant sounds of cheers as the French steeled themselves for an attack. The infernal drumming began once more, and two pristine columns lurched into motion, Summer sunlight flashing off shako badges and bayonets, and dust rising round the columns' front and flanks like seawater disturbed by a rowboat's motion, spreading outward from their passage, and hanging low in the air.

What happens over there, *out of range, is exciting,* Lewrie told himself; *but what comes right at you can frighten the* piss *out of you.*

The French looked to be coming straight at him, and he felt the need to pee.

The French artillery opened up a minute or two later after he had come back to the crest, their roundshot howling and moaning overhead, tweetling up the musical scale as they approached to go silent as they drummed into the ridge below the crest, and one or two lucky shots skimming the crest to pluck unfortunate soldiers away as they stood two ranks deep, and it was British sergeants who bawled out for the survivors to close ranks, this time.

Then British guns barked when the range had fallen to about six hundred yards, and the shrapnel shells began to *Crack* and *Crump* over the French columns spreading death in all directions.

"Wonder what it feels like," the Lieutenant said with a touch of nervousness to his voice as the French columns kept up their implacable advance. "Surely, they must be able to *see* the fuse trails coming at them, *knowing* they're going to burst above them!"

"I'd expect they've *very* loose bowels, and wouldn't trust their arseholes with a fart," Lewrie hooted, raising a titter of laughter from the officer's company. "The French have never experienced bursting shot before . . . never come up against British soldiers before, and must be in dread, by now, after what happened to the first attack."

"We'll *maul* them!" the Lieutenant declared, sounding confident, but Lewrie noted how white his fingers were round the hilt of his scabbarded sword.

"Damn right we will!" several soldiers barked in agreement.

"Silence in the ranks, stand steady," the company's Captain growled, casting a dis-believing eye on Lewrie for a second.

The nearest column looked as if it would reach the ridgeline about one hundred yards East of where Lewrie stood, thinned though it was by the artillery fire. The drums were urging it on, the French were shouting praise of their Emperor in unison, and they were nearing, within about four hundred yards. Lewrie slung his Ferguson on his shoulder and made a point of *ambling* down the company's front as if he had not one care in the world.

I'm such *a sham*, he told himself; *but I've gotten good at it, play-actin' for people's benefit, by now. They* all *are*, he thought, glancing down the company front to see how the soldiers were taking the French approach. Everyone in sight, even the French, were playing bold and brave! There were some pale faces, some gulps of awe, and some fondling of talismans, but they *looked* ready.

What a damn-fool *idea this is*, he further thought, shaking his head over his stupidity for coming ashore; *this is the* last *time I take part in a shore battle! By choice, I hope!*

He reached the left flank of the infantry company, into open ground where one of the sheltering companies would form when called up to the line. It felt very lonely and vulnerable to be out there on his own, of a sudden, and he understood a common soldier's assurance of having others at his sides, and his rear-rank man backing him up.

Boom-boom-boom, buh-buh-buh-boom-boom-boom "Vive l'Empereur!"; it was very close now, the nearest column panting and gasping for air as it struggled to climb the slope to the British lines. Musketry erupted downslope from the skirmishing companies as they fired, then fell back, re-loading on the go. The front of the column looked to be about two hundred yards away, and Lewrie nodded, then un-slung his Ferguson, looked for an officer to target, and put the butt to his shoulder, looking down the barrel.

There! He spotted a French officer with a dark red sash round his waist, his sword out and waving to urge them on. He had one of those long mustachios. Lewrie drew his weapon back to full cock, and took aim. The late Major Patrick Ferguson, inventor of his rifled musket who had died at the Battle of King's Mountain in the American Revolution, might have intended long-range accuracy, but he hadn't done much by way of improving front and rear sights to achieve it.

Lewrie held aim above the officer's shako, drew a breath and let it slowly out, then pulled the trigger, just as the officer turned to face his men and march backwards to say something to them. The bullet, fired downhill, didn't follow the usual descending arc, and struck him square between the shoulder blades, punching the Frenchman facedown dead.

Here, that's *cheerin'!* Lewrie told himself as he opened the breech and tore a fresh cartridge open with his teeth. In a trice, he was loaded again, seeking a new target, and finding one, this one a senior officer with lots of gold-lace on his coat and a fore-and-aft bicorne on his head, adorned with egret plumes. He aimed smaller, this time, taking advantage of the flatter trajectory of a round fired downhill, holding only a foot above the egret plumes and firing. He hit the officer full in the cheek below his left eye and saw the back of his head explode into his soldiers' faces!

A very young junior officer stepped forward to lead, and he went down with a bullet in his chest; then it was a great, hulking older sergeant who stepped out in front, bull-roaring defiance and courage loud enough to be heard over the din of gunfire, and Lewrie shot him just above his shirt collar and neck-stock, driving the man to his knees in surprise, and fountaining gouts of blood from his mouth.

"Up, form line, odd-numbered companies!" some senior British officer was shouting. "Up, form line and stand ready! Front ranks will kneel!"

The skirmishers were back on the crest and taking their places at the left flanks of their regiments. Grenadier companies were forming at the right ends, and the line companies were now shoulder-to-shoulder. Lewrie got off two more quick shots as the French got within one hundred yards, and beginning to swing out into a firing line.

Haven't shot this well in years! he congratulated to himself as he tore open another cartridge; *I may take up duck-hunting, next!*

He'd run out of obvious officers in front of the French column, so he settled for a tall soldier in the centre of the first rank, and dropped him with a shot just below his brass cross-belt plate.

"Get out of the way, you bloody damned fool! We volley, and we will cut you down!" someone was shouting behind him.

Lewrie assumed that that was addressed at him and spun about to realise that he was looking down the muzzles of over six hundred levelled muskets. "Oh, *shiiitt*!" he yelled as he hastily flung himself to the ground!

"Front ranks . . . fire!" came a second later, and all Hades erupted. The whole ridge roared with noise, and spurting powder smoke blanked out his view, from an ant's level, of an entire regiment delivering a massed volley. "Second rank, fire!" and by then all that he could make out were trouser legs and boots below the smoke pall.

He could hear the balls rushing overhead like a swarm of bees, screams and shouts from the French down-slope, even the meaty thumps of bullets tearing into enemy bodies.

"Front ranks . . . level!"

He stayed where he was, wishing that he could dig deeper, for though British troops were the only ones in the world who actually practiced at live musketry, the Tower musket, "Brown Bess," had even more rudimentary sights than his Ferguson, and the command was "Level," not "Take Aim." Rapidly delivered massed volleys at sixty to seventy-five yards was the desired effect, "shotgunning" fire in the foe's general direction! And, as he'd seen at the firing butts at Gibraltar, some soldiers did not even *bother* to aim, turning their heads as far from the flash and smoke in the priming pans as possible, with their muskets pointed in the general direction. He heard one ball hum disturbingly close to his head, just inches above him, and squirmed to make himself flatter.

He also had another desperate urge to pee!

"Regiment will . . . advance!" some senior officer bawled out. "Fix . . . bayonets."

Captains of companies shouted their own orders for the first ranks to stand, and to fix bayonets, and close ranks.

"Regiment . . . twenty paces forward . . . march!"

Marching men weren't likely to be shooting, or so he thought, so Lewrie warily got to his feet, still lost in the powder smoke fog, hearing the swish of boots through grass, and the tramp of marching men in lock-step, the pace being called out by sergeants.

He wanted to be out of their way, but had no clue as to where to go. An instant later and he was blundered into by a young Private who let out a screech of fright, almost dropping his musket.

"Frog!" the soldier squeaked, "A Frenchie, roight 'ere!"

"British officer!" Lewrie shouted back, almost nose-to-nose.

"Sykes, ye silly sod!" his Sergeant yelled. "Pick up yer damn musket!"

Lewrie turned sideways to sidle 'twixt the soldiers of the first rank, then their rear-rank mates, all of whom were laughing at their unfortunate companion.

"Silence in the bloody ranks!" an officer demanded.

The two-deep line of troops seemed to be marching into clearer air, so Lewrie ambled along behind them a little way as the regiment began to descend the crest of the ridge.

"Regiment will halt! Load cartridge! By platoons, level . . . fire!" a senior officer ordered very loudly. Lewrie looked around to see a Colonel near him, a short fellow who was on his tiptoes, hopping in the air to see downslope past his soldiers, which Lewrie found a funny sight.

The regiment, and the others on that part of the ridge, opened fire down on the struggling French column, and any hope of a view of the results was blotted out. The platoon volleys rippled down the regimental line, four rounds per man per minute, from the Grenadier Company on the right to the Light Company on the left, repeated as soon as the right of the line was re-loaded. Now and then, one better-trained company's volley didn't sound like a long crackle, but a muted *Chuff!* as every trigger was pulled at the same second.

That Colonel bulled his way through the ranks of his taller soldiers, drew his sword, and cried "Cease fire! Poise bayonets, and . . . Charge!" as he rushed out ahead of his men, whirling his sword about and shrieking like a banshee. With wild, feral howlings, his troops raced down the hill with him, and Lewrie was left alone at the crest of the ridge, again.

"Bugger *that* for a game o' . . . soldiers," he said aloud, wishing no part of the melees to come.

But, it was an awesome sight to see. The French drummers were whacking away on their skins with urgency, but the column was having no more of it. The front six or seven ranks, thirty or so men across, had been shot to a reef of dead and wounded against which the French behind could make no progress. There looked to be an attempt to fan out from column to line and respond with musketry, but that had also been shot to a halt, and when the British regiment began its charge downhill with wickedly sharp bayonets, all order dissolved, and the French turned their backs and began to scramble over each other to get away, some tossing aside their muskets in their haste.

What Lewrie had seen through his telescope of the first two-column attack to the West was being repeated close up here. It was an un-controlled rout, a stampede of survivors, that ran back downhill. Off to Lewrie's left, the other column that had come uphill alongside this one was also retiring, though in better order. Over there, the British troops had not launched a charge, but had kept up a steady rolling fire that stopped that column in its tracks and decimated it, convincing its surviving officers that staying and dying was futile. Those French soldiers were skulking off to the rear, defeated, and pursued by derisive cheers and curses from the victors.

Downslope, now that the gunsmoke was clearing, the regiment had stopped its charge, having run out of Frenchmen available to skewer, butt-stroke, or shoot. They were coming back to the ridgeline laden with quickly snatched souvenirs; shakoes or brass regimental shako plates, the short infantryman's swords, the *sabre-briquets*, bloodied epaulets torn off dead men's shoulders, pipes and tobacco purses, and what little solid coin they could find in dead Frenchmen's pockets, no matter how officers and sergeants railed against the practice.

Young subalterns were crowing and congratulating each other in high spirits, passing leather or metal flasks of brandy to toast their success. Lewrie had not brought any of his aged American corn whisky, so he had to settle for several gulps of water from his borrowed canteen.

"Saw you, sir, potting away at the Frogs," one Lieutenant brayed. "Get any?"

"A few, thankee," Lewrie replied, "just before I had t'throw myself flat so I'd not get shot, then nigh got trampled. So much for the French and their famous columns."

"By God, you're right, sir, absolutely right!" the young officer crowed. "Why, I can't recall the French *ever* being stopped so surely."

"I'll thankee for my flask back, Snowden," another young man grumbled. "Stopped? Here and there, rarely, on a *part* of a battlefield one of their attacks might have been held off, but never like this. Let them keep it up, and we'll slaughter the entire lot of them by sundown, hah hah!" he boasted, then took a deep sip from his flask.

"If they've the bottom t'keep it up," Lewrie cautioned, wishing for some of their camaraderie, and a sip of something stronger than water. "They've most-like never known defeat. Bashed straight through the Spanish, the Portuguese, Austrians, and God knows who else. I'd expect their soldiers're not feelin' all that plucky anymore."

"By God, he's right, gentlemen!" the one named Snowden cried. "We could inflict the first defeat that 'Boney's' ever suffered!"

"Well, there was Egypt, and the Holy Lands," another quipped. "Maybe Marshal Junot will send Paris a letter *calling* it a victory!"

"See to your men, sirs!" a Major snarled at them as he passed. "There's wounded to be seen to, and the day's not over, not by a long chalk. Leftenant Acklin?"

"Sir?" the young fellow who'd demanded his flask back replied, stiffening.

"You will take command of the Light Company," the Major said. "Captain Ford's wounded, and doesn't look long for this world. Belly wound, the worst kind. Off with you, now."

The subalterns scattered, shame-faced, as the regimental bands-men and the regiment's wives went past to begin recovering the wounded and the dead. Walking wounded, aided by their mates, began to struggle to the top of the ridge from their charge, some chattily happy to have taken survivable wounds, yet most ashen, and fearful of what they faced with the surgeons. Some whimpered, some wept, and some unharmed soldiers shared tears with them over the loss of good friends.

And the day was not over, Lewrie realised as he heard trumpets or bugles, and turned to look down over the ridge to the land below. Another pair of those massive French columns were forming up to make a fresh attempt near the village of Vimeiro, and a whole three fresh columns were assembling farther to the East. He pulled out his watch and found that it was not quite ten in the morning.

"I need a sit-down, somewhere," he muttered.

CHAPTER THIRTY-TWO

*T*here was no way that Lewrie could walk all the way to where the fresh French attacks would come; that would be asking too much of a sailor's legs. Un-employed, he drifted to the back slope of the ridge to see if his horse was still there, or had galloped off in fear. It was restive, but glad for some stroking and nose rubs, and the men who served as grooms had provided it with oats and water, and assured him that his mount was fine.

Further down the slope, on a flattish ledge, the surgeons were doing their grim best under a series of canvas awnings, shirtsleeves rolled to their elbows yet still bloody, their leather aprons from upper chests to their knees slick with gore.

Lewrie had been taken down below to the cockpit surgery a few times in his life, and could sympathise with the soldiers undergoing the surgeon's ghoulish ministrations. He could appreciate his ship's surgeons' wit and civility . . . but he had no wish to witness them at work. Already there was a small pile of amputated legs, arms, and hands laid out on a tarpaulin, gruesomely near wounded men who waited to be seen to, a wailing, cursing, praying lot. He heard the rasp of a bone saw, the screams of the soldier losing his right arm, and his ability to work, his regimental home, and most likely his life if his wound festered, and turned away.

There was a row of wounded men laid out on blankets, men who had been seen to, operated on, or given up as lost causes. A kindly looking older Sergeant with white hair was tending them, ladling water or rum to those who were awake and able to swallow, and Lewrie felt drawn to that group, no matter his distaste.

"Yessir?" the old Sergeant asked, looking up from his chores.

"There's a Captain Ford?" Lewrie said in a croak.

" 'E's over 'ere, sir, poor fellow," the Sergeant, said. "Goin' game, unlike some. You should face h'it as brave as th' Captain, you lot," he gently admonished the dying. "You'll be with th' Lord in Paradise, some o' you, an' there's still time t'ask forgivness fer your sins, th' rest o' you. Want some 'elp prayin' do you, lads?"

Lewrie slowly paced down the row of wounded, unable to hide a grimace 'til he discovered Captain Ford, propped up on a field pack, and nude under a blanket. Some effort had been made to staunch his bleeding, but the bandages and cotton batt were soaked.

"Captain Ford?" Lewrie began, kneeling down beside him. "I *am* sorry, sir."

"Ah, Captain Lewrie," Ford said in a weak voice, though his face lit up with joy to have someone visit him. "I'm glad to see that you've come through unscathed, so far. We saw the French off right smartly, did we not?"

"In a panicked rout, sir," Lewrie tried to assure him, and give him some cheer, "flyin' like flushed quail. That's four of their columns smashed, so far."

"Ah, good," Ford said in a sigh. "It appears that the column cannot prevail against the line. My First Leftenant, Acklin. Do you know if he is well?"

"I met him, briefly," Lewrie told him. "Aye, he's whole, and your regimental Major told him to take command of your company."

"Good, good," Ford said, "young Acklin can be a thoughtless fellow, but he's shaping well as an officer. My men will be in good hands, thank the Lord. I'd *dearly* like to see how the battle goes, but—" Ford cut off with a wince and a stifled groan of pain. "I'm done for, you know." To which Lewrie could only nod. "A belly wound. You don't come back from those. There's nothing the surgeons can do for you, but make you comfortable. God grant me a quick exit, for I fear I might un-man myself does the pain get much worse . . . Aaahh!"

He stiffened as another wave of pain took him.

"I enjoyed our discussion this morning, Captain Ford," Lewrie said, knowing full well that men wounded like Ford could linger for days, screaming in agony as their stomachs and bowels went gangrenous. "It was delightful to hear such a fine exposition on the units of the French army."

"Always was a quick study," Ford said with what sounded like a deprecating laugh, even as his pain ravaged him. "I knew when I went for a soldier that one must learn all one can about the enemy . . . unlike some," he added, making a face, then turned serious and looked Lewrie directly in the eyes. "I am ready, you know, Captain Lewrie. My will is made, and my last letters to my parents written. They might not recoup all the costs of purchasing my commission, not in a fielded regiment, but, today's laurels *may* encourage some young fellow to buy into a successful regiment. If we'd only managed to capture one of their damned eagles . . . aahh! Damn!" He broke off, groaning and gritting his teeth.

"Is there anything I can do for you, Ford?" Lewrie asked him. "Water, or some rum, or . . . ?"

"Just enough to wet my mouth, I fear," Ford said with another stoic grin as the pain passed for a moment. "The surgeons say that I'm not to drink anything. The bowels, you see."

Lewrie offered him his canteen, which Ford used to dab at his dry lips, and swirl round his parched mouth.

"If someone could prevail upon the butchers to allow me a dose of laudanum," Ford supposed, looking skyward. "I am *trying* to go game, but, Lord, it is hard!"

"I will ask them for you," Lewrie promised, feeling a cowardly urge to get away from Ford, as if dying was catching. Men who'd died aboard his ships passed away out of sight on the orlop, unseen if not unheard, mourned later, after they'd been committed to the sea. He had never sat with one of them, not for long.

"I'd admire if you did, Captain Lewrie," Ford said, extending his right hand. Lewrie took it, and felt him squeeze as his pains gnawed harder for a moment. "Buzzards, or kites? Or are there vultures in Portugal, do you know?"

"What?" Lewrie gawped.

"Those foul birds circling up there," Ford said, jutting his chin skyward, and Lewrie looked up to see a whole flock of scavenger birds gyring about. "Wish they were larks, or something else. Just waiting for their feast, the horrid things. I wonder if you could tuck me up, Captain Lewrie. I'm feeling a bit of a chill."

Lewrie lifted the rough army blanket up to pull it higher to cover Ford's chest, noting that his thick pad of bandages were soaked red and dripping. He drew the blood-wet blanket up under Ford's chin. "That better?"

"Yes, don't know why . . . such a warm morning . . . ," Ford dreamily said. "If you'd hold my hand awhile longer, sir?"

Lewrie took hands with him, waving his left to atract the old Sergeant's attention, who came over with his ladle and pail.

" 'E ain't t'have no water, sir."

"His wound's bleeding heavily, and he says he's cold," Lewrie told him. "One of the surgeons—"

"Won't do no good, sir," the old Sergeant said, shaking his head and whispering. " 'At's a blessin', an' God's mercy 'at 'e's bleedin' out. 'E'll go quick, all fer th' best, 'at is."

Lewrie could feel Ford's hand go slack in his, and lowered it to the blanket, then stood up. "A brave fellow."

" 'E was, sir," the Sergeant agreed. "A friend o' yours?"

"Only met him this morning," Lewrie said, feeling bleak.

"You did a kindly thing fer 'im, sir, God bless you, an' sure when h'it's your time, you'll be rewarded," the Sergeant said with a pious bob of his head. "You run along, now, sir, an' we'll see 'im inta th' ground proper. Wot was 'is name?"

"Captain Samuel Ford, of your regiment's Light Company," Lewrie told him. "You said you knew him by name."

"Make a note of h'it, I will."

Lewrie took off his hat and laid it on his chest for a moment, then clapped it back on as the sounds of battle swelled. Cannonfire, bursting shrapnel shells, French drums and *"Vive l'Empereur!"*, and the long crackling of rolling volley fire from thousands of muskets.

He went back to the crest of the ridge to look both East and West to see French columns sway-marching into battle, unwilling to admit that they had met their match, and that their vaunted tactics no longer prevailed.

Horses neighed, drawing his attention down the line where Sir Arthur Wellesley and an older, stouter General in a red coat dripping with gold-lace sat their mounts in discussion.

"Captain Lewrie?" someone called out.

"Hey?" he called back, swivelling round to see who spoke.

"You came up to see the battle, *too*, sir?" Lt. Beauchamp, who had been his guide the day before, said in delight as he reined his horse over from the generals.

"Still an aide, Lieutenant Beauchamp?" Lewrie asked with a grin.

"A galloper today, sir, one end of the ridge to the other," the young fellow breezily boasted.

"Who's the stout fellow yonder with Wellesley?" Lewrie said, pointing.

"Oh Lord, that's General Sir Henry Burrard, sir," Beauchamp said in a lower voice, pulling a face, "come to see how our General's running the battle."

"Hope he leaves well enough alone," Lewrie commented, not liking the look of the newcomer, and his skeptical scowling.

"Amen, sir, we seem to have the French well in hand, so far," Beauchamp agreed quickly. "Unless they come up with a new tactic, it looks as if they'll throw their army away trying to batter against us. We're reaping a wondrous slaughter!"

"So it seems, sir," Lewrie agreed. "You know, Burrard is known as 'Betty' Burrard?" he added with a sly grin.

"Well, he's in a bad position, Captain Lewrie, sir," Beauchamp said, idly flicking his reins. "If Sir Arthur wins, he'll get no credit for it, and I hear that Lieutenant-General Sir Hew Dalrymple will be coming from Gibraltar to take charge in the field, and Burrard'll have to play second to him, and if something goes wrong after that, Burrard might end up with the blame for it."

"Not exactly Admiral Nelson's 'band of brothers,' is it, sir?" Lewrie commented with a guffaw. "Though it makes me wonder if those gentlemen in my Service ever *really* eschewed playin' personal politics all that long. No one's *that* un-ambitious."

"Our officer's mess in the Ninth has made *me* more cynical," Lt. Beauchamp replied with frank honesty. "God help our army do some of my fellows gain high rank."

"Galloper, here!" General Wellesley barked out. "Beauchamp! Quit that prittle-prattle with the *naval* person. I've a directive for Ferguson, out beyond Ventosa. He's to shift positions Eastward and prepare to receive a fresh attack."

"Very good, sir!" Lt. Beauchamp loudly replied, stiffly formal and tossing off a quick salute as he took the folded-over despatch and reined his mount about to gallop off.

The naval person, am I? Lewrie thought, grinning over that description. He ambled back up to the crest of the ridge, near where the two generals sat their horses, noting that Wellesley and Burrard were observing the battle below, without saying a single word to each other, studiously avoiding even looking at each other.

Lewrie pulled out his pocket watch to note the time; just 11 A.M. The French had been shoving their massive columns forward for nigh two hours, now, with nothing to show for it. He traded his watch for his telescope and looked West to the latest attack near Vimeiro.

Good God, are they fightin' hand-to-hand? he gawped. Red coats and blue coats looked mingled, with a lot less musket smoke than before. Even as he realised the fierceness of the fight, though, blue-uniformed soldiers began to fall back, to turn and run, far enough for a brace of British guns to open upon them again, and the wide defile into which the French had attacked was now lined with green-coated Riflemen on either side, sniping at the confused mass and making a rich harvest.

"Rifles," he heard Wellesley grump. "Damned useful."

"Primadonnas," Burrard commented, squirming in his saddle but not looking at Wellesley, and ignoring that fight as well, looking to the far distance to the South. "Too slow to fire, too."

Lewrie swivelled about to look East to where three French columns had launched their attack, but that looked to be pretty-much over, too, shelled then shot to pieces at close range and thrown back in confusion. The two fresh columns forming to make yet another attack beyond the little village of Ventosa had yet to move forward.

"You, there," Lewrie heard from his right side as the soft clops of an approaching horse pricked his senses. "Whatever are you *doing* here, sir?"

"Trying t'make sense of how the French fight, sir," Lewrie re-joined, lowering his telescope and turning to face Wellesley, looking up a considerable distance, for the General was a rather tall man on a tall horse. He doffed his hat in salute. "Captain Sir Alan Lewrie, of HMS *Sapphire*, at your service, sir."

Wellesley's salute was a riding crop tapped on his plain, and unadorned bicorne. "You have powder round your mouth, Sir Alan. Done some shooting, have you?"

"As the attack came up the ridge just yonder, a few minutes ago, Sir Arthur," Lewrie told him. "Seemed a good idea to contribute."

"With a Sea Pattern musket?" Wellesley sniffed, sounding dubious.

"A breech-loading rifled Ferguson, sir," Lewrie informed him, unslinging the weapon and holding it out for Sir Arthur to inspect. "Good for at least one hundred fifty to two hundred yards."

"Formed any opinions of the French, have you, Captain Lewrie?" Wellesley asked after looking the rifled musket over and handing it back. His eyes had lit up in enthusiasm to see such a rarity; perhaps that was why he seemed less stiff. That thin-lipped, imperious mouth of his al-most showed a faint smile.

"Well, it strikes me that the column is all they know," Lewrie com-mented, removing his hat to ruffle his sweaty hair. "Once stopped, they just keep on doin' the same old thing, hopin' for the best. At Trafalgar—I wasn't there, but my son was, and wrote me of it—Nelson attacked with *two* columns, took horrid punishment to punch through the enemy line of battle, and turned it into a melee, throwin' all he had at 'em at once. Here, though . . . ," he said, tossing in a shrug of bewilderment, "four or five columns, closer together, attackin' at once *might* prevail, but . . . I'm just a sailor, so what do I know of it? Land fighting? You're welcome to it, sir. They keep this up, they'll ruin themselves by dark."

"No," Wellesley countered, turning steely-eyed again. "By mid-day, I fully expect. I hope you enjoyed yourself, Captain Lewrie."

With that, he tapped his riding crop to his hat and kneed his horse away at a trot towards Ventosa, leaving General Burrard behind. Lewrie heard a muffled "Goddamn" as Burrard spurred after him.

Lewrie looked over the battlefield below, suddenly feeling the urge to be away, to be back aboard ship where things made sense, and leave this form of butchery to those more accustomed to it. His right hand felt sticky, and he found that it and his shirt cuff were bloodied with Captain Ford's gore. He would have washed it off, but his canteen, he also discovered, was almost empty, and he wondered where he'd drunk so much of it. His feet complained inside his boots, and he was tired and sore, and wolf-hungry.

He groped for his sausages, bisquit, and cheese, but they were no-where to be found. *Must've dropped 'em when I flung myself flat,* he told himself, envying the soldier who picked them up.

What was left of the battle was happening far to the East beyond Ventosa. There didn't look to be any French threat on the right round Vimeiro; even the battle smoke had cleared over there, so he ambled to the backside of the ridge, found his borrowed horse, and set off at a slow walk back down to Vimeiro, allowing the horse a drink from the Maceira at the ford. He got down from the saddle to wash his hands, dab at his powder-stained mouth, and re-fill his canteen, then went on into the village.

The army's baggage train had come up near the water, a bit to the North of the village. Lewrie supposed that he could cadge some salt-meat and hard bisquit, but, there were some of the Irish waggoners nearby, round a campfire, cooking something that smelled simply amazing, and he led his horse over to them.

"Dere's me passenger from dis mornin'," his pre-dawn carter said, pointing Lewrie out to his mates. "Have yerself a nice battle, did ye, sor?"

"It was an eye-opener, aye, and God help all soldiers," Lewrie replied.

"We winnin' it, sor?" another asked.

"It certainly looks like it," Lewrie told him. "What's cooking, and could you spare me a morsel or two?"

The meat on the spits was not chunks of salt-meat junk; it looked more like rabbit, or chicken. The army had Provosts to prevent looting and foraging, but the civilian carters did not quite fall under their authority, and would have ignored them if they did. Not only did they have rabbit and chicken, but, true to the carter's word, they had baked fresh bread, not the dark army-issue ammunition loaf, but Irish soda bread, and where they had gotten the eggs and milk to make their dough didn't bear thinking about.

Dark meat was most people's preference, but since beggars can't be choosers, Lewrie ended up with a pair of scrawny chicken breasts, and two thumb-thick slices of bread liberally spread with butter for the princely sum of six pence. The carters drove a hard bargain, sniggering in glee to rook an Englishman and an officer, but he paid it gladly, and found himself a low stone wall along the rutted road that ran through Vimeiro for his dining table, washing it all down with canteen water, and not above licking his fingers when he was done, dignity be-damned.

There were rather a lot of flies, though, and Summer swarms of midges or gnats to pester him during his meal. After a long look round, he discovered that there was another field surgery set up in the village, wounded soldiers trickling to it from the last attack by the French on this part of the line; was it his imagination, or did the humming of myriads of flies dominate over the moans and cries of the hurt and dying?

A troop of cavalry came clattering by at the lope, in some urgency, swinging out to the hills to the South. Somewhere, drummers began to beat the Long Roll, bugles blew, and weary soldiers arose from where they rested, armed themselves, and began to form ranks, as if yet another pair of French columns would make a fresh attempt upon the village. Brigadiers and Colonels and their aides left the two-storey house that served as headquarters, quickly saddled up, and loped off to follow the cavalry troop down the road that led to Torres Vedras and Lisbon.

He was tired, yes, but Lewrie's curiosity was piqued, so he mounted his horse and rode South to see what was happening, coming abeam of a clutch of mounted officers busy with their telescopes.

"Bless my soul, it *ain't* an attack," he heard one Colonel say. "There's no more than one squadron of cavalry, flying a flag of truce!"

"Think you're right, Bob," a Brigadier agreed. "Damn my eyes, but I believe there's a General with them. It's Kellermann, by God, the fellow with the white hair? Oh, a clever old fox is Kellermann. Practically saved their revolution in Ninety-Three, when everyone in Europe marched against the French frontiers. Fought them all off with his *levée en masse*."

"Well, he's come to pull their chestnuts from the fire today, sir!" the Colonel whooped. "We've broken them, bloodied every one of their damned battalions! I wonder if His Nibs will settle for a truce, or demand surrender."

"Won't be up to Wellesley," the Brigadier grumbled. "That'll be up to 'Betty' Burrard, he's senior."

Good Christ, we've won*!* Lewrie thought with glee; *They* ain't *invincible!* As hapless as the British Army had behaved in Holland, as disastrous as their efforts had been at Buenos Aires where two armies had been forced to surrender to half-trained, poorly-armed Argentine patriots, no one had given this army, or "Sepoy" General Sir Arthur Wellesley, much of a chance against the French, yet . . . ! The odds had been beaten, the *French* had been beaten, beaten like a *drum*, and Lewrie was suddenly very glad, and proud, to have seen it happen, and take even a minuscule part in it!

I could be dined out on this tale for years*!* he crowed.

Gallopers were headed along the ridge line to pass the word, and Lewrie identified Lt. Beauchamp coming from the opposite direction, with Wellesley and Burrard just crossing the Maceira to come to the parley.

With a sense of satisfaction and conclusion, Lewrie turned his horse about and headed back to the bay, crossing the shallow Maceira and threading his way through the baggage train to the open plain between the hills. It was a long two miles, but he let the horse pick its own way down to the sea. He worried whether there would be someone to take charge of the beast, or would he have to leave it to graze with dropped reins. It had been a poor prad, but it had served him well enough, and he gave the horse an encouraging pat on its neck.

Fortunately, there were soldiers from the Commissariat loading more waggons and carts to bear fresh supplies from the ships up to the army, and one of their officers swore that he'd look after it.

And there were boats plying 'twixt the supply ships and the shore, and Lewrie managed to flag one down and cadge a ride out to *Sapphire*, out where he belonged, waded out to clamber aboard and take a seat on the stern-most thwart beside a Midshipman.

"How goes the battle, sir?" the young lad asked. "No one can tell us anything."

"The French are suing for terms," Lewrie told him, grinning. "We beat the bastards, and broke every one of their battalions."

"Huzzah, sir! Hear that, lads?" the Mid called to his oarsmen. "We've won the battle!"

Lewrie closed his eyes and slumped in weariness, still with a pleased smile on his face, quite enjoying the rock, pitch, and thrust of the boat's motion as it was stroked out into the bay.

Once aboard, I think I'll have me a sponge-off, and a good, long nap, he promised himself.

CHAPTER THIRTY-THREE

*T*he *Phoebe* frigate came into the bay the day after the battle, and a great military show it was to form a grand parade to welcome Lieutenant-General Sir Hew Dalrymple to his new post as Commander-In-Chief of British forces in Portugal. Lewrie watched it from a comfortable sling-chair on *Sapphire*'s poop deck, sheltered from the heat under a canvas awning that spanned the length and breadth of that deck.

He thought it odd, even so, that the army had returned to its en-campments, with only a few regiments still posted to keep an eye on the French. Those officers he had overheard as they had awaited the arrival of General Kellermann and his truce party had opined that once the French were dis-armed, the army would march on Torres Vedras, nearer to the prize, Lisbon, for there were very good defensive positions to be had there and that they should strike while the iron was hot.

That was up to General Burrard, Lewrie supposed, and none of a sail-or's business, but he thought it silly to spruce up and march to band music just to make a show for Sir Hew. Frankly, he, and all his crew were grow-ing tired of idling at anchor off the mouth of the Maceira, watching boats working by day and night to ferry off wounded soldiers to ships that would bear them back to England and proper hospitals. Shouldn't they be going *somewhere?*

⚓

It was a couple of days later before orders turned up to sail, and they came mid-morning during cutlass drill.

"Boat ahoy!" Midshipman Ward shouted overside at an approaching rowboat, using a brass speaking-trumpet to augment his thin shrill.

"Despatches for your Captain!" came the reply, and a side-party was hastily assembled. Lewrie broke off his own sword practise with Marine Lieutenant Roe and went to the bulwarks in his shirtsleeves.

"Oh, Goddamn," he groaned, "it's that damned fool, Hughes."

"It seems he's rejoined Sir Hew's staff, sir," Lt. Roe said, making a sour face. "Better there than in command of troops, I suppose. At least he won't stumble about and get himself captured again, on staff."

"Well, there are proper soldiers, and then there are *clerks*, Mister Roe," Lewrie quipped. "I'm sure he has all his paperwork just tiddly."

Lewrie sheathed his hanger and trotted down to the quarterdeck to welcome Hughes aboard, loath as he was to clap "top lights" on him again. He even plastered on a grin.

"Ah, Captain Hughes! Welcome aboard," he said in greeting as Hughes completed his climb up the battens to the deck.

"Good morning, Captain Lewrie," Hughes purred back, in kind, "though, there was a sudden vacancy and I was able to purchase a promotion. It's Major Hughes, now. Substantive, not brevet."

"Congratulations, Major Hughes," Lewrie amended. "Care for a 'wet' in my cabins? Cool tea, or cool wine?"

"Thank you, sir, I'd much appreciate it," Hughes said with an *harumph*. "Sir Hew has need of you and your ship to bear despatches to Admiral Cotton, off Lisbon, and another set for General Drummond at Gibraltar."

"This way, if you please, Major Hughes," Lewrie bade, waving an arm towards the coolness of his great-cabins.

Once seated on the starboard-side settee, and with a glass of wine in his hand, Hughes gave him a quizzical look. "I heard tell that you were ashore the day of the battle, sir, potting the odd Frenchman alongside the soldiers, what?"

"Curiosity, aye, and I was," Lewrie said agreeably. "Quite the sight to see, Frogs dyin' in droves, and runnin' like rabbits."

Left unsaid was "You should have been there," and Hughes was aware of it. He *harumphed* again and took a deeper sip of his wine.

"Yayss," Hughes drawled, "young Wellesley did well, for his first encounter with the French. His victory convinced them to offer terms, with their fellow, Kellermann, speaking for Marshal Junot, of even greater import. We refer to it as the Convention of Cintra, the largest town nearby. Junot is offering to evacuate all of Portugal."

"Well, just damn my eyes!" Lewrie exclaimed, wishing he had something stronger than his cool tea to toast that. "But, doesn't Junot have the bulk of his hundred thousand troops still whole, and grouped round Lisbon? Why should he just give it all up?"

"Well, he's *surrounded,* Captain Lewrie," Hughes boasted. "He is blockaded by sea, bound in by the Tagus River at Lisbon, and has nowhere to go but to straggle back cross the rough mountains into Spain. Here," he offered, handing over two thick packets of reports and letters. "There is a letter for you, a summary of the terms of the treaty, so you may answer any of Admiral Cotton's, or General Drummond's, questions on the broader points. Yes, it's best that the French evacuate Lisbon, and their other enclaves, before they run out of provisions and Sir Hew's troop positions prevent them from foraging the countryside."

Lewrie opened his letter and scanned down the terms, quickly scowling in dis-belief.

"Mine arse on a *band-box*!" he barked. "Ship 'em home to France, on *British* ships, with all their arms, flags, and personal possessions? They'll be on parole, won't they? Unable to serve against us 'til exchanged for an equal number of British prisoners?"

"Ah, no," Major Hughes carefully corrected. "That would require the existence of an hundred thousand or so British soldiers held by the French, already, and we know *that* ain't so. Equally, there would be no way to enforce that rule once Junot's army is back on French soil, so that demand was not made."

"Good Christ, Hughes, we'll just hand Napoleon a whole bloody army back? 'Sorry 'bout that, just dust 'em off and they'll be good as new, and better luck the next time'?" Lewrie fumed. "Mine arse on a band-box, has Sir Hew addled his brains? If it was up to me, the whole lot'd be stripped naked and sent back over the Pyrenees with their thumbs up their arseholes, and marchin' on their heels and elbows!"

"Colourful," Hughes said, only mildly amused, more simpering than laughing, reminding Lewrie over again how much he disliked the beef-to-the-heel bastard.

"Did Burrard, or Wellesley, agree t'this . . . idiocy?" Lewrie asked.

"The Convention is an agreement 'twixt Sir Hew and Sir Henry," Hughes said with a sniff. "Sir Arthur is greatly out-ranked by years of seniority, and has very little say in the matter. Within a few days, General Sir John Moore is expected to arrive here with additional re-enforcements from England, and will assume overall command in the field, supplanting Wellesley, or reducing him to a divisional commander, anyway, should Sir Hew or Sir Henry deem his continued presence useful."

"Oh, so he's good enough t'be the first British General to beat the French since the war began," Lewrie cynically surmised, "but he's not the established Army's favourite, so he has to go? Is that what you're sayin'?"

"Well, Captain Lewrie, you surely must know that there is an odour round the entire Wellesley clan that makes them not quite . . . *quite,* shall we say?" Major Hughes said with a well-informed simper, idly waving his empty wineglass for a re-fill. "They rankle people the wrong way, and Sir Arthur's reputation *was* made in India, after all, his command there sponsored by his brother, who jumped him over men of longer service. And, he is not an easy man to socialise with, being so stand-offish and severe. He may get some of that from his unfortunate choice of wife, haw haw. A *very* ugly woman to begin with, and one who has turned into the *worst* sort of religious shrew, with few social graces.

"Is it any wonder, then, that Sir Arthur pursues quim hotter than most, on the side, hmm?" Major Hughes intimated, leaning closer and winking. "He may be more circumspect in his dalliances than his brother, who has become a laughing-stock in England, but Wellesley is just as mad for a romp."

"Good God, Hughes, who ain't?" Lewrie laughed off. "Don't tell me you've been got at by the 'Leaping Methodists' of a sudden!"

That rankled Hughes, reminding him of his former mistress, Maddalena Covilhā, and the fact that she was Lewrie's mistress, now.

"A top-up, sir?" Pettus enquired, poised over Hughes's shoulder with the wine bottle. Pettus knew all about it, and was a clever fellow. Servants, at sea or in civilian homes, usually knew everything that their masters and mistresses were doing. Pettus looked at Lewrie with a smirk on his face, unseen by Hughes, finding the subject of Maddalena, and Hughes's sudden huffiness, amusing.

"No," Major Hughes decided of a sudden, setting aside his wineglass and shooting to his feet. "Think I'll return ashore. You have the despatches, and your sailing orders, sir, and I'll not detain you."

"Oh, must you go so soon, Major?" Lewrie asked most blandly, getting up as well to see him out. "Aye, I think I'll sail as soon as I can get the anchors up, gladly. Sitting here too long's turned my crew dull and eager to depart for more excitin' things. I'll see you to the entry-port, sir."

They went out to the quarterdeck, where Midshipman Leverett summoned the side-party back to duty for the departure honours.

Lewrie couldn't help it; as he shook hands with Hughes, he just had to say "Who knows, Major Hughes, I may be able to sail into Lisbon and be 'in sight' when the French and Russian warships there are made prize, if there's time for it, and, it'll be grand to get back to Gibraltar, at long last. Should I give your regards to your regimental mess?"

Hughes went slit-eyed and red in the face as he doffed his hat in parting salute, then descended the battens to his waiting boat, making Lewrie grin widely and chuckle silently.

"Pardon for asking, sir," Geoffrey Westcott idly asked as he sauntered over, "but, did that fellow bring us sailing orders?"

"He did, Geoffrey," Lewrie was happy to tell him. "We'll get under way right after the hands have had their mid-day meal. We done with cutlass drill?"

"Aye, sir, and all weapons returned to the arms chests. Here are the keys," Westcott told him, handing over the keys. "Any chance we might return to Gibraltar? The hands are eager for liberty."

"Count on it," Lewrie assured him, "though we won't be bearing grand news to General Drummond. Dalrymple and Burrard have cobbled up a disastrous agreement with the French. Junot will evacuate all of Portugal, and leave it to us. It's *sort* of a surrender, yet it's not," he went on, drawing Westcott to the chart space on the larboard side of the quarterdeck for a bit of privacy, and laying out the terms that he'd been told, giving him a thumbnail sketch.

"Are they *serious*?" Westcott gawped, almost beside himself in utter astonishment. "Napoleon will have that whole army re-equipped and right back into Spain in three months, maybe send them right back into Portugal to undo everything! Promise me we *won't* be escorting them to France, or have anything to do with this madness."

"First off, we're to meet up with Cotton's blockading fleet off Lisbon, then go on to Gibraltar," Lewrie assured him, "as far as we can get from it, with no blame attached for bein' the messenger."

"Good!" Westcott determined, much relieved. "When news of this gets to London, anyone involved with this so-called . . . Convention, is it, will be ruined, maybe stood up against a wall and shot, like old Admiral Byng was. I was *wondering* why the army wasn't marching on Lisbon straight-away."

"Hughes told me that Marshal Junot was pretty-much trapped with no way out, and runnin' low on supplies. Dalrymple and Burrard *could* march South and close the ring round him, but that'd mean a few more battles, and even with Sir John Moore and his re-enforcements coming in a few days, the old fools . . . how did they put it in the terms of the treaty? 'To avoid the useless effusion of blood'? They probably thought that Welles-ley's victories were flukes, up against Marshal Junot's less-competent fools, and it's mortal-certain that *those* two wouldn't risk their own reputations now *they're* in command, and got beaten. Wait for Moore, the darling of the Army and Horse Guards, and let *him* take the blame."

"'Betty' and 'the Dowager,'" Westcott sneered. "My Lord! Give it a month or two, and they'll be up before a court-martial board, mark my words, sir. Anyone associated with it will be tainted for the rest of their lives."

"They will, won't they?" Lewrie said, suddenly breaking out a crafty smile. "Ye know, Geoffrey, our old friend Major Hughes looked like a preenin' peacock just now, like he'd hitched his waggon to a go-er, back on Dalrymple's staff."

"Thought he'd reverted to a substantive Captain?" Westcott asked, puz-zled.

"Bought himself a jump in rank," Lewrie shrugged off. "Well, he may have promoted himself, but it may be a hollow Majority if no one'll have him after word gets out. I think I may have t'go aft and have me a good laugh over his predicament, in private, hee hee!"

"I'll tell Keane and Roe over dinner," Westcott said, taking joy of that picture himself. "The whole wardroom will enjoy hearing."

"Before you do, pass word that we'll be sailing by Two Bells of the Day Watch, and have everyone make sure that we're ready for sea in all respects," Lewrie cautioned, then paused, cocking his head over. "Why do I have a naggin' feelin' that I'm forgetting something?"

Lt. Westcott frowned, too, as if sharing his concern. "Aha, sir! What about Mister Mountjoy? We can't leave him here."

"Damn my eyes, you're right," Lewrie said, all but slapping at his fore-head. "Ye know, I haven't seen hide nor hair of him since I came back

aboard." He looked about to espy one of the Midshipmen of the Harbour
Watch. "Mister Ward, you are to take boat and go ashore to the army encampment, find Mister Mountjoy, and fetch him back so that we can sail."

"Ehm . . . Mister Mountjoy, sir?" Ward said with a gulp, turning red
in the face, "I, ah . . . he sent a note aboard late last night and I . . . I was
about to stand the Middle, and . . ." He felt himself all over, probed all his
pockets, and finally produced a wadded piece of lined foolscap. "I'm sorry,
sir, I quite forgot about it, being so late, I didn't wish to wake you, and . . ."

Lewrie took it from him, un-wadded it, and spread it flat with his palm
on the nearest bulwark cap-rail. It was written in pencil.

"Well," Lewrie said at last, frowning deeply. "It appears that Mountjoy's left for Gibraltar, already, aboard one of the transports carrying
wounded soldiers to the Navy Hospital. Wanted to carry news of the victory quickest, damn him."

It actually read;

Spies unwelcome, bad food and worse drink, fleariddden straw pallet,
and barred from negotiations by the "proper" sorts. Gibraltar and
Seville must be told at once. See you at the Ten Tuns Tavern,
Mountjoy

"Well, that's a relief," Lt. Westcott said.

"Mister Ward, though," Lewrie growled, rounding on the lad. "You've
been badly remiss, you've denied me what amounts to official communication. You *know* that I should have been roused, or the note sent to my
cabins, at once . . . don't you, young sir?"

"Sorry, sir," Ward said, shuddering. It was rare that the Captain lost
his temper.

"Mister Terrell?" Lewrie bellowed in his best quarterdeck voice. "Pass
word for the Bosun! Mister Westcott, when the Bosun turns up, he is to
give Mister Ward a dozen of his best."

"I will see to it, sir," Lt. Westcott replied.

Lewrie went aft to his cabins, and only heard the whacks as Midshipman Ward was bent over the breech of a gun and "kissed the gunner's
daughter."

CHAPTER THIRTY-FOUR

*I*t really wasn't all that far from Maceira Bay to Lisbon and the Tagus River, and even the usually plodding HMS *Sapphire* fetched sight of Admiral Sir Charles Cotton's blockading ships just after dawn of the next day. *Sapphire* made her identification number to the flag, then hoisted Have Despatches, quickly answered by the flagship's demand of Captain Repair On Board, and Lewrie was off in the 25-foot cutter as soon as his ship could come within rowing distance, with his boat crew in their Sunday Divisions best.

"Welcome aboard, sir," the flagship's Captain said once Lewrie had attained the deck of the towering Second Rate. "The Admiral is aft in his cabins. If you will come this way? Ehm . . . we've heard some rumours that a surrender has been arranged?" he hinted, as eager as anyone for news from shore.

"I shouldn't tell tales out of school, sir," Lewrie demurred, "but aye, there has been. I fear I must leave it to Sir Charles to impart the details, once he's read it over. Let's just say that the French will evacuate the whole country, and leave it at that, if you don't mind waiting a bit more."

"Hmpfh, well . . . here you go, sir," that officer said, irked a bit that Lewrie was not more forthcoming.

He was ushered into the Admiral's great-cabins, a richly and grandly

furnished suite twice the size of his own. Sir Charles Cotton rose from behind his day-cabin desk and came forward to welcome him, a fellow of a
most substantial build suitable to his age and rank.

"Despatches, is it, Captain . . . Lewrie, is it?" Cotton boomed. "Think
I've heard your name somewhere before. Sit, sir, and will you have tea or
coffee?"

"Tea, sir, if you don't mind," Lewrie responded, finding a chair in front
of the large desk. He looped his canvas bag off before he did so, opened
it, and handed over the slim packet inside. "Sir Hew Dalrymple has fi-
nalised the terms of the French surrender, sir, and this is your copy of
the, ah . . . Convention of Cintra."

"That what they're calling it?" Cotton said, eagerly taking it and
ripping it open to read it.

"So I was told, sir," Lewrie replied. "The largest town near Vimeiro,
or something."

"No, it's nearer Lisbon, and the coast, where the negotiations have been
held," Cotton countered, with most of his attention drawn to the despatches.

Hughes needs to swot up on his geography, then, Lewrie thought.

"What in the bloody, pluperfect Hell?" Cotton exploded. "My God, what
a travesty! Send them back to France, with all their arms and personal . . . ?
What a damn-fool joke!" Cotton spluttered. He went red in the face as he
flipped through the several pages, then slammed it atop his desk as if touch-
ing it was dangerous.

"I was given a separate summary of the agreement, sir, should you have
any questions about the broader strokes," Lewrie offered.

"Talk about snatching defeat from the jaws of victory, hah!" Cotton
fumed. "Didn't think him capable, but Wellesley at least beat the French
right proper, and he deserved better than this, *England* deserves better than
this rot. Dalrymple must be going senile, and Burrard, that puff pastry . . . !
Don't tell me that Wellesley signed this willingly."

"I was given to understand that he had very little say in it, sir," Lewrie
told him, "and I don't know, but suspect, that the other gentlemen used
their seniority to press him to it."

Lewrie got his tea from a cabin-servant, a cup and saucer in an intricate
and delicate Meissen china pattern, with a sterling silver spoon to stir with,
and a tray bearing fresh-cut lemons and a sugar bowl was presented him.

"This will be the utter ruin of them all," Cotton predicted. "Even Wellesley's family can't save him from it, this time. I wish I'd been ashore to see
it, though, and how *anyone* beat the French."

"I was, sir," Lewrie said with a grin. "It was all quite cleverly managed. He placed his troops along a long, two-mile ridge, and hid the bulk of his men on the back slope, only summoning them up at the moment the French columns got in musket-shot. Two or three thousand muskets firing down on the front and flanks of the columns just melted them away in a twinkling, and then they followed that up with bayonet charges, for the most part, sending the French stampeding back in complete dis-order. It started round nine in the morning, and it was done by noon, or thereabouts."

"You went ashore?" Cotton marvelled, squinting.

"I wanted to see it, one way or another, sir," Lewrie said. "The slopes were carpetted with French dead, and thirteen pieces of artillery were captured. It was . . . grand!"

"Hmm, well," Cotton said, referring to that damnable treaty once more. "I don't see any mention as to the disposition of the French warships, or the Russian squadron, at Lisbon. What were you told of them, Captain Lewrie?"

"Nothing, sir," Lewrie told him. "I don't believe that they were even considered, but that's the Army for you. Perhaps Sir Hew Dalrymple might've *imagined* that the French ships would escort their army back to France, but that would be ridiculous."

"*Damn* what Dalrymple imagined, or wants!" Cotton said, slamming a fist on his desk hard enough to make his pens jump. "I have long planned to find a way to bring them to action, or make prize of them, and by God, I *will*! As for Admiral Senyavin's Russian squadron, well . . . Russia isn't an out-right belligerent, *yet,* and Napoleon and the Tsar had it out last year at the Battle of Friedland, so it isn't clear if they and the French are allies, either. The Russians might not make Good Prize, but I could force them to intern themselves back in England 'til London tells me different."

"Aye, sir," Lewrie agreed. "No sense in allowin' them to roam free if they are, or will become, French allies."

"Does your summary say anything about what constitutes 'personal possessions,' Captain Lewrie?" Cotton asked, squinting at the documents more closely. "And, what the Devil does it mean, that 'the export of specie will be permitted'?"

"This is the first I've heard of it, sir," Lewrie had to admit, "but it sounds very much like a license to steal. Damned Frogs."

"I've a few sources of information from Lisbon, you know," the Admiral slyly boasted. "That Foreign Office fellow at Gibraltar . . ."

"Mister Thomas Mountjoy, sir?" Lewrie prompted.

"Aye, that's the one," Cotton said. "He recently managed to get one of his skulking types into Lisbon, overland from Ayamonte on the Spanish border, who sent me a note by one of my regular fisherman informants . . . signs himself *Aranha*, which means 'Spider.' He said that the French brought portable mints with them when they invaded. Made no sense at the time, but . . . that would be a sly way to melt down all their loot from cathedrals, churches, monasteries, and wealthy homes, and turn silver and gold to French coins. Just one more way that the Dowager's been gulled. This agent's latest says that Junot is hiring five neutral Danish ships to carry his own personal 'baggage'! They fully intend to make off with the spoils of their conquest in *spite* of this damned treaty! Simply appalling!"

"Ehm, this Spider chap," Lewrie asked, sure that he knew the agent's identity. "Are his messages . . . does he sound a tad insane?"

"As a matter of fact, yes," the Admiral confirmed for him.

"Know him," Lewrie said with a shake of his head. "Well, met him once. He was in Madrid, before the Spanish revolted, and helped it along. He's daft as bats."

Romney bloody Marsh! Lewrie thought; *How's he still* alive?

"But, incredibly brave and clever," Admiral Cotton said with a firm nod of praise.

"Anything else you wish to know, sir?" Lewrie asked, finishing his cup of tea. "If not, I must be off to Gibraltar, to deliver General Drummond his copy of the treaty."

"Good!" Sir Charles Cotton boomed. "I now recall where I've heard your name before, Captain Lewrie. The newspapers, and the *Naval Chronicle*. Quite the dashing and active frigate captain, and more fortunate than most when it comes to prize-money. Not to be uncharitable, but, those French ships are mine, and my squadron's. We've all been banking on them, and I trust you would not wish to dilute the pot and deprive an older man his long-denied due, hah!"

"God no, sir!" Lewrie said with a laugh. "You're more than welcome to the spoils, tempting though it is to see the French humbled, and tour Lisbon, at last."

"So you will be off at once," Admiral Cotton sort-of-asked, one brow up in worry that he might linger, after all, for a few hundred pounds of profit, with a deep scowl to warn him that he shouldn't.

"Can't even stay long enough for a second cup of tea, sir," Lewrie vowed as he got to his feet. "And, may I wish you great joy of your coming success at Lisbon."

"Capital, simply capital!" Admiral Cotton barked with great satisfaction as he, too, rose to see Lewrie to the entry-port.

When HMS *Sapphire* coasted to a stop and dropped her anchor off the Old Mole at Gibraltar, it was evident that the grand news which Mountjoy had carried from Vimeiro was already known from one end of the town to the other. Bands were parading, and all the battlements were fluttering with Union Flags everywhere one looked. The faint sounds of drunken cheers made their way out to the ship, and some daytime fireworks were being let off in enthusiasm.

The mood was not so merry at the Convent, though, when Lewrie handed over the copy of the Convention of Cintra to Major-General James Drummond. Lewrie had had no dealings with the man so far, but that worthy struck him at once as a much more active, intelligent, and capable officer than Dalrymple.

"Hmm," Drummond grumbled as he read it through a second time, still dis-believing. "Quite extraordinary, even astonishing. Not to criticise my predecessor, but . . . it appears the *French* wrote it and our senior officers slavishly surrendered to *them*! Damme, we had them in the bag, then they just let them wiggle free!"

"It's worse, sir," Lewrie gloomily told him, repeating what he had gotten from Admiral Sir Charles Cotton, and Romney Marsh's mystifying despatches. "Junot's loading five ships with his own loot, and the mints have been workin' round the clock. Napoleon may end up with as much solid coin as he got when he sold Louisiana, and gets an entire army back, with all their arms. Well, we get to keep all their artillery, about two-dozen waggons full of powder, shot, all their stores, cavalry mounts and draught animals, and over twenty thousand rounds of ammunition. Once Lisbon harbour is ours, a lot of that could be useful to the Spanish. All in all, though, Portugal ends up completely looted. The cupboard's bare."

"I would have made them *march* back to France," Drummond said with a derisive snort, "if they *had* to be set free. Ideally, I would have imprisoned them all, but for the cost of *feeding* the bastards. Bah! How could we have settled for this?"

"I'd've stripped them naked and made them cross the Pyrenees with their thumbs up their arses, on their heels and elbows, sir," Lewrie said, repeating his jape to Major Hughes.

"That might have gone a *bit* beyond the recognised rules of war, Captain

Lewrie," General Drummond replied, though the comment awoke a wry grin on his phyz. "You've shared this with the Foreign Office agent, yet?"

"Not yet, sir," Lewrie said. "He's my next stop."

"Well, I won't keep you," Drummond said, pacing over to his large map pinned to a board. Instead of Dalrymple's map of Spain, Portugal, and his pet project of taking the fortress at Ceuta, the General's was of Gibraltar and its immediate environs. He pulled a face, not yet dimissing Lewrie, though Lewrie had already risen to his feet, hat under his arm. "At least we have Wellesley's triumph to celebrate, and that's the main thing . . . that, and the ousting of the French from Portugal. This . . . !" Drummond said, waving the sheaf of paper about, "does not affect us here. We shall celebrate and put a good face on it. I'm told that all the regimental messes are co-operating to stage a grand supper ball, a *fête champêtre*, even if Italian sparkling wines must stand in for champagne proper. Are you still in port, sir, be assured that you and your officers shall be invited."

"Thankee kindly, sir, and I look forward to it," Lewrie said, perking up. "I'll take my leave, then. Good day, sir."

It took Lewrie a hot, sweaty hour of walking to hunt up Thomas Mountjoy after that; Pescadore's, Mountjoy's lodgings, the fraudulent offices of his Falmouth Import & Export Company in the lower town, and the Ten Tuns Tavern. He finally bearded him in his den at his upper-town lodgings, having missed him somehow in transit.

"Ah, Lewrie, back at last, are you?" Mountjoy said jovially as he sat out on his awninged gallery overlooking the harbour, and at his ease following a fine mid-day meal. "You look hot. A cool wine?"

"Yes, thankee," Lewrie said, sitting down on an upholstered iron chair and fanning himself with his hat. "I thought you'd use me as your private yacht to get back here."

"News of our success just had to be gotten to General Drummond, and the Spanish *Junta* at Seville. Sorry 'bout that," Mountjoy said.

"You really should have hung around a tad longer," Lewrie chid him as Mr. Daniel Deacon came outside with a freshly-opened bottle of sprightly floral Spanish wine and an extra glass. "Hallo, Deacon, and how d'ye keep?"

"Main-well, sir," Deacon said, pouring all round.

"Celebrating still?" Lewrie asked. "A bit premature, that. As I said, you really should have stayed long enough to hear the details of the terms that Dalrymple, Burrard, and the French thrashed out."

"Mmm, well . . . what are they?" Mountjoy had to ask, and Lewrie took joy of being the source of information that the spy-master did not know; it was rare that *that* shoe was on *his* foot.

"Well, first, the French will evacuate all their troops from every inch of Portugal," Lewrie told him. "We get it all back at one blow." And as they cheered that, he took a welcome sip of his wine. "But . . ." he added, sticking a finger in the air, "they get to sail back to France, in *British* ships, with all their arms, colours, and . . . personal possessions, which means whatever loot they'd stolen from Portugal. And, their *pay* chests," Lewrie said, scowling, as he explained about the portable mints, the ships that Marshal Junot hired for his booty. "I heard that General Wellesley wanted to march down to Torres Vedras at once, keep the initiative, and box the rest of Junot's troops in at Lisbon, but that was scotched. The whole thing has simply turned to shit, a great, steaming pile of it!"

"My God, the lack-wits!" Mountjoy gravelled, after a minute of slack-jawed amazement. He tossed off his wine at one go. "We've been diddled! How incredibly . . . stupid!"

"Still, we beat them, sir," Deacon said. "I would have loved to have seen it, myself. And we get Portugal back."

"I went ashore with my Ferguson rifled musket, and saw it right from the firing line," Lewrie told him, "and yes, it was grand to see. The French column can't beat the British line, and rolling platoon volleys."

"Portugal free, and the Spanish revolt has driven the French North of the Ebro River," Mountjoy stuck in, seeking *any* solace. "If Spanish math is to be trusted, 'Boney's' invasion has cost him over fourty thousand killed, wounded, and captured, and King Joseph Bonaparte's fled Madrid for Burgos, maybe as far as Vitoria."

"And, we've been told that General Sir John Moore is on his way to Lisbon," Deacon added, looking for another bright spot. "General Sir David Baird is to land another army at Corunna in Northwest Spain, too, and they might be able to unite and drive the French from the rest of Spain."

"Lisbon's where your boy, Romney Marsh is, now," Lewrie took a great joy in relating, loving Mountjoy's astonishment. "However he managed that. He's been sending Admiral Cotton useful news."

"I'd rather *not* know," Mountjoy gawped. "The details would scare me out of a year's growth! I got one note from him from Seville, then another from Ayamonte, then he dropped off the face of the earth. I didn't know he was fluent in Portuguese, but then he would be, wouldn't he? French,

Spanish, Latin, Greek, he's as daft as you are, Lewrie. The two of you are of a piece! Playing private soldier, my Lord! You do anything to relieve your boredom, anything to smell gunpowder."

"Nonsense, I was just witnessing history," Lewrie demurred.

"Well, *there's* a faithless bitch that'll put you in the ground, if you're not careful," Mountjoy cautioned. "History, hah!"

"Can't do without me, is it?" Lewrie teased as he sat back down with his re-fill. "Me, or your private navy? Speaking of that, I suppose I'm still under your orders? Do ye have anything in the works for me to do?"

"More arms deliveries," Mountjoy idly said with a shrug. "Do some scouting of the cities along the coast where the French are holed up, the forts. I may have you sail to Lisbon to retrieve our mystery man, now that we occupy the place."

"I promised Maddalena that she'd see Lisbon someday," Lewrie said with a fond smile. "Speaking of, if ye have no more questions for now, I'll see you both at the ball."

"What ball?" Mountjoy asked with a scowl.

"The garrison officers are poolin' resources t'throw one, and I'm told I'll be invited," Lewrie said, tossing off the last of his glass and getting to his feet again. "I expect you both will be, as well, so . . . shave close, bathe, and brush your teeth, hmm?"

Back on the street, Lewrie set a fast pace South along the quayside, threading his way impatiently through carters, barrow men, and half-drunk sailors. As *Sapphire* had come in under reduced sail, he had peered closely at the rented lodgings, and, sure enough, Maddalena had come out onto the balcony and had enthusiastically waved a tea towel in welcome.

Kept her waitin' long enough, he thought as he increased his pace as he got closer to her building; *Kept me* deprived *long enough!* He felt at a pocket of his coat to assure himself that he had brought a full dozen fresh cundums ashore.

Suddenly, he was there, *she* was there, at the balcony rails, up on tiptoes, bouncing with eagerness with a wide smile on her face, and as he waved widely back, she reached up to the back of her neck and freed her hair to fall long, lush and lustrous. *Yes!*

Some bystanders might laugh, but Lewrie didn't care a fig for their opinions, didn't care if he was making himself the biggest fool. He practically burst through the ground-floor doors, and pounded up the stairs in a growing eagerness of his own, and it was more than a simple, raging lust; that sudden swelling of intense affection struck him in a rush, almost making him utter "Whoo!"

Down the long hallway to the door that was already swung wide, and there she was with her arms out-stretched, her expression between utter delight and a crumple into tears of joy.

"Alan, *meu amor,* you are back!" she cried as he hungrily swept her into his arms, lifted her off her feet, and danced her round the parlour, burying his face in her neck.

"Maddalena, *minha doce,* Lord how I've missed you!" he declared. "It's been too long!" Then he could not say more as she rained kisses on his face almost frantically, 'til he found her mouth and pressed her to a long, deep soul kiss that made her moan and giggle.

"I have missed you so *much!*" Maddalena whimpered and cooed.

"I bring good news, grand news, *minha querida,*" he tried to impart. "The French have been beaten, Portugal is . . . let me tell it, first. The French are leaving Portugal, Lisbon will be ours, and your country's free, again! We've won!"

"*Que ke?*" she squealed in astonishment. "*Sim? Maravilhoso,* oh praise God!" she cried, reverting to English.

"You still have that pink gown ye wore when we met Sir John Moore?" he asked with a laugh. "There's t'be a grand victory ball, sure t'be fireworks with it, and we're goin' t'be invited."

She leaned back a bit in stupefaction, then broke out an even wider smile, and used one hand to brush away more tears.

" 'Less ye'd like a new'un?" Lewrie offered.

"My country is free," she whispered, marvelling, "my people are free." Her face screwed up as she began to bawl in his arms, and Lewrie held her close, lost and unable to understand all that she managed to say, all in Portuguese. Her cat, Precious, now a mature young tom, sensing her distress, came to paw at the bottom of her gown, and bat at the gilt tassels of Lewrie's boots.

She calmed, finally, stepped back and reached down to lift her cat to her breast to cuddle it and stroke its head, slowly pacing about the parlour, as if finding comfort, or giving comfort. Lewrie went to close and lock the door.

"*Agradececer tu,* Alan," Maddalena said in a meek voice, looking at him with frank adoration. "Thank you for the finest gift you could ever give me, *meu amor.*"

"I live to please," Lewrie japed with a lop-sided grin.

She sat her cat down on the settee and came to his arms once more, sliding into his embrace, wrapping her arms round his neck and kissing him long and deep, and her breath went cow-clover musky.

"It has been too long, *meu querido*," she whispered. *"Vamos para a cama,"* she cooed as she un-did his neck-stock.

He knew the word *cama*; it meant "bed."

"Hell yes, we will!" he growled in delight.

BOOK FOUR

There are some defeats more triumphant than victories.

—MICHEL DE MONTAIGNE
(1533-1592) *ESSAIS*

CHAPTER THIRTY-FIVE

September mostly was spent at sea, along the coast of Andalusia to probe at Málaga, Cartagena, even as far East as Valencia, to discover if the French garrisons were still there in the forts, and how active they were. Mountjoy's able assistant, Daniel Deacon, went with Lewrie for most of those probes, so he could be rowed ashore to speak with local Spanish insurgents and get the lay of the land. Deacon was so casual when he spoke about his movements, and the great risks that he faced, that Lewrie feared that he had another Romney Marsh on his hands. Here it must be confessed that, in point of fact, Lewrie was of half a mind to go ashore with Deacon, now and then, for a closer look at Spain than the one from his quarterdeck several miles seaward, or the view through Mountjoy's rooftop telescope.

Satisfied that he'd done all that he'd been asked to perform, Deacon decided, at last, that *Sapphire* should return to Gibraltar to impart all that he'd gathered to his superior.

Three days in port, though, to re-provision and provide shore liberty to the jaded crew, three brief nights with Maddalena, and Mr. Mountjoy expressed an urge to go himself to Lisbon, and with a breezy, "I say, Lewrie, might you oblige me with passage to call upon our army in Portugal?" they were off.

⚓

"A pretty place," Lt. Westcott commented as he peered shoreward with his telescope. "Rather steep going, though. I can see narrow lanes practically zig-zagging uphill."

"Good," Lewrie commented, taking a good, long look of his own. "That'll keep the hands closer to the seafront so they can't desert. *If* we give 'em shore liberty here."

"We might *not,* sir?" Westcott asked, a tad disappointed.

"Too many soldiers, and that's a bad mix," Lewrie explained, recalling the melees and near-riots between bored soldiers and touchy sailors when *Sapphire*'s people were allowed liberty at Gibraltar.

"I don't see that many," Westcott pointed out.

Indeed, the long shorefront teemed with local Portuguese dock workers, busy ferrying mostly military goods from the many supply ships anchored in the Tagus, or berthed alongside the docks, then loading hired waggons and carts to trundle everything elsewhere. But for some officers and enlisted men from the Commissariat, most of the people in sight were civilians.

"Most of Sir John Moore's troops must be quartered out in the countryside," Westcott went on, "to keep them from obtaining so much drink that they collapse, or drink themselves to death."

"Well, we could, I suppose," Lewrie grudgingly allowed.

"Ah, Lisbon!" Mountjoy exclaimed, coming to the quarterdeck from his borrowed dog-box cabin off the wardroom. "One of the most impressive cities of Europe, gentlemen, one of the most beautiful. I have always longed to see it."

Almost gushingly, Mountjoy pointed out the sights, the Praça do Comércio by the riverfront with its mansions and vast square lined with pale lemony facades and mosaic cobblestoned streets, the Baixa district where the world's first gridded streets had been laid out after the destruction wrought by the earthquake, fires, and floodwaters of the All Saints' Day disaster of 1755. "Upwards of ninety thousand people, one-third of the city population, perished, don't ye know," Mountjoy told them, "but thank God for New World gold and silver to pay for the rebuilding. That's the Barrio Alto, up above, and off to the right is the old Moorish quarter, the Alfama. Had it for ages, they did, 'til Dom Afonso Henríques took it . . . with the help of mostly British Crusaders. I read that the pillage after was horrid, though."

"British soldiers, well. What did they expect?" Lewrie japed, sharing a look with Westcott. "They'd steal the coins from their dead mothers' eyes."

"I wish to go ashore and see what Marsh has been up to. Might you wish to accompany me, sirs?" Mountjoy asked.

Lewrie shared another look with Westcott, who, in his eagerness, was almost prancing on his tiptoes, and had his brows up as if to plead.

"Aye, I think we will," Lewrie relented, after pretending to mull that over. "We'd best go armed, even so. Swords, and hidden pistols. You might wish to fetch your own, Mister Mountjoy. Bosun Terrell!" he boomed of a sudden. "Muster my boat crew and bring the cutter round to the entry-port!"

He spotted Lieutenant Harcourt further forward along the larboard sail-tending gangway and summoned him aft to tell him that he would be in temporary charge, then went aft to fetch his own hanger and the brace of single-barrelled pocket pistols.

He found it almost comical to see the younger "master spy," Mountjoy, with a sword belted round his waist, two obvious bulges in the side pockets of his natty grey coat, with a wide-brimmed Summer straw hat on his head.

"My word, sir," he commented before they took deparure honours at the entry-port, "what a piratical picture you make. A freebooter, a Spanish *filibustero* . . ."

"A British pillager-ruffian?" Westcott slyly added. "Come to emulate Lisbon's ancient conquerors?"

"Just for that, *you* buy the wine," Mountjoy shot back. But he did so with a droll roll of his eyes.

"Good God, what is that appalling stench?" Lewrie said as he pinched his nose shut, once they were ashore.

"That, I suppose," Westcott said, pointing to an enormous pile of garbage that almost blocked the entrance to a side street off the impressive plaza. "It looks as if the rains have washed it all down to where it ended up, like a log jam."

Rather large rats and lesser mice could be seen rooting through the mounds, and it swarmed with thousands of flies. Uphill along that steep side street, it did indeed look as if something had moved that disgusting mess downhill, leaving bits, and a slug trail of filth, in its wake.

"I say, soldier!" Mountjoy called out to a passing member of the Commissariat, a stout little fellow with a sheaf of manifests and ledger book, with a scented handkerchief pressed to his own nose. "Doesn't anyone tend to the garbage?"

"Sorry, sir?" the soldier said, stopping in his tracks and coming to a rough stance of Attention. "The garbage? That'd be up to the Portygeers, sir. They're the filthiest folk ever I did see. My officer says 'twas the French did it, shooting all the dogs, soon as they took the place. The Portygeers let thousands of stray dogs do the work for them, if ya can imagine it."

"Shot the *dogs*? Why?" Lewrie demanded, astonished.

"Heard they did the same with all the stray cats, too, sir," the soldier replied, standing a bit stiffer to address an officer. "Feared they was all mad and frothing at the mouth, I reckon."

"Is the whole city like this?" Mountjoy pressed, whipping out a handkerchief of his own and wadding it over his lower face.

"Well sir, I don't see all that much of it, but I reckon that it is, or so I hear," the soldier told him. "The Portygeers live in a pigsty, and think nothing of it. Ehm, beg pardon, sirs, but I've chits to deliver, and my sergeant—"

"Aye, carry on, lad," Lewrie told him, lifting his hat to salute.

"How horrible!" Mountjoy almost moaned in disappointment.

"The dogs and the cats?" Lewrie asked. "Hell of a waste of ammunition. Damn the fastidious French."

"No, I mean . . . the whole, beautiful city just tosses all their offal and garbage out the windows into the *streets*," Mountjoy mourned, "and leaves it for the beasts to eat before it stinks. What sort of a civilised people *do* that?"

"They might've let hogs roam free, too," Lewrie attempted to joke. "Fond as they are of ham in Spain and Portugal. Don't see any, so the French must've eaten them, *then* shot the dogs and cats."

"Catholic countries, sir," Westcott reminded with a sneer.

"Dear God," Mountjoy muttered with sad shakes of his head. "I imagined so much more of this wondrous city."

"We should've asked that soldier where the army has its headquarters," Lewrie said. "They might know where your man Marsh might be found. Unless he's gone so native that *nobody* knows, of course."

With no better idea, they strolled North from the river to the far end of the Praça do Comércio, where they were met by a party of Provosts doing their rounds, and discovered that the Commandant of Lisbon,

General John Carr Beresford, was ensconced in the Castelo, an ancient fortress a *long* way uphill.

"Beresford!" Lewrie griped once they were on their way. "That fool! Remember him, Geoffrey, from Buenos Aires? He was the one in command, and surrendered his whole army to the Argentine rebels."

"Wasn't that much of an army, really," Westcott scoffed, "or much of a battle when it came."

"And he couldn't even manage that," Lewrie continued in some heat. "Garrison duty's all he's good for, though I thought that the Army would've sacked him by now. Christ, but they cling to their lack-wits like burrs to a saddle blanket!"

They could see the towers and battlements of the Castelo high above them, but it was a long, slow climb, and the cobblestones were treacherous footing. They passed homes with drying laundry strung cross the streets, tiny shops jammed between, slowly re-filling with foodstuffs from the countryside but still offering little, and an host of locals shopping for what little there was so far, and at inflated prices at that. People swarmed round moneychangers, pawn shops where family treasures were exchanged for money to keep body and soul together, people everywhere making their ways with sacks, crates, and kegs on their shoulders in search of better deals.

Even so, some of those tiny shops were aromatic with the smells of cooking, and Mountjoy would peek in to see what was offered, getting some of his good humour back as he extolled what he found; *caldeirada de peixe*, a fish stew with tomatoes, potatoes, and rice; *cataplana*, a shellfish stewed with wine, garlic, and tomatoes; *ensopada de enguias*, an eel stew; and *acorda de camarrãoes*, shrimp, garlic, and cilantro thick with bread crumbs. There some grilled strips of spicy chicken, another wee shop no wider than eight feet char-grilling sardines fresh from the sea. There were wine shops selling *vinho verde*, a crisp white, and reds by the meagre glass. Breads of various sorts, of course, and vegetables, were in others. Pastry shops were laying out hot custard tarts, some sort of cheesecake, and almond and egg custards.

"Damn my eyes, Mister Mountjoy, but you must stop," Westcott insisted. "No more thrilling descriptions. You're making me hungry!"

"Well, it ain't as if we've an *appointment* with Beresford," Lewrie pointed out, coming to a full stop. "Why *not* have a bite or two? Look, we're almost to the Castelo, and there's a tavern there, where the square opens up, right near one of the gates."

"You're *still* buying the wine," Mountjoy insisted, this time in wry humour as they entered, took off their hats, and adjusted their eyes to the sudden dimness. The windows were few and small, though the double doors of the entry were as broad as the kind found in a barn. There were tables scattered about, a brace of opposing fireplaces for Winter days, a fair number of candles lit, and several Portuguese scattered about at their sublime ease, or indolence, listening to a musician; sipping wine, snacking on what fare the tavern offered. They found an empty table and sat down.

"That's a *fado* he's singing, by George," Mountjoy said with a broad grin on his face.

"What, that caterwaulin'?" Lewrie scoffed.

It was in Portuguese, of course, slow for the most part, veering into a minor key, and both ineffably sad and haunting, then suddenly forceful and urgent, with many flourishes on the singer's guitar.

"Sorrowful as all Hell, but most engrossing. *Fados* are a fascinating part of the country's culture," Mountjoy praised on.

"Then God help the Portuguese," Westcott said, chuckling.

"Bom dia, senhores," a waiter said as he came over.

"Ehm, *bom dia,*" Lewrie ventured, "ah . . . *alguem aqui fala inglese?*"

"Speak *inglese, senhor?*" the waiter puzzled over Lewrie's horrid accent. "*Sim,* I do, *falo um pouco* . . . the little?" He launched into a lengthy explanation of how he'd become bilingual, all in fast Portuguese, of course, which went right over everyone's heads. "*Ja decidiram* . . . what I get for you?" which sounded very much like *zha-dee-see-dee-rowng,* he asked at last.

The guitarist must have completed the long, long *fado,* for the locals in the tavern wearily clapped and whistled their appreciation. He began another tune, much faster paced, with many strums, plucks, and finger-drums against his instrument, head down in deep concentration, with a wide-brimmed country hat hiding his face.

"What the Devil?" Mountjoy asked as the musician began "Rule, Brittania!"

"Somebody likes us," Lewrie said, turning to the waiter to ask for *vinho verde.*

"Viva Inglaterra!" the musician shouted, still head down. *"Viva las inglese!",* and the local patrons raised a mild cheer to that, too.

"Maybe it'll be their treat, hey?" Lewrie said, with a wink.

The guitarist suddenly looked up, then stopped playing, sprang off the tabletop to his feet, and swept off his hat. "Hallo, Mountjoy, and how d'ye keep, my good man?"

"Marsh?" Mountjoy blurted, stumbling to his feet and over-turning his chair in his astonishment. "How did you . . . ?"

Knows how t'make the grand entrance, damn him, Lewrie thought as he stood as well.

"Have my ways, don't ye know," Romney Marsh/The Multitude said as he came over to shake hands, unable to help himself from dropping into his various guises as he explained himself. *"Primero,* I left Madrid as ze *pobre musico,* joos me an' my *guitarra,* then from Seville to Ayamonte, I played ze *gran caballero,* wees deespatches from ze Seville *junta.* A fisherman, to cross the river and row up the marshes to Portugal . . . the French pay well for fresh eels and sardines, ye know . . . switched from Spanish to Portuguese, grounded the boat and walked off homeward with my nets and oars over my shoulder, and just kept on 'til I could steal a cassock and hat, some sandals, and became a Romish priest for most of the way, beggin' my way, no problems at all, 'til I got close to Sentubal and the French patrols.

"Then, I made myself into a French cavalry officer from near Sentubal to the Tagus," Marsh preened, changing his accent.

"You *what?"* Mountjoy exclaimed again.

"Well, the damned fool was just ambling along without a care in the world, looking for old Roman or Moorish ruins to sketch, and with an eye for available young women, too, I expect, as if he was in a park in Paris, not a hostile country. An *extreme* young'un, no error," Romney Marsh said with a laugh as he sat down at the table with them and claimed a wineglass and the fresh-fetched bottle. After a deep sip, and an appreciative sigh, he continued his tale.

"I passed myself off to him as a Jesuit who had studied in Paris," Marsh went on with a sly grin, "which explained my perfect French. There *were* some ruins, a mile or so off the main road, so I spun him a tale of their antiquity. He on his fine charger, me on my humble donkey, we rode up there. I *warned* him that what he was doing was dangerous, so . . . after he hopped about, sketching like mad, and we shared some bread, cheese, and wine, I fulfilled my warning.

" 'Twas a warm day, so he'd taken off his coat, laid aside his sword," Marsh said with a titter, "and I slit his throat and became . . . *him,* hah hah! Didn't even get any gore on his trousers!"

"You got into Lisbon as an enemy officer?" Mountjoy gasped in shock. "Just . . . killed the bastard and . . . ?"

Good thing he works for us, Lewrie thought, astonished by the callous way that Marsh described his murder; *Was he back in London, there'd be* nobody *safe! He's* seriously *twisted!*

"No no, old fellow, I couldn't do that," Marsh pooh-poohed. "But I could make faster progress on a good horse than I could with a burro. There was a spot of bother when I came across a French cavalry patrol, but I had his sketch pad case, and claimed that I was going to Lisbon with despatches to report the presence of those evil British at Ayamonte, and we rode along together for a bit, and a grand time it was, too, for their officer and his troopers were jolly sorts, and we all knew the same French tavern songs, as it turned out. I got to Montijo, got a remount, and headed for Sentubal, their lodgement South of the Tagus. Around dark, I ran into some armed Portuguese patriots, sold them the horse and the whole uniform kit, got some peasant clothing and this fine new *guitarra* from them, and took the Lisbon ferry as an itinerant musician, serenading the locals, and the French garrison, for my up-keep, 'til the bastards left and our army marched in. Ah, Alfonso," he called to the waiter, "another bottle of this excellent *vinho verde,* and these gentlemen will have . . ." He ordered for them in fluent Portuguese, which resulted in a pot of sardines, shrimp, and mussels in wine sauce, with crisp bread and smooth cheese.

"Well, I never heard the like," Mountjoy marvelled, between bites of food. "You astound me, Marsh, you really do. But, how did you manage to turn up at this very tavern the same time as us?"

"Serendipity, Mountjoy," Marsh told him with a sly grin. "I've been haunting Beresford's garrison headquarters, and Sir John Moore's outside town, for nigh a fortnight, trying to get someone to listen. The Castelo's not a hop, skip, or jump from here, you were obviously on your way there, and the rest was fortunate happenstance. What say we order more grilled shrimp, hey?"

"Listen to what?" Lewrie asked, still puzzled. "Now the Frogs have gone, what information do you have for them?"

"Yes, what you learned was most useful, and allowed us to keep the French from making off with *all* their loot," Mountjoy praised, "but, now they've gone, I'd think you of more use back in Madrid."

"Madrid, hah!" Marsh objected. "There's nothing but a circus going on there, full of boasting and self-congratulatory blather! We need solid information for Moore's thrust into Spain, assurances of Spanish support, and we have neither."

"You don't intend to ride into Spain ahead of the army and do a scout, do you?" Lt. Westcott asked.

"No, sir, I'll leave that to our army to do," Marsh dismissed the notion with a hoot of mirth. "But, someone should, and soon, but that fact doesn't strike our generals as important, and what they've gotten from Hookham Frere is so much moonshine."

"Who the Devil's Hookham Frere?" Lewrie said, scowling.

"John Hookham Frere," Marsh said with the sarcasm dripping, "is a clueless, inexperienced, fool who believes everything the *juntas* tell him, and passes it on to Moore. Lord Canning sent him to Madrid to be Ambassador, and a worst choice I can't imagine. One just *can't* believe a word the Spanish promise, but *he* does. Except for General Castaños at Bailén, the Spanish armies have been beaten like whipped dogs, and the posturing, braggart idiots in fine uniforms claim that they'll do just as well, when their soldiers are without shoes, shot, powder, weapons, horses, and bread. Frere promises them all they lack, then promises Moore that he'll find proper allies over the border.

"They can't arm, feed, or train their own troops, but swear that our army will be amply supplied in Spain," Marsh sneered, "and on the strength of those empty promises, Frere is urging Moore to get going as soon as dammit, and all is in place, just waiting for him, when nothing has been done to *begin* to gather any supplies!"

"I cannot believe that Sir John Moore will assume that his march into Spain will be that easy, or so well assisted," Mountjoy said with a disbelieving shake of his head. "He, and we, well know not to put so much trust into our allies, by now. His Commissariat, his baggage train—"

"Inherited from General Wellesley," Lewrie interrupted.

"Yes, very well thought out," Mountjoy quickly agreed. "He's the best we have, is Moore, the chief reformer of our armies into the modern age. Why, I should think that he has cavalry vedettes out in the field this instant, scouting the roads, making maps . . ."

"Ever *seen* Spanish maps, of their *own* bloody country, sir?" Marsh sneered some more. "Even *they* don't trust them, and they show nothing of how passable the roads are, how steep the elevations and descents are, whether the bridges are wide enough to take wheeled waggons or guns, or if they're even still standing! Cattle paths one steer wide they *call* roads!"

"You say you've tried to speak with Beresford and Moore, sir?" Lewrie asked him, beginning to get a bad feeling.

"I have, Captain Lewrie," Marsh archly and sarcastically told him, "but, I am a *spy*, sir . . . a despicable, sneaking, lying hound not worthy of *associating* with proper English gentlemen, or of being given the *slightest* note. Their aides openly sneer at my arrival."

"Perhaps if you changed your clothes . . . ," Westcott suggested, a bit tongue-in-cheek, which earned him a sudden squint of anger and warning. Romney Marsh was not quite the half-mad theatrical *poseur* living out a great game of intrigue; he was murderously dangerous.

"Perhaps if I spoke with our generals of this matter, along with the other topics I came to Lisbon to discuss with them, I might make them see reason," Mountjoy supposed.

"Someone must, sir," Marsh agreed, settling back and making free with the wine bottle again, turning in an eye-blink to a mild and reasonable fellow. "You know that General Sir David Baird is to land eight or nine thousand men at Corunna, in Northwest Spain, and is to march to collaborate with Moore's army? I gather from what I have picked up at headquarters, *despite* my shunning by one and all, that both armies are to meet at Salamanca, cut the French lines of supply, co-operate with Spanish armies, and drive the French out of Spain altogether.

"Hah!" Marsh erupted in sour mirth, loud enough to startle even a few sleepy whores in the tavern. "With no aid or support from the Spanish, with poor, or only imagined roads to march on, campaigning into Midwinter . . . in the mountains of Spain in Midwinter? My *Lord*! They've no idea where the remaining French armies are, and how they might move against them. It's daft, daft as March hares . . . as daft as I am!"

"That's assumin' that Napoleon'll let Spain go without a fight," Lewrie stuck in, feeling even more gloom and trepidation. "He can't hold his empire if he's seen bein' defeated."

"That's right, sir," Mountjoy agreed. "We in the Foreign Office are aware of growing dis-content in his possessions already, nationalist movements growing. Why, he'd have riot and revolution facing him from here to the Russian borders!"

"The French will be back in strength in the Spring, is that what you're saying?" Westcott asked, equally gloomy. "'Boney' has untold thousands of fresh troops available, his own, and thousands of troops from the other countries he's conquered. He *has* to come back and finish off the Spanish for good."

"Then, God help the Spanish," Lewrie gravelled, "even if they can't seem t'help themselves."

"And God help *our* armies, if they cross the border, trusting the Spanish," Westcott sorrowfully agreed.

"Hmm, well," Lewrie summed up, pushing his empty plate aside. "What's it t'be, Mountjoy? A tour of fabled Lisbon, or will you go see General Beresford or Moore?"

"You weesh zhe grand tour, *senhores?*" Marsh offered, tittering and off in one of his guises, again. "I am expert guide!"

"Only if you can steer Westcott to the prettier whores, sir," Lewrie said with a snigger.

"No, dear as I wish," Mountjoy said, torn between finally seeing Lisbon's impressive attractions, and duty, "I must go talk with our generals, first. A tour, later, if you're still offfering, Romney."

"My delight," Marsh agreed, beaming.

"I suppose we should get back to the ship," Lewrie told his First Officer. "Will you be staying on, Mountjoy, or should we wait for you and carry you back to Gibraltar?"

"Let you know later," Mountjoy said, digging coins out to pay the reckoning. "I may only need to stay a day or two."

"You'll not be haring off to see another battle ashore, will you, sir?" Lt. Westcott asked as they made their way back downhill to the seafront.

"Too far inland for me, if one comes, no, Geoffrey," Lewrie scoffed. "I've seen my share, and those are enough."

"If half of what Marsh says is true, I'd not wish to go off with our soldiers, either," Westcott said, displaying a deep scowl that made some Libson passersby duck away from him, in fear of the Evil Eye. "Maybe General Moore should wait 'til Spring."

"But, the *French* will be back by Spring," Lewrie pointed out.

"Marsh," Westcott mused aloud, still scowling, "do you really think he murdered that French officer as he claims?"

"We've only his word for that," Lewrie replied, shrugging. "I always thought he was much like a half-insane version of Mountjoy, an inoffensive sort who perhaps enjoyed playing some great, dangerous game a tad *too* much, but . . . now I wonder if he is *indeed* capable of violence, like that old spy-master, Zachariah Twigg, who'd cut your throat just t'watch you bleed. You saw that look he gave you when you remarked about his clothes?"

"Aye, I did, sir," Westcott heartily agreed, "and it made me wonder if there's a knife in my back, in future."

"*Tortas, senhores?*" an old woman in widow's black weeds cried from a *pastelaria* set between two tumbledown houses. *"Tortas laranja, de Viana, tortas de limao?"*

"Tarts!" Lewrie enthused. "Orange, lemon, and I think some with jam fillings. We didn't have dessert, did we, Geoffrey? Ah, *senhora, queria dois, dois,* and *dois,*" he said pointing to each variety in turn. *"Quanto custa?"*

"Eh . . . *vinte centimos, senhor,*" the old lady dared ask, not sure if that was too much in these troubled times.

"Twenty of their pence, is it?" Lewrie said, digging out his wash-leather coin purse; he had no Portuguese coin, but he did have two six-pence silver British coins, and handed them over. The sight of silver almost made the old lady faint.

"Aqui esta, senhor, bom apetite!" she exclaimed, wrapping his selections in a sheet of newspaper.

"Obrigada, senhora," Lewrie replied, "thankee kindly."

"Viva Inglaterra!" she shouted in departure.

"I say, these are tangy," Westcott said as he bit into one of the orange-flavoured tarts as they resumed their downhill stroll for the docks. "But, just when did you become fluent in Portuguese, sir?"

"Fluent, *me?*" Lewrie laughed off. "Not a bit of it, Geoffrey, ye know how lame I am at languages. But, the best place to learn a tongue, even a little, is with the help of a bidding girl."

"So *I've* always thought," Westcott said with a smug leer.

"Viva inglese, viva Inglaterra!" a pack of street urchins began to chant, skipping and prancing behind them, and begging for *centimos*.

"It appears we've made some Portuguese happy," Lt. Westcott said, looking over his shoulder at them.

"For now, at least, Geoffrey . . . for now," Lewrie mused.

CHAPTER THIRTY-SIX

*A*ll this will fill the cisterns, sir," Pettus commented as he came back into the great-cabins from the stern gallery, where he had been trying to dry some washing in the narrow, dry overhang of the poop deck above. "Still damp, sorry," he said of Lewrie's under-drawers and shirts.

"Well, hang them up in here, then," Lewrie told him, looking up from his reading, "and we'll hope for the best." When last the planking seams of the poop deck had been stuffed with oakum and paid over with hot tar with loggerheads, some wee gaps had been missed, so spare pots and wooden pails stood here and there on the deck chequer, and the good carpets had been rolled up, to catch the dripping, and save expensive Turkey or Axminster rugs. He looked upwards as the incessant Winter rain increased and began to seethe on deck. It was December at Gibraltar, nigh Christmas, which usually had a mild Winter, but this year was damper, and colder, than what he'd experienced last year.

It wasn't raw or chilly enough to wish for a Franklin-pattern coal stove to heat his cabins, but Lewrie did his reading fully dressed, less uniform coat, and with a loose-sleeved, ankle-length robe made from a wool blanket. It was white wool with red and green stripes at both ends, and upon first exposure to cabin visitors, Lt. Westcott had japed that he looked like an Indian who'd swapped furs for a Hudson's Bay Company blanket.

The weather at sea had delayed many ships' arrival, but Royal Mail packets had managed to come in, bringing him letters from home, most of which were pleasant, and some outright delightful.

Both James Peel at Foreign Office Secret Branch, and his old school chum, Peter Rushton, had written of the scandal, and the court of enquiry, into that disastrous Convention of Cintra. Dalrymple had been removed from command in Spain and Portugal, his career at an end, and General Burrard had been reduced to domestic duties only, never to serve abroad again. Wellesley was the only one of them who had gotten off rather mildly, and the papers championed the real victor, claiming that Dalrymple and Burrard had ordered and brow-beaten him to sign the damned thing. He was idle in Dublin, with no real harm done to him.

Both of his sons were well. Sewallis was still on the Brest blockade, bored to tears with the incessant plodding in-line-ahead for months on end, standing off-and-on the French coast with no sign that the enemy would ever come out to challenge them, with only the rare week or so in an English port to re-provision and have a run ashore where, admittedly, he had taken strong drink aboard and attended some lively subscription balls; he boasted that he was one of the best dancers aboard, had instructed the younger Mids in his mess in the art, and had been quite taken by more than a few pretty girls.

His younger son, Hugh, was still in the Mediterranean aboard a frigate, and as he described it, a taut and happy ship led by an energetic and daring captain. They had done some cutting-out raids in Genoese harbours and had seized merchant prizes right from under the noses of the French and their grudging Italian allies, had made chase of several others off Malta, taken two more, and had fought a spirited action with a French *corvette*, made prize of her, and Hugh suggested that his father should look into the latest issues of the *Naval Chronicle* in which Midshipman Hugh Lewrie was mentioned by his captain as having shown pluck, courage, and skill!

There's one that didn't fall far from the tree! Lewrie told himself with rightful pride.

There was a letter from his father, more an advertisement for the new plays, symphonies, and entertainments of the season. There was one from his former ward, Sophie de Maubeuge, now married to his old First Officer in the *Proteus* frigate, Anthony Langlie, with the thrilling news that her husband had been "made Post" and awarded the command of a Sixth Rate frigate, and would be home for a couple of months as she recruited and outfitted, after nigh a year of separation and anxiety.

There was nothing from his daughter, Charlotte, but, by then, he had no expectations that she would ever write him. Oddly, there was nothing about her from his former brother-in-law, Governour Chiswick's, latest letter, but then, Governour was all about himself and his new prospects; old Uncle Phineas Chiswick had finally died, and he'd left all of his estate to Governour, elevating him from a much-put-upon estate manager to master of all he surveyed, a wealthy man with thousands of acres. Old Sir Romney Embleton had also passed in the Autumn, so *his* son, Harry, was now Sir Harry, Colonel of the Yeomanry militia, and the borough's nigh-permanent representative in the House of Commons, for the very good reason that no one would dare run against him. With Harry so busy, Governour had been asked to be the local Magistrate in Harry's place, too.

God help Anglesgreen, then, Lewrie thought with a scowl, in need of a brandy to wash the sudden sour taste from his mouth; *That brayin' bastard'll run his court like Tsar Ivan the Terrible!*

The read and discarded letters were piling up beside Lewrie on the settee cushions, they were crinkly, daubed with patches of sealing wax, and . . . chewy. Chalky made a prodigious, tail-wiggling leap from the brass tray table to the pile like diving into a snow heap and pawed right and left, unsure which he'd shred first.

"Those ain't good eatin', Chalky," Lewrie chid him, "better ye come here and keep me warm."

Chalky would have none of it. The lure of wagging fingers to tempt him only prompted the cat to plop on his back and wriggle atop the letters, paws out to bat at him, his tail thumping on the papers.

"Have it your own way, then," Lewrie said, opening the last of his personal correspondence. "Well, just damn my eyes!" he had to exclaim once he had opened it.

Percy, Viscount Stangbourne, had written him to announce that his self-raised light dragoon regiment had been selected to be part of General Sir David Baird's army, selected personally by Lord Henry Paget, one of England's most distinguished cavalry commanders, to be in his two-thousand-man brigade! He'd written from shipboard, just hours from sailing, about a fortnight before.

He's probably already ashore, Lewrie thought.

Percy and his troopers were to land at Corunna in Northwest Spain, and march upon Salamanca, unless there was a change of plans, he'd penned; he was bursting with pride for his unit to be selected, to be given the chance to prove their worth, and his own, upon the field of battle, and meet the much-vaunted French cavalry, sabre to sabre! What a chance for glory had been missed, he thought, that at Roliça and Vimeiro, General Wellesley had had so little cavalry, else the battle would have been a clean sweep, and a joyous rout of the defeated French, and that ridiculous Convention of Cintra would not have even been contemplated!

Percy was now the proud father of two fine sons, Eudoxia was well and happy, his father-in-law, Arslan Artimovich Durschenko, was staying in England to recruit remounts to be shipped to Spain later, and that Horse Guards had seen fit to take his regiment into full military service, allowed its own home barracks and second battalion cadre to form a full-strength replacement unit recruited from the Reading and Henley-on-Thames region. He couldn't be prouder that his patriotic efforts, and his great fortune he'd used to raise, mount, arm and equip his regiment, had finally borne fruit!

By the way, he wrote, we're no longer Stangbourne's Horse but the 38th Light Dragoons. Oh, and Lydia is well and content living in the country, with all her childhood friends and their children to spoil, and her good works. She would have come to Spain, but . . .

Hmm, Lewrie thought at the mention of his former lover's name; *I don't feel even the* slightest *twinge.*

He had, at the time, been extremely fond of her, almost at the verge of real love, and even at the moment in that bleak Winter garden when she had rejected him and vowed to live alone, and safe, the rest of her life—the moment that he'd recklessly proposed marriage—had experienced the stumbling of his heart, the sinking of his stomach so keenly that he'd thought he would sicken of his loss.

Months later, after taking command of *Sapphire* and returning to the sea and an active commission, the pangs would disturb him . . . yet now? Lewrie glanced at Percy's letter once more, and found that Lydia had asked him to express her fond regards.

Fond regards, and it don't hurt. Well! he mused. All he did was shrug. Chalky, tired of scattering paper, crawled into his lap with some mews for attention, and a *Mrrk* or two, and settled down to be stroked and petted, slowly beginning to rumble and go slit-eyed.

There was a rap of a musket butt on the deck, the stamp of the Marine sentry's boots, and a shout to announce Yeovill, his cook.

"Enter!" Lewrie called back, not rising.

Yeovill came in, shaking water from his tarred sailor's hat and dripping raindrops from his tarpaulin coat. Chalky perked up in a trice, uttered a glad mew of welcome, and went dashing to Yeovill; Yeovill was food, and good smells.

"Fickle," Lewrie chid him after the cat leapt away. "What is it, Yeovill?"

"Ah, I was wondering about the holidays, sir," Yeovill began, "and what you might have in mind to serve to dine in our officers and such, sir. With the trade cross the Lines so free, now, I can find almost anything you wish . . . hams, geese, ducks, even turkeys."

"Hmm," Lewrie happily pondered for a moment, "smoked Spanish hams are always fine, but . . . a really big Christmas goose'd go down well. Devil with it, you might as well pick up one of everything, and we'll have a two-day feast!"

"Ehm, I was also wondering if we could do something special for the ship's people, too, sir," Yeovill went on with his eyebrows up in hope. "A goose or turkey for each eight-man mess, perhaps, with shore bread, puddings or duffs, and fresh vegetables?"

"Good Lord, how would Tanner ever cook all that?" Lewrie jeered. "The only method that one-legged twit knows is 'boil,' and boiled goose is worse than cold, boiled mutton!"

"I was thinking I could find someplace ashore, sir, to roast whatever I could find, and have it rowed out," Yeovill went on.

"Hmm," Lewrie pondered, again, considering the drawbacks of that. On the days that salt-pork or salt-beef was issued to the hands, it came in the form of eight-pound chunks or joints chosen by weekly-appointed mess-men from every eight-man dining arrangement. Once chosen, the meat went into that mess's string bag with a numbered brass tab to identify it, and once boiled to a fare-thee-well, it and the accompanying bread or bis-quit, duffs or hard puddings, soup, beans or pease, were hand-carried from the galley to the messes. The meat was sliced into roughly one-pound portions—less all the bone and gristle that the crooked jobbers left on—and doled out.

" 'Oo shall 'ave this'un, then?" Lewrie said, chuckling, in an approxi-mation of lower-deck accents. "Only two legs on a duck or goose, Yeovill, and everyone'll want one. Then there's the problem of how they'd deal with the carving, *and* what you'd do with the left-overs."

"Well, perhaps they'd stuff themselves so full, there wouldn't be any, sir," Yeovill suggested, "and if they slice it off in slabs, they could reach over for seconds."

"I don't know . . . ," Lewrie fretted, stroking his chin. "Sailors are a conservative lot, and not exactly welcoming to new foods, as we have learned, hey?"

When his old frigate, *Reliant,* had been off the American coast, the crew had turned their noses up at plain boiled rice, and now his people aboard *Sapphire* weren't fond of *couscous,* either, and had sent a round letter aft to complain, the spokesmen's names arranged in a circle round the margins of the paper so no one could be singled out as the instigator.

And when it came to drink, well! The Navy could substitute wine in foreign waters for their rum, but to do that too often could result in loose cannon balls rolling over the lower decks, an ancient precursor to out-right mutiny. No, Jack Tar would have his rum and his small beer, and all else was so much foreign fiddle-faddle!

"Ah, well, sir, it was only an idea," Yeovill said, slumping.

"Fresh-slaughtered bullocks'd be best for the holidays, shore bread, and sweet duffs . . . *and* of course we could 'splice the mainbrace' for the rum issue on Christmas Day," Lewrie decided.

"Real ale with the meal, sir, not small beer," Yeovill suggested quickly, "a pint apiece with no 'sippers' or 'gulpers,' and that might make them happy. There's pasta available by the bushel, too, and I doubt Tanner could ruin big pots of cheesy pasta. I could see to the melting of the cheese, as a side dish."

"*Small* beer with the meal," Lewrie countered. "I'll not have 'em suckin' ale down in one go, then turnin' angry when they don't have anything more t'drink with their beef. God, next thing ye know, I'd be labelled a 'Popularity Dick,' and discipline'd go straight to Hell. By the by, Yeovill, you've a cat ready t'climb your leg," he slyly pointed out.

Yeovill reached down and swooped Chalky up to cradle against his chest, where the cat sniffed eagerly at all the galley aromas on his clothing, then just as quickly tired of being held, and fussed and wiggled to be freed.

"Like I just said, Yeovill . . . fickle," Lewrie said, grinning.

"Aye, sir," Yeovill said with a grin of his own.

"Yes, we'll think of something t'brighten their lives when the holiday comes round," Lewrie began to sum up, but stopped and cocked an ear as someone on deck challenged an approaching rowboat, yelling over the loud drumming of the rain, but impossible to make out what was said in the snug great-cabins.

A moment or two later, though, and the Marine sentry was reporting Midshipman Griffin to see the Captain. Lewrie bellowed for him to be admitted, and rose to his feet as the lad came in, dripping even more rain-water from his tarpaulin coat.

"A letter from shore for you, sir," Griffin announced, handing over a sealed square of paper.

"Thankee, Mister Griffin, you may return to duty," Lewrie said as he tore it open, "and try not t'drown out there."

"Aye, sir!" Griffin replied with a laugh.

"Mine arse," Lewrie said, groaning after he had read it. "Get out my boat cloak, if ye please, Pettus. It seems I'm summoned out in the rain. Pass the word for my boat crew to muster, Yeovill."

"Yes, sir. Uh . . . your supper?" Yeovill asked as he threw on his tarpaulins once again.

"Not a clue, sorry," Lewrie said as he fetched his own coat and donned it, and selected his oldest, foul-weather, cocked hat from the pegs. "If I'm back aboard in time for it, I may have t'draw whatever the crew's havin', else I may dine ashore if anyone's feelin' charitable after."

The summons had come from General Drummond, now the commander of the Gibraltar garrison and defences, for him to attend that worthy at the earliest possible moment. It was a miserable and soggy trip ashore in his cutter with his voluminous boat cloak wrapped round him and covering his thighs; even so, water had trickled down the back of his neck, and when the wind got up in a gust or two, and the rain came half horizontal, almost blinded him and soaked his face and his shirt collars. After that, it was a long, wet plod up to the Convent, almost wading through some patches and puddles as rain sluiced downhill along the steep cross streets.

Wonder what the bloody rush is about? he wondered as he handed his hat and cloak over to an attendant, shooting soggy cuffs and readjusting his neck-stock, and looking round. The army headquarters was as hushed as a church on Monday, not stirring to some alarm over a sudden crisis. His boots rang on the stone flooring, though in point of fact, doing so rather squishily as he approached Drummond's office doors. Lewrie announced himself to a junior officer in the outer office, and was seen in.

"Ah, Captain Lewrie," Drummond said, looking up from papers on his desk, and rising to greet him. "So sorry to have sent for you on such a day, but . . . there it is. Tea, sir?"

"Most welcome, sir, thankee," Lewrie replied.

Uhoh, Lewrie thought, almost wincing as he spotted Mountjoy and Deacon seated apart from the desk, in front of the large fireplace; *it must be something hellish if* they're *here, too!*

"Afternoon, Captain Lewrie," Mountjoy said, getting to his feet to come shake hands. "A wet day, even for a sailor, hey?"

"Hallo, Mountjoy. Aye, so wet I could paint you a water colour," Lewrie rejoined, "Mister Deacon, how d'ye keep?"

"Main-well, Captain Lewrie, sir," Deacon replied, nodding and beginning to rise 'til Lewrie waved him to stay comfortable.

"So, what's so important, then?" Lewrie asked, going towards the fireplace. There wasn't much of a fire laid, more for atmosphere than anything else, but he wished it was roaring—if only to dry his clothes out.

"Of late, we've received some disturbing, possibly some very bad information," Mountjoy hesitantly began, looking towards General Drummond for permission to speak first.

"Tell him, sir," Drummond gruffly said with a nod as he came to join them with his own fresh cup of tea. "It was your people who first alerted us."

"Very well, sir," Mountjoy said, then turned to Lewrie as he took a seat near the meagre fire. "Our source in Paris—"

"That bitch," Lewrie growled. "Charité, again?"

"Yes, sir, that . . . bitch," Mountjoy said with a wince, and another look to General Drummond. "Captain Lewrie and our agent in Paris have crossed swords, as it were, in the past, do you see. She has sent word that the Emperor Napoleon will not let Spain go quite so easily, and is sending massive re-enforcements over the borders to re-conquer what was recently lost, some sixty thousand, doubling his numbers North of the Ebro River. What's worse, Napoleon *himself* is coming South with another hundred thousand, with his best marshals . . . Lannes, Soult, Ney, Victor and LeFebre, to erase any resistance in Spain, for good. And, might I conjure everyone in this room to ignore Captain Lewrie's out-burst and forget that our agent's name was ever uttered?" Mountjoy added, casting a stern look in Lewrie's direction.

"Sorry . . . heat of the moment," Lewrie said, abashed, busying himself with his offered tea, cream and sugar. "Damn my eyes, 'Old Boney's' takin' the field himself?" he blurted again, suddenly realising the import of that move. "Christ, Moore and his army'll just be trampled in the rush! Is she . . . is this confirmed?"

"We've agents in Northern Spain, and it *is* confirmed, sir," Mountjoy told him, rather severely. "The report from Paris, for once, comes behind the times. The Spanish General, Blake, moved to block the French advance, but his army was nigh-massacred at Durango, and we have it on solid terms that Napoleon is already at Vitoria."

"See here on the map, sirs," Drummond said, finishing his tea and leading them to his massive map of Iberia. "We don't know whether Moore and Baird have united their forces or not, round here at Salamanca, as they had planned. If Napoleon is already at Vitoria, he'll most likely march on Burgos, next, then right on South to re-take the capital, Madrid. He could, however, move from Burgos to Valladolid to face Moore, first, depending on how threatening he imagines a British army is to him."

"He may not think much of us, even after Roliça and Vimeiro, are you saying, sir?" Mister Deacon asked sharply.

"Napoleon doesn't think much of the Spanish, even after the defeat at Bailén, either," General Drummond gravelled back, appearing miffed by the slur on his service's record against the French. "It is hoped that he considers Moore a side-show to his need to seize Madrid, and thrash what forces the Spanish have in the field. Way off here," Drummond said, sweeping a hand to the East, over near Zaragoza, "the Spanish Generals Castaños and Palafax, we believe, managed to extract their armies from the disaster at Durango, and *might* be able to operate against the French supply lines. A damned desolate and forbidding place for the French to be, in the mountains of central Spain in Midwinter, with nothing coming from France to succour them. Should they make the attempt, successful or not, they *might* draw Napoleon away just long enough for Moore and Baird to retreat back into Portugal. I sincerely hope that they do so, soonest."

"Though there's no way to get a rider to warn them, or order them to retreat," Lewrie said in a grave tone.

"No, Captain Lewrie, there is not," Drummond bleakly agreed. "Sir John Moore is senior to me, and Supreme Commander in Portugal and Spain, so I can but advise. Since Moore departed Lisbon I have not heard one word from him."

"What are these marks, at Lugo and Léon, sir?" Deacon asked.

"Those?" Drummond said with a faint sneer on his face. "Those are two more Spanish armies, one under a General Barclay at Lugo in central Galicia, already defeated and licking their wounds by the way, and the other represents an army under a General de la Romana at Léon."

"It would seem that *they* are in as good a position to interdict the French supplies as Castaños and Palafax in the East," Deacon commented.

"Hah!" Drummond said with a derisive toss of his head. "I'll lay you any odds that they won't, sir. Barclay's army, as I said, has been trounced and mauled quite badly, and Romana, so the *junta* in Madrid informs me, may have, ehm . . . inflated his numbers just to look good to them. They *do* that, you know, perhaps to continue receiving the soldiers' *pay*! Our military attaché in Madrid writes me that it's a safe bet that if a Spanish general reports thirty thousand men on hand, he's more like to only have ten or twelve, and half of them are without proper arms.

"An example, if you will, gentlemen," Drummond sourly went on. "This year, the returns upon the Spanish cavalry reported a bit over eleven thousand troops . . . yet they had only a little more than nine thousand *mounts*! God only knows why my predecessor, General Sir Hew Dalrymple, put so much faith in Spanish promises, for I surely don't. Neither does London. Moore and Baird were warned not to attach themselves to Spanish armies, or expect too much from them."

"Anything from Lisbon, Mountjoy?" Lewrie asked the spy-master.

"Hand wringing and fretting, mostly," Mountjoy told him, "viewing with alarm. They don't know much more than we do, having gotten the same despatches that we have, and hopefully sending it on to the Army."

"Napoleon will go after Moore, first," Lewrie said after a long peer at the large map.

"How come you to that, sir?" General Drummond snapped.

"I've met the bastard twice, sir, and he's all for honour and glory . . . his, mind," Lewrie said with a wry smile. "As you say, he's a very low opinion of Spanish armies, and can trounce them any day of the week. He surely knows Moore's reputation, though, and is anxious to avenge how a British army embarassed him at Roliça and Vimeiro, and Marshal Junot's ouster from Portugal. We made him look weak and bad, and that preenin' coxcomb can't abide that. He'll go for Moore with all he's got."

"He's more than enough troops to re-take Madrid *and* take on Moore, both," Mountjoy pointed out. "He'll give that task to another of his Marshals, but, you may be right, Captain Lewrie. The honour of defeating a British army in the field will glitter before him like the biblical Star in the East."

"One would hope that Sir John *is* in contact with the Spanish at Lugo and Léon, then," Deacon said, "and has been informed that the French are in force, and hunting him, before he blunders into them."

"Amen," Lewrie seconded. "Ehm, given all this new information, why am I here, then?"

"If given sufficient warning, there is a possibility that Sir John won't have to retreat over the mountains back into Portugal, but may be able to move from Salamanca, where he expected to link up with General Baird, to Valladolid before the French get there, and get on some halfway passable roads to the Galician ports of either Vigo or Corunna, and be extracted by sea, Captain Lewrie," General Drummond told him. "I am formulating orders for General Fox on Sicily, and to our garrison at Malta, to send as many troop transports as they have to Gibraltar. I am also sending requests to Admiral Cotton, and Admiral de Courcy off Galicia, to ready themselves for an evacuation. As soon as we have a reasonable number of transports assembled here, along with sufficient escorts, I would wish that you take charge of them and sail to join Admiral deCourcy and place yourself and your transports at his disposal."

"Aha?" Lewrie said, startled. "Well, there goes our plans for Christmas geese," which comment forced General Drummond to peer at him in intense scrutiny, as if Lewrie was not of sound mind.

"Game for it, are you, Captain Lewrie?" Drummond demanded.

"At your complete disposal, sir," Lewrie insisted. "And I shall begin provisioning for a lengthy time at sea, at once."

And a miserable time it'll be, Lewrie grimly told himself, for this time of year there would be strong Westerly gales and high seas along the Portuguese and Spanish Western shores, which could drive any number of struggling ships onto the rocks. He recalled a peek he'd had at the sea charts, just a casual glance, really, in quieter times; from Cape Fisterre to Corunna and Ferrol the Spanish called it the *Costa da Morte,* the Coast of Death! He assumed that the Dons knew what they were talking about!

"Sir Alan won't let the Army down, sir," Mountjoy felt need to declare. "He's game, and more than game, for anything."

So long as I don't drown myself, yes, Lewrie thought.

CHAPTER THIRTY-SEVEN

*T*here had been four "troopers" in port at Gibraltar when Lewrie had gotten his initial orders from General Drummond, and over the next week, a dozen more had come in in answer to Drummond's urgent summons, all of which needed victualling, for Lewrie was certain that the army would be desperately short of rations when, or if, it managed to make its way to Corunna or Vigo to be evacuated.

For once, Captain Middleton, the Dockyard Commissioner, was all open co-operation, throwing open his warehouses and fulfilling every request, though his insistence on strict accounting for each jot and tittle could almost drive everyone involved mad. Captain Middleton also fretted over whether the one-thousand-bed naval hospital would be called upon to tend to God only knew how many injured and sick soldiers, sure that his small medical staff would be swamped.

Drummond did receive assurances from London that the Government was at last aware of the pending disaster, and was also assembling a large fleet of transports in British ports to take off the army, but no one could say just when that fleet would sail, or arrive, making the departure of Lewrie's small contingent even more vital, no matter how few soldiers could be rescued by a mere sixteen ships. He would be lucky to take off a little more than 2,100, if the usual loading of 150 soldiers to each transport was followed, the equivalent of a three-regiment brigade!

Escorts, though, were another matter. There was a brig-sloop from Admiral Cotton's squadron that had come in with sprung masts in need of repair, the *Blaze*, under a Commander Teague who was working his crew day-and-night to set her to rights. There was another brig-sloop belonging to the Mediterranean Fleet that had come to Gibraltar from the Toulon blockade; unfortunately, the *Peregrine* had not come in response to Drummond's requests, but to repair storm damage she'd suffered off Cape Sepet, and had been looking forward to a spell of shore liberty after making her own repairs. Commander Blamey had been stunned by the news, and his new duties, but had also pitched in to ready his ship for departure.

Lewrie was sure that he needed more, for the Nor'west coast of Spain was uncomfortably close to the French ports of Bayonne and Bordeaux, the safe anchorages up the Gironde River, where privateers and French warships were based. If word got out that Sir John Moore's army was counting on a transport fleet for their salvation, it would draw them out like a disturbed swarm of bees. The weather would be abysmal, the Winter Westerlies might be "dead muzzlers" to pen them in port, but, if they did get out somehow . . . ?

On top of all his frets, there was Maddalena, too.

He had been ashore to deal with the Dockyards for extra blankets and hammocks, just in case *Sapphire, Blaze,* and *Peregrine* had to take soldiers aboard and quarter them any-old-how, arseholes to elbows. He had reported to Drummond at the Convent to fill that worthy in on his progress, and how soon his escorts could be ready to sail. And, he had gone to Maddalena's lodgings to speak with her, perhaps for the very last time.

"If I don't return for some time, dear girl, or . . . don't return at all . . . ," he had said as calmly and logically as he could.

"Don't *say* that, Alan!" she had countered, tears already coursing her cheeks, and laying a finger on his mouth to shush him. "You *will* come back, you always come back!"

"I'll do everything in my power to do so, *querida*, but, if the sea goes against me . . . ," he had cautioned, shrugging off the possibilities, "it's a foul Winter, full of storms, and a lee shore all the way there and back. If something *does* happen, the branch of Coutts' Bank here has a tidy sum for you, and if you need any help in the matter, go see Thomas Mountjoy and Daniel Deacon. I've spoken with them, and they'll see you right. Your lodgings are paid for through next year, and—"

"I do not care for lodgings, or sums, or . . . !" Maddalena had rejoined with a visible shudder. "I only care about *you, meu querido! Meu amor!* You are so good . . . you have been so good to me, I cannot think of life without you."

"I've been my happiest with you, too, Maddalena," he assured her, embracing her more snugly and burying his face in her sweet-smelling hair. "We both know, though, that I wouldn't be at Gibraltar forever. My Navy has a way of callin' people away, just when they feel happy, or comfortable, or . . . snug, I s'pose. We both knew it, goin' in . . . didn't we?" he had tried to tease. "That we could make the best of it 'til that happened, or . . ."

I don't much care for thinkin' of my own death, either, he had thought, pressing even closer to her body, as if the physical act of moving was proof against that.

"How many days do we have, Alan?" she had whispered against his bare shoulder. "You will be busy? Too busy for me?" she had said, making it sound like a plea, not an accusation.

"A day or two, at most," he had to confess. "Once the other escorts are repaired, I'll *have* t'sail with what little I have got. I can't wait for late arrivals. Duty's a demandin' bitch, but there it is."

"This may be our last time?" Maddalena had whimpered, and he had to nod yes, and she had peered him right in the eyes, so gravely, and had whispered "Then, make love to me, one last time, *meu amor.*"

And that had been frantic, thrashing, panting, and *searingly* passionate. There was no bed, no tangled sheets, nothing in this world but the sensation that they floated on a supportive and ephemeral cloud, all of Lewrie's senses tunnelled down to his member, her sweet, hot wetness and her tightening, 'til he had exploded in her, so pleasurably that it almost hurt, and seemed to last forever, each after-thrust a re-awakening. Maddalena had cried out and had clawed at him at that same moment, wrapping her legs about him, seizing his buttocks to drive him deeper and keep him there to savour every last wave, rolling her head from side to side and gasping for air.

That's one for the memoirs, he told himself as he lay spent, at last, slowly going flaccid and hating the moment to come when he would have to withdraw.

"My Lord, girl!" he croaked, *"Foi extraordinário!"*

"Sim, selvagem," she agreed as he slid to her side to hold her, and rained slow, lazy, lingering kisses on him.

Boom! from the harbour, beyond the balcony, then *Boom!* again, as steady as a metronome.

"What the Devil?" he had groused, sitting upright and grabbing his discarded shirt to hold before his groin to go see what the noise was all about. He flung one of the double doors open. "Hell, yes!"

There was a frigate standing into port, firing her salute to the garrison commander, announcing her presence, wreathing herself in powder smoke.

"If she isn't comin' in on purpose, then I'll have her, no matter!" Lewrie had exclaimed, going back inside to hunt up his clothing. "I'm sorry, Maddalena, but I have t'speak with her Captain. I need her for my escort force, just *perishin'* bad!"

"I go with you, Alan," she had replied, though looking so very sad and disappointed. "I walk you to the landing."

"I'd love it if you would," he had told her.

By the time they were both properly dressed and presentable in public, the arriving frigate had come to anchor and had handed all of her sails up in harbour gaskets. Lewrie could see that she had two of her boats down, a small jolly boat for her Bosun to row about the ship to assure himself that all her yards were squared, and a gig that was headed for the main landing stage, and by the look of her passengers, bearing that frigate's captain ashore to report to General Drummond.

"She may have come under orders t'join me," Lewrie eagerly said, increasing their pace, "and if Middleton has the other two set to rights, I could be out to sea and on my way by dawn tomorrow!"

He spared a bit of his attention to glance at Maddalena, who was practically trotting to keep up with him, and noted her stricken expression.

"Sorry, my dear," he told her, "but events are bigger than we are. I *have* to—"

"I understand, Alan," she replied, "but I do not have to like it." She flashed him a brave smile that both knew was a sham.

Lewrie made it to the top of the quay and the head of the landing stage ramp just as the newly-arrived frigate's gig came alongside the lower stage. He felt a sudden qualm as he clapped eyes on the Post-Captain in the boat, and suddenly wished that he had left Maddalena at her lodgings.

This could be awkward, he thought; *I wonder what he thinks of mistresses?*

The officer in the boat was getting to his feet and about to step ashore. He was a striking fellow, slim, tall, broad-shouldered, and rather handsome, nigh-dashing it could be said. He paused to exchange words with a Midshipman in the boat's sternsheets, who pointed at Lewrie as if to make his superior aware of Lewrie's presence. . . .

What the Devil? Lewrie thought; *Is that . . . ?* Can't *be!*

The Midshipman dared wave to him, beaming fit to bust.

Awkward, mine arse! Lewrie quailed; *It is Hugh! How's he vote on kept women?* This'll *be embarrassin'*!

His youngest son, Mr. Midshipman Hugh Lewrie, exited the boat first, following naval protocol; senior officers were first in to boats, but last out. But Hugh didn't wait for his Captain to step ashore, but came dashing up the ramp from the landing stage shouting "Father, at last!" bubbling over with joy of their *rencontre.*

"Well, hallo, son, where did you spring from?" Lewrie cried, glad to see him, of course, but caught in a cleft stick. He flung his arms wide in welcome, anyway. "Damn my eyes, but you've grown! I almost didn't recognise ye!"

And that was certainly true, for when he'd seen Hugh off into his first ship in 1803, the lad had been a thirteen-year-old stripling, and here he was five years later, eighteen now, and damned near a man grown, taller and filled out, sun-bronzed and tarry-handed. Hugh had inherited his mother's hair colour, but years of ocean sun had turned his light brown hair almost blond. He'd gotten his father's eyes, though, stark grey-blue against a seaman's tan.

Hugh didn't come to his embrace, though, but doffed his hat in salute first, to which Lewrie responded in kind, *then* they met close, heartily shaking hands. If he could not hug him, then at least Lewrie could thump him on the shoulder.

"It's been too damned long, Hugh, a dog's age and more," Lewrie told him, smiling widely, even as he dreaded the consequences to come.

"Aye, it has, sir," Hugh eagerly agreed, then turned serious as he sensed his Captain behind him. "Ahem, my pardons, Father, but, do you allow me to name to you my Captain . . . Captain Richard Chalmers of the *Undaunted* frigate. Captain Chalmers, sir, allow me to name to you my father, Captain Sir Alan Lewrie, Baronet, of HMS *Sapphire.*"

At least he sounded proud to do so.

"Honoured to make your acquaintance, Captain Lewrie, and the very

man I was ordered to seek out," Chalmers said in a forceful baritone, chin
up, and doffing his hat in salute.

"Honoured t'make yours, Captain Chalmers," Lewrie said back, "and
from what I've read of your exploits in my son's letters, a man after my
own heart."

Hugh called him a high-minded sort, too, Lewrie recalled; *whatever that
means. Here comes the embarrassin' part.*

He turned to include Maddalena, plastering a grin on his phyz and striving to make a bold showing.

"Captain Chalmers, son, allow me to name to you Miss Maddalena
Covilhā," he began. "Miss Covilhā, allow me to name to you Captain Rich-
ard Chalmers, of the *Undaunted* frigate, and my son, Midshipman Hugh
Lewrie, also of the *Undaunted.*"

That's enough, no explanations, he thought, waiting for the reaction.

Before they had attended the supper ball to welcome General Sir John
Moore to Gibraltar the year before, Maddalena had fretted over her social
graces, and had sought out a tutor. Her curtsies, and her address to them
were perfectly refined. "Captain Chalmers, Midshipman Lewrie, I am
pleased to make your acquaintances, gentlemen, though I fear it will be
of a brief nature, given the urgent matter which brings you to Gibraltar."

Captain Chalmers tried to hide a scandalised frown, looking as if he
knew for certain what Maddalena was, and did not appreciate being introduced to a doxy. Hugh stood and nodded with his mouth open, an un-
certain smile on his face.

What, she's a cundum stuck to her hair? Lewrie groused to himself; *Are
my breeches buttons undone? Aye, he's high-minded for sure!*

"Miss Covilhā," Hugh hesitantly responded, doffing his hat to her in
involuntary courtesy. "You . . . ehm . . . are . . . ?"

"Portuguese, young sir," Maddalena said with a sweet and disarming
smile. "There are many of us here at Gibraltar, who fled the French invasion."

"Ah, Portuguese, aye," Hugh flummoxed, casting a startled look at his
father.

"But, I delay you gentlemen," Maddalena went on, bestowing one more
smile on one and all. "You must prepare to sail to rescue brave General
Sir John Moore and his gallant army, and there is no time for the social
niceties. With your permission, I will take my leave of you, *sim?*"

By God, an English *girl presented at Court couldn't do that better!* Lewrie
thought with pride, and surprise of her diplomatic skills.

"Miss Covilhā," Lewrie said, sweeping off his hat and laying it upon his chest as he made a leg to her. *"Meu amor,"* he silently mouthed to her, though, with a brief, impish smile. His bow prompted the others to follow suit, no matter what they thought of her.

"Gentlemen, Captain Lewrie," Maddalena said, dipping them all a departure curtsy, low, long, and with a graceful incline of her head. As she looked up at last, she mouthed *"Fofa"* to Lewrie in a shared jest; "Sweetie!"

"Well, what's first on the menu, sir?" Lewrie asked Chalmers in a sudden, business-like tone. "Firewood and water, provisions from the dockyards, or will you wish to speak with General Drummond to be apprised of the latest information regarding the mess the Army's got itself into?"

"Saving the Army, is it?" Chalmers gruffly asked with a confused look on his face. "I was only told that a convoy forming here was in need of additional escorts, and my Commodore offered my ship for the task. Frankly, I'd hoped I'd be bound for England, but . . ."

"You heard that we have two armies in Spain, sir?" Lewrie asked him. "Good. Well, so do the Frogs, and Napoleon *himself* is over the border with nigh a quarter-million troops. We've less than thirty thousand, *somewhere* round Salamanca, we *think*, smack in the middle of the Spanish mountains in Midwinter, runnin' for Vigo or Corunna, we *hope*, t'get taken off before 'Boney' catches up with 'em. We've sixteen troop ships, and have t'get 'em North as soon as dammit, or we lose the whole army. London's sendin' more, but how soon they arrive is anyone's guess. And, welcome to Gibraltar, by the way," he concluded with a cynical grin.

"Egad!" was Chalmers's drawn-out, stunned comment. "Then, it appears that we must be about it, what?"

"Amen!" Hugh Lewrie whispered, though still looking off to follow Maddalena's receding figure. To Lewrie's eyes, the lad didn't look disappointed in his sire, but . . . appreciative.

"Let's get on to the Convent, then," Lewrie suggested, "and let General Drummond fill you in. There's little he can do to help, from here, and explainin' it to you will make him feel better, I'm sure." He led off but Chalmers paused long enough to send Hugh back to the boat, and back to the ship.

"I hope to dine you and the Commanders off our two other ships aboard this evening, Captain Chalmers," Lewrie bade, "and I wonder if you might allow my son to come, too. Catch up on old times, and see some of my retinue he knows."

"It would be grand to see Desmond and Furfy, again," Hugh said, casting a pleading look at Captain Chalmers.

"Well, somebody has to sit at the bottom of the table and pose the King's Toast, I suppose," Chalmers relented.

"Chalky'll be glad t'see ye, too, Hugh, him and Bisquit. He was a good companion when I was laid up healin' at Anglesgreen last year," Lewrie said. "And, you can fill me in on what you've heard from Sewallis, and what he means by claimin' he's become a champion dancer, hah!"

"I look forward to it, sir," Hugh said, beaming as he doffed his hat to his Captain and his father, and dashed back to the boat.

A whole two minutes passed in silence as Lewrie and Chalmers ascended the cobbled street uphill towards army headquarters.

"I am given to understand that your eldest son is also in the Navy, sir?" Chalmers at last enquired. He didn't sound too pleased.

"He is," Lewrie had to admit. "He's spent the last five years aboard two-decker seventy-fours. He's twenty-one, now, but lacks the last two years before he can stand for his Lieutenancy. His present ship pays off next year, and I hope he's appointed into a brig-sloop or something below the Rates. I've always thought that smaller ships are the best schools for seamanship."

"How did he . . . ?" Chalmers asked, curious. In proper British families, it was the younger sons who went off to the Army, Navy, or the Church, sparing the heir and guarantor of the continuance of the family line.

"Sewallis found a way round me and his grandfather, and wrote an old friend of mine, gaining his own berth," Lewrie sketchily explained, leaving out the lad's forgeries. "He saw us sendin' Hugh off and wanted his own chance to get vengeance against the French for the murder of his mother during the Peace of Amiens. They were shooting at me, but hit her, instead, the bastards."

"Ah?" Captain Chalmers commented, sounding as if he found the account a bit too *outré*. "I do recall a comment your son, Hugh, said once. Tried to murder you? Who, and why?"

"Napoleon's orders," Lewrie told him. "Though I still don't know why or how I rowed him at a *levee* at the Tuileries Palace in Paris. He fussed about our keepin' Malta, interferin' in how he was runnin' Switzerland, why we hadn't sent him a proper ambassador yet, and I suspect it was the sword exchange that pissed him in the eye," Lewrie supposed, explaining how he had swapped half a dozen swords of dead French Captains and officers for the one he'd surrendered to Napoleon the first time he'd met him at Toulon in '94, when he could not give Napoleon his parole and abandon his surviving crew, some of whom were French Royalists, sure to be executed on the spot.

Captain Chalmers followed all that with many a sniff or gasp, as if the tale was just too fabulous to be believed.

"That night, Caroline and I were warned t'flee Paris if we valued our lives, and made it to Calais before they caught up with us," Lewrie related, leaving out the juicier parts concerning wigs, and costumes, play-acting, and the aid they'd gotten from a man who'd whetted his skills during the Terror of '93, and styled himself the Yellow Tansy; Chalmers already sounded dubious enough.

"Whatever it was I did to set him off," Lewrie concluded with a grin, "I pissed him in the eye once. With any luck at all, do we pluck our army from his clutches and get 'em clean away, we'll piss him in the eye, again!"

CHAPTER THIRTY-EIGHT

*W*hen Lewrie's little convoy had at last sailed from Gibraltar, its pace was heart-breakingly slow. It took a few days to breast the in-rushing current through the Strait, short-tacking into the stiff Winter winds, then bashing Westward many leagues to round Cape Finisterre and gain enough sea-room to avoid being blown onto a lee shore.

Once safely far out at sea, the struggling ships should have been able to turn North on a beam wind and rush on to Vigo, where information had it that part of the army was being evacuated, but the prevailing Westerlies turned into one howling gale after another, and the seas were steep, forcing all ships, transports and escorts alike, to reduce sail, brailing up to second or third reef lines, striking top-masts, and slowing them even more, and scattering them wide over many miles of sea. Even stout and slow HMS *Sapphire*, at over 1,100 tons burthen, rolled, pitched, and hobby-horsed like the merest wee gig, pricking every hand's ears in dread to the great groans and moans of her hull timbers and masts, to the thundrous slamming and jerking each time the bows ploughed into the tall, disturbed waves, flinging icy water high over her beakhead rails and forecastle, and anyone in need of the "seats of ease" for their bowel movements risked being flung right off the ship!

No matter how tautly the deck seams had been tarred, the upper gun-deck berthing dripped cold water on hammocks, blankets, and wildly swaying men who tried to snatch a few hours' rest from it all. Wood buckets were used for toilets, but no matter how often they were taken to the weather deck, dragged overside to clean them, then hauled back in, the stench became almost unbearable. The sailors who berthed on the lower gun deck might be drier, but their air was even closer, and foetid, to the point that serving watches in the open air, rain and cold and spray, was reckoned refreshing.

Despite tarred tarpaulin over-clothing, everyone's shirts and trousers got soaked when on deck or aloft tending sail, and there was no way to dry anything out below, or in the great-cabins or the officers' wardroom, either, and every morning's sick call featured people with salt-water boils where their salt-crystal laden clothes chafed them raw. Even boiling rations in the swaying, rolling, pitching galley proved extremely risky. Christmas supper was a Banyan Day, with only oatmeal, cheese, hard ship's bisquit, small beer, and a raisin duff for each mess to liven it.

Lewrie was amazed each raw dawn to see that all sixteen of his transports were still with him, and that *Undaunted*, *Peregrine*, and *Blaze* were still with him, dutifully chivvying stragglers back into their columns and urging the more widely scattered ships to rejoin.

They weren't wanted at Vigo, though; *Blaze* had dashed inshore and had returned with word that Admiral de Courcy had been replaced by Admiral Hood, and that Moore would be making for Corunna, where there were yet only about thirty transports awaiting him, and that Hood would be sailing to there with nigh a hundred ships. It had taken *Blaze* a very long and frightful day to beat her way off a lee shore to bear word, and Lewrie had to order his convoy to come into the wind and claw out even more sea-room off the coast of Galicia to get above Cape Fisterra before he'd dare to risk the Costa da Morte, and a run Due East into Corunna.

"It's clearing a bit, sir," Sailing Master George Yelland said as he sniffed the winds and rubbed his chilled hands. "The wind and sea are almost moderate, thank God."

"Is that a lighthouse I see on yon headland?" Lewrie asked, his telescope to his eye. "To the left of that inlet?"

"Ah, hmm," Yelland pondered, employing his own telescope for a long moment. "Aye, it is, sir, the lighthouse at Corunna. The port will be round the other side of the heights. This inlet, Orsan Bay, is a dead-end, don't be fooled by it. We're almost there."

"At last!" Lewrie breathed with relief that the ship could be brought to anchor, and blessed stillness, after too many days of risk. He had spent so much time on deck that he still felt chilled to the bone, and so in need of missed sleep that he could nod off on his feet and jerk back to wakefulness.

"Hawse bucklers removed, cables seized to the anchors and free to run, sir," a weary and storm-ravaged First Officer, Lieutenant Westcott, came aft to report. Shaving had been such a deadly endeavour that everyone had given it up, so he looked as if he could have been a bearded courtier to Henry VIII.

"We'll stand off a bit, and let the transports have the best anchorages nearest the town," Lewrie told him. "Mister Kibworth?" he shouted aft to the Midshipman at the signal halliards. "Bend on a signal hoist for the transports to go in first, and for the escorts to stand in trail of us."

"Aye aye, sir!" Kibworth shouted back.

Slowly, slowly, the little convoy, with *Sapphire* in the lead, rounded the tall headland and wore away South, standing into the harbour bay, with the escorts swinging wider out into the sheltered bay while the transports angled in round the fortified San Antonio Castle on a small island off the tip of the town.

Corunna was laid out in an *L*, with another fortress, the Citadel, dominating the short leg of the L to the North, and the civilian part of town angling off along the seashore behind tall sea walls to the Southwest. Even further along near the bottom of the harbour, near San Diego Point, was a commercial port of piers and warehouses close to a village of Santa Lucía; and all of it swarming with soldiers, ship's boats beetling back and forth under oars, and anchored troop ships.

"Christ, what a pot-mess," Lewrie wondered aloud. "Who's in charge, and who do I report to?" He could see several ships of the line anchored, mostly Third Rate 74s, but only one larger Second Rate, so far. Admiral Hood's armada of troop ships must still be working their way out of Vigo, or thrashing North through the same strong gales as *Sapphire* had.

"You'll take time to shave and freshen yourself, first, sir?" Westcott asked.

"No time for the niceties," Lewrie said with a shake of his head. "I may

have to go ashore t'find where they want our ships to anchor . . . off the
town here, or close to the piers down yonder."

"Taking your Ferguson along, too?" Westcott teased.

"I'll leave soldierin' to the people in red, this time, no, Mister Westcott,"
Lewrie said with a chuckle. "Though I *would* wish to see the ground. Why?
Ye wish t'borrow it and shoot a few Frogs, yourself, sir?"

"Signal from the Second Rate, sir!" Midshipman Kibworth called out.
"The Interrogative."

"Make our number to her, Mister Kibworth, and add that we've sixteen
transports with us."

"Aye, sir!" followed moments later by the news that the Second Rate
had a Rear-Admiral aboard, and was showing the summons of Captain
Repair On Board.

"Damme, we'll have t'fire him a salute suitable to his rank," Lewrie
groaned. "Pipe hands to the twelve-pounders, Mister Westcott, and fetch
up salutin' charges from the magazines. And have a cutter brought round
to the entry-port."

Have to follow the traditions, Lewrie groused to himself; *even if we were
comin' in half-sunk or on fire!*

Matters were out of his hands, he learned after a brief talk aboard the
Second Rate flagship. The captains of the anchored Third Rates and other
escorts were already assigned roles to organise the boats from their own
ships, and the transports, into flotillas to ferry soldiers and their gear out
to the chosen troop ships, sick and wounded first, and those the regimental surgeons had determined to be utterly exhausted and useless for further
fighting later. It was only then that fit troops would be sent out to other converted merchantmen for evacuation.

General Sir John Moore was in a cleft stick, really, for though he must
rescue his army quickly, a French army under Marshal Soult was pressing close, and if he reduced his strength too quickly, he faced the risk that
those still ashore might be overcome and taken, or massacred! Lewrie
was told that there might be at least fifteen thousand British troops left
from the thirty-two thousand that he, General Sir David Baird, and General Sir Henry Paget's cavalry, had led into Spain. Some thirty-five hundred had been gotten off from Vigo. He also learned that during the long
retreat, many artillery pieces had been abandoned, guns, caissons, limbers, and all as they broke down or the horse teams died. What was left to

Moore had to be deployed in defensive positions to counter the French when they arrived, but *must* be evacuated as a point of honour, finally; the loss of one's artillery was too shameful to be borne!

Even worse, Moore's remaining army was in terrible shape, low in morale, dis-spirited and nigh-un-disciplined, the bright uniforms ragged, torn, and filthy, and their footwear (for those who still had them) worn through. Until the lead units had met a large supply convoy of waggons meant for the Spanish armies on the road from Corunna, they had also been starving, and badly in need of greatcoats and blankets, to boot.

General Sir David Baird had set up a large supply depot when he had landed his smaller army at Corunna, and Moore was drawing on that, stretching what was left out to feed and re-equip his own men as liberally as he could for as long as it lasted; what his troops ate, wore, and carried would not be left to the French, not one loaf of bread or side of bacon. Lewrie was also told that he'd missed all the fun from a few days before; there were four thousand kegs of powder that had been landed to be given to the Spanish, and General Moore had ordered it blown up in one spectacular blast. Every glazed *miradore*, the glass-enclosed balconies, in Corunna had been shattered! Not that there were many complaints from the Spanish owners, for the very good reason that most of them had packed up their valuables as soon as the first ragged regiments of the British army had shambled into town and fled into the bleak Winter countryside with as much food and drink as they could carry!

Once back aboard *Sapphire*, Lewrie had gathered his officers and Midshipmen together in his great-cabins and had given them the orders he'd received from the flagship. They would have to be rowed over to a specific set of troop ships that had come into port with them, get all their ship's boats and the transports' boats arranged into one group, and row ashore to the quays by Santa Lucía, and pick up soldiers from one certain regiment, then see them aboard those transports and keep it up 'til every last man of that regiment was accounted for and safely aboard. Lewrie volunteered himself to go ashore with the first boats; he was just too curious to sit idle and let events occur round him with nothing to do about them!

"A damned imposin' place," Lewrie said to his Cox'n, Liam Desmond, as the cutter was stroked towards the quays.

"Aye, sor," Desmond agreed. "Fortified walls right down to th' docks. Like they don't much care f'r visitors."

"Might be pretty, in Summer," Lewrie speculated.

"If ye like rocks, sor," Desmond slyly teased.

The foul weather might have moderated, as the Sailing Master had said, but Corunna, its harbour, and the surrounding country was bleak, and very rocky; it was no wonder that the Spanish called this part of Galicia the "Coast of Death." The long fortifications that ran from the Citadel in the upper town down to Santa Lucía were grim, grime-streaked pale tan, seated atop darker brown and massive slabs of stone, fouled with dead seaweed at low tide, green with a mossy ocean growth. Beyond and over those fortified walls, several ranges of hills rose to the West and South, all of them strewn with large boulders. What trees there were were dead Winter grey and bare, or the darkest, dullest green pine groves. Beyond those hills lay the formidable mountains of inner Spain, as stony and steep and impressive as any he'd seen at Cape Town two years before. And over all were grey and threatening cloud banks scudding low over those hills. Lewrie had never seen such a depressing place in his life!

Once he set foot atop the quays he became even more depressed. There were still wounded men laid out on carrying boards and their own blankets awaiting treatment aboard the transports. Beside the obvious combat wounds, there were fellows without shoes or boots, or wool stockings, their toes blackened by frostbite; those who had lacked gloves or mittens showed fingers or whole hands turned blue-black as well, and sure to suffer amputations before the poisons of their frostbite killed them. Once back in England, the army would discharge them with pittances for pensions, where, unable to work to support themselves, they might starve to death in a year.

"You, sir! You, there! Do you have a hospital ship for my wounded?" an army surgeon demanded as he came up to Lewrie.

"I've a transport, sir, not a hospital ship," Lewrie had to tell him, doffing his hat in salute despite the fellow's rudeness. "My own Ship's Surgeon and his Mates can be sent aboard her to aid you, but . . ." He had to end with a helpless shrug.

"Well, Goddamnit!" the peppery little fellow swore. "I've done the best I could for them, God witness. There wasn't much fighting, and those wounds I've treated, and those poor fellows that lived to this point only need rest. The exposure cases, though . . . yes, do send me your man. I fear there will be quite a number of amputations before the day's done."

"All these are from your regiment, sir?" Lewrie asked. "We've been told t'keep 'em together. Good. Mister Hillhouse?" he called out to his senior Midshipman. "Let's get all the wounded in this lot into the boats, then make for the *Prosperity* transport."

"Aye, sir," Hillhouse replied, looking round, appalled for a moment before springing into action.

"You've attendants t'care for 'em aboard the ship, sir?" Lewrie asked the surgeon.

"Yes, a dozen bandsmen, they'll help with the loading, and tend to them," the army surgeon told him. "The rest of the battalion is still up in the hills, yonder, with Hope's Division."

"Is there anyone I could speak to who knows what's going on?" Lewrie asked him. "Some staff officers, or . . . ?"

"My dear sir, *nobody* knows what's going on here, or has since we began our bloody retreat!" the surgeon snarled, then turned away.

"Carry on, Mister Hillhouse," Lewrie called over his shoulder. "I'll remain ashore for a while and see if I can find anyone who can make sense of this mess."

"Aye, sir," Hillhouse said, then paused. "Ehm, if *Prosperity* isn't full, do we ferry un-wounded troops out to her?"

"Fill her to capacity, then begin on the next ship, the *Blue Bonnet*," Lewrie told him. "Ah, and here come boats from *Undaunted*, and our brig-sloops. And Captain Chalmers appears just as curious as I am," he added as he spotted that worthy in the lead cutter's sternsheets, already standing and impatient to set foot ashore. He waited for Chalmers to make his way to the top of the long quay, then greeted him.

"Lord, what a shambles, Captain Lewrie," Chalmers said as they exchanged salutes.

" 'Deed it is, sir," Lewrie agreed, wishing he could stuff a handkerchief to his nose to stifle the stench of gangrenous wounds. "I'm going to find someone in authority. Care to join me?"

"Delighted, sir," Captain Chalmers eagerly said back.

They made their way through the pallets and litters bearing wounded men, and worked their way into the village of Santa Lucía, in a seemingly aimless mob of ragged soldiers. Abandoned mansions and storehouses had been requisitioned for barracks, with cryptic chalk marks on the doors, like 20/Ist Co./1/29, which meant that twenty men of the Number One company of the First Battalion of the 29th Regiment of Foot would be billeted there. The doors stood open and men lounged about on the steps or stoops, wrapped in new blankets, smoking pipes or chewing tobacco quids. Smoke plumed from chimneys, giving the first real warmth to soldiers who

had nigh-frozen to death in the Spanish mountains. Looted tubs and cauldrons steamed outside over large fires made of smashed furniture and
ripped-down wall panelling, some of it quite fine. Even whole paintings
were being ripped apart so the gilt frames could be used for firewood, and
the paintings, rolled up like logs, burned well, too. Shirts and under-
drawers, stockings and small-clothes were being washed for the first time
in weeks, and over some fires, wool uniform coats and trousers were being given a smoking to drive out the lice, fleas, and other pests. Some
of the soldiers waiting for their cleaned clothes looked so riddled with
wee red bite marks that Lewrie at first suspected them stricken with the
measles!

"Seems there is some order about, after all, Captain Lewrie," Chalmers pointed out, extending an arm to several companies of Highlanders
practicing close-order drill, with their Sergeants and Corporals scurrying about them and barking orders like so many terriers. Further on,
several companies of green-jacketed Rifles were marching and counter-
marching under arms.

"Like the Admiral told us," Lewrie commented, "discipline fell apart
on the retreat. If the French arrive before we get 'em all off, they'll have
t'fight. Is that a Colonel, yonder?"

"A Major, I think," Chalmers said with a shrug. "Think we can question him?"

"Aye, let's try," Lewrie agreed, increasing his pace. "Sir!" he called out.
"Major? Could you talk to us?"

"Hmpf? What?" the stout fellow asked with a snort as he turned about
to see who was calling him. "Ah, the Navy's here, is it? At last . . . even if
it is in mere dribs and drabs, so far."

Lewrie was quick to assure him that Admiral Hood and nigh one hundred transports were coming from Vigo, and asked if he knew the dispo-
sitions of the army, and the location of the French. He took time to introduce
himself as Major Phillpot, of General Sir David Baird's staff, before
explaining things to the naval officers.

"The last of our troops crossed the Mero River, and we demolished
the only bridge, so that will slow the damned French down," he said. "It's
beyond the second range of hills, the Peñasquedos, yonder. We don't
have enough troops to hold those hills, but we do have cavalry vedettes
out to keep watch. The nearest range of hills, there, is the Monte Mero,
rocky as anything, with so many large standing boulders that it might as
well be fortified. General Hope's Division is on the left, Sir David Baird's

Division holds the centre, near a village called Elvina, and the Guards hold their right flank. General Edward Paget is near Santa Lucía in reserve, and Frasier's Division is posted on the road to Vigo and Santiago de Compostela on the far right."

"The French?" Lewrie asked.

"No idea yet, sir," Phillpot replied with a toothy leer. "As bad as we had it, the French must have had a worse time, for once we left any town through which we marched, there wasn't a crumb, or a flagon of wine, left, hah hah! *Shameful* looting and in-discipline, our men got to, burning anything to keep warm, no matter how grand. Pianos, harps, bed-steads, God knows what all. The weather, and the roads, my *word*! One-lane bridges slick with thick ice, and hardly any kerbings. Why, it's a wonder *any* of our carts and waggons survived. And, you ought to see some of the mountain villages we went through . . . lanes so narrow, and winding at odd angles, bound in by stone walls that hand-carts had to be un-loaded and stood on their sides to get them through!

"The French will have it just as bad," Phillpot prophesied, "and struggle, as we did, along the same routes, through the snow, ice, and mud, perhaps all three conditions in the same *day* in those mountains, their own supplies far behind and starving, and every hamlet plucked as clean as a chicken. Damn them all, they are *welcome* to it!"

"So, you believe the army can hold for a while?" Captain Chalmers asked him.

"Frankly, sir?" Phillpot posed with a scowl, thinking that over. "For one day, perhaps, after the French catch us up. After that? Well, the Navy will just have to get us off or the entire army's lost, what's left of it."

Major Phillpot offered them a tour of the defences up on the Monte Mero, though the retreat had cost so many horses that they would have to accompany him on foot while he rode his own worn-out prad; he was seeing a column of hand-carts up with fresh ammunition from the depot. They both decided not to.

"Save a place for me in one of your boats, will you, sirs?" Phillpot asked, and it was not in a parting jest. "Good day."

"And good luck," Lewrie bade him. Under his breath to Chalmers, he added, "I think they're going to need all the luck in the world."

As he and Captain Chalmers made their way back to the quays it began to drizzle an icy rain, quickly turning to sleet, then just as quickly to another bout of snow that began to blanket the ground, which had already been whitened, then churned to a slushy, muddy, muck by the thousands of soldiers. They passed a narrow church, where soldiers were quartered, and paused as they heard a flute and fiddle playing a tune inside.

"What's that?" Lewrie asked.

"I think it's 'Over the Hills and Far Away,'" Chalmers said as he cocked an ear. "It's from *The Beggar's Opera,* as I recall." As the tune continued, Chalmers "um-tiddlied" 'til he got to a part he recalled. "'And *I* would love you all the day, *all* the night we'd *laugh* and play, *if* to me you would fondly *say,* over the hills and *far* away.'"

"I wager that's their fondest wish, right now," Lewrie wryly said, "for them to *be* 'over the hills and far away' from here!"

He recalled that he *had* heard it long before, when he had had the *Proteus* frigate, escorting a convoy of "John Company" ships, and the ship that carried Daniel Wigmore's Circus/Menagerie/Theatrical troupe that had attached itself as far as Cape Town. They had staged a performance of *The Beggar's Opera* when they broke their passage at St. Helena Island, and Eudoxia Durschkeno had sung it as part of the chorus, back when she'd been enamoured of him, and long before she'd discovered that he was married.

The quays were empty when they arrived, and a gaggle of rowing boats were scuttling out into the harbour bearing the last of that surgeon's regimental wounded.

"Mister Hillhouse," Lewrie said, tapping the finger of his right hand on his hat by way of casual salute. "Last of 'em off, I see?"

"Aye, sir," Midshipman Hillhouse replied, doffing his hat in reply. "I was told by an army officer that there are more wounded men coming to be got off. The *Prosperity* and the *Blue Bonnet* are now full, so when the boats return, I thought to send the new batch out to the *Boniface,* if you think that right, sir."

"Quite so, Mister Hillhouse," Lewrie said with a nod of agreement, then looked about to determine the arrangements that the Army might have made for their soldiers. "Damme, but it's cold. Perhaps we should fetch pots, firewood, and tea leaves ashore after our boats make their first run out to *Boniface*. It's shameful t'let the poor devils lay here and shiver in the open, in this snow."

"Perhaps 'portable soup' might be more welcome, sir," Captain Chalmers suggested. "One would think that the army would see to such. Aha, here comes the next batch."

Lewrie turned about to see wounded men being brought to the quays, some being trundled in hand-carts, but most, those called the "walking wounded," astride horses, some clinging to healthy men.

"Cavalry, aha!" Chalmers said. "With all their saddles and such. I suppose we must attempt to salvage all that," he added with a frown, and a sigh.

"Light Dragoons," Lewrie noted aloud, taking in the fur-topped leather helmets, short jackets, Paget-model carbines, and sabres the healthy troopers wore. "Aye, I suppose we must get all their gear off, though God knows if we've any horse transports, and they may . . . Percy? Percy Stangbourne?" he shouted as he recognised the officer leading the column.

Colonel Percy, Viscount Stangbourne, looked up from his dour and weary musings, startled, looked about, then spotted him.

"Alan? Alan Lewrie?" he perked up. "Where the Devil did you spring from? Here to get us off, are you? Thank God!"

CHAPTER THIRTY-NINE

*B*elieve it or not, I was just thinking of you, Percy," Lewrie told him after Stangbourne had sprung from his saddle and had come to not only shake hands warmly, but thump him on the back in a bear-hug.

Well, yer better half, really, Lewrie thought.

"What? Why?" Percy asked, head cocked over in puzzlement.

"That tune," Lewrie told him. "I remember Eudoxia singin' it, on the way to Cape Town. How is she?"

"Safe in the country, thank God," Percy answered. "Oh, she *was* of a mind to take the field with me, same as Lydia, but in her condition . . . we're due another child, perhaps even now, so far as I know . . . and her father and I talked her out of it, again thank God!"

"And Lydia?" Lewrie asked of his former lover, thankful that he no longer felt a twinge in doing so, surprised again that mention or thought of her no longer caused a lurch in his innards.

"She's well," Stangbourne said, half his attention on his restless mount that was butting its head on his back. "Hunting and shooting round the estate, by herself if she can't convince anyone else to join her. Horses and dogs, and her new hobbies . . . church work, ministering to the wives and children of the regiment who didn't get to come along to Portugal, raising funds and such for the needy."

Just as I thought, Lewrie told himself; *it'll be missionary work and soup kitchens in the stews, you just watch!*

"That's good, I suppose," Lewrie opined.

"Yes, well," Percy agreed, with a roll of his eyes.

"Boats are coming for your wounded men. Have many, do you?" Lewrie asked, peering at the men being lowered from horses, or borne out of the hand-carts.

"We've more sick than wounded," Stangbourne told him with a bleak expression. "The badly wounded, and the very ill, died along the way, or had to be left behind in the villages we passed through. And, there were some who got so drunk off looted wine stores that we just had to leave them where they lay! Oh, the damned French *loved* that! We could hear them, when we stood as the rear-guard, *butchering* them without an *ounce* of mercy!"

"Good Lord!" Lewrie exclaimed.

"Laughing their evil heads off as they did it, too," Viscount Percy spat, "my troopers, soldiers, and the women and children with the army, too, all murdered. Now and then, though, we caught them at their games, and made them pay, blood for blood," Percy vowed, in such heat that made Lewrie re-consider his opinion of Percy. He was not a rich and idle *dilettante* playing at soldiering any longer, but a blooded veteran.

"I hear it was horrid," Lewrie lamely said.

"You don't know the half of it, Alan," Stangbourne mournfully said. "I've lost a third of my regiment, and a quarter of my horses! No grain, thank the bloody Spanish very much! No grass for them to eat, no rations for my troopers, damn Spanish promises, again! There were steep places where the ice was so thick that the horses couldn't even stay on all four hooves, fell, broke their legs and had to be put down . . . fell off the sides of the damned arched bridges into the ravines, horse and trooper together, or grew so weak that they just lay down and died. *Damn,* but half-cooked horse meat is just *foul,* an abomination to every good Englishman."

"Well, we'll get your sick and wounded out to the *Boniface* and let them heal up," Lewrie promised. "Warm, dry berths, hot food and drink?"

"We've tried to salvage as much of our saddlery as we could. I hope there's room for that," Stangbourne demanded, waving at carts filled with sabres, carbines, broad saddle-cloths with the regimental badge embroidered upon them, and heaps of leather goods.

"I'm sure there'll be room in the holds," Lewrie said to assure him. Now that Percy's regiment was no longer Stangbourne's Horse but officially on

Army List, anything lost would be made good by the Government; it wouldn't come out of Percy's purse. He'd lavished thousands to raise, equip, mount, and train his Dragoons in 1804, so many thousands of pounds that Lydia had feared that he would squander his wealth on it . . . that, or his penchant for gambling deep.

"They're holding the cavalry ashore, for now," Percy went on. "If the French get here before enough transports arrive . . ."

Lewrie assured him that over an hundred ships were coming, and that the Navy would do its best to get everyone off before the French arrived in force.

"Horse transports?" Stangbourne pointedly asked.

"Ah . . . that I don't know, Percy," Lewrie had to admit. "We don't have any among the ships we brought from Gibraltar. But surely, that'll have been thought of, by Admiral de Courcy, Admiral Hood, and London."

"Well, just Merry bloody Christmas, and Happy Fucking New Year!" Percy exclaimed, quite out of character from the proper fellow that Lewrie had known before. "Haven't we left enough behind, already? Guns, carriages, waggons, even the pay chests that got tossed into the steep ravines! Come Spring, some damned Spaniards might find them and make themselves rich! *Then* maybe the bastards will offer us even the *slightest* bit of aid!"

"Ready, sir," one of Stangbourne's officers interrupted.

"Right, coming. Excuse me for a bit, Alan," he said, stomping off, and leaving the reins of his horse to a trooper.

"No help from the Spanish, I take it, sir?" Lewrie asked the junior officer.

"Those pusillanimous bastards, sir?" that worthy spat, brows up in surprise at the question. "Not a morsel. There was only one Spanish general willing to come join us, *if* we could feed, arm, and clothe *his* soldiers for a Winter campaign! All that talk of proud, armed civilian bands defending their own blasted country is just so much moonshine. Every village or town we came to, the Spanish had packed up and carted everything away, leaving us scraps, offering us nothing! Well, they left the wines. Benavente, Astorga . . . Bembibre was the worst. Rum stores, wine vats, got staved in and it ran in the filthy streets like floodwater, and our poor fellows scooped it up, dirt, mud, animal waste and all, and drunk themselves simply hoggish. Even flogging couldn't control them. It was abominable. You ask me, sir, Spain and its idle people aren't worth the effort to save, for they won't save themselves."

Percy came back to rejoin them as the last of his wounded and sick men were laid out on the stone quays. At least the depot that General Sir David Baird had established could provide them blankets, replacement great-coats, and capes.

"I thought to send out for kettles, to brew up tea or soup," Lewrie said as Percy took back his horse's reins, and stroked its nose and muzzle.

"Ah, thankee, Alan, but I've already seen to that," Percy told him, gesturing to some troopers removing kettles from the hand-carts and passing among the sick and wounded with tin mugs. "The depot has lashings of rum that will most-like be burned up or dumped into the harbour, so they'll all get a portion in their tea, orders and regulations be-damned. They've more than earned the wee comfort, the poor devils. Like my horse, do you, Alan?"

"Aye, he looks a go-er," Lewrie agreed, appraising the grey gelding.

"Thunder, here, is a stout and brave beast," Percy said, stroking his horse's neck. "He's the last of mine that still has shoes. Another of our torments, that . . . the farrier waggons lost, no nails or horseshoes, along with no grain and no grass to graze. We simply had to shoot the lame ones.

"I started with a string of five in Portugal," Percy went on, fondling his mount's forehead and muzzle, "and now I've two left, and my mare is lame, and without shoes, so I suppose it's be kindest to shoot her, too, but . . ." He broke off and buried his face against his horse's neck.

"The depot, surely . . . ," Lewrie tried to encourage.

"They've no grain," Percy told him, leaning back. "We were told the Spanish would provide, and I doubt they could shoe no more than a single squadron before running out, and most of the farriers marched with the army, anyway . . . dead back in those damned mountains," he said as he waved towards the far, forbidding heights.

"The big convoy's due any hour," Lewrie promised, hoping that there were horse transports; he was an Englishman, a horse-lover from birth, and despised the thought of Percy's magnificent horse being shot to keep it from the French, or to keep it from starving.

"I must get back to my post," Percy announced, after a grim look-over the so-far-empty harbour. "We're brigaded with Fraser's Division, to defend the open country and the road from Vigo. That's about the only place where French cavalry could attack. I'd offer you a supper in our regimental mess, but I doubt you'd care for oat meal and hard bisquit."

"I get enough o' that aboard ship," Lewrie said with a little stab at humour, then offered his hand. "You take care, now, Percy. We'll do what we can to save you and your men."

"I count on it, Alan," Percy replied, shaking hands strongly. "I wonder . . . if anything does happen to me, would you see to . . . ?" He reached inside his ornately trimmed tunic and withdrew a packet of wax-sealed letters, bound in a short stack with ominously black ribbon.

"Christ, Percy, how would I know when t'mail 'em, not knowin' whether you're alive, or fallen?" Lewrie exclaimed. "I might frighten Eudoxia and Lydia to death with false news!"

"Nothing that grim, no, Alan!" Percy told him with his first sign of good humour. "Merely last expressions of love, just in case. I didn't write me *will*, for God's sake, no 'by the time you get this' nonsense!"

"Alright, then," Lewrie promised, taking the packet and putting the letters in a side pocket of his coat. "Though, you'll be on some transport, and I don't know *where* I'm goin' from here, but I'll post 'em for you."

"That's true, but mail them anyway," Percy told him, stepping back near his horse's saddle and gathering up the reins. "I suppose this will be the last chance to see each other, as you say, so . . . do you take care, yourself, Alan."

"If the French come, give 'em Hell," Lewrie replied.

"We've already done a good job of that, and I intend to if they dare. Goodbye, old son," Percy said as he mounted. "And, I think my sister a damned fool for her choices."

There was no reply that Lewrie could make to that statement; all he could do was doff his hat as Colonel Percy, Viscount Stangbourne, wheeled his mount about and cantered off.

"Boats are coming back, sir," Midshipman Hillhouse reported as Lewrie paced to the seaward end of the stone quays. "Fresh oarsmen, it looks like."

"Excellent," Lewrie told him, looking over the harbour waters. The snow had stopped, and the scudding clouds appeared higher, and lighter in colour, as if the Winter gloom might abate.

"There, sir!" Captain Chalmers shouted, pointing seaward. "See there, sir! Damme, why did I not bring my glass with me?"

Lewrie went to his side and cupped his hands either side of his eyes. "Yes, by God! Yes, thankee Jesus!"

Admiral Hood's vast armada of over an hundred transport ships was sailing into sight, sail after sail, mast after mast, stacked up against each other from one end of the vista to the other, and stretching far out to sea as if the on-coming columns of ships would never end. The nearest would come to anchor within two hours, whilst the farthest out to sea might take 'til dusk to get into Corunna.

"Gad, what a magnificent sight!" Chalmers crowed.

"About bloody time," Lewrie added with less enthusiasm after his initial outburst.

"Oh, surely, Captain Lewrie," Chalmers countered, "one simply must be awed by such a sight."

"Oh, I'm awed, no error, Captain Chalmers," Lewrie said, "but, if the French get here before the army can begin to evacuate, they'll have to stand under arms, where they are, and perform a fighting withdrawal before we can get 'em into boats and safely aboard all those transports. This ain't over, not by a long shot."

"One might think you a pessimist, sir," Captain Chalmers said rather stiffly.

"Just a simple sailor, me," Lewrie rejoined with a grin.

CHAPTER FORTY

All the sick, wounded, and exhausted soldiers were aboard the transports, as much of the depot's supplies were either removed to the ships, and the rest scandalised. The Spanish artillery in the Citadel, the little island castle of San Antonio off the town's defences, and along the long sea walls were either spiked, levered over into the harbour waters, or turned about to face landward.

Yet, as Lewrie suspected, General Sir John Moore's army still stood in their positions along the Monte Mero, on Santa Lucía Hill, and upon the Vigo Road approaches. The transports were waiting, the twelve sail of the line were anchored to provide fire should the French swarm over the defences and gain the town, but . . . everyone waited, and no one would, or could, tell anyone *why*.

Moore had brought the remnants of his army to Corunna on the 11th of January, Lewrie's convoy had come in on the 13th, and defencive positions had been taken up on the 12th, but . . .

"Good morning, sir," Sailing Master Yelland said, tipping his hat as Lewrie left his great-cabins for the quarterdeck on the morning of the 16th. "It looks to be a brighter day."

"Hmmph," was Lewrie's comment. The skies *were* clearer, and a weak Winter sun now and then peeked through the grey clouds slowly scudding inland. The harbour waters were chopped with short, steep waves, strewn with white-caps and white-horses, and were a tad more green than the steel grey of the day before, a sure sign that out to sea there had been heavy weather. Lewrie went to the bulwarks for a look seaward, then to the Second Rate flagship for any signals that might tell him anything, but finally turned his telescope shoreward to see if he could make out what the army was doing, or if the enemy had arrived in the night.

He finally lowered his telescope and collapsed the tubes so he could stow it in a coat pocket, shaking his head in weariness, and disappointment. He heard a hopeful whine by his right knee, and felt a muzzle touch his leg. Bisquit had come for a snack, and a touch of human comfort.

"Yeovill *already* cooked you a warm breakfast," Lewrie said to the dog, "and you're *still* hungry? Oh, here, then." For just such an eventuality, he'd put a spare sausage in his pocket, and held it out for Bisquit to whine and jump at, balanced on his hind legs. "Might be too spicy for ye."

No, it wasn't, for Bisquit chewed up the token morsel and went puppy-eyed for more, licking his chops and sweeping the deck clean with a rapidly wagging tail.

"Good morning, sir," Lieutenant Harcourt greeted him, doffing his hat. Greetings also came from Marine Lieutenants Keane and Roe.

"On deck for the chilly air, sirs?" Lewrie asked them. "Or, to satisfy your curiosity?"

"Curiosity, sir," Lt. Keane allowed, followed a second later by his subordinate, Lt. Roe, who confessed, "Bored, sir."

"I know it's not our proper place," Lt. Keane went on, "and I know that our meagre Marine contingent would make no difference if a battle is to be fought . . . sometime . . . but I do wish that we were ashore with the army."

"If only to see what's happening, sir," the younger Lt. Roe added. "If all the warships present mustered their Marines, we might amount to a battalion."

"They'd only put you in reserve, sirs," Lewrie had to tell them, "guardin' what's left of the depot, or mannin' the sea walls. You have just as good a view from here of . . . whatever."

"Ah, good morning, sir," Lt. Westcott said as he, too, came to the quarterdeck from the wardroom below. "Good morning, gentlemen."

"Good morning, Mister Westcott," Lewrie said. "Bored, or just curious? There seems to be a lot of both, this morning."

"Both, sir," Westcott said with one of his fierce, brief grins. "Though I could use a long nap after cutlass drill. That still on?"

"Aye, if only t'keep the hands awake," Lewrie said. "Have 'em work up a mild sweat, keep warm . . ."

"Hark, sir!" Mr. Yelland interrupted, going to the bulwark facing the shore, and cupping a hand to his ear. "I could swear that I hear cannon fire."

That made them all peer round the vast anchorage to see if one of the ships of the line was holding live-firing practise, or if a storm might be coming, one with thunder and lightning; but there was no sign of either.

"Aye, I thought so!" Yelland said, pointing ashore. "There's gun-smoke rising along yon line of hills."

That prompted everyone to fetch out their telescopes, or grab a spare from the compass binnacle racks, and crowd the bulwarks for a good look. Slowly, the sound of cannon rose in volume, and spent powder smoke spread along the whole length of the Monte Mero, sickly yellow-white and lingering, merging together into a long pall that hardly seemed to move despite the breeze off the sea, with taller thunderheads of smoke rising to mark the positions of enemy batteries and British batteries as they duelled with each other for supremacy.

"Well, the French have come at last," Lewrie summed up. "We can only hope they arrived in as poor condition as our army when it got here. Hah! Maybe they're so hungry they're fightin' to seize what's left of the food in the depot!"

"I simply don't understand this, sir," said Midshipman Leverett, who was standing nearby without even a pocket telescope to watch events unfold. "The army's had bags of time to evacuate, long before the French showed up. Why are we still here, why's the army still here?"

"Well, the depot had to be emptied to supply, feed, and re-equip the troops, first," Marine Lieutenant Keane said, "and there were the sick and wounded to be seen to. That took time. General Moore *had* to set out defences should the French arrive in the middle of that. If he had begun the evacuation, yesterday say, his defence line would now be a lot closer to the town and the docks, and the French would capture half the army . . . just roll over the few regiments still on shore."

"And, perhaps it's because the *French* are starving, frozen solid, their own cavalry and artillery lost in those mountains in pursuit," Marine Lieutenant Roe, Keane's second-in-command, added, "and Moore now has the upper hand. If he holds, and bloodies them, the French can't interfere when he *does* begin to evacuate."

"Or, maybe General Moore is tired of being chased all round Spain, and wants to get in a hard lick at them to show the French, and Napoleon, who's the better soldier," Lt. Westcott commented with one brow up. "What? Just saying," he had to add, after almost all officers on the quarterdeck turned to look at him, amazed by such a suggestion. "In his shoes, wouldn't *you* want to get in the last blow?"

We do insane things for our pride, Lewrie thought, peering intently shore-ward; *for God, King, and Country . . . and ourselves.*

The sound of the bombardment, and counter-bombardment was louder, now, the concussions spreading out from the Monte Mero ridges to make the bare limbs of trees ashore tremble, to create wee ripples of harbour water that spread outward from the docks at Santa Lucía. He cocked an ear and imagined that he could almost hear the twigs-in-a-fire crackling of musketry, but he shook his head, thinking that it was much too soon for the French to advance their infantry columns and come down from the further ridges of the Peñasquedo to attempt to march up the slopes of the Monte Mero. He hoped that Moore was husbanding his soldiers on the reverse slopes, as Wellesley had done at Vimeiro, even as Sir Brent Spencer had planned at Ayamonte.

They'll keep bangin' away with artillery for a time yet, he told himself; *unless they really* are *starvin'! If the French* do *get atop the ridge . . . hmm.*

"Mister Yelland," he called out over his shoulder, his view intent upon the near shores, "those transports East of the quays at Santa Lucía . . . they're anchored rather close to shore. How deep are the waters there, d'ye think? Do your charts show?"

"Close to shore, sir?" Yelland asked, rubbing his chin.

Always was slow on the up-take, Lewrie thought.

"Should it be necessary to close the shore and fire our guns to support the army should it be driven back, how close could we get, I'm asking," Lewrie patiently told him.

"I'll go look, sir," the Sailing Master said, taking off his hat and scratching his scalp for a second; "Close" and "Shore" together in one sentence put the wind up every officer responsible for the safe navigation of a King's Ship.

"I will join you," Lewrie said, closing the tubes of his telescope and steeling his nostrils for an assault as he went to the improvised chart space.

As Lewrie expected, the shore was steep-to, sloping off sharply, and littered with large boulders, but the old Spanish charts did show at least five
fathoms of depth within a quarter-mile of the coast. East of the commercial piers of Santa Lucía there was a deep notch, a cove or inlet that re-
sembled a large, circular bite out of a sandwich, just beneath the heights
of Santa Lucía Hill, which was the end of the Monte Mero ridge. With the
use of a long brass ruler, Lewrie could determine that if they entered that
cove, they would have a direct line-of-sight to the Monte Mero, and could
take any French mass of troops, advancing triumphantly on Corunna, in
enfilade, and if they came on in their massed columns, *Sapphire*'s guns could
rake their flanks with all her weight of metal.

"There's this little stream that runs down from the hills, from Elvina
to spill out into the bay below Santa Lucía," Lewrie pointed out with a pencil stub. "If Moore is dis-lodged from the ridge, that'd be a good line t'try
and hold, and we could smash the French columns right on their right flank.
It's what . . . hmm, five fathoms, or the Spanish equivalent . . . a quarter-
mile from the rocky shore . . ."

"At mean low tide," Yelland dubiously agreed, "though there're these
two rocky outcrops, wee islands, and the depths between . . ."

"We get between 'em, right here," Lewrie said, making an *X* to mark
the place on the chart. "If we have to, Mister Yelland."

"If we can thread our way through the transports crammed about the
quays, sir," Yelland cautioned. "They are anchored close to ease the rowing distance from shore to ship. Corunna's as crowded as the Pool of
London, or worse, even with the loaded ships moved seawards."

"It'd take some crafty ship-handlin', aye," Lewrie said, standing erect
from leaning over the inclined chart table, and tossing the pencil into a
low shelf on the back edge. "But, if the army runs into trouble, I'll not
have it said that the Navy let 'em down. That's what they pay us for . . .
crafty ship-handlin', right?"

"Right, sir," Mr. Yelland said, looking as if he had been ordered to thread
'twixt Scylla and Charybdis, hunt up the fabled Northwest Passage through
Midwinter icebergs, or sell his first-born son; that glint in his eyes, and
the way he licked his lips, told Lewrie that Mr. Yelland was badly in need
of a stiff "Norwester" glass of grog.

Lewrie stepped back out onto the quarterdeck, took a deep and refreshing breath of clean air, then trotted up the ladderway to the poop deck for
a better vantage point. The cannonading was continuing, with no sign of
a French breakthrough . . . yet. When he swivelled to look to the West,

where Percy Stangbourne's cavalry guarded the road from Vigo, he could not spot any sign of a French attack. Whoever was in command of the French troops looked as if he was throwing all he had at the Monte Mero, so far.

Can't be Napoleon himself, then, Lewrie thought; that *bastard would be sneaky enough t' feint an attack where Moore's strongest, and hit him where he's weakest.*

Lewrie returned to the quarterdeck after a break to warm up in his great-cabins, and have Yeovill fetch a pot of hot tea from the galley, and, admittedly, to visit his quarter-gallery toilet. He saw his crew gathered all down the bulwarks facing the shore, half-way up the shrouds, in the fighting tops to watch what was happening ashore. Some men of the off-watch division had eschewed four hours of sleep below, and were on deck in their warmest clothing, with their blankets wrapped round them.

"Any change?" Lewrie asked the First Officer, who was sipping a cup of tea himself, with his own boat cloak wrapped round him for warmth.

"It gets louder, now and then, sir, then fades out a bit," Lt. Westcott said with a bored expression on his face. "Every now and then I *think* I can hear musketry, but, who knows?" he said with a shrug. "We *seem* to be holding them in check."

Lewrie pulled out his pocket watch to note that it was a little past 10 in the morning of the 16th of January, and the fighting had begun just round 9 A.M. He looked shoreward with his telescope for a long minute, then lowered it and looked round his own decks. Hands were looking aft at the quarterdeck, now that he was back.

Lewrie made up his mind with a firm nod, then went to the edge of the quarterdeck to lean on the cross-deck hammock stanchions.

"Lads!" he called out loudly, drawing everyone's attention to him. "The Army's holding the damned Frogs, so far! I'll tell you what I know from when I was ashore at Vimeiro!"

He described the French column formations, and how they marched shoulder to shoulder like a massive blue carpet, how the British Army kept their men safe behind the ridges yonder 'til it was time to come up and shoot those columns to a bloody standstill; how the exploding Shrapnel shells would burst over them and scatter bodies about; how a reef of dead and wounded would pile up knee or thigh high, when the French would stall, unable to step over those reefs, even though the drums and the officers would still urge them forward; and he told them how the French had broken and run, at last, and how vain those shouts of *"Vive l'Empereur!"* would be.

"Long live the Emperor," he said in a comically shaky voice, "and let *me* live t'get *outa* this place! *Mon Dieu, Mort de ma vie!* I am *running* now, *toot sweet!*"

That had them roaring with laughter.

"I was told that those ridges yonder, the Monte Mero, are steep, and so full of boulders, it might as well be a stone fort," he went on. "The Frogs'll be out of breath by the time they're halfway up, and dyin' by the dozens at every step. All the gun-smoke is over on the *other* side, so far, so . . .'til we see red coats fallin' back, and blue carpets on this side of the ridges, all's well. If we *do* see that, then we'll sail over to that inlet, yonder," he said with one arm pointing towards the foot of Santa Lucía Hill, "and use our cannon t'slaughter 'em by the hundreds!

"Our first year in the Med," he exhorted, "you shot the Devil out of forts and batteries . . . this Summer, we took on that column of Frogs marchin' along the coast road from Málaga, you shot the *guts* out of two Spanish frigates. You're the best set of gunners ever I did see in the King's Navy. If called to do it, can ye shoot Hell out of a French *army?*"

Eager cries of agreement and cheering greeted his exortations, and he waited 'til it died down before continuing. "For now, we will wait t'see what happens. You off-watch men, you really *should* go below and get some sleep, but I can't *order* ye to. So . . .'til the rum issue and dinner, let's have a Make and Mend, and stand easy."

They cheered that, too. The keenly curious could stay by the bulwarks and up the masts, while others could read, write letters, or mend their clothing, fiddle with their craftwork and carvings, whilst a fair number would indeed nap on deck wrapped in their blankets, or go below to turn into their hammocks.

The rum issue at Seven Bells of the Forenoon came and went, as did the hands' mid-day meal, the change of watch from Noon to four, the change of watch at the start of the First Dog, and even the approach of the Second Dog at 6 P.M. The army was holding, it seemed, as the sun sank low and dusk began to dull the view of the shore. Lewrie had been aft in his cabins, catching up on the never-ending paperwork associated with a ship in active commission, when he took note that Pettus and Jessop were lighting more lanthorns.

And the sudden silence.

"What the Devil?" he asked himself as he rose from his desk, cocking his head to listen more closely.

"Think it stopped, sir," Jessop commented. "Quiet-like."

Wonder if that's good, or bad, Lewrie asked himself as he went for his hat and boat cloak, and hastened out to the quarterdeck, where he found his officers gathered in puzzlement, up from the wardroom in curiosity, instead of preparing for their own suppers.

"There are boats coming off from the quays, sir," Lt. Westcott pointed out. "More wounded men, it looks like."

"Any summons from the flag for us to send in boats?" Lewrie demanded.

"Not yet, sir, no," Westcott answered, totally mystified.

"I can't see any French infantry on the ridges, sir," Harcourt, the Second Officer, reported. "Ours, mostly, some hand lanthorns, and litter parties, I think. The light's going."

Boom-Boom! There were two guns fired aboard Admiral Hood's flagship, the General Signal to all naval ships present to watch for a hoist of signal flags, which would be hard to make out in the gloom of dusk.

"I can make out . . . Send Boats," Midshipman Hillhouse slowly read off with a telescope, "and Wounded, spelled out, sir."

"Let's be at it, then, gentlemen," Lewrie snapped, "man all boats and get them on their way. See which transport shows a night signal that she's to receive wounded. Bosun Terrell? Muster all boat crews!"

"What of the hands' supper, sir?" Westcott asked. "What should Mister Tanner do, hold off serving out, or—?"

"Damn," Lewrie spat. "He's to serve those men still aboard, and let the meat simmer awhile longer for the rest."

He dearly wished that he could hop into the pinnace or the launch and go ashore to discover what had happened, but, for once he held himself to a tighter rein. He would have to be *patient*!

"Mister Hillhouse, still here?" he called out.

"Aye, sir?" the Midshipman replied.

"Take charge of one of the cutters, get ashore, ferry wounded men out to the transports ready to receive them, but . . . report back to me as soon as you can as to what's happened ashore," Lewrie ordered.

"Aye aye, sir!" Hillhouse said, doffing his hat before dashing off, eager to shine, happy to be singled out, and just as curious as his Captain in that regard.

Who the Hell am I dinin' in t'night? he had to remind himself; *Sailin' Master, Marine officers, Purser, and Mister Elmes, and two of the Mids? Well, the Mids are out, they'll all be busy.*

He thought better of that.

"Gentlemen, I will be dinin' later than normal," he announced. "We'll put it off 'til the Mids invited are back aboard. I will be aft."

As soon as he was in the privacy of his cabins, he tossed off his hat and boat cloak and cried for whisky, listening to the clack of his chronometer as it measured the un-ending minutes that he had to bide.

"Midshipman Hillhouse t'see the Cap'm, SAH!" the Marine at his door shouted.

"Enter!" Lewrie barked back, much too loud and eagerly.

Mister Yelland the Sailing Master, Marine Lieutenants Keane and Roe, Mister Cadrick the Purser, and Lieutenant Elmes were already in the great-cabins, sitting or standing round the starboard side settee with wineglasses in their hands. Their already-muted conversations were hushed as Hillhouse entered, hat under his arm.

"Well, Mister Hillhouse?" Lewrie demanded.

"Beg to report, sir, all wounded are now aboard the transports, and our boats are returning," Hillhouse began, very aware that all eyes were upon him. "The army beat off every French attack, and hold the same positions that they did this morning. I was told it was touch and go round some village called Elvina, the French would take it and we would shove them back out, several times. I was told that they're fought out . . . the French, I mean, sir. Shot their bolt, was the way an officer described it. We've *won*, sir!"

Sapphire's officers began to cheer at that news, but Hillhouse was holding up a hand to indicate that there was more to be imparted.

"It was dearly won, sir," he said at last when the din had subsided. "General Sir David Baird is among the wounded, had his right arm shattered, and General Sir John Moore, sir . . . he was hit by a cannonball, and he passed over, just after the French retired from the field. General Hope is now in command of the army, and he wishes the army evacuated, now the French are so badly mauled. I am told that we should begin just after first light, tomorrow, sir."

"Baird, good God!" Lewrie gasped. "I knew him, from Cape Town. Poor fellow! I hope he survives his wounds."

"And, we all met Sir John last year, sir," Lt. Elmes lamented. "A Devil of a fine fellow, a gentleman, and a soldier."

"Amen t'that," Lewrie agreed, taking a sip of his wine that had suddenly lost its sprightly lustre. "Hope is sure that the French are done, they've shot their bolt, and can't interfere with the evacuation?"

"I gathered that they were in very poor shape when they arrived, and fought out of sheer desperation for our rations, sir," Hillhouse told him, "much as you speculated this morning, that they were fighting for a spoonful of food!"

"Well, then, sirs, let 'em starve some more round their cheerless camp-fires tonight," Lewrie said with a grin, "and let *us* make a point to dine exceeding *well*! You'll join us, of course, Mister Hillhouse?" And the Midshipman nodded his thanks, Lewrie raised his glass and proposed a toast; "To Victory, gentlemen!"

"Victory!" his officers shouted back.

"And Confusion, and Famine, to the French!" Marine Lieutenant Roe added on, crowing with glee.

"Ah, supper is laid and ready, sir," Pettus reported.

"Good! Let's dine, then, sirs," Lewrie bade them, waving them to the dining-coach and their places at the table.

Some victory, though, he thought as he took his seat at the head of the table; *too dearly won, and we're still slinkin' off like thieves in the night. And, there's still tomorrow. The army ain't away Scot free, yet!*

CHAPTER FORTY-ONE

*T*he 17th of January dawned cold, mockingly clear, but with boisterous seas out beyond the harbour. It appeared almost too cheerful and sunny, as the day progressed, to shine so on the scene of such a dreadful and desperate battle. Upon mounting the poop deck for his first look-round with a telescope, Lewrie discovered that the number of transports huddled in Corunna's harbour had been reduced. During the night, those ships with the sick and wounded, and the remnants of the army's wives, children, and camp-followers, had departed.

Word had come during their supper the night before that all of the evacuated troops would not be returned to Lisbon, where they had started, but would be borne back to English ports, as if the entire expedition had been given up as a failure. That prompted speculation that the ten-thousand-man garrison left in Portugal might be withdrawn, as well. "Keep it to yourselves," Lewrie had cautioned, though "scuttle-butt" would spread, as it usually did, to every man and boy aboard as if he had stood on the quarterdeck and bellowed the news to one and all!

Make the best of your way to English ports, is it? Lewrie reminded himself as he scanned the fleet, and gave out a derisive snort; *Well, which bloody ports, hey? Regimental sick, wounded, wives, and kiddies end up at Falmouth, and their men end up at Sheerness? What idiot decided that, I wonder? England, well! It* would *be grand to be home for a while.*

He spotted some movement among the transports anchored close to the quays at Santa Lucía; several were hauling themselves to Short Stays, and beginning to loose canvas, now full of soldiers and whatever of their weapons, gear, and rations that they could carry away. The quays and the commercial town round the village seemed to have turned red with all the regiments queued up and waiting to begin embarkation into others.

"Good morning, sir," Lt. Westcott said, looking up from the quarterdeck. "The evacuation has begun, then?"

"Good morning, Mister Westcott," Lewrie replied in kind. "Aye, so it appears. I think I can make out some defensive lines out beyond the town. Come on up and have a look for yourself."

Westcott joined him and stood by the bulwarks, slowly panning his own telescope back and forth. "Looks as if they're coming down to the quays by whole brigades. Soon as their ships are full, they'll be off. Hmm, no sign that the French mean to have a go at them, *yet.*"

"No, not yet," Lewrie glumly agreed, scanning back and forth. Bisquit came to the poop deck and sat on his haunches between them, uttering wee whines for attention. Lewrie leaned down to pet him for a bit.

"I say, sir," Westcott said, "but is that a *French* flag atop Santa Lucía Hill, yonder? Our troops must have left it during the night. Yes, yes it *is* a French flag. Damn my eyes, I *think* I can make out artillery pieces!"

Lewrie straightened up and leaned onto the bulwarks with his telescope to his eye, again, straining to confirm Westcott's observation. "Damme, you're right. They've a whole battery up there, the snail-eatin' bastards!"

As they watched, they could hear the rustling of sail-cloth, the distant rumbling of anchor cables, as more transports began to get under way, along with the approved capstan chanties allowed aboard Royal Navy warships as they, too, began to get under way to escort this clutch of ships out to sea and back to England.

"They're opening upon our transports," Westcott spat as they both saw the first puffs of gunpowder smoke from Santa Lucía Hill, followed seconds later by the reports of discharges, and the keens and moans of incoming roundshot.

"Aha!" Lewrie shouted as he spotted the Sailing Master, Mister Yelland, coming up from the wardroom below, still chewing on a last bite of bacon. "Mister Yelland, fetch yer sextant and come up!"

Yelland had to duck into his starboard-side sea cabin for his sextant, and a slate and chalk, before he ponderously mounted the ladderway to join them on the poop deck. "Aye, sir?" he asked.

"Where we intended to go yesterday and fire on the French if they gained the Monte Mero," Lewrie impatiently pressed, "if we go there this morning, can we elevate our guns high enough to engage that damned Frog battery?"

For a seasoned sea-captain, Lewrie would be the last to claim that he was a dab-hand at mathematics, not like his past Sailing Masters during his career. He was forced to wait while Yelland hefted his sextant to his eye, took the measure of the hill's height, then scribbled on his slate with many a cock of his head and some "Ah hums" thrown in for good measure. At last, he announced, "Not as deep into the inlet as you proposed yesterday, sir, no." Yelland rubbed his un-shaven chin and allowed "If we come to anchor nearer the mid-way point 'twixt that point and the quays of Saint Lucía, about two-thirds of a mile off from the hill, would be best, and that at *extreme* maximum elevation of the guns."

"Good enough, then," Lewrie said, slamming a fist on the cap-rails of the bulwarks. "Mister Westcott, pipe All Hands to hoist the anchor and make sail. We'll beat to Quarters once we're under way!"

"Aye aye, sir!" Westcott said, looking positively wolf-evil as he bared his teeth in a wide, brief grin.

"Bless me, are they actually *aiming* at any ship?" Captain Chalmers observed from the quarterdeck of his *Undaunted* frigate, as French shot rumbled into the harbour waters, raising great pillars and feathers of spray and foam. "Why, they're all over the place!"

"That will most-like change, sir," his First Officer opined. "Cold barrels and ranging shots, what? Oops, oh my!" he added, as the French artillery scored a hit on a departing transport, splitting the ship's main tops'l and leaving a large hole in the canvas. A second or so later, and that transport was struck, again, this hit just a bit wide of the mark and scoring down her larboard side, and raising a great cloud of dust and engrained dirt from her timbers.

"Damned plunging fire!" the Third Lieutenant exclaimed.

"I will thank you to mind your tongue, sir!" Chalmers snapped. "You know my views on curses, and blasphemy."

"Sorry, sir."

"There's *Sapphire* getting under way, sir!" the First Officer pointed out.

"Mister Lewrie?" Captain Chalmers called out. "Has there been a signal from the flag for our group to make sail that you missed?"

"No, sir," Midshipman Hugh Lewrie quickly answered. "The last signals to that effect showed the numbers for other ships. She is getting under way on her own, it appears, sir!"

HMS *Sapphire* was ringing up her best bower, even as she began to make sail; spanker, stays'ls, tops'ls, and jibs. She was turning slowly, wheeling away as if to make for the lower end of the harbour and the French battery. *Undaunted* was near enough to her former anchorage for everyone aboard to hear her Marine drummers beating out the Long Roll, and her fiddlers and fifers starting to play "The Bowld Soldier Boy."

"And just what does he intend, I wonder?" Chalmers asked the aether. "Should we join him? Any signal to us?"

"That's my grandfather's favourite tune, sir," Midshipman Hugh Lewrie said with a wistful note to his voice. "My father's, too. He is going to fight!" he said with pride. "*Sapphire* makes no signal, sir."

"Do you imagine, sir," *Undaunted*'s First Officer asked, "that Captain Lewrie intends to draw the French battery's fire upon his ship? She's stouter than us. She can take their eight- and twelve-pounder shot better than we could, perhaps even the plunging fire from their howitzers."

"Spare the transports?" Captain Chalmers wondered aloud, even as the French found the range upon another departing transport ship and scored several damaging hits. "I must say that Captain Lewrie has 'bottom,' in spades!"

"Yes, he does!" Midshipman Lewrie seconded that impression, if only under his breath.

"The ship is at Quarters, sir," Lt. Westcott reported in his most formal and grave manner, then cast an eye towards the Sailing Master and his Master's Mates, Stubbs and Dorton, all of whom were busy scribbling on their slates, their sticks of chalk squeaking in urgency between quick sights with their sextants.

"Soon, Mister Yelland?" Lewrie called to them.

"Soon, sir," Mr. Yelland assured him, sounding anxious.

"There's not enough room for us to go about," Lewrie said to Lt. Westcott, waving an arm round the harbour. "We can't stand close to the quays, wear about, and engage with the off-side battery. We would spend all our time at it. We'll have to anchor, with the best bower and kedge, with springs on the cables."

That drew a wince from Westcott, and a sucking of breath over his teeth. "Play target, to spare the other ships? Aye, nothing for it, then. Let go the kedge, first, and hope it finds good grounding, as rocky as the harbour is."

"And use the best bower at a very short scope t'keep us from swinging, aye," Lewrie grimly agreed. "Stand by to let go the kedge when Yelland decides we're at the best place, then send topmen aloft as we free the bower."

"Aye aye, sir," Westcott said, doffing his hat most formally, again, sure that this would be a *very* hot business. He turned away to begin issuing Lewrie's orders.

The French battery atop the hill had been busy during their slow approach, sending roundshot chasing after departing transports, but, after finally taking notice of such a big and tempting target, they began to shift the aim of their guns, even before *Sapphire* got to her optimum firing position.

"I think this will do, sir," Yelland said at last.

"Very well, Mister Yelland. Let go the kedge, springs on the cable!" Lewrie cried. "Topmen aloft, trice up and lay out t'take in sail! Open the gun-ports and run out!"

Shot keened overhead, and the main tops'l puckered as a shot punched clean through it. Another roundshot snapped the halliards of the middle stays'l between the main and foremast, bringing it down to drape the waist.

Sapphire rumbled and groaned as the kedge anchor cable paid out the stern hawsehole, squealed as the sheaves of the gun-port blocks lowered the ports, roared and drummed as the larboard guns were run out to thud against the bulwarks and hull. She snubbed as the kedge bit into the rock and sand of Corunna's harbour, and began to ghost to a stop.

"Seize, and bring to!" Lt. Westcott could be heard yelling to snub the kedge cable. "Breast to the aft capstan bars! Mister Ward!" he called to the forecastle with a brass speaking trumpet. "Let go the bower!"

A 12-pounder shot passed close over the poop deck, clearing the larboard bulwarks by inches, but smashing the cap-rails of the starboard bulwarks as it caromed off. The Sailing Master and his Mates came tumbling down from where they had been making their calculations in a trice.

"Pass word to the gun-decks," Lewrie ordered, "quoin blocks all the way out, load, and lay the guns!"

The first serge cartridge bags were being rammed down muzzles, followed by wadding, then roundshot. Lewrie leaned over the side to see the 12-pounders and lower deck 24-pounders jutting from the side, barrels jerking upwards as the wooden elevating quoin blocks were withdrawn, allowing the breeches to rest on the truck carriage beds.

Westcott was back at Lewrie's side, speaking trumpet still in his hand, and they shared a look in the moment it took for Mids to dash up from below and report the guns ready. Lewrie gave him a nod.

"The larboard battery will open," Lewrie gravely ordered, "by broadside. And *skin* the sons of bitches!"

"*Larboard* battery . . . by *broadside* . . . *fire!*" Westcott yelled.

Unconsciously, Lewrie crossed the fingers of his right hand along the side of his thigh as the guns lit off in a titanic roar, a sudden fog bank of powder smoke, and amber-red flashes of jutting flame that erupted from her side.

"Two-thirds of a mile, you made it, Mister Yelland?" Lewrie asked, turning to look for the Sailing Master.

"Aye, sir, about that," Yelland said through a dry throat.

"Can't see a bloody thing," Lewrie groused. "Mister Harvey," he called to the nearest Midshipman. "Aloft to the cross-trees with a telescope, and spot the fall of shot!"

"Aye aye, sir!" the lad said, snatching a glass from the binnacle cabinet rack and making his way to the larboard main mast shrouds.

The first broadside's smoke was wafting away over San Diego Point, and Santa Lucía Hill was emerging once more.

If we can't take their fire, we can get the bower up and the wind'll blow us back on the kedge, then wheel back out to sea, he thought, taking time to look over to starboard at the other ships in port. Fully laden ships were shifting their anchorages further out of range of the French guns, some in groups that were leaving the harbour to stand off-and-on outside. The one transport that had been hit several times looked to be in a bad way, her main topmasts hanging over, her yards a'cock-bill in disorder, and listing a bit to starboard. At least the French weren't firing at her, anymore.

"Run out yer guns!" Lieutenants Harcourt and Elmes could be heard from below as they pressed their gun crews to prepare for one more broadside.

"Shot was high, sir!" Midshipman Harvey yelled from aloft. "High and right!"

"Quoin blocks in a bit, Mister Westcott, and take in on the kedge cable spring!" Lewrie snapped, impatient for the adjustment in aim to be completed.

"Ready!" was shouted up to the quarterdeck.

"By broadside . . . fire!" Lt. Westcott yelled, and *Sapphire* shook and roared as the guns lit off, as the truck carriages came rushing back in recoil. "Better aim as the barrels warm up, sir," he said to Lewrie, with a confident wink.

A full battery of French artillery consisted of several 8-pounder guns, at least six of their famed 12-pounders, and a brace of howitzers. All were firing at a fixed target. Shot splashes towered close to the larboard side, *Sapphire* drummed to a solid hit, and a howitzer roundshot crashed down onto the starboard sail-tending gangway with a raucous shriek of rivened, splintered wood.

"Still *high*, sir!" Midshipman Harvey shouted over the din to the deck. "Traverse is still just a *bit* to the *right*!"

"Pass word, quoins in another inch," Lewrie snapped, "and take another strain on the kedge cable spring!"

"Ready?" Westcott demanded after the adjustments were made. "By broadside . . . *fire*!"

What I'd give for fused shells! Lewrie bemoaned as the broadside bellowed, flinging heavy shot shoreward through the sudden pall of smoke. He'd dealt with fused mortar shells and bursting shot when he'd been at Toulon; he knew the dangers of such tricky, delicate shells being rammed down hot barrels, perhaps lighting the fuses as they were rammed down and bursting, destroying the guns and killing gunners. As he wished that he had stuffed some candle wax in his ringing ears, he began to imagine how that could be managed, despite the risks.

"Traverse is *true*, sir!" Harvey screeched, sounding triumphant. "Our shot is *skimming* the hill, by *inches*, I think!"

"Quoins out half an inch!" Lewrie shouted. "Serve the whores another!"

"Ready? By broadside . . . *fire*!" Westcott roared.

"Yes! Yes, that's the way!" Midshipman Harvey yelled, far above the massive smoke clouds and able to see.

French shot was still striking close aboard, the ship boomed to hits crashing into her thick timbers and stout scantlings, and wood shrieked and squawked as the lighter upper bulwarks were ravaged. The fore course yard was hit, amputated just below the foremast fighting top, and both ends of the yard sagged downward in a steep *V* to drape furled canvas, and snap brace line, clews, and jeers. A Marine tumbled from the foremast fighting top with a thin scream, crashing to the deck in a pinwheel of arms and legs.

"*Spot . . . on,* sir!" Harvey reported, going hoarse.

"Pass word below," Lewrie yelled, "our aim is spot on, and no adjustments are needed! Pour it on, Mister Westcott, pour it on!"

He lifted his telescope as the smoke thinned once more, peering hard to see the results of that last broadside. He saw raw divots in the slope just below the French guns, where roundshot had hit short and buried themselves, some lines ploughed a bit further upslope where other shot had ripped long troughs in the earth, as if God had drawn His fingers to rake at the French.

Damme, is that an over-turned gun yonder? he wished to himself.

Two-thirds of a mile range was just too far to make out close details, even with his strong day-glass, but he could make out French gunners scurrying to fetch powder cartridges from the limbers, which were hidden behind the crest of the hill. Their cannon and their wheeled carriages were little black *H*-shapes, surrounded by gunners who wheeled them back into position, fed their maws with powder and fresh shot . . . all pointed directly at him; he was looking straight down their muzzles!

"By broadside . . . fire!"

"Dammit!" he spat as his view was blotted out, lowering his telescope in mounting frustration. He wanted to *see!*

Climb the shrouds, high as the cat-harpings? he thought; *No, it wouldn't be high enough. I'd have t' join Harvey, and I've not been in the cross-trees in ages!*

There were some good things about being a Post-Captain, or pretending to be one, after all!

"A gun dis-mounted, sir!" Harvey yelled down.

Lewrie whipped up his telescope again as the smoke cleared to a haze and did a quick count of the little *H*-shapes. Yes, there *was* one of them leaning to one side, with no one standing round it!

"Serve 'em another, Mister Westcott!" he roared.

Firing, running in, swabbing out, loading, then running out and shifting the aim with crow levers; he lost track of how long *Sapphire* kept up her fire; he lost count of how many times his ship was hit. After a time, though, reports of damage came less often, and Midshipman Harvey's shouts became more excited, raw and rasping as his throat gave out. Finally . . .

"Deck, there!" Harvey cried. "They are bringing up *limbers*! *Three* guns dis-mounted . . . they are *retiring*!"

Lewrie took a long, hard look, even though his eyes burned from all the irritants in gunpowder smoke, blinking away tears, swiping at his face with the cuffs of his coat sleeves.

Yes, by God! he told himself; *They've had enough of us, they're pullin' out!*

Horse teams, which had been sheltered near the caissons of shot and powder cartridges, could be seen near the surviving guns, being hitched up; carriage trails were being lifted to re-assemble guns to the limbers. One by one, the French battery was withdrawing to the shelter behind Santa Lucía Hill!

"Cease fire, Mister Westcott," Lewrie bade in a croak through his dry and smoked throat. "Cease fire, and pass word below that we shot the living *shit* outa those bastards! Damn my eyes if we don't have the best gunners in the whole bloody *Fleet*, tell 'em!"

"Took the better part of two hours, but we did it, sir," Westcott said, grinning fiercely, his white teeth startlingly bold against the grime of gunsmoke that had coated him from head to toe.

"It *did*?" Lewrie said in wonder. "I didn't keep track. Secure the guns, see that the hands have a turn at the scuttle-butts, then let's take in the bower, make sail, and fall down on the kedge."

"Aye, sir, I'll see to it," Lt. Westcott promised.

"Mister Yelland, still with us?" Lewrie asked, turning round to survey the quarterdeck.

"Here, sir," the Sailing Master said. "My congratulations to you, sir."

"Mine to you, sir," Lewrie replied, shrugging off the compliment with a weary modesty. "I wonder, sir . . . might you have a flask on you?"

"Just rum, sir," Mr. Yelland said, sounding apologetic.

"I think we've earned ourselves a 'Nor'wester' nip, don't you, Mister Yelland?" Lewrie asked.

"Why, I do believe we have, sir!" Yelland cried, breaking out into a wide smile as he handed over his pint bottle.

"There is a hoist from Admiral Hood's flagship, sir!" one of *Undaunted*'s Midshipmen announced to the officers on her quarterdeck. "It is . . . *Sapphire*'s number, and . . . Well Done, no . . . spelled out . . . Bravely Done!"

"And so it was," Captain Chalmers said with a vigourous nod of his head, "though I do wish that Captain Lewrie had summoned us to aid him."

HMS *Sapphire* was standing out from her close approach to the shore, gnawed and evidently damaged, but putting herself to rights even as she made a bit more sail. Captain Chalmers could hear the embarked soldiers and transport ship sailors raising cheers as the old 50-gunner Fourth Rate passed through their anchorages. Ship's bells were chimed in salute, clanging away tinnily like the parish church bells of London. Chalmers's own crew was gathered at the rails waiting for their chance to cheer, her, too. He looked round cutty-eyed to seek out Midshipman Lewrie, and found him up by the foremast shrouds, safely out of earshot.

"Pity that the 'Ram-Cat' is such a rake-hell of the old school," Chalmers imparted to his First Officer in a close mutter. "He don't even have a Chaplain aboard! From what I've heard of him, it's doubtful if one could even call him a Christian gentleman. A scandalous fellow, but a bold one. Runs in the family, I've heard."

"Surely not in his son, sir," the First Officer said.

"Perhaps we've set him a finer example, and altered the course of his life," Chalmers said, congratulating himself for being one of the principled, respectable, and high-minded sort.

Then, as HMS *Sapphire* began to come level with *Undaunted*, about one cable off, Captain Chalmers doffed his hat, waved it widely, and began to shout "Huzzah!", calling for his crew to give her Three Cheers And A Tiger!

Scandalous reprobates still had their uses.

CHAPTER FORTY-TWO

*N*ight on the open sea, as dark as a boot, with the Westerlies keening in the rigging, and HMS *Sapphire* plunging and hobby-horsing under re-duced and reefed sail. The clouds overhead were thick, and there was no moon. Captain Alan Lewrie was on deck, bundled up in his boat cloak, with a wool muffler round his neck, and his oldest hat on his head, peer-ing into the darkness to count the many glowing taffrail lanthorns of the transports ahead of his ship to make sure that none of them were veering off, or lagging. There were even more astern, a second convoy low on the Southern horizon, with its own escorts over-seeing its safety. And, far out on the Northern horizon, beyond his own group, hull down and barely guessed at, there were even more, their night-lights winking as the sea surged ships atop the long rollers, then dropped the trailing ships into the deep troughs. All bound for some port in England.

He paced about, from the windward side which was his, alone, by right, to the helmsmen at the massive double-wheel, then down to leeward for a bit, where the officer of the watch, Lt. Elmes, stood.

Looking forward along the length of his ship, he could see a wee glow from the lanthorn at the forecastle belfry, and the ruddy square glows of the hatchways that led down to the upper gun-deck.

England, my God, he wearily thought. He had no idea if Percy Stangbourne had survived the last French assaults, and wondered what would happen when he mailed that promised packet of letters for him. Most of the army was off and away, large clutches of ships sailing as they were filled and sorted into convoy groups. There were still ships waiting at Corunna for the rear-guard, for the men who spiked the guns and despoiled what was left in the depot that could not be carried away. He had no idea what *their* fate might be.

At least the people are in good takings, he noted as the sound of music came wafting up from below through those hatchways. "Spanish Ladies," "The Jolly Thresher," "One Misty, Moisty Morning" were being sung in hearty bellows. The crew was happy; they would be in England soon.

He frowned, feeling very glum, as he speculated if he would be going back to Spain, to Gibraltar, or Lisbon anytime soon. Would Thomas Mountjoy still have need of him and his ship, or would he and *Sapphire* be sent halfway round the world to do something else? And, there was Maddalena to gloom about. If there was no return to Gibraltar, they would never see each other, again, and he would have to send her a very sad letter and a note of hand with which to support her 'til she managed to find someone else who would see to her up-keep.

"Damn, damn, damn," he growled.

To make things worse, the musicians below struck up a new tune, and a strong tenor voice, he thought it might be Michael Deavers from his boat crew, began to sing "Over the Hills and Far Away."

He only could recall the few lines that Captain Chalmers had sung, even though he had tried to play the tune on his penny-whistle that afternoon.

"'And *I* would love you all the day . . . *all* the night we would kiss and play, *if* to me you would fondly *say*, over the hills and far *a-way*,'" he mouthed along under his breath, humming the tune at the rest. "Oh, damn, but I'm sorry, girl," he whispered. *"Minha doce . . . meu amor."*

Over the hills and far away.

AFTERWORD

Napoleon Bonaparte, self-crowned Emperor of The French, must've been very bored when he decided to overthrow the Spanish Bourbon king and conquer the Iberian Peninsula. Oh, there was still England to be invaded (he hadn't completely given up on the scheme) but he'd beaten everybody else in Europe, had Russia cowed and allied (sort of) with his Empire, and ruled the roost from the Atlantic to the Germanies, Poland (still beholden to Russia, anyway), and most of Italy.

There was Portugal, long a friend of England, that must have her ports closed and all her trade with Great Britain shut down, to complete the implentation of his Berlin Decrees and establish his Continental System to destroy British–European trade and bankrupt his last enemy. Fine and dandy, but, why Spain?

After all, Minister Manuel Godoy had cozened his country into an alliance with France in late 1804, had handed over good warships, money, food, and access to Spain's overseas colonial ports, not that the French were in a position to take advantage of that after losing control of the seas after the Battle of Trafalgar. Spain was supine, a lick-spittle ally, and as said in *A Hitchhiker's Guide to the Galaxy* . . . "mostly harmless." Napoleon was allowed to march an army through Spain into Portugal and conquer, but occupied cities in the North and centre of Spain. Did he *really* imagine that by conquering Spain he also gained every Spanish colony in the *world,* including the Phillipines in the Pacific? Or, was Spain merely a stepping-stone to *grander* ambitions, like seizing both Gibraltar and Ceuta, then crossing into North Africa, marching East to Egypt (again!) and even to British-held India? You have to give it to him; the little bastard dreamed big!

There was no real point to it, but, perhaps Napoleon thought it would be a walk-over. He did not take into account the Spanish people, nor did he take into account, or thought very little of, the British, who thought it possible to confront Napoleon on land, at last.

Everywhere that French armies went, once they had conquered a new province or country, they usually found quick-thinking collaborators who'd go along with them, and populations so weary of all those Thirty Years' Wars and Hundred Years' Wars that had plundered their lands and wealth that they would meekly succumb and try to make the best of things. Garrison duty was usually dull for the French, and they could quickly enlist, or conscript, young men into "allied" militaries who could police their own countries, and march to flesh out the already-massive French armies.

Nobody, anywhere in Europe, had ever cut a French throat in their sleep before, rebelled against them, ambushed their couriers and supply convoys, and armed themselves. General Castaños's victory against French General Dupont at Bailén must have been an embarrassing shock to Napoleon's pride in his armies. Unfortunately that victory made the Spanish think that they were invincible, which led many of their other Generals to lead Spanish armies to utter catastrophes, later on. The introduction of self-organised, self-armed bands of *guerrillas, partidas* who fought the "Little War" as they called it, was another shock; why, it was against the very rules of war, as they were understood in Europe, as chaotic as war on the frontiers against savage Red Indians! (Politically Correct types may blow it out yer arse.) Except from people like the bum-licking Godoy and the elite classes of Spain, the Anfrancesados, Napoleon and his men could not find very many collaborators, or recruits to serve alongside their own soldiers, either; the guerillas saw to that, making it very bloodily clear that co-operation or collusion with the invaders could be fatal. There were very few Quislings in Spain!

Napoleon's expected quick conquest was turning into a steaming pile of *merde*. His trusted Marshal Junot had his can kicked at Roliça and

Vimeiro, his other Marshals had retreated to the North of Spain, and his lacklustre brother, Joseph Bonaparte, now King of Spain, had to abandon Madrid and run for his life!

Enter the unfortunate General Sir John Moore. He didn't ask, and no one told him, how desolate central Spain could be in the middle of Winter, or just how bad the roads were. Mr. John Hookham Frere took all the empty Spanish promises as Gospel, and eagerly passed them on to Moore; his only qualification for his important post at Madrid as a diplomat to the Supreme Junta was his friendship with Foreign Secretary George Canning! "Old School Tie," or "Arse-Hole Buddies," don't make the most effective, or useful, representatives.

Actually, HM Government in London thought that invading Spain would be as easy as a stroll in Hyde Park . . . minus the rain! When Moore and Sir David Baird's separated wings of the army realised at last that Napoleon had come to Spain himself with massive re-enforcements, they had no choice but to retreat to the coast and try to save the army, especially when Napoleon realised that he might be facing Sir John Moore, and got on a tear to be after him, thirsting for a victory over the British. He pushed his troops so hard, in the same horrid conditions as Moore and Baird experienced, that he was stranded for hours in a raging blizzard in a mountain pass, urging his men on, and earned a shout of "Convicts suffer worse than we do. Shoot him down, damn him!"

The glittering prize of destroying a British field army was too tempting. Napoleon abandoned any plans to continue marching South to polish off the Spanish rebellion, which left half the country free of him, which in the long run proved fatal. Then, after sitting before the city of Benavente for two days waiting for bridge repairs, and getting urgent despatches from Paris warning him of new problems with the Austrians, Napoleon turned the pursuit over to Marshal Soult and left Spain forever, never to return.

With the excellent help of the Royal Navy, Moore's army was plucked from disaster, from Vigo and from Corunna in an operation likened to the miraculous evacuation of the British Expeditionary Force from France in 1940, Dunkirk.

By drawing Napoleon upon him, Moore saved Spain from utter disaster and collapse in the last month of 1808, and January of 1809. Historians reckon that the resistance, and the introduction of a new British army into Spain under the returned Sir Arthur Wellesley in the Spring of 1809, created a "Spanish Ulcer" that was the turning point in the long Napoleonic Wars, and cost France more in the long run than the disasters in Russia of 1812!

Even if the Spanish never could do much to aid that eventual victory; Wellesley, later Lord Wellington, never could quite trust them to do what they boasted.

Lewrie, and the crew of HMS *Sapphire*, are not to know this; as they sail away through stormy seas from Corunna to land their transports in English harbours, and shelter, the whole thing looks as revolting as a stray dog's dinner, and yet another shameful defeat at the hands of the "Corsican Ogre" and his invincible armies. Moore is dead, a sacrificial hero slain at the moment of his last success, the best hope of Britain gone. His Majesty's Government may toss up their hands and cut their losses, abandoning both Spain *and* Portugal to their own devices.

Will Alan Lewrie get a few days of shore leave, long enough to catch up with doings in Anglesgreen, post those letters from Viscount Percy, or, if Percy fell in the fighting at Corruna, must he deliver them by hand to help Percy's widow, Eudoxia, and his sister, Lydia, grieve?

Might he have time to really catch up with his son, Hugh, who seems to be doing quite well at his early naval career, or discover what's up with his other son, Sewallis, and all his talk of *dancing,* carousing at subscription balls, and taking aboard strong *drink*? Is he no longer serving willingly, and might want out of the Navy?

Once back in England, and in Admiralty's clutches, what fresh orders might await him, and where might they send him, this time? No more Independent Orders, no being seconded to the needs of Secret Branch, and Thomas Mountjoy's whims or needs . . . no more returning to Gibraltar, and Maddalena Covilhã! Why, his new duties might be as bad as commanding that squadron of bloody gunboats, *without* the comfort of a fond and affectionate young woman!

And what's that rot about "high-mindedness," and getting the "Stink Eye" from the upright and high-minded Captain Chalmers? Has Respectability reared its ugly head, again, and when back in England, what social changes might Lewrie encounter. Will he be in the same bad odour as his father, Sir Hugo?

Hint-hint!

Fare-well, and adieu, to you, ladies of Spain,
For we've received orders to sail for Old England,
but we hope very shortly to see you, again!

Lewrie may be a cad, but he's a useful cad. This time, though, he may have enough sense to stay aboard ship and not go haring ashore with the Army . . . maybe. You'll simply have to wait and see.